VISION OF DESIRE

As Rachel watched, the man slid a finger under the neckline of the woman's bodice, tugging the material downwards until her breasts were on full view. He caressed the smooth skin, then rolled each nipple in turn between his thumb and forefinger, until her breasts began to swell under his ministrations and the dusky nipples grew even harder and longer.

Rachel swallowed hard. The weirdest thing wasn't the tableau in front of her: it was that she could feel everything that he was doing to the beautiful Egyptian princess, exactly as she'd felt it when she'd blacked out and seen them by the pool. It was as though her own skin were being caressed, his fingers brushing the soft undersides of her breasts in the way that she liked and pulling at her nipples in a way that made her warm and moist with desire . . .

Mirage

Evelyn D'Arcy

NEW ENGLISH LIBRARY
Hodder and Stoughton

Copyright © 1997 Evelyn D'Arcy

First published in 1997 by Hodder and Stoughton
A division of Hodder Headline PLC

A New English Library paperback.

The right of Evelyn D'Arcy to be identified as the Author
of the Work has been asserted by her in accordance with the
Copyright, Designs and Patents Act 1988.

10 9 8 7 6 5 4 3 2 1

British Library Cataloguing in Publication Data
A CIP catalogue record for this title is available from the
British Library

ISBN 0 340 68267 1

Typeset by Palimpsest Book Production Limited,
Polmont, Stirlingshire
Printed and bound in Great Britain by
Mackays of Chatham PLC, Chatham, Kent

Hodder and Stoughton
A division of Hodder Headline PLC
338 Euston Road
London NW1 3BH

For Wendy

ONE

It was a typical Saturday afternoon in the British Museum, full of Japanese tourists with video cameras and Bible Tour groups. The Egyptian section was a heaving mass of people, with harassed-looking curators at the doors repeating 'Go in on the right and out on the left, please,' in an irritated monotone. Rachel half-wished that she had chosen somewhere different to spend a hot and airless spring afternoon. On the other hand, wandering around the Egyptian section was her favourite way of spending a spare afternoon, and she'd learned virtually to ignore the crush of the tourists.

She was walking through the inner rooms when she sensed it – something calling her attention, demanding that she look. As she turned and saw it, goose-flesh crept up her arms. It was in a glass case on its own, set back in a small dark recess, the spotlights on either side of it drawing her eyes to its beauty: a golden mummy-case, with black 'hair' and striking black kohl-rimmed eyes. Rachel couldn't help going closer to it, admiring the raised designs on the gilded case and those beautiful, beautiful eyes. They seemed yearning to her, drawing her in to their blackness . . .

She was kneeling next to a shallow pool, scooping up the clear cold water in her hands and splashing it against her face. The water was so clear that she could see herself in it, her reflection shattered by the small ripples she'd caused by dipping her fingers into the pool. She was naked, her skin pale and creamy against the blackness of her hair. Her lips were red and slightly swollen, and her dark eyes glittered as she cupped her breasts in her hands, bringing them up and together to deepen the vee between them. Her hair swung freely, black as an ibis wing, framing her face.

She knew that she was beautiful. Many men had lusted after her; many men had wanted to make her their own. And yet she had held apart, waiting for . . . She hadn't known what she had been waiting for, until she had met him. The handsome stranger, so unlike her own people. The man who'd taught her body to sing with pleasure, who'd stroked her and caressed her until her body had rippled and foamed beneath his fingers.

Suddenly, a second reflection appeared in the water, behind her own. A naked and obviously male reflection. A smile crossed her lips. She had known that he would come to her, here. Forbidden or not, he couldn't help himself: he couldn't stay away from her. From the first time their eyes had met – his own eyes so strange, so un-Egyptian, an aqua grey – he had been lost. And from the moment that his mouth had first touched hers, so had she.

His arms curved round her body, his fingers seeking hers and lacing between them; he pulled her back against him, his hands locked around her waist. She could feel the beating of his heart against her skin, a steady and rapid thudding which betrayed just how excited he was. She tipped her head back to rest against him, and his lips feathered a trail along the sensitive cord at the side of her neck.

She sighed with pleasure, and he began to stroke her

breasts, his fingers still interlaced with her own: lifting the soft globes, judging their weight, and then tracing the faint blue veins with wondering fingers, the dark pimply flesh of the areolae, and then finally touching the hard rosy peaks at the centre, pulling gently at them so that she arched her back in pleasure.

She drew his fingers down over her belly to tangle in the dark fleece of her pubic hair; he shivered, and began nibbling her shoulder, his lips and tongue caressing her skin. Gently, his fingers drifted lower, between her thighs, exploring the folds and crevices of her quim, seeking out and then caressing the hidden nub of flesh, the centre of her pleasure.

Her sex grew warm and moist under his ministrations, receptive; he guided her onto her hands and knees, making sure that the ground beneath her was smooth and firm, with no stones to cut into her delicate flesh. She could feel the hard jutting muscle of his erect penis nudging against the cleft of her buttocks; then he slipped his hand between their bodies, repositioning his cock against the entrance of her sex.

She almost cried out when he penetrated her: had it not been for the soft pads of his fingertips on her lips, warning her that they had to be silent, she would have betrayed their presence to the guards who were just around the corner. She clenched her teeth hard, biting back her pleasure, and pushed back against him, so that he filled her to the hilt. He smiled against her shoulder, and began to thrust.

Unable to help herself, wanting to see what was happening, she looked into the pool. She could see their reflection, their limbs entwined and his long thick cock pushing in and out of her, his balls slapping against her as he slid into her. Their gazes met in the water, and he smiled at her. What they were doing was forbidden, but neither of them cared. All that mattered was the way their bodies were joined, the network of nerves and muscles straining into convulsions of pleasure.

She bit on his fingers, hard, as warmth bubbled up from the soles of her feet, centring in her solar plexus and then exploding. The aftershocks of her orgasm fluttered around his cock, warm silky contractions on his skin, tipping him into his own release. He rested his smooth cheek against her back, holding her close, and she closed her eyes, wanting the moment to last for eternity ...

The next thing that Rachel knew, she was being supported by unfamiliar arms. She looked up, blinking, into a pair of grey-green eyes. Aqua grey. Eyes exactly the same as the eyes of the man that she'd seen by the pool.

Colour drained from her face for a second time. She was in the British Museum, among hundreds of tourists, and yet she'd been making love by a pool in an unknown land, with a complete stranger. At least, it had felt like she'd been making love: and yet the hair and eyes of the woman reflected in the pool had been different, not her own. It had been her, and yet not her. She swallowed. Just what the hell was happening to her?

'Are you all right?' the stranger asked, his face concerned.

'Yes, I think so,' she lied.

'You blacked out,' he told her. 'Luckily, I was behind you, to break your fall.'

Rachel flushed. 'I'm so sorry to have been such a nuisance.'

He smiled. 'No problem. You weren't a nuisance.'

He was, Rachel thought, the most beautiful man that she had

ever seen. He was a little under six feet tall, with straight dark hair parted at the side and brushed back from his face, and a sensual curve to his lower lip. He had an olive complexion, which made the colour of his eyes more of a shock: with that skin tone, she had expected his eyes to be a typical Mediterranean deep brown, not that unusual and beautiful aqua grey.

He had an almost classical profile: his nose neither too large nor too small, his jaw-line strong but not stubborn. It made her wonder what the rest of him was like, beneath his cream cotton poloneck sweater and slightly baggy dark grey trousers. Was he the same as the beautiful man who'd been making love to her by the pool, with a flat hard torso, and a muscular yet not over-developed chest? And such a long, thick, rigid cock?

She realized that her nipples were beginning to harden at the thought, and that she was still in his arms – close enough for her arousal to be blatant, and for him to notice. She pulled away, embarrassed, and hoped that he hadn't noticed; or, at least, that he didn't realize the reason for her arousal. 'It must have been the heat,' she said apologetically.

'Mm, it's pretty stuffy in here.' He smiled at her. 'Would you like a glass of water or something?'

She shook her head, and immediately wished that she hadn't when another wave of dizziness shot through her. 'I'm fine, thanks,' she lied.

'No, you're not,' he said, taking her arm. 'You're as white as a ghost.'

Rachel couldn't help herself. 'Shouldn't that be "white as a sheet"?'

He gave her a sidelong look. 'Not everyone sleeps in white sheets, you know.'

A picture of him, naked and erect, lying on navy blue silk sheets, came into her mind. Her eyes darkened as she involuntarily reworked the picture to include herself, equally naked, straddling his thighs, his cock just about to slide into her . . .

She swallowed hard. God, this was ridiculous. Anyone would think that she'd taken something – first of all fainting, and then having erotic dreams and projecting them onto the man who'd come to her rescue. Had it not been for the fact that none of her friends took drugs, either, she would have been convinced that someone had slipped something into her drink at the party, the previous night.

'I'll see you home,' he said.

'There's no need. I'm quite all right, thank you.' She winced inwardly at the prim note in her voice, knowing how rude she must sound to a stranger who was only being kind.

He didn't seem to notice her rudeness. 'Fainting can catch you unawares. I'd hate to think of you falling under a bus or a tube or whatever.'

She took a deep breath. 'Look, I don't even know you.'

'That's easily remedied.' He gave a short bow. 'Daniel Sinclair at your service, madam.'

He was irresistibly appealing, she thought. She'd always been a little careful of strangers, in London, but someone as polite and gorgeous as this man simply couldn't be a potential knife-wielding maniac – could he? She held out her hand. 'Rachel Meaden.'

He took it and kissed it, then glanced at her through his lashes and grinned. 'Corny, but . . .'

She couldn't help smiling back. 'Mm.'

'So come and have a cup of coffee with me,' he tempted. 'Sit down for a while. *Then* I'll see you home.'

His smile won her over. 'All right. Thank you.'

They walked to the Museum café in easy silence; Daniel settled her in a chair, then went to fetch them both a cup of coffee.

'Better?' he asked as she took a sip of the dark steaming liquid.

'Better,' she admitted.

'I hate to say "I told you so . . .",' he teased.

'We don't know each other well enough,' she reminded him.

'That's easily cured, if we give each other brief potted histories.' He took a deep breath. 'Daniel James Sinclair, aged thirty, history lecturer, living in a Victorian terrace in Walthamstow. Single, youngest of three boys, two nieces, no children of my own, no pets – though I'd love a dog if I ever escape from London, probably a chocolate labrador. Completely addicted to pasta, cheese, blueberries, Chablis and Margaux – though not all at the same time; favourite colour iris blue. Favourite music Mozart or Fleetwood Mac – from the Peter Green years, I mean, not the later poppy stuff. Favourite author Thomas Hardy; favourite film *It's a Wonderful Life*. Into films, reading, and skulking round the British Museum, wishing that I'd been an archaeologist. Not into body-building, junk food or decaffeinated coffee. Ambition: to enjoy life.' He tipped his head slightly to one side. 'Now, you?'

She found herself warming to him; even without that sexy smile, his personality attracted her. 'Rachel Lois Meaden, aged twenty-eight, copywriter, living in a flat in Islington. Single, only child, no children, half-share in a stray cat with my next-door neighbour. Addicted to good coffee, white Belgian chocolate, Brie and Chablis. Favourite colour lapis lazuli; favourite music Bach or Joni Mitchell. Favourite author Margaret

Atwood; favourite films *When Harry Met Sally* and *Amadeus*. Into the theatre, walking, and Egypt. Not into aerobics, or queuing up. Ambition—' she paused '—I don't know, at the moment.' She'd been coasting for a while, putting off deciding what to do about her career. She liked her job, and there was no point in changing just for change's sake, she justified to herself.

He nodded. 'Well, now that's out of the way.'

'What is?'

'Getting to know each other.'

She laughed. 'I think that it takes more than a few minutes to get to know someone.'

'Does it?' he asked softly.

Rachel avoided his eyes. She had the strangest feeling that she knew him from somewhere. Just as she'd known the man in her dream. And yet she'd never met Daniel Sinclair before that day. Which meant . . . what? There was something odd about this whole thing, and it unnerved her. Suddenly uncomfortable, she drained her coffee.

'Would you like another?' he asked.

She shook her head. 'Thanks, but I'm fine, now.'

'Let's go, then.'

They walked to Holborn station, chatting easily. Rachel felt fine, until the train started moving. As soon as they were in the tunnel, she made the mistake of glancing at the window. The figures reflected there were not the exotic-looking Daniel and herself. They were the people she'd seen by the pool.

She stared, fascinated, at the glass. The woman looked like her, albeit with dark hair cut in a Cleopatra bob, dark eyes, and a slightly haunted smile. This time, she wasn't naked, but was clad in a white robe made of fine linen and a lapis-lazuli and gold necklace. The linen clung to the contours of her body, almost translucent in the light, revealing the dark triangle of her pubic hair and firm high breasts. Her nipples, too, were visible, showing dusky and erect through the pale cloth.

The man sitting beside her reminded her of Daniel, with an olive complexion and those strange eyes: though the smile was different, the hair longer. He was wearing nothing but a white linen loincloth. The thin material did nothing to hide the size of his cock – or the fact that it was erect.

As Rachel watched, the man slid a finger under the neckline of the woman's bodice, tugging the material downwards until her breasts were on full view. He caressed the smooth skin, then rolled each nipple in turn between his thumb and forefinger, until her breasts began to swell under his ministrations and the dusky nipples grew even harder and longer

Rachel swallowed hard. The weirdest thing wasn't the tableau in front of her: it was that she could feel everything that he was doing to the beautiful Egyptian princess, exactly as she'd felt it when she'd blacked out and seen them by the pool. It was as though her own skin were being caressed, his fingers brushing the soft undersides of her breasts in the way that she liked and pulling at her nipples in a way that made her quim moisten.

He changed position, then, gliding smoothly to his knees in one moment, facing the woman on the throne. Rachel's throat dried as she saw his hands disappear under the hem of the robe, pushing the material back. And then she felt his fingers gently walking up her legs, stroking her thighs until they parted for him.

Her quim was already wet with anticipation; she felt rather than saw his smile as he discovered the fact, his lips caressing her thighs while his fingers traversed the length of her quim, exploring her folds and crevices. One clever finger circled her clitoris, rubbing it gently with just the right amount of pressure and speed to make her even wetter.

She could feel the warmth of his breath against her thighs, and almost whimpered with longing. He made her wait until she was literally thrusting her pubis at him; then, with a gentle and knowing laugh, he finally gave her what she wanted.

She gave a little moaning sigh as she felt his tongue against the warm moist flesh of her sex, moving from the top to the bottom of her slit in one lithe movement. His face was perfectly smooth, no roughness of stubble dragging against her soft delicate skin, and she gripped the arms of her chair hard as pleasure lanced through her ...

'Rachel? Rachel?'

She became aware that Daniel was shaking her. 'What?' she asked, slightly dazed.

'It's our stop,' he said quietly. 'I think that you just blacked out again.'

Rachel flushed. Blacking out wasn't the phrase she would have used. Her internal muscles were still contracting, and she was glad that she was wearing a tunic-style sweater over her leggings, which was long enough to hide the fact that her crotch was decidedly wet. She only hoped that she hadn't been acting out her dream, or whatever it had been, on the tube.

'I'm all right, Daniel, honestly,' she said softly.

'I don't know whether we should get a taxi, or whether the fresh air will do you more good.'

She smiled at him, touched by his concern. 'Fresh air, I think. I don't live that far from the station.'

They relaxed into easy silence, Daniel slowing his pace to match hers; after a few minutes, they reached her flat.

Rachel paused on the doorstep. 'Would you like to come in for a coffee, Daniel?'

He looked at her. 'Are you sure that you're up to having a guest?'

'I think that I can just about cope with a kettle,' she said lightly.

'Then thank you, I'd like that.' He followed her into her flat.

The first thing that struck him as he stood in the living room was how many Egyptian things there were in the place. There were framed prints of hieroglyphs and illustrations from Egyptian manuscripts on walls; small statues of Egyptian black cats sitting and stretching out were dotted on the pine bookshelves. He scanned the titles of the books lazily: Rachel had an eclectic collection of literary novels, French poetry, and books about Egypt, from scholarly tracts about women's daily lives to glossy coffee-table reproductions of *The Book of the Dead*.

A reproduction of Tutankhamun's death-mask stood in the centre of the pine mantelpiece. On one side of it was a reproduction of a painted outer mummy case for a cat, and on the other was a brass-framed portrait of Rachel, made up as an Egyptian princess. The picture was head and shoulders only, but he could imagine what the rest of her looked like: she'd be wearing a loose white dress, belted in gold, and her feet would be bare.

'Fancy dress party?' he guessed, picking up the picture.

'Oh, that.' She laughed. 'No. Charlie at work did it on the computer. He's my creative partner at the agency – I'm the wordsmith, and he's the one with the magic markers,' she explained.

'Oh.' Daniel studied the picture. It had a haunting beauty, her glossy dark hair and dark kohl-rimmed eyes making him want to reach out and touch her face, bring those lips closer to his. And yet the woman standing next to him had shoulder-length fair hair, pulled back from her face by a navy velvet Alice band, and iris-blue eyes. 'How did he do it?'

'Photoshop,' she said.

'Hm?'

She smiled. 'Sorry. I was talking jargon. He used a computer program. He scanned in a photograph of a mummy case from one of my books – it's actually the inner case of Henutmehit – then scanned in my face over hers. He did a little bit of tinkering with his computer program to wipe out the rough edges between the photographs, and that's the end result.'

'It's very good.' It was also very erotic, and Daniel was uncomfortably aware that his cock was hardening. He swallowed hard, remembering that he was supposed to be playing the good Samaritan. Rachel had fainted in the museum, and had almost blacked out again on the train. It was unfair to leap on her, much as he would have liked to do so.

'Well, now you know why they call me Cleo, at work,' she said flippantly, going into the kitchen.

He followed her, leaning against the worktop. 'Yes. All you need is the violet eyes, and you could be the young Elizabeth Taylor.'

She chuckled. 'Hardly. But thanks for the compliment.' She made the coffee swiftly. 'Milk or sugar?'

'I prefer my caffeine unadulterated, thanks,' he said with a smile, taking the mug from her.

She added milk to her own cup, and ushered him through to the living room again. He noticed with wry amusement that she didn't sit next to him on the sofa, or meet his eyes. He had a feeling that his attraction to Rachel was mutual, and she didn't know how to deal with it, either.

He decided to change the conversation, to make her feel more at ease with him. 'So what started you off on Egypt, then?'

She shrugged. 'I don't know, really.' She laughed. 'Would you believe, I've never even been to Cairo or Luxor? The nearest I've been to Egypt is Greece and Turkey.'

'There's an ambition for you, then,' he said softly.

'Mm. One I'd better not leave too long, with the whole lot crumbling further every year. I'd be so disappointed to get there, finally, and discover that all the tombs were closed to protect them.' She pursed her lips thoughtfully. 'What started me off? Well, I've always been interested in Egypt, ever since I was a child. My parents took me to see the Tutankhamun exhibition at the British Museum – I can't have been much older than about five, but I think I was interested even before then.' She nodded at the framed prints and Egyptian artefacts. 'I bought some of them, but most of them are presents from indulgent friends. Carrie – my best friend – found the cat mummy case in a junk-shop when she was in Suffolk, last weekend, and brought it back for me.'

'It's a good reproduction,' he said. Something about it made him feel slightly edgy, but he put that down to being more of a dog-lover than a cat-lover.

'Mm.' She coughed. 'So what about you? Why didn't you become an archaeologist?'

He smiled. 'When I realized that it meant digging up dead

13

bodies, I decided to stick to the paper version. That was gory enough for me.'

'So you lecture in ancient history, then?'

He shook his head. 'I'm afraid not. I specialize in Victorian history, though I've also taught a bit of medieval. Ask me about Disraeli or Gladstone or the Irish Question, and I can rattle on for hours; but ask me about Tutankhamun or Alexander the Great, and I'm just your average man on the street.'

'I don't think that there could be anything average about *you.*' The words were out before she could stop them.

Daniel looked at her in surprise.

'I'm sorry.' She flushed. 'My brain's not in gear with my mouth, right now. I don't usually say things like that.'

He smiled. 'I could ask you to explain what you meant.'

Her flush deepened. 'Do you want another coffee?' she asked, hoping to change the subject.

He shook his head. 'No, thanks.'

'Do you mind if I do?'

'Not at all.' He followed her back into the kitchen. 'Well, since you're obviously feeling better, I'll be on my way,' he said softly.

She nodded. 'Well, thanks for rescuing me.'

'My pleasure.'

He held out his hand, and she took it, with the intention of shaking hands, but the moment that his flesh touched hers, she shivered with desire.

His fingers stroked her palm. 'Are you sure that you're really all right, Rachel?'

'Yes,' she lied. Then she made the mistake of looking him in the eye. His pupils had expanded so that his eyes were almost black, leaving her in no doubt that he felt the same heady attraction.

He cupped her face, drawing it closer to his; her skin was soft, and she smelled of honey and something else he couldn't define, but found very arousing. He touched his mouth lightly to hers; she tipped her head back slightly, her lips parting, and he nibbled at her lower lip. He slid one hand down to cup the nape of her neck, and the other stroked gently down her spine, coming to rest at the soft swell of her buttocks.

Rachel slid her arms round his waist, pressing against him; he nudged her thighs apart with one knee, sliding one leg between hers. She murmured slightly, and he kissed her properly, his tongue flickering against hers.

With an effort, he remembered that she was ill, and broke the kiss. 'I'm sorry,' he said. 'I'm rushing you. You should be in bed.'

'That,' she said lightly, 'is the best idea you've had yet.'

He grinned. 'Freudian slip. I meant, you should be resting.'

She stroked his face, tracing the bone structure before running one finger along his lower lip. 'I feel fine, really.' He caught her finger between his lips, sucking it into his mouth, and her eyes darkened. 'Daniel.'

'Mm?'

'Don't think me cheap – I know we've only just met – but I'd like to go to bed with you. Now.'

He kissed her palm. 'Rachel, are you sure?'

She nodded. 'I just want you to know that I don't make a habit of it.'

He smiled. 'Funnily enough, neither do I. In fact, I have a reputation among my colleagues for being boring, bookish, and a would-be Trappist monk.'

She laughed. 'With those bedroom eyes? There must be hundreds of disappointed students all over London.'

He rubbed his nose against hers. 'I don't know about that, but I never go to bed with my students. It's unprofessional.'

'Colleagues, then,' Rachel suggested with a grin.

Daniel rolled his eyes, remembering the last departmental party and how he'd narrowly evaded the desperate clutches of a recently divorced middle-aged colleague. 'Let's just draw a veil over it, hm?'

'Then, Mr would-be Trappist Monk, how about acting out of character?'

'I was hoping that you might say that.' He smiled broadly, and allowed her to lead him through to her bedroom.

She drew the curtains, and switched on the bedside light before coming back to stand before him. Gently, he pulled off her sweater, and removed the navy velvet Alice band which held her hair back from her face, rearranging the fair tresses so that they fell over her shoulders. Her skin was creamy against the navy silk and lace of her bra; he drew one finger through her cleavage, revelling in the softness of her skin and her immediate reaction to him, the way she tipped her head back slightly and lifted her chest as he touched her.

He kissed the curve of her throat, nibbling at the hollows of her collarbone, then rubbed his face against her breasts, taking in her perfume. The hard peaks of her nipples thrust at him through the silk and lace; he undid the clasp of her bra, letting the garment fall to the floor and cupping her breasts in his hands, his thumbs idly teasing her nipples.

Rachel tugged at the hem of his sweater, and he smiled wryly, releasing her for a moment while he removed it. His torso was lean and firm, and his chest well-developed with a light sprinkling of dark hair; Rachel appraised him briefly and approvingly. He wouldn't have disgraced the latest ad she was working on, she thought, tracing the outline of his ribcage. He was beautiful, with the sort of body women would fantasize about.

Again, the vision of the man she'd seen by the pool and reflected in the window of the tube flashed into her mind. This man looked almost identical to Daniel, with the exception that he was slightly smoother-skinned: no doubt down to the Egyptian tradition of sugaring away their bodily hair. She blinked hard, to dispel the vision, and again it was Daniel smiling down at her, his fingers caressing her skin.

Gently, he cupped her chin in both hands, drawing her face towards his; he nibbled softly at her lower lip, running his tongue along it before kissing her deeply. His hands slipped down to her waist, and he slowly eased her leggings down, sliding one hand between her thighs to cup her mons veneris. Through the thin silk of her knickers, he could feel the heat of her quim pulsing over his fingers. It made him want to taste her properly, the sweetness of honey and the tang of the seashore in his mouth.

He knelt before her, removing her leggings as he did so; she stepped out of the clinging material, and stood before him clad only in the navy silk knickers. Slowly, he eased the garment over her buttocks, revealing soft globes of creamy flesh, and let the thin silk drift to the floor. He rubbed his face against her thighs, breathing in her musky scent.

Rachel felt herself grow wet at the thought of what he was about to do; she murmured softly, shifting her position slightly to give him easier access. She felt him smile against the soft skin of her inner thigh, and then at last she felt the slow stroke of his tongue as he parted her labia, searching through her intimate folds and crevices until he found her clitoris.

He teased it out of its hood, his tongue flicking rapidly across it, and then he drew the small hard bud into his mouth, sucking gently at first, and then harder. Rachel moaned softly, sliding her hands into his hair and digging the pads of her fingers into his scalp. Daniel, tasting how much pleasure she was receiving, continued to lick and suck at her until his mouth was full of her musky juices, and he could feel her sex-flesh quivering against his mouth.

He dropped a kiss against her quim, then slowly got to his feet again, caressing her cheek. 'OK?'

She nodded, opening her eyes and looking at him. Her pupils had expanded until her eyes looked almost black. 'Definitely OK,' she said. Her voice was husky still, her breathing slightly ragged. She traced his lower lip with a fingertip. 'Thank you.'

'I haven't finished yet,' he said softly.

Rachel flushed as she realized that he was still wearing his trousers. 'Oh, God, we really did get carried away.'

'It was entirely mutual, believe me,' he reassured her, removing his trousers and pulling off his cotton boxer shorts. He took her hand and curled it round his erect cock. 'This is going to sound ridiculously corny, but you turn me on in a big way,' he told her quietly.

'I'm glad to hear it,' she said, a smile spreading over her face. She tipped her head back in the direction of the duvet. 'And still on the corny note: time for somewhere more comfortable, do you think?'

He grinned. 'Sounds good to me.'

To her mingled relief and disappointment, he didn't try

anything macho, like picking her up and carrying her to the bed; rather, he let her lead the way. She pushed back the duvet, feeling suddenly shy; as if he could read her feelings, he slid his arms round her, pulling her back against his chest and wrapping his arms around her ribcage and kissing the nape of her neck. The cherishing gesture gave her courage, and she scrambled into bed, patting the empty space beside her and smiling at him.

Daniel smiled back, and moved to lie next to her, tracing the soft curves of her body with the palm of his hand. 'You're one beautiful woman, Rachel Meaden,' he said softly, pulling her closer to him. He shifted, rolling over and pulling her with him so that she was straddling him, the ends of her hair brushing his face as she tipped her head down slightly. He could feel the moist heat of her quim against his cock, and opened his mouth in a wordless sigh of longing.

Rachel lifted herself slightly and slid her hand between their bodies, guiding the tip of his cock to the entrance of her sex. Then, slowly, she lowered herself onto the rigid muscle. Daniel groaned as his flesh was encased in warm liquid velvet.

His hands spanned her waist, and he lifted his upper body from the bed so that he could kiss the soft creamy flesh of her breasts, drawing the tip of his nose down her cleavage. 'You smell and taste beautiful,' he said, licking her skin until she shivered. The tip of his tongue traced the veins of her breasts until he reached the darker pimply skin of the areola; she arched backwards as he took each nipple into his mouth in turn, sucking on the sensitive flesh.

She began to move over him in small circles, lifting up from him until he was at the point of slipping out of her, then pushing back down hard until her pubis ground against him. He tipped his head back, squeezing his eyes shut tight and opening his mouth as his orgasm grew nearer.

Pleasure bubbled through her veins, pooling in her solar plexus; as it exploded, she felt his cock throbbing inside her, and the warm wet gush of his seed filling her. Daniel wrapped his arms round her, drawing her down on his chest and stroking her hair.

'What a beginning,' he said softly.

Rachel only just stopped herself from informing him that the beginning had been a long time ago. She frowned. This was crazy. It was the first time she'd met Daniel Sinclair, she was sure. So how come she felt as though she'd known him for a long, long time?

Dozens of other questions crowded into her mind. Why had she suddenly started having these blackouts? Who were the man and woman she'd seen? And what did they have to do with her – or Daniel?

She made a conscious effort to blank them out. She didn't have any answers; and until she had at least some ideas, she didn't want to discuss them with Daniel. Like he said, this was a beginning, and she didn't want to spoil it.

This time, her treacherous mind added.

TWO

'Well, Cleo, you're looking pretty pleased with yourself,' Charlie remarked, coming to stand by his creative partner's desk. 'Good weekend, was it?'

'You could say that.' Rachel gave him an enigmatic smile, and returned to the pile of papers in front of her.

'Oh, come on. You can't leave it at that!' Charlie pushed some of her files to one side and perched on the edge of her desk, pushing his dark curly hair back from his forehead. 'Tell me.'

Rachel played it cool. 'Tell you what?'

'What, precisely,' Charlie enunciated crisply, 'you got up to this weekend, to put a smile like that on your face.'

'Don't I always look happy?' Rachel fenced.

'No. Nobody's *always* happy. And you certainly don't go around with a smile that wide on your face, without a damn good reason.' Charlie removed the pencil from her fingers. 'So what's he like, then?'

'Who?'

He rolled his eyes. 'The bloke who's put such a smile on your face, of course.'

She lifted her chin, giving him a coquettish look. 'And who says that it was a man, Charlie-boy?'

He laughed, his green eyes sparkling. 'Nice try, Cleo, but I know that you're a hundred per cent straight. There isn't a dykey bone in your body.'

'Mm, I suppose not.' Rachel had no prejudices about other people's sexuality, but she'd always considered herself strictly heterosexual. Although she could see the attractions of other women, it was purely from an artistic point of view. Rachel had never, ever fancied another woman.

'So come on, then, what's he like?'

She sighed. 'I give in. You're not going to let me do any work until I tell you, are you?'

'Nope,' Charlie confirmed, with a grin.

'OK. His name's Daniel, he's a history lecturer, and I met him in the British Museum.'

Charlie groaned. 'Oh no. No, no, no, no, no.'

'What?'

He rolled his eyes. 'Please, just don't tell me that he's another Tutankhamun groupie!'

'No, he's not.' Rachel laughed. 'Though he wanted to be an archaeologist when he was a kid.'

'An archaeologist,' Charlie repeated, pulling a face.

'Mm. Nothing wrong with that, is there?'

'I suppose not.' Charlie was thoughtful. 'Though the British Museum isn't exactly what I'd call a cruising ground. What happened? Did he come over to you and say that you looked like one of the beautiful Egyptian princesses on the mummy cases, or something?'

She flushed. 'Nothing of the kind.'

'What, then?'

'Actually, I fainted, and he caught me.'

Charlie's teasing manner dropped, and he became all concern. 'You fainted? Rachel, are you all right?'

'Yes, I'm fine. I suppose that the place was just a bit stuffy, that's all.'

'Fainted?' Sara, the departmental secretary, overheard the last bit. 'Cleo, don't tell me that you've fallen victim to the baby boom.' Half the women on their floor of the office had become pregnant in the previous six months.

Rachel pulled a face. 'Not unless it's by immaculate conception! No, it's my own fault – for not bothering with lunch and then spending my afternoon in a stuffy room.' She shrugged. 'Low blood sugar and not enough oxygen. There's nothing more to it than that.'

'Pity. I'd have liked to be a disreputable honorary auntie,' Sara said with a grin.

'Well, she's met a new man, so don't give up hope yet,' Charlie informed her.

Rachel groaned. 'Oh, honestly, you two, you're a pair of old gossips. Some of us have work to do around here. Though I need a caffeine fix, first.' She stood up. 'Anyone else for coffee?'

'Cleo, my sweet, I thought that you'd never ask,' Charlie said, giving her a beatific smile and a dirty coffee mug.

'By rights, I should let you get botulism,' Rachel said, pulling a disgusted face at the mould which was beginning to grow on the surface of the half-inch of liquid in the bottom of the mug. Charlie had taken the previous Friday off, and obviously hadn't bothered washing out his mug before he'd left the office on the Thursday night.

He blew her a kiss. 'But as my wonderful partner, and with the deadline we've got on the perfume brief, of course you won't . . .'

A few minutes later, Rachel was reading the file on their

perfume project, sitting in her usual working position, with a mug of steaming coffee in one hand and her other hand pushed up through her hair, resting her weight on her elbow as she pored over the papers.

Then her office vanished. She wasn't in London, with Charlie and Sara and the rest of her department at the agency, sitting in front of a bleached oak desk with papers spread in front of her. She was in much warmer climes. Egypt.

Again, she saw the beautiful couple who had haunted her in the museum and on the train. They were outdoors; although, this time, they weren't near water. They were lying in long lush grass, in each other's arms, and laughing at some shared joke. They were naked and, from the slight rosy flush still mottling the woman's body, Rachel knew that they'd just been making love.

She leaned her head against his shoulder, still smiling; then she turned her face so that her lips just touched his skin. The smile died from his lips, and the look in his eyes rapidly changed from laughter to passion, their colour becoming more grey than aqua. He laid his hand tenderly against the curve of her cheek, then tilted her face so that he could nibble at her lower lip, teasing her with tiny kisses.

She closed her eyes, opening her mouth and rubbing the tip of her nose against his. He shifted onto his back, drawing her on top of him so that she was on all fours. She straightened up slightly, straddling his thighs with her hands on her hips. He sighed in contentment as he felt the heat of her moist quim against his hard rigid cock.

Her breasts hung down, pendulous and ruby-tipped; he reached up to cup them, the sun-darkened skin of his hands contrasting sharply with her pale breasts. He ran his tongue along his lower lip, then lifted his upper body so that he could circle her areola with the tip of his tongue, before drawing the hard flesh of her nipple into his mouth. She tipped her head back, exposing her throat to him; he pressed her breasts together, deepening the valley between them, then ran his nose along the line of her cleavage, breathing in her scent and then nibbling along her collar-bone.

Her hand slipped between their bodies, and she grasped his cock firmly, lifting herself slightly and guiding him to the entrance of her sex. Slowly, she pushed down on him, enveloping his cock in her wet velvety folds. Then she put her hands on his shoulders, gently pressing him back down to the ground and rubbing her nose against his in a gesture of affection.

He smiled up at her as she placed her hands either side of his head, letting the erect tips of her breasts just touch his chest; she moved her upper body sinuously, brushing against his body. Her hair hung down, straight and black, the ends tickling his face as she moved over him.

Then she lifted herself up straight again, and began to move over his cock, pushing down hard and then pulling up so that he was almost out of her before pushing down hard again. She ground her pubis hard against his, putting a delicious pressure on her clitoris, and tipped herself back slightly, changing the angle of his penetration to increase her pleasure. She flexed her internal muscles, massaging his cock as she moved. His hands spanned her waist, and he urged her on, helping her move in tiny circles. Their rhythm grew wilder, faster, until at last she gave a loud cry; she slumped on top of him, the spasming movement of her internal muscles tipping him into his own release . . .

Evelyn D'Arcy

*   *   *

The next thing that Rachel knew, she was sitting with her head between her knees. She groaned, and straightened up, lifting her head. She blinked hard as her surroundings swam back into view: not the lush green grass of the Nile delta, but the modern and discreet decor of the London advertising agency's office.

'Are you feeling better now?' Charlie asked, fanning her.

She smiled weakly. 'Yes, I'm fine, thanks.'

He frowned, looking worried. 'I dunno, Cleo. You still look positively ashen; and you hit the desk with a hell of a thump. Is this how you blacked out at the weekend, when this new man of yours rescued you in the British Museum?'

'Mm.' She hated to admit it but, in the circumstances, she could do nothing else. What she wasn't prepared to tell him was what she'd seen, the sheer eroticism of the visions.

'Look, I really think that you ought to see a doctor.'

She shook her head, and immediately wished that she hadn't when the room swam again. 'I'm all right, Charlie, really.'

He gave a disbelieving snort. 'If you were all right, Cleo, then you wouldn't be fainting all over the place, would you?'

She was in no mood to argue. 'All right, all right, I'll ring up and make an appointment when I get home.'

'You'll make one,' he said, picking up the phone, 'right now. And if you don't, I'll do it for you. I mean it.'

She wrinkled her nose. 'Charlie, don't fuss. I'll do it when I get home.'

'Hm. Well, I'll ask you about it tomorrow.' He replaced the receiver. 'And I warn you, if you haven't made an appointment, I'll set Sara on you – in her most ferocious rottweiler mode.'

She smiled weakly. 'Oh, Charlie. You're such a clown.'

'Should've been Chaplin, I know,' he quipped. 'Do you want a coffee, or some water?'

'Water would be nice. Please.'

He patted her hand, relieved. 'OK, Cleo. Water of the Nile, it is.'

In the circumstances, Rachel thought, *that isn't particularly funny*. All the same, she smiled, as he expected her to. As he turned away, her face darkened. *What the hell is going on?* she thought. *Why do I keep seeing these visions? Who are those people? What's their connection with me? And why does the man have Daniel's eyes?* She squeezed her eyes tightly shut, and then opened them again. Visions or no visions, she had work to do. When Charlie returned with the glass of water, she was deep in the perfume brief again, scribbling down a few ideas on the pad beside her. He set the glass in front of her without comment, and picked up his own copy of the brief.

'You look beautiful,' Daniel told her, appraising Rachel's black tailored jacket and the matching straight skirt which came to just above her knee. Rather than the flat and sensible shoes that she'd worn to the museum, she was wearing black patent leather court shoes with narrow high heels, and her hair was caught back in a black velvet Alice band. Her demure cream silk shirt was buttoned to the neck, and the only hint of colour was in the string of lapis-lazuli beads she wore. Her make-up was minimal, but effective in the way that it widened her eyes and emphasized the beautiful curve of her lips.

'They're my office clothes,' she told him with a smile. 'If you're likely to see clients, you have to dress up a bit. They expect people in advertising to be a bit glam.'

'Yes. Have you had a good day, then?' Daniel asked, kissing her lightly.

'Pretty average, thanks.' She decided not to tell him about the blackout. Having her creative partner nagging her to make a doctor's appointment was bad enough, without her lover nagging her as well. She slipped her arm through his. 'How about you?'

He pulled a face. 'Let's just say that first year students aren't my favourite.'

'They think that they know everything, right?'

He was surprised. 'How did you know?'

'Because one of my tutors said exactly the same thing to me, years ago. Though I should add that I was a third year, at the time, and she was supervising my dissertation. She was more of a friend than a tutor, by that point.' She smiled wryly at the memory. 'So what are the plans for tonight?'

Daniel put his mouth close to her ear. 'First of all, I'm going to feed you; and then I thought that I might fuck you silly.'

'Daniel!' She coloured beautifully.

He nibbled her earlobe. 'Well, you did ask.' Straightening up again, he slid his arm round her shoulders. 'Where do you fancy eating? I know a very nice place in Islington High Street, if you want to head back to your part of town; or we could eat *chez* Sinclair.'

She slid her arm round his waist. 'Don't tell me – pasta, cheese, blueberries and Margaux?' she teased.

'Something like that. How does pasta, garlic bread, salad and praline ice-cream sound? Followed by Blue Mountain coffee?'

She gave him a sidelong look. 'Very New Mannish.'

He grinned. 'If I cook for you, Princess, you do the washing up.'

'Deal,' she said. 'If you do the drying.'

They took the tube back to Walthamstow, and walked along the streets to his house, their arms wrapped round each other.

'Well, this is it,' he said, leading her down a black-and-red chequered tile path towards one of the middle houses in a Victorian terrace.

The door-knocker was brass Arts and Crafts, in the shape of a woman's face; Rachel ran her fingers over the flowing hair. 'This is beautiful, Daniel.'

He coughed. 'Um. I suppose I have as much of a thing about the Victorians as you do about the Egyptians.'

'The Victorians,' she reminded him, 'had a lot to do with the excavations of the tombs. Mind you, some of them were more professional than others.'

He grinned. 'Who's going to lecture whom tonight, I wonder? Will it be you telling me about Egypt, or me boring the pants off you about the Arts and Crafts movement?' He opened the door, and ushered her inside.

Rachel looked round the hall. 'Very nice,' she said, running her hand down the polished mahogany banisters. 'And I love the border.'

'Designer's Guild. Their Morris collection,' he told her. 'Do you want a tour of the place before I feed you?'

'Oh dear. Is it that obvious, or do you just think that all women are nosy?'

'A little of both. Plus,' he admitted, 'I poked around your flat. It's only fair to give you the same chance to look round my place.'

The recesses around the cast iron fireplace in the living room were filled with history books, plus the complete works of Thomas Hardy and a shelf of obscure Victorian novels. The sofa was covered in dark green Morris-patterned fabric, and matching curtains hung at the large bay window, with a matching border round the pale green walls. A reproduction Burne-Jones hung on the wall in a mahogany and gilt frame, a Turkish rug in green and blue was spread in front of the fire on top of the toning pale green velvet-pile carpet, and a small but powerful stereo was tucked away in the corner of the room, together with a small television and a video recorder.

'It isn't what I'd expected,' Rachel said.

'Oh?' He tipped his head slightly to one side. 'Tell me more.'

'Well – apart from the fact that it's tidy, it's . . .' She sighed. 'Don't take this the wrong way, Daniel, but most men don't have a clue about whether carpets and curtains and sofas match or clash. These are absolutely perfect. My designer friends couldn't have done better.'

'So you detect a woman's touch, then?' he asked.

She nodded.

'Well, as I told you, I'm single, and I live on my own.'

'Ex-girlfriend?' she hazarded.

He chuckled. 'My mother, actually. When I moved in, this place needed a fair bit doing to it. She's an interior decorator, and she had a whale of a time sorting this out. Especially when I told her I wanted it done in period style, though I'd prefer plain walls to heavy paper. She went potty with her suppliers, finding the right sorts of borders and what have you.'

'It's lovely. She's very talented,' Rachel said honestly.

He led her into the dining room. The large oak table was partly covered with papers, and a computer sat at a smaller oak table in the corner of the room. 'It doubles as my study,' he explained. 'I was going to use one of the bedrooms, but I really couldn't be bothered to trek downstairs every time that I wanted a coffee. This is more convenient.'

The kitchen, to Rachel's surprise, turned out to be modern in design, rather than Victorian. The units along one wall were bleached pine, and the walls and work-surfaces were covered with Delft blue ceramic tiles. A large pine dresser stood on the other side of the room, adorned with blue and white plates. There was a small pine table in the centre of the room, with two chairs, and the floor was made of shiny red pamment tiles.

'Sit yourself down,' he said, gesturing to the chairs. He turned to the small CD player on one of the worktops, and the strains of a string quartet floated into the air.

'Mozart?' she guessed.

He was impressed. 'Do you know it?'

She shook her head. 'You said that you like Mozart, so I suppose it was a bit of an educated guess.'

'It's the Hunt quartet,' he told her. 'One of my favourites. Now, would you like a coffee, or would you prefer something alcoholic?'

'Coffee would be lovely, thanks,' she said, taking off her jacket and hanging it on the back of the chair. 'Can I give you a hand?'

He shook his head. 'There's not much to do, really, apart from opening a bag of salad, cooking some ravioli, and putting the garlic bread in the oven.' He smiled at her, and put the kettle on. 'White, isn't it?'

'Yes, please.' She nodded.

'You know, the best way to drink coffee is unadulterated,' he told her.

'You mean, you're too absent-minded to put milk in it,' she teased.

'For that,' he said, 'you can do the wiping up as well.'

She stood up and slid her arms round his waist, resting her head on his shoulder. 'Sorry,' she said.

'Creeping isn't going to get you out of it,' he said, putting his arms round her and stroking the soft curve of her bottom.

'No.' She could feel his cock hardening against her, and deliberately rubbed her hips against his.

'Tease,' he said, rubbing his cheek against hers and then licking her earlobe.

'And who was it who said that he was going to fuck me silly?'

'Oh, I am.' He drew his mouth down the sensitive spot on her neck. '*After* I've fed you, Ms Meaden.'

She caressed the outline of his cock through his dark trousers. 'Oh, yes?'

'Yes.' He brushed his thumb over one hardening nipple. 'My bed is a hell of a lot more comfortable than the floor – or the kitchen table, for that matter. Besides, I'm starving.'

She pouted at him. 'So am I.'

'Fifteen minutes, and we can eat,' he promised. 'Then we can take the ice-cream to bed with us.'

'Into messy games, are we?'

He smiled, kissing her lightly on the lips. 'There's only one way to find out, isn't there?'

She laughed, and let him extricate himself from the embrace. 'The kettle's boiled.'

'I know.' He took some ground coffee from the freezer. 'One of my American colleagues told me that this keeps it fresher,' he explained, at her surprised look; then swiftly made the coffee, added milk to hers, and handed her a steaming mug. They chatted easily while Daniel sorted out dinner; finally, he uncorked a bottle of Chablis, poured them both a glass, and sat down with her at the small pine table.

'Mm,' Rachel said after her first mouthful. 'Gorgeous.'

'Only the salad dressing's home-made,' he said. 'Next time, I'll do it properly.'

She gaped. 'You mean, you make your own pasta?'

He grinned. 'You must know some very undomesticated men.'

'I do indeed,' she said, thinking of Charlie – who lived on peanut butter sandwiches and takeaway pizza, unless he could persuade the latest girlfriend to cook for him.

'Well.' He forked up some more ravioli.

Daniel had a beautiful mouth, Rachel thought, watching him eat. His lips were soft and well-shaped, revealing even white teeth when he laughed. She remembered how he'd used his mouth on her, that Sunday afternoon, and it made a delicious shiver run through her. She longed to feel his mouth on her body again, bringing her to another climax and another and another, until they were both sticky and sated ... She smiled. Later.

From a purely professional viewpoint, too, Daniel was very attractive. He would have made a good model, she thought. For something expensive, something luxurious. A good aftershave, or a watch, maybe.

'What's up?' he asked.

'Hm?'

'You were staring. Is there something on my face?'

She shook her head, smiling. 'No.'

'Then what?'

'Do you really want to know?'

He nodded.

'I was thinking what a beautiful mouth you have. You'd make a great ad,' she said. To her amusement, he actually blushed. She reached out and stroked his hand. 'I mean it. You'd be perfect for an aftershave ad, or maybe for designer watches.'

'Well, I'm afraid that I'm just a boring old history lecturer,' he said lightly, 'not one of your male super-models.'

'Don't fish.'

He laughed. 'You started it.'

'Mm.' She kicked off her shoes, and slid one foot under the bottom of one trouser-leg, stroking his ankle with her toes.

In response, he bent down to pick up her other leg, resting her foot in his lap and stroking her calves. His eyes held hers, watching the way her pupils expanded as desire flooded through her. 'This isn't going to work, is it?' he asked wryly.

'What isn't?'

'Eating, first.' He caressed the hollows of her ankle. 'How about we take a little break somewhere more comfortable, and I'll reheat this stuff in the microwave, later?'

'That sounds like the comment of a man who's obsessed with sex.'

He laughed. 'And that, Princess, is entirely your fault.' He released her foot, and stood up.

'What about the ice-cream?' she teased.

'Later.' He pulled her into his arms. 'At the moment, I'm more interested in eating you.'

'Promises, promises.'

'Promises,' he said softly against her ear, 'I always keep.'

A shiver ran down her spine. There was something so

familiar about his words, and the way he said them . . . She swallowed as a picture suddenly flashed before her, of the beautiful Egyptian man who looked so much like Daniel. His face was serious, his pupils expanded so that his eyes looked dark and sombre: and he was saying the same thing. *Promises, I always keep.*

'Rachel?' Daniel was concerned. 'Are you all right? You're not having another one of those dizzy spells, are you?'

'I'm fine,' she said, reaching up to tangle her hands in his hair and bring his face down to hers. She rubbed her nose against his, then lightly ran her tongue along his lower lip. His mouth opened involuntarily, and she took advantage of it, kissing him deeply.

Daniel was shaking when she broke the kiss.

'I believe you said that your bed was a tad more comfortable than the kitchen floor,' she said huskily against his ear.

'It is,' he said with an effort, sliding his hands down her back to cup her buttocks. He released her, then took her hand and led her upstairs.

His bedroom was again in Victorian decor, in blue and cream; Rachel noted with approval that his bed was king-sized. Daniel swiftly drew the curtains, and switched on the bedside lamp before coming back to stand before her. 'You're so bloody beautiful, Rachel,' he murmured, sliding his hand under her hair and stroking the back of her neck.

'Would you still have done your knight in shining armour act, if I'd been middle-aged and a raddled hag?' she asked.

'Of course I would.' He smiled. 'Mind you, I don't think that we'd be in this situation now, if you had.'

'That's ageist. Not to mention unfair to the decoratively-challenged,' she teased.

'That's as maybe . . . Oh, Rachel, just shut up and kiss me,' he said.

She smiled, and tipped her face up to his, doing as he asked. While she kissed him, he unzipped her skirt, gently easing it over her hips, and unbuttoned her shirt. 'Oh, wow,' he said, as she broke the kiss and he realized what she was wearing underneath: an ivory stretch lace teddy, and hold-up black stocking with lace welts.

'It goes with my work suit,' she said.

'Oh, really?' he said in tones of disbelief.

She grinned. 'All right. I guessed that we'd end up taking each other's clothes off, at some point this evening, so I wore it as a surprise for you.'

He stroked the creamy skin at the top of her thighs. 'And what a surprise.'

She undid her necklace. 'Can I put this somewhere safe?'

He nodded and took it from her, placing it on the bedside cabinet before turning back to her. Gently, she unbuttoned his shirt, removing it and letting it drop to the floor while she concentrated on the buckle of his belt. She slid her hand down his groin, caressing the outline of his engorged cock. 'Mm. This feels nice. Verrry nice indeed.' Giving him a completely over-the-top pout, she undid his trousers, and inched the material down. He stepped out of the garment, removing his socks at the same time; gently, she removed his silk boxer shorts.

'Are you quite sure that you don't want to be in one of my ads?' she asked, appraising his body.

He laughed. 'Thanks for the offer, but I think I'll stick to being a boring history lecturer.'

'Don't say that I didn't offer.' She cupped his balls with one hand, stroking his cock with the other. 'Mm. Nice.'

'Then what are you going to do about it?' he asked.

'That,' she said, 'is entirely up to you.'

Gently, he slid the thin shoulder-straps of the teddy down her arms, drawing the garment down until her breasts were exposed. 'Mm,' he said, bending down to kiss their rosy tips, suckling each nipple in turn until they were hard peaks. He buried his face in her cleavage for a moment, breathing in her perfume, then continued to roll the teddy down her body, exposing her abdomen and finally the fluffy triangle of hair at the apex of her thighs.

He let the material fall to the floor, but he couldn't resist leaving the stockings, liking the contrast between the dark sheer material and the creaminess of her skin. He slid one hand between her thighs, cupping her mons veneris; he could feel the moist heat of her quim against his fingers. Gently, he probed the satiny cleft, and was gratified to hear Rachel's breathing grow uneven as he worked on her clitoris.

They walked backwards until they reached the bed; Daniel threw off the duvet, and picked her up, laying her down gently on the bed. Rachel tipped her head back onto the plump feather pillows. 'Mm. You're right. This is *much* more comfortable than the kitchen table,' she pronounced.

'I'm glad to hear it,' he said, stretching out on his side next to her and stroking her skin, his fingers moulding themselves to her soft curves. 'God, you feel so good.'

Her eyes darkened as she curled her fingers round his cock. 'So do you.'

He shifted so that he was lying between her thighs, his weight all on his elbows and knees. 'Oh, Rachel, I need this so much,' he said softly, closing his eyes in bliss as the tip of his cock nudged against her entrance.

She curled her legs round his waist, and pushed up hard so that he sank into her wet velvety depths. They lay together for a moment, Rachel glorying in the way that he filled her to the hilt, and Daniel loving the way that her musky sex-flesh enveloped him; and then he began to move with soft, unhurried thrusts.

The hairs on his chest created a delicious friction against her swollen nipples; she groaned with pleasure when he slid one hand between them to seek out and pleasure her clitoris, manipulating the sensitive nub of flesh until it seemed that fire streamed through her veins. She cried out his name as pleasure pulsed through her, making her head spin, and felt rather than heard his answering cry as he, too, reached a climax.

What seemed a long time later, Daniel finally withdrew from her, his beautiful aqua grey eyes tender as he looked at her. 'Do you fancy a shower before we finish dinner?' he asked, getting off the bed.

She smiled, stretching like a cat and then joining him. 'Sounds good to me.' She bent down to peel off her stockings. He took her hand and they wandered through to the bathroom. As she'd half expected, it was distinctly Victorian in style, down to the carved feet on the bath and the old-fashioned taps. Even the shower over the bath – which should have been a glaring anachronism – was in keeping with the rest of the room.

Daniel switched on the water, tested the temperature, and lifted her into the bath, climbing in beside her and pulling the shower curtain across. He took a bar of lemon-scented soap and lathered her back, smoothing her muscles at the same time. Rachel waited for him to rinse the suds off her skin, then turned round to face him. 'I take it that the rest of me gets the same treatment?' she asked.

'What a good idea, Princess,' he said laconically, lathering his hands and soaping every inch of her breasts, playing with them before moving on to the rest of her body. He lingered in the curve of her waist and over the soft roundness of her belly: she was all woman, he thought, soft curves and not trying to look like an ironing-board – unlike half of his colleagues, who were more obsessed with working out in the university gym than with their work.

'My turn,' he said, handing her the soap and turning his back on her. She lathered his back, enjoying the opportunity to stroke his flanks and feel the muscles in his back move under her fingers. He turned round again, with a smile, and she was amused and flattered to see that his cock was hard again.

With a smile, she lathered his chest, rinsed the soap off, and then turned to his abdomen. Before he had any idea what was in her mind, she knelt down, taking his cock in one hand and cupping his balls in the other.

She circled his glans with her tongue, flicking the sensitive groove at its base; at his muffled groan, she took the whole of his cock into her mouth, sliding her lips along it and sucking hard. With her other hand, she gently massaged his balls.

The fine spray of water fell on her back, wetting her hair as she worked on his cock, her lips and tongue probing his sensitive spots as her fingers caressed him. Daniel's legs were suddenly weak, and he leaned against the tiled wall for support. He felt his balls lift and tighten, and finally his creamy seed jetted into her mouth. Rachel swallowed every drop, then caught his eye and licked her lips, before standing upright again.

'I think that I've worked up a bit of an appetite, now,' she said with a grin.

He laughed, and leaned forward to kiss her lightly. 'What a woman,' he said admiringly.

He switched off the shower, and climbed out, grabbing one of the large bath sheets from the pine towel-rail and wrapping it round Rachel before lifting her out of the shower. He wrapped another round himself, and then dedicated himself to drying her, the soft fluffy towel mopping up the moisture from her skin.

Rachel was touched by the cherishing gesture: even more so when he wrapped another towel round her, sarong style. 'It saves you having to dress for dinner,' he said with a grin. 'Besides, if you were sitting opposite me in that lace confection again, we'd never get to eat dinner.'

She slid her arms round his neck. 'And that would never do, would it?'

He laughed, and kissed her. He dried himself swiftly, wrapped another towel round his waist, and shepherded her out of the bathroom. 'Come on, Princess. Food. And I think that we should drink a toast to the British Museum – or whatever it was that made you faint in my arms.'

'Mm.' A small coil of fear knotted in Rachel's stomach, but she forced it away. She was with Daniel, in Walthamstow, near the end of the twentieth century – not somewhere on the Nile, in the past. Nothing could happen to her. Not here. She made herself smile back at him. 'To the British Museum,' she said softly.

THREE

Rachel looked at her watch in surprise. It was later than she'd thought: and she was supposed to be elsewhere, twenty minutes ago. She stretched luxuriously, yawned, and stood up. She replaced her papers in the file and put them, together with her pad and pen, into the middle drawer of her desk – unlike her creative partner, who preferred working in chaos, she believed in keeping to their office's clear desk policy – and ruffled Charlie's hair on her way out of the office. 'See you tomorrow, then.'

'Huh?' He glanced at his watch. 'Oh, yeah. I think it's time that I was out of here, too.'

Rachel grinned at him. 'I'll just finish this last little bit, before I go,' she mimicked. Charlie always ended up staying late, 'just to finish' something or other. Not because he was a slow worker – far from it – but because he adored his job.

'If I don't, I'll brood about it all night,' he protested.

'Even so, you work too hard.'

'Says you.' Charlie pulled a face at her. 'Well, see you later, Cleo. Have a good evening.'

She gave him an over-emphasized wink. 'I don't think that that'll be a problem, somehow.'

'Going out somewhere nice with this new man of yours, are you?'

She shook her head. 'It's Wednesday, Charlie.'

'Oh, yeah.' He suddenly remembered. 'Your girly night with Carrie.'

'You bet it is.' Wednesday nights were almost an institution; she and Carrie always met up after work on Wednesdays for a girly gossip, a drink and something to eat. It had started when they had first worked together at DFA, and had continued long after Carrie had left the agency.

'Give her my love, then. And have a drink for me.'

She grinned. 'I think it might be a little more than one.'

He grinned back. 'Drink loads of water before you go to bed – otherwise you'll have a hangover, and I can't cope with you when you're being grumpy.'

'Grumpy? *Moi?*'

'When you've got a hangover, yes.'

She pulled a face at him, and left the building, heading for the small wine bar where she and Carrie usually met. Carrie was already there, with an almost-full bottle of wine and two glasses sitting on the small polished table in front of her. She raised her hand as Rachel walked into the bar and glanced round the room, looking for her friend.

'Hi.' Rachel hurried over to the table and threw herself into the chair opposite Carrie. 'Sorry that I'm a bit late. I was working on something, and I just lost track of time.'

'You mean, you were slaving for David again, on yet another tight deadline.'

'Something like that.' Rachel smiled. David Foster, the head of their agency, had clashed spectacularly with Carrie on more than one occasion; theirs was a love-hate relationship, even now. 'But at least I'm here, now. Charlie's still working.'

'Charlie ought to ask for a pay rise, or an assistant. So

should you, for that matter. If you've got too much to do, you're either not up to the job – which certainly isn't true of you, or of Charlie – or you've got far too much to do, and your manager isn't doing his job properly in allocating the work.'

'Yeah, well. It's the same everywhere, nowadays. There are plenty of places that are a lot worse than DFA. Anyway, Charlie and I both like what we do.' Rachel leaned over, and kissed her friend on the cheek. 'So how are you, then?'

'Fine.' Carrie scrutinized her friend. 'But something good's obviously happened to you.'

Rachel tipped her head on one side, her eyes narrowed. 'How do you mean?'

'Well, your eyes are sparkling, and you've got that satisfied look about you. The proverbial cat and cream look, I'd say.'

Rachel grinned. 'You mean, I'm looking smug.'

Carrie shook her head. 'No, nothing like that. It's a nice look. Sort of happy and contented and excited, all at the same time.'

'Well.' Rachel shrugged. 'It's just life, at the moment.'

'What's his name?'

Rachel played dumb. 'Sorry?'

'Oh, come on, Rach. I've known for you long enough to be able to tell when a man's involved.'

'True.' Rachel and Carrie had met, seven years before, when they'd both joined David Foster Associates as graduate trainees. Carrie had specialized in account handling, and had eventually been head-hunted by a rival agency; Rachel had been promoted to senior copywriter, and had turned down half a dozen offers, preferring to stay where she was. She liked her job, and knew that if she went much further up the ladder, she'd have to spend more of her time managing people and balancing budgets, and less of her time doing what she enjoyed most – creating. Carrie had often teased her friend about her lack of ambition, but the teasing was completely good-natured. Both of them accepted the other's differences, and didn't begrudge them.

'OK, OK, you're right. I've met someone,' Rachel admitted.

'Not just someone, either, by the look of you! Come on, tell all.' Carrie filled a glass for Rachel, and topped up her own glass. She lifted her glass in a toast. 'Well, cheers.'

'Cheers,' Rachel answered, sipping her wine. 'Mm. Chardonnay.'

'What else?'

Rachel grinned. 'They don't call you the Chardy Queen for nothing.'

'Don't change the subject,' Carrie admonished her, laughing. 'Just tell me about this new man of yours.'

Rachel spread her hands. 'What do you want to know?'

Carrie groaned. 'Rach, don't be so mean. *Tell* me.'

'His name's Daniel, he's a history lecturer, and he's a couple of years older than I am.'

'Looks?'

'Ten out of ten. He's tall, with dark hair, and these incredible eyes – a sort of aqua grey. Long lashes – the sort to kill for. A gorgeous mouth.' Rachel's lips twitched. 'And a nice bum.'

Carrie chuckled. 'What about the rest of his anatomy?'

'If anyone else had asked me that, I'd have told them where to go.'

'But as *I've* asked you?'

Rachel chuckled. 'Let's just say that you'd approve of him, Carrie.'

'So how did you meet him?'

'Ah.' Rachel rubbed her jaw. 'I fainted, in the British Museum, would you believe? Anyway, he caught me.'

'You *what*?' The teasing light left Carrie's face, and her dark eyes were filled with concern. 'Rach, are you OK?'

'Yes. I think that it's just because it was so hot and stuffy in there. There's nothing to worry about, honestly.'

'It was just a one-off, then?'

Rachel decided to lie. 'Yeah, yeah. It was my own fault, for not bothering with lunch. Low blood sugar and no oxygen has the same effect on most people – you start feeling dizzy and a bit faint. Anyway, like I said, he caught me, and took me for a cup of coffee. And . . . Well, it just went on from there.'

'Don't tell me that he's into Egypt at well?'

Rachel shook her head. 'Not Egypt, exactly: pretty much the museum in general. He lectures on Victorian history. He wanted to be an archaeologist, until he discovered that it meant digging up dead people.'

Carrie chuckled. 'Yeah, he has a point. I don't think that I'd like to do that.'

'How about you?' Rachel asked. 'You're looking pretty happy, yourself.'

'I'm fine. Work's going well. Actually,' Carrie confided in a much lower voice, 'I'm up for promotion. They're thinking about making me a junior partner.'

'That's great,' Rachel said warmly. 'About time, too.'

'Mind you, I very nearly screwed it up.' Carrie rolled her eyes. 'You know I've always had a rule never to sleep with colleagues or clients.'

'Carrie – you didn't!'

'Not a colleague.' Carrie lifted her chin, a flash of anger

crossing her face. 'I won't let anyone say that Caroline Taylor fucked her way to a promotion.'

'You don't need to screw your way up the ladder. You're bloody good at what you do, and everyone knows it,' Rachel said, laying a placatory hand on top of her friend's. 'I assumed you meant that you ended up in bed with a client, anyway.'

'He wasn't *exactly* a client.'

Rachel tipped her head on one side, intrigued. 'What, then?'

'I suppose you could say that he was an almost-client. We blew the pitch.' Carrie wrinkled her nose. 'It was for one of these luxury ice-creams, a new brand on the market. God, I would have liked to get that one – if only for all the product testing my team would have had to do. For the sake of the brief, of course. Can you imagine, indulging yourself every single day with a huge tub of decent ice-cream?'

'And someone nice to share it with,' Rachel said. 'Mm. My idea of bliss.' She smiled at her friend. 'And now you're the one changing the subject. So what happened?'

'Well, the day after the client gave us his decision ...' Carrie's dark eyes sparkled. 'I had this phone call.'

'Tell me more.'

'Not here,' Carrie said.

Rachel looked around, and realized that she recognized nearly half the people in the wine bar. There were too many people from rival agencies around them for Carrie to risk telling such an intimate story. In their business, gossip travelled faster than anything else, and had ruined more than one career. Carrie had worked too hard to let her career slide in that way. 'Dinner at my place, or at yours?' she suggested.

'Takeaway pizza, at mine,' Carrie said decisively.

'Sounds good to me.'

They continued chatting lightly and inconsequentially, avoiding anything they didn't want reported over the grape-vine. When they'd finished the bottle, Rachel followed her friend out of the wine bar. Unsurprisingly, a large number of male heads turned to watch Carrie's exit. Carrie had jet black hair, dark almond-shaped eyes and olive skin, inherited from her Italian mother, and she was wearing a sharply-tailored, short-skirted red suit, teamed with very high-heeled black patent leather shoes. Daily workouts meant that her figure was absolutely perfect: a narrow waist, softly curved hips, and generous breasts, with long, lissom legs. Rachel often thought that if she didn't like Carrie so much, she could easily have hated her, for looking so glamorous and being so talented.

Theirs had been an unlikely friendship, with Rachel being quiet and a little on the shy side, while Carrie was extremely confident and outgoing, the sort who organized office parties and was the life and soul of every occasion. With the exception of Daniel, Rachel rarely slept with a lover within a month of starting the relationship; whereas Carrie, who was dedicated to pleasure, had as many lovers as she pleased, whenever and wherever the fancy took her, and she wasn't particularly fussy about how well she knew her lovers beforehand. Rachel knew that Carrie had made love with more than one man at the same time, too, and suspected that Carrie had also made love with other women. Her experience was so much broader than Rachel's that, although Rachel was no prude, she felt like a prim little virgin, compared to Carrie.

And yet they'd clicked, from the first moment that they'd met at DFA. They'd started chatting, discovered that they had similar tastes in music and art and food and books, and had become close. Even though Carrie was much more ambitious than Rachel, they'd stayed best friends over the years.

They caught a cab back to Carrie's Docklands flat. Carrie opened the door, and kicked off her shoes; Rachel followed suit, and padded into the sitting room. She sank into one of the soft white leather chairs, and groaned. 'Bliss. If you ever want to get rid of this suite, Carrie, I want first refusal.'

Carrie chuckled. 'It wouldn't suit your flat, Cleo. It's too modern, too stark.'

'I don't care.'

'I'm not getting rid of it. Remember how long it took me to find it?'

'Yes. And how many pairs of shoes we both went through, when you dragged me off shopping.'

Carrie laughed. 'Considering that you're as much of a shopaholic as I am, Rach . . .' She picked up the cordless phone. 'Right, let's get the pizza sorted. We took a client to this place in Mayfair, the other day, and I was introduced to a new topping.' She gave Rachel a sidelong glance. 'Fancy trying it?'

Rachel returned her friend's glance. 'That depends on what it is.'

'It sounds weird – the sort of thing a pregnant woman would crave, even – but trust me, you'll love it. I did.' Carrie smiled winningly at her friend.

Rachel, knowing that Carrie was in persuasive mode, and there was no point in arguing, gave in gracefully. 'OK, then. Let's give it a whirl.'

'Good.' Carrie rapidly dialled the number of the pizza delivery place, and smiled in satisfaction as the phone was answered within three rings. 'Yes, hello. I'd like a pizza delivered some time in the next twenty minutes, please. It's Carrie Taylor.' She gave the address. 'I'd like two large Margherita pizzas, with extra dolcelatte, olives, avocado and smoked salmon, plus a portion of garlic dough sticks. That's great, thanks.' She smiled at Rachel as she replaced the receiver. 'That's that sorted, then. There's a bag of salad in the fridge, and we can be lazy and have ice-cream for pudding.'

'Sounds good to me. But talking of ice-cream – what happened with this almost-client of yours, the other day? You said that were going to tell me, once we were somewhere private.'

'Ah, that.' Carrie stretched. 'Let me get us some more wine, first.'

'Need a hand?'

Carrie shook her head, and disappeared in the direction of the kitchen, returning a few moments later with a bottle of chilled chardonnay, two glasses, and a corkscrew. She opened the bottle, poured them each a glass, and lifted hers in a toast. 'Well – to us.'

'To us,' Rachel echoed. 'Now, are you going to tell me about this man, or not?'

Carrie took a leisurely sip of wine, her dark eyes sparkling. 'Well, like I told you, it was a pitch for a company who are launching a new luxury ice-cream. The account itself isn't that huge, but—' she shrugged '—it could have led to more things. And, like I said, it would have been nice to have a supply of good ice-cream on tap for a while. Anyway, we stuffed up the pitch. I don't know what went wrong, because I thought we'd done a good enough job to get it, but they decided not to give us the account. Immediately after the pitch, the client asked me if he could take me out to dinner. I turned him down nicely, but . . .' She sighed. 'I suppose I wish that I'd broken my principles.'

'You what?' Rachel was surprised. Carrie was ambitious, and her career took precedence over everything. Even if she found someone attractive, she'd turn them down if it meant compromising her principles and her career.

'Well, Ralph was pretty much my type. Tall, dark hair, cornflower blue eyes. He looked a bit like Charlie Sheen.'

Rachel groaned. 'Oh, God. I should have known that *that* was coming. You're the only person I know with a copy of *Hot Shots, Part Deux* that's unplayable for about three minutes in the middle, because you've played your favourite scene so much, you've worn it out!'

'Says the woman who did the same with her favourite *X files* episode, fantasizing that she was the vampire being kissed very thoroughly by Fox Mulder.' Carrie grinned, unabashed. 'I tell you, if that was Charlie Sheen on the bed under me, giving me that shy yet pleased little nod . . .' She moaned, an expression of bliss crossing her face.

'Behave yourself, Taylor,' Rachel said, laughing. 'You're telling me about Ralph, not your favourite lust-objects.'

'He really was nice, though, Rach. Ten out of ten for looks. He dressed well, too. Dark grey suit – well cut, and obviously not off-the-peg stuff – a crisp white shirt, a sober and very tasteful silk tie. Armani aftershave, and hand-made well-polished shoes. I tell you, the moment I met him, I could have eaten him for breakfast. I could hardly keep my eyes off him, all through the pitch.

'I think he knew that I was interested, even though I told him that I wouldn't have dinner with him because I don't mix business and pleasure. Anyway, when the news came through that we'd lost the pitch to Barker's, he rang me again and asked me if I'd changed my mind about dinner. So I said yes. He took me to this fabulous place in Mayfair – the kind of place where they give women a menu with no prices on it. It was obviously expensive, and the food was excellent.' She swallowed. 'Though all the way through dinner, neither of us could concentrate on the food. We didn't lay a finger on each other, but, my God, did he smoulder. I think that we could read each other's minds – and it was bloody interesting reading. Then he asked me back to his place for coffee.'

She licked her lower lip. 'He lives in Regent's Park – a top floor apartment, in the most incredibly beautiful building. There was so much space, huge rooms with high ceilings; I loved it. Everything was expensive, from the curtains to the carpets to the furniture, and he had a few original water-colours. It was done in perfect taste, though. Nothing vulgar, nothing ostentatious. You could just see that it was all top quality, the kind of stuff that lasts almost forever.

'Anyway, he put the espresso machine on in the kitchen. I don't think either of us could wait for the coffee. The next thing I knew, we were kissing, and he was bunching up the hem of my dress – you know, my favourite little black one.'

'Your pulling dress,' Rachel teased.

'Yeah, well. I wasn't leaving anything to chance. Like I said, I found him attractive. I didn't want him going all prissy on me and saying he didn't sleep with a woman on a first date.'

Rachel chuckled. 'Oh, Carrie. That's real man-eater talk.'

'Believe me, any woman I know would want to eat that man.' Carrie licked her lips again. 'He slid his hands up my thigh, stroking me.' She swallowed hard. 'He slid one finger along the gusset of my knickers; God, how I wanted him to touch me! I would have begged him to do it, but he was kissing me so thoroughly, I couldn't speak. My nipples were so hard, they hurt, and I just wanted to feel him inside me. I think he could tell how hot and wet I was. Anyway, I was wearing silk knickers . . . and he just ripped them off me.'

Rachel's eyes widened. 'You're kidding!'

Carrie smiled. 'Don't worry. It was controlled violence, something we both wanted – and he more than made up for it later, believe me. God, it made me so wet when he did it. He had my dress pushed up to my waist, so I was exposed to him: he broke the kiss, then, and held me at arm's length, just looking at me. It made me so excited, seeing the desire in his eyes; he wanted me as much as I wanted him. And then he took my dress off. He was more careful with that.'

'I should think so. It cost you a fortune.' Rachel had gone shopping with Carrie on enough occasions to know just how expensive her friend's taste in clothes was.

'Mm.' Carrie almost purred at the memory. 'I knew we were going to do it, there and then, on his kitchen floor.'

'Wasn't it cold?' Rachel asked with a grin.

'Terracotta's cold, yes – but I didn't care. You wouldn't believe how good it felt, Rach. He took my bra off, very gently, and let it drop to the floor with my dress. He left my stockings on, though. And then he stripped in front of me. Very professionally: it was obviously not the first time he'd done it.' She took a sharp intake of breath at the memory. 'My God, it makes me feel hot now, even to remember it. I don't think I've ever seen a man with such a gorgeous body – or such a gorgeous cock.' She licked her lower lip again. 'I was expecting him almost to take me then and there, but he had other ideas. He was very inventive.'

'Come on, Carrie. You can't stop, now,' Rachel said. 'Tell me.'

'Well, he had this vase of white lilies on the windowsill.'

'Hang on – a bloke with flowers in his flat?'

'Mm. I think that he has a housekeeper, and she deals with that sort of thing.'

'A housekeeper.' Rachel whistled. 'He's way out of the normal run of the men we meet, then.'

'Absolutely.' Carrie almost purred. 'He walked over to the lilies, and removed one of the buds. You know what they're like, in bud: hard, about four or five inches long, like a small cock. Anyway, then he walked back over to me, and drew me down to the floor. Then he started tracing complicated patterns over my skin with the tip of the lily bud. He traced the outlines of my breasts, and the edges of my areolae, teasing me until my nipples hurt, I wanted him so much. Then he let it drift southwards, down over my midriff.' She paused. 'I had a feeling that I knew what he was going to do next; I was a bit shocked, in a way.'

'Shocked? You?' Rachel said, the affection on her face softening her scoffing tone. 'Come off it, Carrie. You were more likely to shock *him*!'

'Maybe.' Carrie closed her eyes in bliss as she remembered what had happened. 'He stroked my thighs apart, and I knew what he was going to do. I felt him slide the lily over my cunt; it was waxy and hard, like a tiny cock. The next thing I knew, he pushed the bud inside me, and withdrew it again, soaked with my juices. He rubbed it over my clitoris, moving it back and forth, then pushed it back inside me again, simulating

Evelyn D'Arcy

what he would do to me later, with his cock. All the while, he rubbed my clitoris with his thumb; just when I was at the point of coming, he dropped the lily and crouched between my legs, hooking my thighs over his shoulders and lifting me up so that he could eat me. I don't think I've ever come so hard under a man's tongue.

'And then, when I'd calmed down, he produced the lily bud again, running it over my lips so that I could taste myself. Then he licked the remaining juices himself, like a cat. God, he looked so sexy, I almost came again.' Carrie's voice became husky. 'It didn't stop there. He stood up, drew me to my feet, and led me to his bedroom. We forgot the coffee; all we wanted to do was to fuck each other silly.

'His bed was amazing, one of those wrought iron four-poster things draped in white muslin. There were thick feather pillows, and the mattress was so comfortable, you wanted to stay there forever.' She licked her lower lip. 'Even thinking about it makes me wet – what we did, the rest of the night. We made love all night, in every possible way.'

'Shaykh Nefzawi, eat your heart out?' Rachel teased.

Carrie grinned. 'I dunno about reading things like the *Perfumed Garden* – I think he could have written it.'

'That good?'

'Mm. His mouth's amazing. He made me come, time and time and time again. My stomach muscles hurt, afterwards, I'd come so much. I didn't think that I'd be able to walk, the next morning, but I still didn't want it to stop. I wanted him to make me climax again and again, filling his mouth with my juices and then kissing me hard, so I could taste myself on him. And his fingers . . . they were so expressive.' She swallowed hard. 'He used every orifice, as well.'

'You're kidding!'

'No, really. He made love to my mouth; he used his hands and his mouth and his cock on my cunt; and then, he turned me over. I mean, I've never really been a devotee of anal sex, but the way Ralph touched me ... Well, it was incredible. He'd put a pillow under me, for support, and he had me almost in a slave-girl position, kneeling with my head on my hands. But there wasn't anything submissive about it: although I was exposing myself to him, we both wanted it. He started touching me, stroking me, kissing me. He kissed up and down my spine, and I wanted to feel his mouth on my arse. I wanted him to lick me.'

Carrie's voice grew husky as she remembered. 'Then he did. I felt his tongue against me, and it was so good. Then he pressed his little finger against me; I was so ready for him, he slid in easily. He began to pump his finger in and out, until I was moaning. I think I even begged him to do it – and then he did. I felt him withdraw his finger, and then I felt something else press against me, something big and thick and hard. I wasn't sure if I could take him, he felt so big: but he was so gentle, so considerate.

'He pushed in so very slowly, stopping every so often to let me get used to the feel of him stretching me; and then, when he was in me up to the hilt, he began to move. He was rubbing my clitoris, at the same time, until I was bucking and moaning under him. I came so hard, I almost passed out.' She coughed. 'Anyway, that was my affair with the almost-client.'

Rachel whistled. 'Don't tell me that it was a one-nighter, Carrie.'

'No.' Carrie grinned. 'Far from it. The next morning, he sent me home in a cab. I had a cold shower, and drank about four cups of double-strength coffee; all I wanted to do was go to sleep and dream about the night before, but I had some important meetings. I don't think I could have cancelled them, even if I'd had a better excuse than the fact that I had spent the entire night fucking the most gorgeous man I've ever met. Anyway, I dragged myself into work; by the time I got to the office, I was more or less over my tiredness. I looked knackered – which wasn't surprising, as I'd had about ten minutes' sleep, if that – but I was glowing. I felt so good. And there, on my desk, was this huge bunch of white lilies, from him.' Her lips twitched. 'And a small box containing a pair of black silk knickers, to replace the ones he'd ruined.'

'Very stylish,' Rachel agreed. 'And I bet that your office was buzzing with gossip.'

'It was. But because he'd only signed the card with the initial R, no-one had any idea who he was.' Carrie grinned. 'They're still guessing, as a matter of fact.'

'So no-one else knows about him? Why?'

Carrie pursed her lips. 'Well, it's none of their business. It's between me and Ralph.' At Rachel's sceptical look, she sighed. 'I just don't want anyone thinking that we lost the account because I screwed Ralph.'

'You didn't. It was because one of the other agencies did a better pitch. You can't win everything, no matter how good you are,' Rachel said gently.

'I know.' Carrie shrugged. 'But it's my business, and nothing to do with the agency.'

'I take it that you're still seeing him?'

'Every night since – apart from tonight, of course. I told him that Wednesdays were reserved for you.'

Rachel's eyes widened. 'It's serious, then?' It was more of a statement than a question.

'I dunno,' Carrie said, 'but he's the first man I've ever met who can satisfy me.'

'He's worth holding onto, then,' Rachel said.

'More than holding,' Carrie said, with a wicked chuckle.

The doorbell rang, heralding their pizzas and interrupting the conversation. Both of them were hungry, and ate with gusto.

'This is brilliant,' Rachel admitted. 'I have to admit, that when I heard you say avocado and smoked salmon, I wasn't quite sure. I mean, I like my smoked salmon cold. And as for hot avocado . . .'

'Avocado's becoming quite trendy again. Like fondues, black forest gateau and prawn cocktail,' Carrie said. Her lips twitched. 'I read an article the other day – apparently, the Aztecs called the avocado the "testicle fruit", because of its shape.'

'Trust you to know that!'

'Well. I adore avocados.' Carrie gave a lascivious smile. 'I'm not sure what I like most about them, the texture or the taste.'

Rachel groaned. 'If this is going to turn into another story about your gorgeous man, I'm going.'

Carrie grinned. 'No, but you've just given me one hell of an idea . . .'

They both laughed, and finished their pizza. When they'd finished eating, Carrie made a pot of coffee, and they returned to the sitting room, curling up in comfort. 'You didn't tell me that much about your new man,' Carrie said.

'There isn't that much to tell. He's not quite as inventive as yours.'

'You mean, you've slept with him already?' Carrie was surprised. Rachel usually kept her lovers at arm's length, until she knew them a lot better.

'Um. Yes.' Rachel flushed. 'I don't know what it is about him.' She swallowed. 'Actually, there's something else I didn't tell you. When I fainted, I had this weird vision. It was all set in Egypt, and somehow, I was there. I don't know if I was a princess, or a daughter who was having a forbidden liaison with a strange man – but it was incredibly erotic. It was so real.'

'If that's what the British Museum does to you, maybe it's about time that I paid the place another visit,' Carrie quipped. 'Rach, you were probably reading something steamy the night before, and when you blacked out, your brain scrambled it up a bit and re-translated it, dragging in your surroundings.'

'Yeah.' Rachel bit her lip. 'The only thing is, I've experienced it a couple of times since – on the tube, and in the office.'

'What, fainting? I thought you said that it was just the once?'

'Um.' Rachel flushed. 'A couple of times.'

'Where?'

'In the office. I didn't feel as though I blacked out: just that I saw things. I kept seeing this woman, who was like me but not like me, and a man . . . He looked like Daniel.'

'Well, that's your subconscious projecting.'

'No.' Rachel shook her head. 'The man's eyes . . . They were the same as Daniel's. And I hadn't met Daniel when I first saw the Egyptian man in the British Museum.'

'Maybe you'd seen him – you know, noticed someone out of the corner of your eye – but hadn't realized it,' Carrie suggested.

'I don't know. Maybe. But it's weird, Carrie. I don't just see things – I feel them, too. When he touches her, it's like he's touching me. When Daniel took me home, I seemed to see the Egyptian man, reflected on the window. And I was sitting on a throne, not on the Central line. He was crouching between my feet, stroking my thighs and then nuzzling his way under my robe, licking me.' Rachel shivered. 'I could feel everything that he was doing. And I came, right there and then, on the tube – though, thank God, I didn't make a sound.' Rachel paused. 'Then, I blacked out in the office, yesterday.'

'Maybe I should have made you eat lots of spinach, instead,' Carrie said.

Rachel caught her friend's inference immediately. 'I'm not anaemic, Carrie. I probably eat a better-balanced diet than you do.' She pulled a face. 'I don't understand what's happening to me, though.'

'You ought to get to a doctor and check it out.'

'That's what Charlie said. I promised him I'd make an appointment. He said, if I don't, he'll set Sara on me to make sure that I do.'

'Good. And I'm going to ring you tomorrow, to make sure you have.'

Rachel smiled. 'Carrie, don't fuss. I don't think anything's wrong with me, physically. It's just ... I keep having these weird dreams. They're all linked up with Egypt, and sex.'

Carrie was thoughtful. 'In that case ... Maybe you should try a hypnotist, instead of a doctor.'

'Why?'

'You could be seeing some kind of past life.'

'Regression, you mean?' Rachel shook her head. 'Carrie,

you've got to be joking. You don't believe in all that mumbo-jumbo, do you?'

'All I'm saying is that there might be something in it.'

'Come off it! There are always articles in magazines about celebrities who've lived before, as part of King Henry's court or a medieval knight. It's all hype,' Rachel said.

'I don't know about that. There are more things in heaven and earth, Horatio,' Carrie quoted.

'Maybe, but I still don't believe in reincarnation.' Rachel sipped her coffee. 'Now, do you mind changing the subject?'

'All right, all right.' Carrie held her hands up in mock surrender.

Rachel had consumed enough wine with Carrie that evening to make sure that when she finally got home and went to bed, she fell asleep almost immediately. She was dimly aware of a cat mewing; expecting it to be the cat she half-shared with her neighbour, she turned over, sticking her head under her pillow. The last thing she wanted was a cold and wet cat squeezing into bed beside her and drying itself off on her.

The tapping and the faint mewing continued for a while longer; then, it was almost as though the cat had realized that she wasn't going to let it in, and had sloped off to try the neighbour, as everything was silent again. Rachel, who was only partly awake, gave a small murmur and turned over again, falling into a deeper sleep.

The next morning, after a shower and a promise to herself that she wouldn't drink that quantity of wine again on a night before she had to go to work, she grabbed a bowl of cereal. Then she wandered into the sitting room to pick up the book she'd been reading the day before. Something in the room seemed different. She frowned, unable at first to work out what it was; then she realized. The cat mummy-case that usually sat on her mantelpiece had moved, and there was a trail in the dust, showing its path.

But how on earth had it moved? Nothing else in the room had been touched. Her frown deepened. What the hell was going on? Was this another of her weird hallucinations? Or was there something more to it than that?

She grimaced. She'd been drunk the previous evening. She'd probably come home, decided to move the cat, and forgotten about it in the morning, she told herself crossly. 'Stop being such a drama queen, Meaden, and grow up,' she said loudly. She moved the cat back to its usual position, blew the dust from the mantelpiece, and closed the sitting room door.

FOUR

By the time that she got to work, Rachel had managed to put the incident completely out of her mind. It was going to be a busy day on the perfume brief. She and Charlie had presented the visuals and the copy of their proposed creative treatment to the client, who had loved it, and had agreed that the photography could go ahead. They were due in the studio that morning.

When she walked into the office, she was surprised not to see her creative partner already there. Charlie was a night person, and usually had a struggle to get up in the mornings: unless he had a photo shoot with one of his old college pals, when he'd be in at the crack of dawn, looking forward to a day of working and reminiscing. 'Where's Charlie?' she asked Sara.

The departmental secretary winced. 'Bad news, Rach, I'm afraid. He's got that awful twenty-four hour bug, and he says he feels like death warmed up.'

'It must be bad if he's missing a photo shoot and a gossip about old times with Matt. Poor old Charlie.'

'Mm. He sounded terrible,' Sara told her.

'I'll give him a ring later. Once I've rescheduled the shoot, that is.'

Sara shook her head. 'I've already tried that for you. It has to be today. Matt says that he can't fit you in for another three weeks, if you have to reschedule.'

Rachel grimaced. 'Oh, hell. That's way too late – everything has to go to print next week.'

'I know – I looked in your files. Thank God you're more organized than Charlie-boy, and I can at least read your handwriting. Anyway, I rang Charlie back to tell him, and he says do you mind going along and sorting it for him? I mean, you've worked with him on the brief. You know the sort of look you want.'

Rachel lifted her hands in mock surrender. 'Hey, I'm a word-smith. I can't design to save my life.'

'Oh, come on, Cleo.' Sara gave her a pleading look. 'You know you're talented. If you won't do it for Charlie, do it for me – or he'll make my life hell when he gets back.'

Rachel grinned. Sara was more than a match for Charlie, and they both knew it. 'Yeah, yeah,' she said.

'Seriously, Rach.' Sara looked sidelong at her. 'Think about it. You'll have to pay the model fees for today whether you shoot or not – and David's trying to make us a low-cost organization. Extra model fees will put you over budget.'

Rachel rolled her eyes. She'd almost forgotten their boss's latest dictat, that they had to save money wherever they could. Clients were cutting budgets, left, right and centre, and the agency had to do the same if they wanted to remain competitive. 'OK, OK. I'll do it. But I hope that it doesn't have to be re-shot – or the budget really will be blown.'

'It won't. Have confidence in yourself,' Sara urged, smiling at her. 'Charlie said to tell you that when he's better, he owes you a Thai meal, to make up for this.'

'I'll hold him to that,' Rachel said. She glanced at her watch. 'I'd better get going, then. I'll see you later.'

'See you,' Sara echoed. 'Hope the session goes well.'

The photographer's studio was only a couple of tube stops away. It was a nice day, so Rachel decided to walk. It might clear her head, she thought, and give her the breathing space she needed. She'd never been a hundred per cent comfortable with the design side of her work. Although she and Charlie worked as a team – and Sara was right about Rachel knowing exactly what Charlie wanted from the shoot – it still felt strange for her creative partner not to be there with her, making half a dozen seemingly tiny adjustments that she would never think of, and which always made such a huge difference to the end result.

She wasn't surprised that the photographer was booked up for weeks. Matt Harston was extremely good, and the only reason he'd managed to fit them in at short notice in the first place was because he was an old friend of Charlie's from their design college days. She'd met him a few times, and liked him; all the same, she would have been happier if Charlie had been there, too. It just didn't feel right, doing the whole thing on her own.

Matt was a nice bloke; he was also very attractive. Carrie's usual type, she thought with a grin: tall, with dark hair brushed back from his face, very blue eyes and a big nose. Nice bum, too. Her grin broadened into self-deprecation. And why she was thinking about Matt in such a way, when she'd met Daniel, God only knew. She wasn't like Carrie, able to conduct several no-strings relationships at the same time. Besides, Matt was a supplier and came under the 'don't sleep with colleagues and clients' rule.

She turned into the small side street and rang the bell. After a long pause, the intercom clicked in, and she heard Matt's deep voice. 'Yeah?'

'Hi, Matt, it's Rachel. Rachel Meaden, from DFA,' she said quietly.

'Cleopatra! Come up, sweetheart. I'm on the third floor.' She heard a buzz, then the door clicked. She opened the door, then walked up the stairs to the studio. The walls were painted stark white, and the narrow windowless passage was lit by steel tungsten lights. On the walls, on the way up, there were several of Matt's best photographs, shot in black and white and framed carefully behind non-reflective glass. She smiled to herself as she walked up the stairs. Matt really was a talented photographer. Although she suspected that he'd much rather do arty work to his own taste rather than the advertising bread-and-butter work, he was still a complete professional and delivered things exactly to brief and to deadline.

When she got to the third floor, Matt was waiting for her. He shoved a styrofoam beaker of coffee at her; she smiled ruefully. 'Oh, dear. Do I look that jaded?'

'You do look slightly hung over, yes,' he said, returning her smile. 'Anyway, time for introductions. Rachel, this is Jasmine, our model; Jasmine, this is Rachel Meaden, who works for the ad agency.'

Rachel smiled at the young woman who sat cross-legged on a bean bag on the other side of the room. She was exactly the model that Rachel would have chosen for the new perfume launch. Rachel judged her to be about twenty-six or twenty-seven. She was about five feet ten, and had jet black hair, very pale skin, and stunning green eyes. Lilith personified, Rachel thought.

Jasmine uncurled herself from the bean bag and walked gracefully across the room, holding out her hand. Rachel took it, and found her hand being shaken in a surprisingly firm grasp. 'Hi,' Jasmine said. Her voice was rich and slightly deep; it was also completely accentless. Rachel had no idea whether Jasmine was from the Home Counties, Manchester or deepest Devon.

'Hello,' Rachel said, feeling suddenly shy, and cross with herself at the same time for being so gauche.

'Matt's shown me the brief, and I think I can deliver what you want. Do you mind if I get on with my make-up?' Jasmine asked, smiling.

'No, no, that's fine.'

'See you in about five minutes, then.' She smiled again, and walked out of the room. Rachel couldn't help watching her as she walked out, noticing the smooth way that Jasmine sashayed out of the room, the clean lines of her body.

'Yeah, she's gorgeous, isn't she?' Matt said softly, breaking her thoughts.

Rachel flushed. 'I wasn't thinking about her in *that* way. I was just thinking how good she'd be in the ad – she's perfect for Lilith.'

'Oh, really?' Matt breathed against her ear. 'Come on, Rach. You can feel the effect that she has on me.' He took her hand, sliding it gently down his body until she reached his groin. His cock was already hard, throbbing against her fingers. 'I wouldn't mind betting that she has exactly the same kind of effect on you.'

Rachel flushed. 'I'm a hundred per cent heterosexual, Matt.'

'Even so, she's dynamite.' Matt's voice was husky with desire. 'I think that she could turn a straight woman into a dyke; if I were a woman, I think I'd want to make love with her. Touch her, taste her ... I don't think I could get enough of her.'

'Charlie said you had someone good lined up, but I wasn't expecting her to be *that* near to our brief. Where did you find her?' Rachel said, trying to keep her voice steady and changing the subject before Matt could make her admit that, yes, she found the model sexually attractive. She could feel her nipples hardening, and hoped that Matt hadn't noticed – or, if he had, that he put it down to his own charms rather than jumping to the right conclusion, which was that Rachel found Jasmine very attractive, and in a sexual sense.

'Through one of the agencies I use. She's done some work for me before – and I can vouch for the fact that her hair's naturally that colour, not a dye-job.'

Rachel grinned. 'This is such an incestuous business. Everyone knows everyone else.'

'That's how we all get work, isn't it?' His blue eyes sparkled as they held hers.

She chuckled. 'Stop fishing, Matthew. You know that you're good, and that's why we wanted you to do the shoot.'

'Thank you, sweetheart.' He gave her an exaggerated bow. 'Anyway, Cleo, just what have you been doing to Charlie-boy, then?'

'Nothing. He has one of those twenty-four hour bugs.'

'More like he had too hot a curry and too many beers last night.' Matt, remembering past evenings out with Charlie, raised an eyebrow. 'Were you with him, to get that kind of hangover?'

She shook her head. 'No. Anyway, who says I have a hangover?'

'I've had enough of them in my time to spot one at fifty paces.'

She smiled wryly. 'All right, all right. I'll admit I've felt better. I was out drinking with Carrie Taylor, last night.'

Matt whistled. 'That's one high-powered lady.'

'Yes, but she's a hundred per cent genuine. You always know where you stand with her.'

Matt held his hands up. 'OK, OK. There's no need to defend her to me. I know Carrie, and she's a good woman.'

'Yeah. Sorry.' Rachel coughed. 'I didn't mean to bite your head off.'

'Besides, I think that she's more than capable of fighting her own corner,' Matt added softly.

Rachel flushed. 'She's my best friend. I'm not going to sit by and listen to someone slagging her off.'

'I wasn't slagging her off.'

'I know. I'm sorry. I suppose I'm just used to people making comments like that, then sliding into bitching about her.'

Matt's smile broadened. 'I wouldn't dare bitch about Carrie. Apart from the fact that she's very good at her job, she can be one hell of a scary woman, when it suits her.'

Rachel relaxed again. 'Yes, that's true. But only when someone deserves it.'

'Mm. Thank God I've never been on the receiving end of the rough side of her tongue.' Matt gave her a teasing look. 'Not that I'd mind her using her tongue on me in more pleasurable ways, that is.'

Rachel rolled her eyes. 'Matt Harston, you old tart, keep your mind on the job in hand.'

He gave a throaty moan, and clutched his hands to his heart dramatically. 'Oh, yes, the idea of Carrie Taylor in my hands . . .'

Rachel chuckled, her bad mood forgotten. 'What's it worth not to tell her that?'

'And have her being scary next time she sees me?' Matt

laughed back. 'How about a good shot for your perfume ad?'

'Deal,' Rachel smiled. Actually, she thought, Carrie would probably be flattered to know that Matt fancied her, rather than annoyed. But with Ralph on the scene, Rachel had a feeling that Carrie would be too busy to do anything about it – even if Matt could get past Carrie's inflexible rule of not sleeping with anyone in the business.

Jasmine came back into the room, her make-up finished. She'd outlined her eyes with kohl and darkened her lips, giving her almost an Egyptian air. She was wearing a very sheer green chiffon dress, fashioned in Egyptian style; Rachel felt a pulse begin to hammer between her legs.

Stop it, she told herself. *You don't go for women.* Yet Matt was right. Jasmine was irresistible. She'd sprayed herself liberally with the new perfume; obviously, Charlie had given Matt a sample earlier. It was a heady, bewitching scent, and Rachel found herself responding to it. God, if they could capture this in the shoot today ... She smiled to herself. It would be one of their best ads yet, and Lilith would be a raging success.

She retreated to the bean bag Jasmine had been sitting on, earlier, and just watched as Matt turned into a human camera, directing Jasmine's position and altering the lights. Jasmine was a particularly good model, doing everything that Matt told her and interpreting his commands perfectly.

Rachel took another sip of the coffee, and pulled a face, putting the cup to one side. It had been kind of Matt to offer it to her. He was a damn good photographer and a nice bloke to boot, but Rachel had forgotten just how awful his coffee was. She didn't know what he did to coffee, but the end result was even worse than the near-undrinkable sludge she'd had from clients' vending machines.

As she watched the shoot, the scene seemed to blur in front of her eyes. Suddenly, she was with the beautiful aqua grey-eyed man again. They were in water, bathing in a lake; but this time, they weren't alone. There was a woman with them: a very beautiful woman, with dark hair and dark eyes. She was between the pair of them; they were swimming round her, touching her and arousing her, but teasing her by swimming away before she could touch them in turn. A gentle squeeze of a breast or a buttock, a stroke of the thigh, a gentle tweaking of her nipples ...

Rachel shuddered, suddenly aware that both Jasmine and Matt were kneeling beside her, looking concerned.

'Rachel, are you OK?' he asked.

'Yes, I'm fine. I just felt a bit strange, that's all.'

'You're not going down with this same thing that Charlie's got, are you?'

She shook her head. 'I don't think so. It's happened a couple of times, lately; it's nothing to worry about.'

Matt stroked her hand. 'Is there something you want to tell us, Cleo? Like a little addition to the Meaden household, perhaps?'

She rolled her eyes. 'I'm not pregnant, Matt. Carrie says that I'm probably just anaemic.'

'Could be,' Jasmine said. 'A few of my friends have had the same sort of thing – not eating properly, then feeling faint. From what Matt told me about you, you're a bit of a workaholic.'

'Well, I've been eating properly,' Rachel said defensively. 'There's nothing wrong with me.'

'Get it checked out by a doctor,' Matt advised her.

'I will.'

She was aware that Matt was still stroking her hand, running his thumb and forefinger down each of her fingers in turn. Jasmine was doing something similar with her other hand, rubbing her thumb against Rachel's palm. The air was suddenly electric, and Rachel's eyes widened. This was exactly the feeling she'd had in the dream – about herself, the strange man and the beautiful woman. Exactly the same deep sensuality that was spreading between Jasmine, Matt and herself.

And then Matt was kissing her very gently, his lips touching hers; he nibbled at her lower lip, coaxing her mouth open so that his tongue could explore her properly. She realized that he was undoing her shirt, revealing her bra, and then giving a sharp intake of breath as he saw her breasts swelling, her hardened nipples showing clearly through the white lace of her bra.

Jasmine gently drew Rachel to her feet, and Matt finished taking off her shirt, hanging it neatly over the back of a chair. Her skirt followed, and her half-slip, leaving her only in her stockings, knickers and bra. Matt didn't take his eyes off her, but stripped swiftly; and Jasmine just seemed to touch the top of the Egyptian-style dress and it fell to the floor, leaving her wearing only a pair of very brief lacy knickers. She, too, was obviously aroused, her nipples hard and dark and her breasts slightly swollen.

Rachel swallowed hard. She'd never made love with another woman – or with more than one person at the same time. Part of her was shocked; but part of her welcomed it, welcomed the reliving of her dream. She wanted Jasmine to touch her; she wanted Jasmine to take off her bra, to stroke her breasts and knead them gently, then to suckle on her nipples. She wanted Matt to stand behind her and slide his hands between her legs, stroking her quim and easing a finger into her, while Jasmine slipped one hand inside the front of her knickers and stroked her clitoris.

Rachel wasn't sure whether she'd said it aloud or whether they'd just read her mind, but the next thing she knew, Matt was standing behind her, pulling her back against his body so that she could feel his erection pressing against her buttocks, and Jasmine was standing in front of her, pulling down the cups of her bra to reveal her breasts.

She closed her eyes as Jasmine lifted her breasts in turn, almost weighing them, and squeezed them gently. Matt was kissing the nape of her neck, and stroking her buttocks; her quim felt hot and wet and swollen, and she wanted one of them – both of them – to touch her more intimately. She felt Jasmine trace her areolae, her fingers brushing teasingly against Rachel's throbbing nipples; and then, at last, she felt the other woman's hair brush against her skin as Jasmine bent her head. A moment later, she felt a mouth sucking rhythmically on her breast; she slid her hands into Jasmine's hair, massaging her scalp and urging her on.

At the same time, Matt eased a finger under the elastic of her knicker leg, and she felt his finger start to explore her.

'Mm, Rachel, you're all wet and hot and ready for us,' Matt murmured in her ear as he stroked her quim. 'Your cunt's dripping for me, Rachel. And for Jasmine. You want us to touch you, to fill you, don't you?'

'Yes,' Rachel hissed softly. 'Yes.'

'You want this, don't you?' He pressed his finger to the entrance of her sex. 'Or do you want more?'

'Oh, yes,' Rachel moaned.

Matt nibbled her earlobe. 'How about I fuck you from behind while Jasmine rubs your clit? Or would you like her mouth there, to feel her eating you while I'm filling you?'

Rachel's pulse began to beat faster at the scenario he was describing. 'I . . . I . . .' She swallowed, not knowing what to say. She wanted him to do it – she wanted *them* to do it – but it was so far outside her experience that she didn't know how to tell them.

He chuckled, and Jasmine dropped to the floor in front of Rachel, hooking her thumbs into the sides of Rachel's knickers and easing them down. Rachel shivered, and Jasmine crouched between her thighs.

'Easy, easy. This is going to be nice, for all of us,' Jasmine said softly. She stretched out her tongue, licking Rachel's inner thigh, and Rachel moaned, widening her stance.

Matt held her steady, and Jasmine began to explore Rachel's quim, first with her fingers, and then bending her head and using her mouth. Rachel moaned again as she felt the soft stroke of Jasmine's tongue against her musky divide, exploring her folds and crevices; she felt hot and wet, and she wanted something more, more.

'Easy,' Matt whispered, stroking her breasts with one hand and sliding his other down her back, over the curve of her buttocks.

Jasmine drew back slightly and concentrated on Rachel's clitoris, her tongue flicking cleverly across the hard nub of flesh at just the right speed and pressure; Matt let his hand drift further, and slid his finger into Rachel's quim, dipping into the moist heat of her flesh and coating his finger with a thin film of creamy juice.

'Oh, yes,' Rachel breathed, and Matt let his hand piston in and out, arousing her even further. Jasmine was still sucking Rachel's clitoris, and Matt's other hand was still playing with her breasts, pulling at her nipples in a way that made her arch against him.

'Lovely Rachel,' he murmured, and withdrew his finger, stroking her perineum. Almost at the same time, Rachel felt another finger insert itself into her quim: Jasmine's. And then Matt was pressing his lubricated finger very gently against the puckered rosy hole of her anus; she moaned, and Matt pressed harder, his finger sliding into her up to the middle joint.

'Oh, God,' Rachel moaned, half-shocked and unbearably turned on at the same time.

'Like it, do you?' he whispered.

'Yes,' she breathed hoarsely.

'My finger up your pretty little arse, and Jasmine's up your cunt, her mouth on your clit. What a beautiful film you'd make, Rachel. If only I had a camera handy – then I'd set it up so you could see what we're doing to you. I'd project it onto the wall over there, so you could see exactly how we touch you, how your body reacts.' His voice was husky with arousal. 'You'd like that, wouldn't you? Watching us finger you and fuck you and bring you to climax?'

The combination of his words and their actions were enough to make Rachel come; her internal muscles spasmed wildly round Jasmine's fingers, and Matt laughed softly. 'Oh, Rachel. I can feel you coming. I can feel the pulse beat in your arse, and the way you're coming round Jasmine's fingers.'

'I . . .' This was what the people in her dream would

be doing, Rachel realized with shock. Touching each other, making love – with her as the central pivot.

Gently, Matt withdrew his finger. 'Lean forward,' he said softly.

Rachel froze. Was he planning to do what Carrie had described Ralph doing to her in such graphic detail? But she'd never done that before: she wasn't sure that she wanted to.

'I'd like to feel your cunt flexing round me,' he informed her, licking her earlobe. 'So stop worrying. We won't make you do anything you're not ready to do.'

She flushed. God, if her doubts were that obvious, he must think she was so gauche. Not like the women that Matt was used to. She licked her suddenly dry lips. 'I . . . I'm sorry.'

'Don't be. You're lovely, Rachel. I love the idea of exploring all sorts of things with you, and introducing you to new pleasures. But I need to feel my cock in you, Rachel, right now. I need to feel you wrapped round me, like warm wet silk.'

It was an irresistible appeal; Rachel bent forward slightly, and Matt slid the tip of his cock over her still-flexing quim, the hard rounded tip brushing against her clitoris and making her quiver. Then he moved, and pushed easily into her, up to the hilt; she groaned, and Jasmine stroked her thighs, soothing her. Rachel closed her eyes, concentrating on the intensity of the way Matt and Jasmine made her feel; as Jasmine began to rub her clitoris, she moaned, her orgasm reaching a higher plateau. Matt continued to thrust in a slow, measured fashion, his cock penetrating her deeply; Rachel thought she was going to pass out, the sensations were so strong.

The next thing she knew, she was kneeling on the floor between Jasmine's thighs, and Matt was kneeling astride the model's chest, his thick cock jutting towards her mouth.

Jasmine lifted her head and shoulders, licking her lips and taking the tip of Matt's cock in her mouth. He made a small sound of pleasure, and Rachel could feel Jasmine's body rocking slowly as she fellated the photographer, her head moving back and forth.

Jasmine's legs were splayed widely; Rachel stared at her moist, intimate flesh. Jasmine was very obviously aroused, her vulva glistening and turning a deep vermilion, and her clitoris becoming long and erect, peeping from its hood. Rachel swallowed. She knew what was expected of her: to touch Jasmine as intimately as Jasmine had touched her, to use her mouth to drive the model to a higher peak of pleasure. And yet she was unsure, feeling inexperienced and gauche. How would she know if she was doing it right? How would she know if she was pleasuring Jasmine, or merely teasing her?

As if Matt felt her hesitation, he reached backwards to take her hand, rubbing his thumb across her palm. 'Relax, sweetheart,' he breathed.

'I . . .'

He turned his head to smile at her. 'Don't worry. Just do what you'd like someone to do to you.'

Rachel felt suddenly shy. 'But . . .'

His smile broadened; and yet it was gentle, affectionate rather than mocking. 'If you don't feel comfortable using your mouth on her, there's something in that box in the corner which might help.'

Rachel was glad of the breathing space, and stood up, going to the wicker box in the corner of the room. Her eyes widened as she lifted the lid and saw the contents: obviously these props were for Matt's very private collection of photographs. Black silk scarves, used as blindfolds or restraints; a white leather basque, which would reveal more than it concealed; a couple of pairs of high-heeled black patent leather stilettos; and a number of vibrators in a variety of colours, from black to clear to gold. There was also a pot of cream: Rachel felt a pulse beat hard between her legs as she guessed how it was used. Lubrication, so that the biggest cock or vibrator could be accommodated. And the lubrication would be used in more than one orifice . . .

On impulse, she picked up the clear plastic vibrator; then she walked back over to Matt and Jasmine. She paused for a moment, watching them; Jasmine was obviously enjoying herself, her eyes glittering with pleasure as she took Matt's cock as deeply as she could into her mouth. Matt, too, was abandoned to pleasure, his head tipped back and his eyes closed, and his fingertips playing with Jasmine's dark nipples, pulling at the hard peaks of flesh.

It was a pretty scene, Rachel thought, returning to her place between Jasmine's thighs. And now she was part of it, too. Gently, she rubbed the tip of the vibrator against Jasmine's quim, sliding it down the length of her musky furrow; Jasmine's quim flexed, and Rachel smiled. She used the tip of the vibrator to tease Jasmine's clitoris, rubbing hard; the model splayed her legs wider apart and rocked her hips.

Jasmine had obviously stopped sucking Matt for a moment, as Rachel heard her say huskily, 'Oh yes. Do it, please, do it. Do it now.'

Rachel did as she was asked, pressing the vibrator against the entrance to Jasmine's sex; the model gave a groan of pleasure as the vibrator slid deep inside her, stretching her. Rachel began to simulate the way Matt had made love to her, using the vibrator as a dildo with long and leisurely strokes.

Jasmine gave another moan and resumed the way she'd been sucking Matt, using a similar rhythm to Rachel's.

Rachel grinned as Jasmine began to use her internal muscles, pulling in as Rachel withdrew the vibrator, then opening herself more widely as Rachel pushed it back in again. Rachel's smile broadened, and she spun the bevel at the base of the vibrator, turning it on full. Jasmine's hips bucked, and Rachel quickened the pace, manipulating the vibrator deftly. Jasmine shuddered, and her muscles tensed for a moment; Rachel didn't stop, but continued thrusting with the vibrator, bringing Jasmine to another climax, and another.

Almost at the same time, she saw Matt's body grow rigid; he cried out, and came, filling Jasmine's mouth with creamy salty liquid. Gently, Rachel reduced the speed of the vibrator, turning it off and withdrawing it; Matt rolled onto his side, taking Jasmine into his arms and kissing her deeply.

His cock was still hard; Rachel was impressed. He'd already come twice; maybe it was because he was so young that he could recover so quickly, she thought. Young, and very talented – in more than one way.

He manoeuvred Jasmine so that she was sitting astride him; she rocked back and forth with a wicked smile on her face, letting him feel how hot and wet she was. Rachel sat on the floor beside them, her knees drawn up and her arms wrapped round her legs; Matt reached out to stroke her face. 'Rachel. Come here.'

She leaned forward to kiss him; she could taste the salty flavour of his seed on his mouth, and it sent a thrill through her.

'Nearer,' Matt said as she broke the kiss. 'Sit across me, and face Jasmine.'

'You sound like a temperamental art director,' she teased.

'You'd better believe it,' he said with a grin.

She did as he asked her, sitting across his chest and facing Jasmine.

'Push your bottom back towards me,' he directed.

Rachel did so, and shivered as she felt his breath fanning against her quim.

Jasmine leaned forward, then, sliding her hands round Rachel's neck and bringing her face close to hers. She nibbled at Rachel's lower lip, and Rachel couldn't help responding. As Jasmine's tongue slid into her mouth, exploring her, so she felt Matt's tongue penetrating her, cleaning her; she moaned, and Jasmine's hands came up to cup her breasts, her thumbs rubbing against Rachel's taut nipples.

Matt worked deftly on her clitoris; Rachel felt herself slide into another climax, her whole body seeming to pulse around Matt's tongue. At the same time, Jasmine was lifting and lowering herself on Matt's cock, her body moving in small circles to change the angle of his penetration and give her more pleasure. They were moving in perfect harmony; Rachel sighed, letting her hands slide down Jasmine's body, her palms flat against the model's fine curves.

She let one hand drift upwards again, touching one breast in the same way that Jasmine had touched her, squeezing the globe of flesh and pinching the nipple between thumb and forefinger in a way that made Jasmine gasp. Her other hand smoothed down over Jasmine's abdomen; now, face to face, she felt bold enough to touch Jasmine in the way she'd shied from, earlier. She cupped Jasmine's mound of Venus, then eased her middle finger between Jasmine's labia, seeking her clitoris.

Jasmine gasped, and continued to rock wildly over Matt's

cock. Rachel grew bolder, rubbing the model's clitoris hard and then lifting her hand to taste the musky juices. Almost at the same time, she felt Matt's tongue flicker backwards, lapping at her perineum, and then finally pressing against her anus. She stilled for a moment, then gave herself up to pleasure, leaning forward to kiss Jasmine hard and slide her tongue into the model's mouth. The movement of her finger over Jasmine's clitoris mirrored the movement of Matt's tongue against her intimate flesh, exactly the same rhythm and pace.

She slowed the pace down, making the movements long and slow so that she could feel Matt's rigid cock as she pushed forward and Jasmine lifted herself up. Matt continued probing her, and she closed her eyes, letting her body melt into another climax; Jasmine seemed to sense the change in her, and slid her hand between Rachel's thighs, rubbing her clitoris to extend her orgasm. The three of them moved in perfect synchronicity: and they came at exactly the same moment, their bodies shuddering together.

At last, when their breathing had slowed, Jasmine kissed Rachel very lightly on the lips, and climbed off Matt. Rachel, too, climbed off Matt, and he sat up, smiling at both of them. 'If that perfume has this effect on everyone who wears it, Rachel, I think you've got a success on your hands.'

'Mm.' She smiled back at him. 'I certainly wasn't expecting it to have that effect on me.'

Jasmine stroked her face. 'You're incredibly sensual, Rachel. I don't think it was just the perfume.'

'I'd agree with you, there,' Matt said seriously. 'I just wish I'd had a camera rigged up. I think the shots would have done my private collection proud.'

'Your private collection?' Rachel queried.

'Yeah. Remind me to show you, some time.' He winked at her. 'Which I suppose is another way of inviting you to come and see my etchings.'

'Indeed,' Rachel said wryly.

'Except that we both know where we stand, beforehand. You've seen my private props box: and I use them all to very good effect, in my portfolio. Though it's not something that I usually show to clients,' he added. 'It's for me.'

'In the meantime, I need a shower,' Jasmine said.

'Well, my flat's upstairs. Turn right at the top of the stairs, and it's the first door on your left,' Matt said. He stretched. 'And I have another shoot in a couple of hours, so I suppose I'd better get this place straight.' He looked at Jasmine. 'I could do with a shower, too, but if I join you, I'll be running way over time.'

'You and me, both,' Rachel said.

Jasmine took her hand. 'I promise not to leap on you again! Just a shower,' she said.

Rachel grinned. 'Just a shower.' She followed Jasmine out of the studio, and up the stairs to Matt's flat.

FIVE

Rachel curled into Daniel's arms as they sat on her sofa.

'So how was your day?'

'Not so bad, thanks.' Rachel flushed. She couldn't tell Daniel what her day had really been like – what had happened between her and Matt and Jasmine. It wasn't that she was ashamed of what she'd done: more that she couldn't explain it, and she still didn't know Daniel that well. She didn't know how he'd react, whether he'd think that she was a raving pervert, someone he no longer wanted to be involved with – or whether he'd find it a real turn-on, and would make love to her for hours after she'd confessed to him what had happened. But it had been a one-off, and she didn't want to risk him walking out of her life. 'I had the photo shoot today, for the new perfume launch.'

He sniffed. 'Are you wearing it now?'

'Yes.' After their lovemaking session, she'd showered with Jasmine, who had been as good as her word. They'd taken a shower together, and it had been a shower only. Although they'd soaped each other's bodies, it had been more like friends washing each other's back than lovers exploring each other. Then, after she'd dried herself, Jasmine had sprayed her liberally with the new perfume. Rachel had worried about it being too heavy on her, but Jasmine had simply grinned and informed her that it would blow the minds of all the men in her office. It hadn't, although Rachel had had more than one passing glance of interest, intense and sexual enough to make her face burn.

'It's very nice,' Daniel said, nuzzling her face and breathing in her scent again.

'Thanks.'

He stroked her face. 'How are you feeling? No more dizziness?'

She wrinkled her nose. 'Not dizziness, exactly.' She took a swig of her coffee. 'Daniel . . .' She tailed off, not sure how to say it.

'What?' He looked at her, his eyes filled with concern.

'Look, this is probably going to sound really stupid but . . . It's not so much dizziness I've been having.' She swallowed. 'I see things, as well.'

'You mean, something like spots in front of your eyes?'

She shook her head. 'Nothing like that.'

'What, then?'

'The only way I can explain it is that it's almost like watching a film.'

'A film?'

Encouraged by the look of mingled concern and interest in his eyes, she continued. 'There are two people, a man and a woman. The woman looks a bit like me, except she has dark eyes and dark hair. The man . . . well, he reminds me of you.' She bit her lip. 'In fact, I saw him, the first time when I blacked out. I saw him before I'd even met you – and that's what made me nearly black out again, the second time. Your eyes were exactly the same colour as his – and it's not exactly a common colour, like blue or brown.'

'Maybe you'd noticed me in the museum, but it was subconscious,' Daniel suggested. 'The mind does funny things when you faint – it picks up all sorts of things and jumbles them together.'

'It's not like that.' She sighed. 'I'm making a real mess of this. And there was I, thinking that I was good at communicating.'

He grinned. 'You have to be, with a day job like yours.'

'Yeah.' She paused. 'Look, Daniel, what I'm trying to say is that I keep seeing these people. They're in Egypt, and it's weird, like I'm hallucinating. When I was sitting with you on the tube, I saw them reflected in the window; but it's not just the fact that I can see them. Everything he does to her, I can feel. When he touches her, when he talks to her – it's like I'm there, hearing him and feeling him touch me. It's so real. It's like it's all happening to me: and yet it's not happening to me, if you see what I mean.'

He frowned. 'Rachel – I'm sorry to have to ask you this, but you're not taking drugs, are you?'

She laughed shortly. 'No. Absolutely not. I sometimes drink too much wine, but I think that everyone does that, at some time. I don't smoke, and I've never taken drugs. I don't believe in them.' She bit her lip. 'I went to a party the night before I met you. When I had that first vision, I wondered if someone had spiked my drink with something, but apart from the fact that none of my friends is into drugs, it's happened too often since then to be that. The dreams, hallucinations – call them what you will – happen during the day, in broad daylight, in public places.'

'So how many of these dreams have you had, and what actually happens in them?'

'Ah.' She flushed. 'Like I said, they're all connected with Egypt.'

He smiled, and gestured round the room. 'With surroundings like this, that's hardly surprising.'

Her flush deepend. 'Yes, but it's not just the Egyptian side of it. It's all very . . .' She swallowed. There was only one word to describe what she saw. 'Erotic.'

'Erotic?' His eyes widened. 'You mean, you saw me making love with you, before we actually did?'

She nodded. 'Something like that. Except that you weren't exactly you, and I wasn't exactly me.' She winced. 'I talked to Carrie about this; she's my best-friend, and she's known me for years. She thinks maybe – oh, no, it's crazy, and I told her so.'

'She thinks what?' Daniel asked gently.

'She thinks that I'm having some kind of regression – that maybe I've lived before, in Egypt, and that I knew you there.' She shook her head. 'But I don't believe in past lives. I think that it's something that's buried in someone's subconscious – something they've read or seen or heard and forgotten about – and when they're hypnotized, the memories surface again.'

'Yes, you have a point.' He nodded. 'Look, one of my friends at the university works in the psychology department. Maybe if you have a chat to her, she might be able to tell you what's going on.'

'Maybe.' Rachel was suddenly embarrassed. She could hardly tell a complete stranger what had happened to her – particularly a stranger who was a good friend of Daniel's. She hadn't even told Daniel the full extent of what had happened, the way she'd ended up making love with Jasmine and Matt in the studio.

'You're probably working too hard, as well,' Daniel said.

'I've already had that lecture from my friends in the office. I may be a bit of a workaholic, but I'm eating properly, and I'm taking regular breaks.' She glanced at the mug of coffee. 'And I drink water in the office, so I'm not overdosing on this stuff, either.'

'I know what you mean. I worked on a book the other year, and I was twitching by the end of it, with the amount of caffeine that I'd consumed.' He ruffled her hair. 'Tell you what, why don't you go and have a shower? While you're freshening up, I'll cook dinner – if you don't mind me taking over your kitchen, that is.'

'Sounds good to me,' she nodded. 'Thanks.'

'Off you go.'

She leaned over to kiss him, then left the room. She walked into the bathroom and stripped swiftly before stepping into the bath. She pulled the shower curtain across, and turned the shower on full flow, at its coldest setting. The temperature of the water made her yelp; but she hoped that it would clear her head, rid her of the visions that had been haunting her for the past few days. 'Whatever it is, it's going to stop, and it's going to stop now,' she said firmly.

She turned the thermostat dial round to lukewarm, slowly increasing the temperature to a more comfortable level; then she soaped herself thoroughly, letting the shower rinse the suds from her skin.

Without warning, everything seemed to blur. She was no longer in her bathroom; she was standing beneath a waterfall, the river cascading down over her naked body, and she wasn't alone. The woman she'd seen earlier that day was beside her, laughing, tossing her long hair back so that the sunlight glinted on it and brought out red lights in her dark tresses. She, too, was naked.

There was no other word to describe what they were doing but 'frolicking', Rachel thought. They were almost dancing under the pouring water, splashing each other and teasing each other. Touching each other. And then suddenly they were kissing, her arms round the other woman's neck and the other woman's tongue parting her lips, sliding erotically into her mouth. The other woman was massaging her buttocks, pulling her closer so that they were belly to belly, breast to breast.

She could feel the other woman's nipples hardening against her skin, and her own breasts were throbbing and swelling, the nipples becoming dark and elongated as her arousal grew. She moaned softly as the woman eased one hand between their bodies and slid it very slowly down over her abdomen, her fingers spread and her palm gently rubbing Rachel's midriff. And then her hand was drifting lower, lower, insinuating itself between her thighs.

Rachel widened her stance slightly, not caring how slippery the rock was beneath her feet; it didn't matter any more. What she wanted, what she needed, was for her lover to touch her more intimately, ease the raging ache in her loins. She gasped as an exploring finger parted her labia, seeking and finding her clitoris with unerring skill. Still, the other woman was kissing her, swallowing her soft moans as her finger travelled further along Rachel's warm moist flesh and slid deep into her vagina.

The next thing that Rachel knew, they'd stepped through the waterfall and into the cave behind, and she was lying on the sandy earth, her head tipped back, her breasts thrust upwards and her knees bent. Her feet were flat on the floor and her thighs were splayed wantonly, so that her moist quim was on full view. She looked up at her lover, half expecting the other woman to kneel between her thighs and start using her mouth more intimately on Rachel; to her surprise, her lover was nowhere in sight.

She frowned and turned onto her side, looking towards the back of the cave. Her eyes widened in surprise as she saw what her lover was doing. She was tying something round herself; Rachel couldn't see what it was, until her lover turned round. Rachel gasped at the sight. Her lover was wearing a large phallus made of very soft leather and bone; it was fastened to her body by a complicated system of thongs, one tied round her waist and others tied round her thighs.

Rachel felt her insides melt with excitement and shock and shame. What they were doing ... If they were caught, it would be seen as worse than depraved. Stroking and kissing and sucking each other's breasts and genitals was one thing, maybe using a dildo by hand; but this, strapping on a dildo to make herself more like a man ... It was more than shocking. They'd be outcast, both of them.

'Relax,' her lover said, coming to lie beside her and stroking her face.

Rachel swallowed. 'If we're caught ...'

'We won't be.' The other woman smiled at her, her dark eyes confident and her voice husky with desire, 'Now, I've wanted to do this with you for a long, long while.'

Rachel realized with shock that it wasn't the first time that her lover had done this. She had done this with another woman – and maybe even with a man, taking him as a man would, pushing the phallus into his anus as deeply as she could and making him moan and writhe beneath her. Her eyes dilated. 'I . . .' Her mouth was suddenly dry.

'Relax,' she said again. 'You're going to like this. We both are.' She leaned over to kiss Rachel. Her mouth was soft and warm; that hadn't changed. Rachel suddenly felt desire jolt through her as her lover kissed her tenderly, nibbling gently at her lower lip and stroking her breasts, teasing her nipples between thumb and forefinger and sliding a hand back down Rachel's body, inserting it between her thighs. 'Lie on your back, my sweet,' her lover directed.

Rachel did as she was told, resuming her former position while her lover crouched between her thighs.

'Yes, that's it. I can see the pretty garden between your legs.'

Rachel chuckled. 'The way you express yourself, sometimes. It's so . . . so . . .' She spread her hands. 'You know what I mean.'

Her lover grinned back. 'Well. I want you. I want to touch you and taste you and . . .' She drew one finger down the satiny cleft. 'You feel so good. So hot and wet. Like warm honey, melting round me. You're ready for me, now. Ready for me to fuck you as if I were a man. And you want it too, don't you? You want me to do it to you. You want me to fill you.'

'Yes,' Rachel breathed.

The phallus was large, slightly longer and thicker than the penises Rachel had seen; she stiffened as her lover leaned forward and she felt the tip of the phallus pressing against her sex. 'Easy, easy,' the other woman soothed; and then the phallus was inside her. She was being penetrated. Rachel closed her eyes, tipping her head back and thrusting her breasts up.

It was a weird sensation, being filled by a thick cock and yet, at the same time, feeling another woman's soft breasts and hard nipples pressing against her own. A shiver of delight ran through her. She opened her mouth invitingly, and her lover took the hint, kissing her deeply and sliding her tongue into her mouth, possessing her mouth as the phallus possessed Rachel's loins.

Rachel reached up to touch her lover's breasts, loving the way they felt against her fingers. She pulled at the hardened nipples, and was rewarded by her lover hissing and arching against her. The way that the phallus was fashioned, Rachel couldn't slide a hand between their bodies and start touching her lover's quim. But what she could do ... She pulled back slightly from her lover's kiss, wetting her middle finger, then began to kiss her lover back, thrusting her tongue into the woman's mouth.

She was rewarded by deeper and faster thrusting; with a grin, she lifted her legs to twine them round the other woman's waist, then she smoothed her hand over her lover's buttocks, sliding her finger down the crease of her cheeks until she reached the puckered rosy hole of her anus.

'Oh yes,' the woman crooned, her voice husky with desire as she realized her lover's intention. 'Do it, do it, do it.'

Rachel pushed, and her finger slid deeply into the other woman's anus. As her lover withdrew the phallus, Rachel pushed in as deeply as she could; and as her lover pushed back in again, Rachel withdrew her finger, her rhythm in perfect timing.

She could feel the pressure of her orgasm spinning up from the soles of her feet, warming her, making her blood feel as though it were fizzing; then finally snaking up to coil in her gut, exploding hard so that her quim contracted sharply around the phallus. Almost at the same time, she heard her lover cry out as she, too, climaxed. She could feel her lover's contracting quim and the pulse beating hard in her anus . . .

Rachel opened her eyes and realized that she was in her bathroom, in the shower, with her hand working madly between her legs, her quim contracting sharply round her fingers.

'Oh, Christ,' she said.

This last vision had been even more outrageous; and this time, they'd been talking to each other. She swallowed hard. What the hell was going on? Was she a lesbian, to be so excited at the thought of making love with another woman? It had never occurred to her before; she'd just never thought of women in that way. Until Jasmine.

She sighed. What she'd done with Jasmine was probably what had triggered off this particular vision. There was nothing more to it than that. And as for being a lesbian . . . If that were the case, she wouldn't have enjoyed the feel of Matt's lithe body thrusting into hers, or Daniel's. Carrie had often said that no-one was a hundred per cent heterosexual. Rachel had always disagreed with her, but maybe it was true. Maybe she was just waking up to one side of her sexuality, a side she'd always kept buried before.

She finished washing herself, then wrapped herself in a towel and padded into the kitchen. Daniel was making a hollandaise sauce to go with the salmon that Rachel had bought earlier; he smiled at her. 'Are you feeling better now?'

'Yes.'

He saw the reservation in her face. 'But?'

She sighed. 'Nothing.'

'You've just had another of those hallucinations, haven't you?' Daniel asked immediately.

'Yes.' She shook her head. 'I don't know what's happening to me, Daniel, and I'm not sure that I can cope with this.'

'Try talking about it. It might help.'

She winced. 'Maybe. But I'm beginning to think that you ought to leave.'

'Leave?' He frowned, not understanding. 'Why? What's wrong?'

'Because something weird is happening to me, and I don't want it to happen to you, too.'

'I rarely dream; and when I do, it's the boring dream of an historian. Pretending that I'm Nelson at Trafalgar, or Wellington at Waterloo – that sort of thing.'

His smile disarmed her. 'Not Ramses the Second or Tutankhamun, then?'

'Definitely not.' His lips twitched. 'Though I've been known to have erotic daydreams. Like this afternoon, at my desk, after a particularly hellish tutorial with students who were too arrogant to do the reading I'd set them, and made it clear that they considered Victorian politics to be boring and utterly useless.'

'Daydreams?' She tipped her head on one side. 'Such as?'

'Let's just say that they involve a certain advertising copy-writer.'

'Tell me more.'

He grinned. 'Over dinner. It's nearly ready.'

'I'd better go and put something on, then.'

'You're fine as you are.' He drew his forefinger along the top of her towel. 'Though I might take advantage of this, later.'

'Indeed,' she teased back. 'Where are we eating?'

'In here?' he suggested.

She nodded, and busied herself laying the table. By the time she'd finished, Daniel had dished up perfectly poached salmon with hollandaise sauce, sauté potatoes, spinach, and baby corn.

Rachel took a mouthful. 'Mm. It's good. And I have to admit, your hollandaise sauce is better than mine.'

'Practice, that's all.'

They chatted inconsequentially during dinner; when Rachel had finished the fruit salad Daniel had made, she gave a sigh of satisfaction and stretched. 'That was really nice. Thank you.'

He smiled at her. 'Feeling better, now?'

'Yeah. I am.'

'Let's go and sit down, then. I'll do the washing up, later.' He led her out of the kitchen into the sitting room, and she curled up on the sofa.

Daniel flicked through her CDs and picked out the Bach double violin concerto, which Rachel had once told him was her favourite piece of music. As the first notes floated into the air, she smiled at him. 'An excellent choice, Mr Sinclair.'

'That's what I thought.' He sat on the sofa next to her, rearranging her position so that she was lying across the full length of the sofa, her legs draped over his lap. He began to massage her feet; Rachel made a small murmur of bliss.

'Oh, Daniel. That feels gorgeous. Where did you learn to do this?'

He grinned. 'I'm not telling you. But I thought that you might like it.'

'Definitely.' She closed her eyes, leaning back against the

arm of the sofa. As Daniel continued the massage, she felt herself relax.

'So,' he said quietly, 'this dream of yours . . . You looked fairly shocked by it.'

'Yeah.' The massage was relaxing her enough to stop her tensing at the memory. Daniel's hands began to drift higher, working on her ankles and her calves.

'Why don't you tell me about it?' he suggested, still using that soft, gentle tone.

'I . . . I don't know if that's such a good idea.'

He leaned over to kiss her mouth lightly. 'I may be a dry old history lecturer—' he ignored her snort of amusement '—but it doesn't mean that I'm easily shocked.' He continued massaging her legs. 'So what was it? Did you imagine yourself tied up to a four-poster bed and blindfolded?'

Her lips twitched. 'Apart from the fact that that wouldn't shock me, Daniel, I told you that it was all based in Egypt. They didn't have four-poster beds in Pharaonic society.'

He chuckled. 'Tied to a stone couch, then.'

'No, nothing like that.'

'Then what?' he persisted.

'All right, you asked for this. If you must know . . .' She paused. 'It was me, with another woman.'

'Another woman, hm?' He caressed her legs. 'So you've never thought about that before, then?'

Rachel avoided the question, not wanting to tell him what had happened between her and Jasmine, earlier that day. 'Let's just say that I always thought of myself as a hundred per cent heterosexual. Anyway, isn't that a man's fantasy, two women together?'

'Not necessarily. It can turn women on, too.' Rachel was surprised. She'd expected Daniel to be ... what, shocked? At the very least, she hadn't expected him to be so matter-of-fact about it. 'But you're right. It's a fairly common male fantasy,' Daniel said, the slight huskiness in his voice betraying his growing excitement.

Rachel could feel his erection rubbing against her, and grinned to herself. The idea was enough to turn Daniel on, too. 'So you really want to know all about it?' she asked.

'Yes.' The pads of his fingers stroked her skin, moving gently upwards above her knee.

'Well, the other woman – she and I were playing in a waterfall.'

'Don't tell me, you were wearing one of those long white shift dress things, and the water made it stick to you and outline your body?'

She shook her head. 'We were both naked.' She opened her eyes and looked at him.

He leaned over to kiss her again, gently placing his hands over her eyes. 'Don't look at me. Just talk to me, tell me what happened.'

Rachel paused, and closed her eyes again. 'Well, we were both naked. She was kissing me, in the waterfall. The next thing that I knew, we were behind the waterfall in this cave, and I was lying down.'

'Indeed.' His hands drifted slightly higher, beneath the hem of her towel. Instinctively, Rachel widened the gap between her thighs, giving him easier access. 'So you were lying on the floor like this?' he asked softly.

'More or less, except that my feet were flat on the ground and my knees were bent.'

'And the other woman – where was she? What was she doing?'

'That's the thing,' Rachel said. 'I was expecting her to be kneeling between my legs, touching me and kissing me – but she wasn't. She'd wandered off towards the back of the cave, and when I turned round to look at her, I saw that she was putting on something.'

'What sort of something?'

Rachel swallowed. 'I . . .'

'What sort of something?' Daniel repeated, his voice gentle yet firm.

'It was a phallus,' Rachel whispered. 'I suppose it was the sort of thing that people would use nowadays, with some kind of complicated arrangement of straps and buckles – except this wasn't a harness. She used leather thongs to tie it to herself: one round her waist, and the others round the top of her thighs.'

Daniel digested this. 'A phallus, you say.'

'Yes. It was big – bigger than the average man. It was made out of bone, covered in very soft leather.'

'And she was going to use this on you?'

'Yes. She knelt between my thighs and she told me that she wanted to fuck me like a man.'

'Indeed.' By now, Daniel's fingers were only millimetres away from her quim. He drew one finger experimentally down her satiny cleft, discovering how warm and wet she was. Rachel may have been shocked by her daydream, he thought, but thinking about it afterwards obviously aroused her.

'What did you feel when you saw her kneeling there like that,' Daniel asked, 'knowing what she was going to do with you?'

'I . . . I was excited,' Rachel admitted. 'And a bit scared. It was the first time I'd done anything like that, but it certainly wasn't the first time for her.'

'How do you know?'

'Because I could see it in her face. She knew exactly what she was doing. She rubbed the phallus up and down my quim, until she thought I was ready for her, and then . . . Then, she fitted its tip to the entrance of my sex.'

Daniel pushed the tip of his finger against her sex. 'Like this?'

'Yes,' Rachel confirmed. 'Then, oh, so very slowly, she put it in me, right up to the hilt. Then she began to thrust, just like a man would, pushing it in and out of me.'

Daniel added a second finger, and a third, and began to move his hand very slowly back and forth. 'Something like this?'

Rachel swallowed. 'Yes. It was so big, I could feel it stretching me.'

'Was it good?'

'Yes, but it was . . . different, somehow. It was strange, feeling her breasts all warm and soft against mine, instead of the hardness of a man's body; and yet, at the same time, the way she moved, with my legs crossed round her waist and her thighs parting mine, it was like making love with a man.'

'Did you come?' Daniel asked.

'Yes. It was the way she touched me – rubbing my clitoris, too.'

Daniel slid his other hand under her towel, and began to rub her clitoris. 'You mean, like this?'

'Yes. Yes. Oh . . .' Rachel cried out as her orgasm took her unawares, her internal muscles contracting wildly and clutching at Daniel's fingers.

He withdrew his hand, licking every scrap of glistening

moisture from his fingers, and then leaned forward to kiss her so that she could taste herself on his mouth. 'Not so bad, was it,' he asked softly, 'telling me about your dream?'

'No.' She opened her eyes. 'But, Daniel – I don't understand what's happening to me. I never used to fantasize like this; and I certainly never found myself almost blacking out in public places, seeing these visions.' She decided not to tell him about the cat moving on her mantelpiece. That sounded almost like she'd made it up, after watching too many science fiction films.

'Why don't you have a word with my friend, Hazel? She might be able to help.'

'Yeah, maybe.'

He kissed her again. 'Don't worry that I'm going to start thinking that you're outrageously kinky, and I won't want anything to do with you any more.'

'I hope not,' Rachel said seriously.

His eyes glittered. 'I have a few mildly kinky fantasies myself. Like tying you to my bed, and blindfolding you, and doing all sorts of pleasurable things to you.' He licked his lips. 'With a pot of whipped cream, some honey, and a banana.'

She chuckled. 'Now, that's corny.'

'Give me a few hours of your time with the said honey, cream and banana, and I'll make you eat your words.' His eyes sparkled. 'And that's literally, too . . .'

She grinned. 'Was this what you were fantasizing about this afternoon?'

'After the tutorial from hell, you mean? No. I had a different scenario in mind.'

'Tell me more.' She levered herself into a sitting position.

'In fact, lie down across me. You'll be more comfortable if you close your eyes.'

'Oh, yes?' He tipped his head on one side. 'And just what do you have in mind, Rachel Meaden?'

She grinned. 'Later. You were telling me about this afternoon.'

'It was pretty boring, really. I just imagined being at my desk, working, and you came into my office. You closed the door behind me, and locked it. You smiled at me, one of those long, slow, sensual smiles, and I knew what you were going to do. You didn't care that I had a tutorial in a few minutes. You said to me that it didn't matter, it wasn't important. This moment was for us.

'You were wearing your hair pinned up. It was fastened at the back of your head by just one pin; you took out the pin, and shook your hair so that it fell down to your shoulders. OK, OK, I admit that it's corny, but it really turned me on. I swallowed, and reached over to draw the blind, but you shook your head. "I don't care if anyone sees us," you said. Then, very slowly, you began to undress. You were humming some kind of Egyptian song, and the way you moved to the music ... I suddenly realized that you were belly-dancing, your body flowing gracefully as you danced for me.

'I licked my lips as I watched you. I wanted to take you into my arms. I wanted to touch you and taste you, but you said, "No, not yet." You were wearing one of your office suits; you took off your jacket, hanging it over the door handle, then your skirt and your shirt. You were standing there, just in your underwear: a pair of white lacy knickers, a matching bra, and navy hold-up lace-topped stockings. You looked so beautiful.

You continued to dance for me, and I felt myself growing hard. I wanted you so much.

'You smiled at me, then, and walked over to me. There were some papers on my desk; you swept them onto the floor, not caring that they scattered everywhere. Then you spun my chair round, and pulled me to my feet. You kissed me, hard, your tongue sliding into my mouth.' His eyes glittered. 'You were the one in control, and you let me know it.'

Rachel was tempted to bend over and kiss him, but she decided not to. She wanted to hear his story. She contented herself with undoing the button of his trousers and sliding the zipper downwards, easing her fingers under the waistband of his pants and freeing his cock. He was already hard. Daniel shivered as her fingers closed round his shaft, and gently began to masturbate him.

'Anyway,' he told her, his voice growing huskier, 'you took off my sweater, and then you undid my jeans, pushing them down over my hips and dragging my underpants down with them in one smooth movement. You didn't undress me properly: you simply pushed me back against my desk, and then straddled me. I could feel the silkiness of your knickers against my cock and it turned me on so much. I could feel how warm and wet you were through that thin silk barrier, and I wanted you. Then you lifted yourself slightly, pulled the gusset of your knickers to one side, and fitted the tip of my cock to the entrance of your sex. Then you eased yourself down on me. You felt so good, so incredibly good.

'You took off your bra, then, and I lifted my head so that I could suckle your nipples. You were really turned on; your nipples were so hard, so dark. I began to suck one nipple, playing with the other, and you started to ride me. You slid your hand between our bodies, and started to rub your clitoris. I could feel the movement of your hand against my cock, and it was driving me mad. I couldn't concentrate on anything except the way you felt, warm and wet and tight around my cock.'

Rachel continued to masturbate him, and he shivered. 'Oh God, yes. It was so good, the way you rode me. With your hair loose, you looked like a Maenad, a wild angel. Then someone knocked on the door. I lifted my head from your breasts. I was about to call out to them, tell them to come back in a few minutes, but you stopped me. You jammed your mouth against mine, kissing me hard, so there was nothing that I could do.

'Whoever it was knocked again, tried the door, and called my name. I couldn't answer: not just because of the way that you were kissing me, but because I was so near to coming. Eventually, whoever it was went away. Still, you rode me, using your internal muscles to massage my cock. And then . . .'

Rachel, recognizing the look on his face, pushed up his light cotton sweater to bare his midriff. 'And then?'

'And then,' he said, 'I came. You came at the same time. I wished that it had gone on forever, the way it felt as if we were melting into each other's bodies.' He groaned, and a jet of pearly white fluid shot from his cock onto his stomach. Rachel, grinning, rubbed the sticky fluid into his skin.

'That's not fair,' he protested.

She chuckled. 'It's meant to be brilliant for the skin, you know. All that protein.'

Daniel reached up to kiss her, sliding his hands round her neck. 'Yeah, well. Looks like I'm going to have to have a bath before I take you off to bed.'

'It does, indeed.' She smiled at him. 'Just out of interest – where is your desk, at work?'

'Right next to my window.'

'At right angles, I hope.'

'Of course.'

She tipped her head on one side. 'And what do you overlook?'

'A courtyard. And I'm pretty sure that anyone on the second floor on the opposite side of the quadrangle – or anyone looking up from the courtyard – can see exactly what's going on in my room.'

She grinned. 'So you're an exhibitionist at heart, then.'

He grinned back. 'I told you it was a fantasy.' He stroked her face. 'And I think I can do better than that, in real life . . .'

SIX

The following Wednesday, Rachel found herself heading for Vivace, an exclusive health club in Chelsea. DFA had recently won the account, and Rachel had been given the job of writing a brochure selling the club's services. She'd been invited for a tour-cum-trial of the club by the owner and had protested, saying that it should really be something for the account director, but Ellis Brown had been adamant.

'Not at all. You're the one who's writing the brochure; so you need to know exactly what the club can offer potential clients.'

The account director, Grace Walker, had agreed with him when Rachel had tackled her, later. 'Honestly, Rachel, he's right. You need to see the place first hand.' She smiled. 'And no, I'm not ragingly jealous; I'm working on getting discounted subscription rates for the team for the next year!'

Rachel chuckled. 'Grace, you're amazing.'

Grace groaned, rolling her eyes. 'I wish you guys would leave off. I hate that nickname!'

'Sorry.' Rachel didn't look in the slightest bit penitent. Grace could more than hold her own where office teasing was concerned. 'I suppose you have a point. Seeing the place can only inspire copy.'

'Exactly. Go and have a nice time. And make sure that Ellis lets you try everything out – and I mean everything!'

When Rachel walked into reception, Ellis was already there; he greeted her warmly, taking her hand and shaking it firmly, his blue eyes sparkling. 'Hello, Rachel. I'm glad that you could make it.'

'Me, too.' She smiled back at him. Ellis really was an attractive man. He was tall, with the sort of physique which suggested that he used the facilities at the health club every day. His shock of blond hair was brushed carelessly back from his face, and his eyes were a deep cornflower blue, fringed by unfairly long lashes. He had a generous mouth; and had Rachel not been involved with Daniel, or stuck rigidly to the same code as Carrie – that you never slept with colleagues or clients – she would have been very tempted indeed. 'Part of me feels guilty about swanning round here, when I really ought to be at my desk.'

'Who says that you won't be working here?' he asked. 'You need to see what the place is like, before you can write about it.' He looked at her. 'Did you bring a swimming costume with you?'

'I didn't think to,' she admitted. 'To be honest, I'm not the fitness type; I haven't seen the inside of a gym since my schooldays, and my swimming's limited to a bit of splashing in a pool on holiday.'

He smiled. 'No matter. I'm sure that we can rustle up something for you.'

'Er – Ellis, if I'm not going to try out the facilities, why do I need swimming things?'

'Even if you don't want to have a swim, I'm sure that you'd like to try out the spa pool.' He grinned. 'And the sauna. Then there's the steam bath, and the aromatherapy steam tube. We also have massage facilities.'

Rachel chuckled. 'If I go back to the office and tell them that I've sampled all those while they've been slogging away at their desks . . . I think they'll have my guts for garters!'

He smiled. 'Well. Would you like a coffee, before I show you round?'

'No, I'm fine, thanks.'

'Tell you what. Let's go for the sauna, first; meanwhile, Sabrina can rustle up a swimming costume for you.'

'But don't I need a costume for the sauna?'

He shook his head. 'A towel will do.' He led her over to the receptionist. 'Sabrina, could you be a darling and sort out a swimming costume for Rachel, please?'

Sabrina smiled. 'Of course. I'm sure we have something in the right size. I'll bring it through to the changing room.' Rachel flushed. She was only too obviously a size sixteen – a good three sizes larger than the receptionist – even though the cut of her office suit helped to disguise her voluptuous curves. Sabrina's smile held no malice, though; she reached under the desk and brought out two thick navy blue bath sheets, handing one to Ellis and one to Rachel.

'The changing rooms are through here,' Ellis said, shepherding Rachel down a corridor. 'I'll meet you here in five minutes.'

'Fine.' Rachel walked into the changing room, and her eyes widened in appreciation. The floor was tiled in pale blue, and the pale walls were marbled with shades of blue, from the deep midnight blue of the towel she was holding, to the pale blue of the floor, and all the shades in between. There were none of the faintly cramped metal lockers familiar to many sports centres; instead, there was a tall pine cabinet, with several doors and good locks.

When she opened one, Rachel found that there were a couple of padded hangers, and the wardrobe space smelled of lemon. She smiled. That was a plus point, being able to hang your clothes up instead of leaving them piled on a coat-hook or squashed into a locker. Another big plus was that the air smelled sweet: from what she could remember of changing rooms, they were either stuffy and reeked of chlorine, or damp and smelled of sweat.

She stripped swiftly, wrapping the towel round herself sarong-style, and hung her clothes up in one of the wardrobe spaces; then she locked the door and removed the key. She walked out into the corridor; Ellis was waiting for her.

'I like the idea of being able to hang your clothes up properly,' she said.

'Well, that's one plus point for you to write about,' he said with a grin.

'Something like that.' She smiled back at him, suddenly at ease. Why the hell should she feel guilty about being pampered here? She was, after all, working; and she'd put in more than enough hours recently to justify any time she spent enjoying herself. *A fair day's work for a fair day's pay*, she thought.

'Some of the rooms along here are for massage and beauty treatments. We offer the full range, from eyelash tinting and eyebrow shaping through the mini-facials, full facials and body-wrap treatments.' He looked sidelong at her. 'And you're welcome to try any of them out at any time. Just ring Sabrina, and she'll sort it out. When you've finished the brochure, I'm sure we can come to some kind of arrangement.'

'Thanks.' Rachel grinned. 'I'll have to tell this to my friend Carrie. She'll go green.'

'Does she work at the agency, too?'

'No. She used to, but Carrie Taylor's what you might call a high-flyer. She moved out and upwards, some time ago.'

'Carrie Taylor?' Ellis smiled back at her. 'Actually, I know her. She's a member here.'

It was Rachel's turn to be surprised. She knew that Carrie went to a gym, but she'd thought that it was somewhere near her flat in Docklands, not here. And certainly Carrie hadn't mentioned that her gym had so many other facilities ... 'She never told me.'

'Well. Maybe she was trying not to make you go green,' he teased. 'Here on the right, we have the spa pool; there's also a relaxation pool, for more serious swimming. At the end of the corridor, there's a gym, and we can offer personal trainers to help people meet their needs.'

'Which are?' Rachel prompted, making mental notes.

'Anything from general body toning or shaping, through to specific sports training. The steam room's here, on the left, and the sauna's right here.' He led her through another door.

Rachel was impressed. The saunas she'd seen before at health clubs were just big enough to hold two or three people; this was big enough for ten, and she told Ellis so.

'It's a good place to hold business meetings,' he said.

'Business meetings?'

'You'd be surprised at what people do in here! Anyway, come and sit down, and I'll tell you a bit more about the club.' He nodded at the coals. 'Do you mind if I add some more water?'

'That's fine.'

Rachel was a little surprised that there was only the two of them; but then again, it was just a little too late for ladies who lunched, and too early for the office directors who could afford the membership of a place like this.

'This is the off-peak time,' Ellis said, as if reading her thoughts. He came to sit beside her on the slatted pine bench, and told her more of the history of the club: why he'd set it up, the sort of clients he had, and the sort of services they could offer.

Then, without warning, the room seemed to spin round Rachel. She closed her eyes. *God, please, no, not again . . .*

She was in a small clearing with her lover, the man with the beautiful aqua grey eyes. There was no wind, and the day was baking hot. He smiled at her, and loosened the white shift she wore, letting it fall to the ground. Beneath it, she was completely naked. He smiled as he realized that she'd sugared herself, and her mound of Venus was completely bare. He ran his finger over the smooth, plump mound, liking the feel of it.

She pushed his hands away, laughing. 'But you're still fully dressed.'

He shrugged, gave her a grin, and stripped swiftly; like her, he was naked beneath his outer clothes, and his sex rose hot and hard from the cloud of hair at his groin. 'The hand of Isis,' he said, taking her hand and folding her fingers round his cock, moving her hand gently back and forth.

She winced. 'You shouldn't blaspheme. The gods will be angry with us.'

He shook his head. 'No. The gods are never angry with lovers. Besides, isn't that what your priests' handmaidens do?'

She flushed, not wanting to talk about secret rituals. 'I . . .'

'It's all right. You don't have to say, if you don't want to.

But I thought that was why they were called handmaidens. Because they use their hands on your priests, who are the instruments of your gods.'

She continued to masturbate him as he let his hand drop, tightening the ring of her thumb and forefinger as she rubbed up and down the shaft. He made a small noise of pleasure, arching his back and thrusting his pelvis towards her. 'The hand of Isis,' she echoed softly, dropping to her knees in front of him.

He tensed with anticipation, knowing what she was going to do next. As she licked her lips and eased her mouth over the tip of his cock, he pushed his hands into her hair, massaging her scalp and urging her on as she began to fellate him. She continued rubbing his shaft, moving her hand in direct opposition to the movement of her mouth, and caressing his balls with her other hand, stroking the soft, silky crease behind his balls.

He groaned, and she began to fellate him more quickly, until she felt his whole body tense and her mouth filled with warm salty liquid. She swallowed every last drop, looking up at him and licking her lips in a mock-lascivious way. He drew her to her feet and kissed her hard, his tongue sliding into her mouth and his hands smoothing their way up her body to touch her breasts. She arched against him as he took one nipple between thumb and forefinger, pulling gently at it . . .

Then Rachel opened her eyes and realized that she was staring straight into Ellis' blue eyes – eyes which had grown hot with passion. At the same moment, she realized that her hands were round his neck, and his were resting on the curve of her hips. Her mouth was only centimetres away from his, and his mouth was slightly swollen and reddened, as though he'd been kissed very thoroughly and very recently. Given their positions, there was only one candidate for who had been kissing him – herself.

She pulled back, embarrassed. 'Ellis, I . . .' She closed her eyes for a moment. 'I'm so sorry.'

'Rachel.' He stroked her face. 'Are you all right?'

'Yes, of course.' She opened her eyes again and forced a smile to her face. 'I'm sorry. The heat in here made me black out for a moment, and I thought I was somewhere else.'

'Look, Rachel, I know I haven't known you for very long, and forgive me for prying, but you don't seem to be the type who'd – well, start kissing someone at the first opportunity, whether you thought you were somewhere else or not. And I don't flatter myself to think that I'm that irresistible to women. One minute I was talking to you, telling you about the club; the next minute, you were sliding your hands round my neck and you started kissing me.'

She couldn't trust herself to speak.

'Did you think that you were with your lover?' he asked softly. She nodded. 'Whoever he is, he's one hell of a lucky man.' He stroked her face.

Whoever he is . . . The phrase echoed through Rachel's brain. Who was he? He was Daniel, and yet not Daniel. And in her dream, she'd brought him to a climax, while she was still barely starting on hers. Almost as if her body wanted her to continue where her mind had left off, she found herself turning her face and brushing her lips against Ellis' palm.

His eyes widened. 'Rachel . . .'

The sound of his voice brought her back to sanity. She pulled back, and stared at the floor. 'Oh, Christ. Ellis, I'm sorry

– I don't know what the hell I'm playing at. You're a client. I should be treating you with the respect you deserve and paying attention to you, not trying to seduce you.' She bit her lip. 'It's the unwritten rule: never sleep with a client or a colleague. I've been in the business long enough to know better.'

'Rachel.' He cupped her chin, turning her face to his. 'Right at this moment, I don't care about rules, written or not. There's just you and me; and we won't be disturbed in here.'

The sensible part of her knew that she should make some jokey comment to lighten the atmosphere, and suggest that they leave the sauna and see if Sabrina had managed to find a swimming costume. Yet her body had other ideas. Her nipples were so hard they almost hurt, and her quim felt liquid, ready for a man. Ellis was right: no-one would ever know. And it was just a one-off. Why should it matter if they both gave each other pleasure?

When he leaned forward to kiss her very lightly on the lips, she didn't pull away; he nibbled gently at her lower lip, and she gave a small sigh, opening her mouth to give him the access he needed. He made a small sound of satisfaction, and began to kiss her properly, exploring her mouth and stroking the back of her neck.

She shivered, pressing against him, and he untucked her towel, letting it slide onto the pine bench. He pulled back slightly to look at her, and gave a sharp intake of breath. 'Christ, Rachel. You're so lovely.' He ran the tip of his middle finger down her cleavage. 'Rachel . . . I want to touch you. I want to taste you.'

His voice was husky with desire, and sent a thrill through Rachel. The amount of women Ellis must meet who spent their time sculpting their bodies and pampering them to perfection . . . and yet he was turned on by her, an ordinary woman.

Then she stopped thinking, as Ellis moved to kneel in front of her. He cupped one breast almost reverently, then lowered his head, taking the hard peak of flesh into his mouth. Rachel tipped her head back, her breath hissing from her as he began to suck, gently kneading her breast at the same time.

He moved one hand to her other breast, pulling gently at the nipple with his finger and thumb – just as the man with the beautiful aqua grey eyes had done to his lover, in Rachel's mind – and she arched against him, wanting more. Ellis' mouth slowly tracked downwards, and Rachel parted her legs. He rubbed the tip of his nose against her abdomen, breathing in the scent of her skin, and she gave a small moan of longing, wanting him to go further, to use his mouth on her properly and bring her to the climax she needed.

Ellis' mouth drifted downwards, and she opened her legs even wider. He rubbed his cheeks against her thighs, and she felt the faint rasp of stubble against her skin, making her gasp. He pressed his palms flat against her inner thighs, and then pulled back slightly to look at her. His breath hissed sharply. 'Christ, Rachel, you're so beautiful.' And then, almost reverently, he drew one finger down the full length of her satiny cleft. She was already wet – very wet indeed – and his finger slid easily down the folds and crevices of her quim. She reached out to slide her hands into his hair, but he shifted back, not letting her. He wasn't ready yet.

He continued his slow, oh, so very slow exploration, brushing his finger up and down her cleft. Every time he brushed against her clitoris, she jerked: his touch was so light, so gentle, and yet it made her feel on fire, wanting more. She wanted him to rub her properly, roughly, bring her to the swift sharp climax she craved so badly. This slow, slow teasing exploration was too much for her: she couldn't handle it.

She slid her right hand over her thigh and cupped her mons veneris; he chuckled. 'Rachel, don't be so impatient. Let it flow. This is going to be so good, so good for both of us.'

He continued teasing her, drawing his finger so lightly and gently up and down. Rachel could feel herself growing wetter, her sex flexing and opening like a flower. And then, at last, he slid one finger into her, staying perfectly still and enjoying the way that the pulse in her sex beat hard against him.

She pushed her pelvis towards him, wanting him deeper; then, at last, he leaned forward, and she felt his breath, cool against her fevered flesh. He stretched out his tongue, and then, at long, long last, he drew the tip of his tongue down her quim. His finger was still deep inside her, not moving; Rachel tightened her internal muscles round him for a moment, impatient and wanting more. He smiled, and then he began to lick her properly, his tongue flickering lightly across the hard bud of her clitoris, teasing it from its hood.

Rachel almost cried out when Ellis drew the hard bud of flesh into his mouth. As he sucked her, his finger began to move in and out, very slowly; Rachel was shockingly aware that he'd added a second finger, and a third. This time, he didn't pull back when she slid her hands into his hair; she revelled in the feel of his clean, silky tresses between her fingers. She began to massage his scalp, urging him on: and then she went completely rigid, her muscles tensing as her orgasm swept through her, so strongly that her whole body quivered afterwards.

Ellis stilled, remaining in his crouched position; he kept his mouth on her flesh, lapping her gently until the aftershocks of her orgasm had died away. Rachel was still shaking when she opened her eyes. 'Ellis . . .'

'Don't say another word,' he commanded softly, reaching up to kiss her.

She could taste herself on his mouth, a sweet-salt musky taste, and it was then that she realized that he was still wearing the towel wrapped round his waist. His erection was obvious beneath it, but she still felt awkward, being completely naked while he was still dressed so demurely. She slid her hands down his back until she reached the edge of the towel, and then she tugged at the impromptu fastening. The towel slid off, and he stood up; it was Rachel's turn to take a sharp intake of breath. Ellis was built very impressively indeed. Clothed, he looked good, his body moving with a fluid grace; naked, he was breathtaking.

His body was firm and well-toned, yet not over-developed. There was a light covering of sandy hair on his chest, and his cock reared impressively from the cloud of hair at his groin. His cock was long and thick, and he was circumcised; his glans was dark and glistening, and there was a clear bead of moisture at the eye of his cock. It was all Rachel could do to stop herself leaning forward, stretching out her tongue, and licking the moisture away.

Almost unconsciously, her tongue slid over her suddenly dry lower lip, and Ellis' cock twitched in anticipation. She was about to repay the compliment and act out the scene she'd seen earlier; as if he guessed her intention, he took her hands and pulled her to her feet.

He kissed her again, this time more deeply, sliding one

hand down her back and moulding her close to him, stroking her buttocks, while his other hand settled at the nape of her neck, holding her to him as he kissed her. She could feel his erection pressing strongly against her; then, suddenly, he was sitting down, and he'd manoeuvred her position so that she was kneeling astride him on the slatted pine bench.

Gently, she lowered herself, sliding one hand between them to position the tip of his cock at the entrance of her still-moist and puffy sex; then she pushed down, feeling his body fill hers and stretch her. She put her arms round his neck for balance and began to lift and lower herself, moving in small circles to change the angle of his penetration and give them both more pleasure. Her movements grew more jerky as her arousal flared again; and this time she was kissing Ellis, sliding her tongue into his mouth and taking the lead as she ground her pubis against his.

She felt the tension building in her body again, to an almost unbearable pitch; suddenly, her climax exploded. She broke the kiss, tipping her head back and giving a small cry as she climaxed, her internal muscles clutching sharply at the thick rod of his cock. At the same time, she heard Ellis give an answering cry, and she felt his cock twitch deep inside her.

When their pulses had slowed down, she climbed off him and took his hand, squeezing it. 'Ellis – God, I don't know what to say.'

He raised her hand to his lips, kissing her palm and curling her fingers over the place he had kissed. 'Rachel, there's nothing to say. I've already gathered that you don't usually behave like this. I don't know what's happening, but I'm glad that I was here to share it with you.' He smiled at her. 'Don't worry, this is just between you and me. I won't say anything to the agency, or to any of my staff.'

'Thank you.' She bit her lip. 'Look, I swear that this won't affect the work I do for you.'

'I didn't think for a moment that it would.' His smile broadened. 'Come on. I think we both need a shower; then we'd better find that swimming costume for you.' His eyes glittered with a mixture of amusement and affection. 'Otherwise, I don't think I can be answerable for what would happen if we climbed into the spa pool . . .'

The rest of Rachel's visit to the club passed as planned, trying out the other facilities and then having lunch with Ellis in his office. He was good company, and although a part of her was still shocked at what she'd done with him, part of her didn't regret it at all. When she returned to the office, she spent the rest of the afternoon working on the rough draft of her copy for the brochure. If Charlie or Sara noticed that she was more subdued than normal, they made no comments.

At half past five, Rachel headed for the wine bar to meet Carrie. This time, it was Carrie who was late, and Rachel had already drunk two glasses of Chardonnay before Carrie appeared at her table, breathless and apologetic. She kissed her friend. 'Sorry I'm late, Rach. I had a meeting with Eddie and the team, and it ran over. I was trying to shut the bastard up, but he kept running on and on and on . . .' She rolled her eyes. 'God save me from male bosses, especially ones who love the sound of their own voices. If I hear one more pointless anecdote from him in the next week, I swear I'm going to slap him, or accidentally-on-purpose spill my coffee in his lap.'

'That'll do your career prospects no end of good.'

'Yeah, but I'd have the satisfaction of seeing the look on his face.'

'Have a glass of wine.' Rachel poured a glass, and handed it to her friend. 'That'll make you feel better.'

Carrie took a deep draught. 'Mm. You're right – much better.'

'Maybe I'd better get another bottle.'

Carrie wrinkled her nose. 'Much as I love this stuff, I have to admit, Rach, I'm starving. I didn't even get the chance to have a sandwich at my desk today. I'd rather just finish this bottle, then get something to eat.'

'How about a Chinese takeway at my place?' Rachel suggested. 'There's a bottle of wine in the fridge.'

'Sounds brilliant to me.'

They finished their wine, then took the tube back to Islington. 'So how are you feeling?' Carrie asked. 'Are you still having these blackouts?'

Rachel had previously decided to lie and tell Carrie that she was fine; but Carrie was the only person she knew who would listen to her without judging her, and come up with a sensible suggestion. 'I don't want to talk about it here, Carrie. Wait till we get to my place.'

'All right. But just tell me that you went to see a doctor.'

'I did. I had blood tests—' Rachel, who was a coward when it came to needles, grimaced at the memory '—and I'm fine. I'm not anaemic, I'm not diabetic, and I'm not suffering from some weird form of epilepsy. So . . . God only knows what it is.'

'Overwork.' Carrie shrugged. 'Par for the course, in our business.'

'We're talking about advertising – people who have three-hour lunches and spend the day floating around chatting about nothing, drinking a lot,' Rachel teased.

'If only. You and I both know that it's not like that any more. It's a hard slog, and if you're not trying to keep the client happy, then you're trying to keep someone else in the agency happy, or spending hours on the phone to sort out temperamental suppliers. And I'd like to have the occasional twenty-minute lunch break, let alone a three-hour session,' Carrie said. 'If I do take a client out to lunch – or they take me – then it's a working lunch, and I end up spending more time taking notes of action points than I do eating or talking.'

'Yeah, I know.' Rachel smiled at her friend as they turned into Rachel's local Chinese takeaway. 'What do you fancy?'

'Lots and lots and lots of food.'

Rachel grinned. 'I mean, do you fancy anything in particular?'

'There's an answer to that,' Carrie said with a grin, 'but I think that you'd probably slap me if I said it.'

Rachel groaned. 'I was talking about *food*, not Hollywood darlings.'

Eventually, they settled on Peking duck, bang-bang chicken, tiny spring rolls, crispy seaweed, sweet-and-sour mushrooms, and fried rice. It was only a couple of minutes walk back to Rachel's place; when they reached the flat, Rachel sorted out the plates and cutlery while Carrie, familiar with the layout of Rachel's kitchen, scooped up two glasses and uncorked the wine. They ate in near-companionable silence; when they'd finally demolished the food, Carrie leaned back in her chair and gave a sigh of pleasure. 'Mm. That's better.'

'Much,' Rachel agreed.

'So now I'm fed, you can tell me everything.'

'About what?'

'These blackouts. I'm worried that you're still getting them.'

'That isn't the worst thing.' The words were out before Rachel could stop them.

Carrie's eyes glittered. 'Then what is?'

'Nothing.'

'Rach, I'm your best friend. Talk to me.'

Rachel sighed. 'All right. If you must know, I think I'm becoming a nymphomaniac.'

Carrie, who had slept with at least a dozen times as many people as Rachel had, chuckled. 'What, you? Never.'

'I'm serious.'

'Okay, so you can't keep your hands off this gorgeous new man of yours. That doesn't make you a nymphomaniac.'

'I know. It isn't just Daniel.'

Carrie, catching the light in her friend's eyes, frowned. 'Not just Daniel? How do you mean, Rach?'

'It's to do with the blackouts. Did I tell you that I kept seeing these erotic visions? A man and a woman?'

'Yes. You said that he was like Daniel – that his eyes were the same.'

'Well, there's a lot more to it than that, now.' Rachel bit her lip. 'And I find myself acting them out. I'm breaking every one of my personal rules.'

Carrie frowned. This sounded serious. Rachel had always been one of the most stable, almost conservative, people she knew. 'How do you mean, acting them out?'

'Well, the other day, we were doing a shoot for the perfume brief with Matt Harston. Charlie was ill, so I went on my own.'

'I know Matt. He's a nice guy,' Carrie agreed. 'And very talented.'

'In more than one way.' Rachel coughed. 'The model was called Jasmine.'

Carrie shook her head. 'I don't know her.'

'You will, when the ads appear. She's going to be in the super-league in a few months,' Rachel said with a wry smile. 'I blacked out while I was there. I had this vision about me and this man – the same one as usual – and a woman. The next thing I knew, Matt and Jasmine were both crouched down beside me, looking concerned and asking me if I was all right. It went on from there, and then I was making love with them.'

Carrie digested this in silence. Not only was Rachel one of her quieter friends, she was also the straightest. And whereas Carrie's sexual experience had been broad, this was the last thing she'd been expecting from someone like Rachel. 'Let me get this straight,' she said quietly. 'You were making love with another woman?'

'Yes.' Rachel rubbed her hand across her face. 'It's not me, Carrie. Or at least, I didn't think that it was. I'm beginning to think that I'm turning into a lesbian because, later that evening, I was having a shower, and I had this vision of a woman making love with me.'

'No, you're not a lesbian. You don't find men unattractive. You know my views about people not being a hundred per cent hetero, anyway.' Carrie took her hand and squeezed it. 'So you met a woman, found her sexually attractive, and made love with her. God, I've done that myself often enough. It's no big deal.'

Rachel ignored the fact that her friend had confirmed one of her long-held suspicions. 'It feels it. And what about Daniel?'

'I take it you haven't told him about this, then?'

'No.' Rachel sighed. 'Though I did tell him about the visions I've been having.'

Carrie's lips twitched. 'I can understand that. Talking fantasies with your lover is even more fun than having the fantasies in the first place.'

Rachel winced. 'Yes, but the way I keep acting them out . . . Today, I was at Vivace.'

Carrie was surprised. 'I didn't know that you were a member.'

'I'm not – we've just won the account, and I'm working on a new brochure for it.' Rachel's lips twitched. 'I believe that you know the owner.'

'Ellis Brown. Mm.' Carrie licked her lips. 'That's one gorgeous man. Even though I don't usually go for blonds, I have to admit that I wouldn't mind having him.'

'That's what I thought.' Rachel paused. 'We had a sauna today.'

'We, as in just the two of you?'

'Well, he had to show me the club's facilities. He thought that we might as well use them as see them.'

Carrie's eyes widened as she realized what Rachel was trying to say. 'You mean, you and Ellis? You made love with a client?'

Rachel nodded. 'We were in the sauna. He was telling me about the club and, the next thing I knew, I blacked out again. I was back in Egypt, with this man. He didn't look anything like Ellis – he still reminded me of Daniel – and he made love with me. He took my dress off, and then stripped, and I ended up fellating him. And then, I came round, to find that I was kissing Ellis.'

'Kissing?' Carrie prompted, her eyes glinting mischievously.

'On the mouth,' Rachel said firmly.

'I see what you mean about breaking all your rules in one week.'

Rachel sighed. 'Never, ever, ever sleep with a client. Or a colleague – and that includes freelancers and suppliers. I know.'

'So what happened?'

'I apologized.'

'And?'

'We were both aroused. I think I tried to be sensible about it, but I couldn't help myself. I was so hot, so horny after that vision: I needed a man. Any man. Even one who was off limits.' She tapped her fingertips on the table. 'Let's just say, I think that Ellis would live up to your expectations. He knows exactly what he's doing, and he's good.'

Carrie gave a low whistle. 'Rach, this isn't like you.'

'Exactly. If I'd seen this stuff once, I could have put it down to drinking too much at a party, or maybe that someone had spiked my drink. But it keeps happening, Carrie. I don't understand what the hell is going on.'

'Have you talked to Daniel about any of this?'

'I told him about your idea of reincarnation. He suggested that I talked to a colleague of his; she works in psychology, and she's interested in hypnosis and regression.'

'Go, then. Talk to her. It can't do any harm.' Carrie squeezed her friend's hand. 'You never know, it might explain what's happening to you.'

'I doubt it. You know what I think about regression. It's all a PR stunt.'

'Don't be so narrow-minded,' Carrie chided. 'Give it a try.'

'I suppose I could.' Rachel was slightly doubtful.

'Well.' Carrie topped up their glasses. 'Come on. Let's go and sit in comfort, stick something good on the stereo – and you can tell me a bit more about Ellis.'

Rachel couldn't help laughing. 'Why? Planning to seduce him, are you?'

'I might do. He'd make a nice contrast to Ralph. And if I introduce them . . .' She gave Rachel a lascivious wink. 'Well. Let's just say that it'd be my kind of evening.'

'You're impossible, Carrie.' Rachel chuckled, and followed her friend into the sitting room.

SEVEN

Later that evening, Rachel decided that Carrie, as usual, was being sensible, and rang Daniel. He immediately agreed to fix up a meeting with Hazel; the following Friday evening saw them walking down a street in Walthamstow towards Hazel's house.

Daniel, noticing how quiet Rachel was, looked sidelong at her. 'OK?'

'Yeah.' She wrinkled her nose.

'Really OK?'

She sighed. 'Well, part of me thinks that this is all going to be a complete waste of time.'

He squeezed her hand. 'Mm, I know that. But Hazel's not a crank, if that's what you're worrying about. She's a trained psychologist. She just happens to be interested in hypnosis and regression therapy.'

'You already know what I think about that. It's a publicity stunt.'

'Just keep an open mind, hm?'

'I'll try.' Rachel frowned. 'Though part of me's scared, Daniel. I know I don't believe in it, but supposing there really is something in this regression stuff, and I really have lived before? Supposing I'm seeing what actually happened to me, years ago?'

'I don't know, Rachel. We'll cross that bridge when we come to it.'

She smiled wryly. 'I still don't know why the hell I let you and Carrie talk me into this.'

'Because we both care about you, neither of us has any idea what's happening to you, and this might just be a way of finding out. If it doesn't work, then we'll try something else until we start finding some answers.'

'Yeah.'

He wrinkled his nose at her. 'Anyway, I quite like the idea of you being regressed into a seventeenth century trollop and talking lewdly to me. A milkmaid pulling down the front of her dress to show herself to me . . . Mm, I like that idea a lot.'

She smiled unwillingly. 'Trust you to think of something like that.'

'Well.' He smiled encouragingly at her. 'It'll be fine. And you'll like Hazel. Everyone does. She's one of these people who puts you at your ease without even trying.'

He paused by a gate, shepherded Rachel through it, then walked down the black-and-red tiled path to Hazel's front door. Like Daniel's house, it was a Victorian terrace, with moulded architraves. There was a door-knocker exactly the same as Daniel's, in the shape of a woman's face, framed with long flowing hair; obviously, Rachel thought, those door-knockers had been the height of fashion in Walthamstow a hundred or so years before.

Daniel noticed the sudden pallor on Rachel's face, and stroked her hair. 'Rachel, you don't have to go through with this if you don't want to. We'll just have a drink with Hazel, and then go.'

'I'm fine. Really. And I need to do this, Daniel. I need to find out if there's something in it – and if that's why I keep seeing those bloody visions.'

'OK. But you can pull out any time you like, remember that. Hazel will understand.' He knocked on the door; a short time later, a kind-looking woman opened it. She had dark hair, which was shot through in places with grey; it was cut into a short bob, and it was pulled back from her face by an Alice band. Her eyes were brown and kind; she wasn't exactly pretty, but there was something attractive about her that made Rachel want to like her. Rachel judged her to be in her late thirties, older than herself and Daniel; she was of average height and build, and was dressed comfortably in a pair of dark tailored trousers and an unstructured tunic shirt.

'Hello, Daniel. And you must be Rachel. Come in.'

Rachel's eyes widened as she stepped into the hall: it was the kind of place that a New Ager would have described as having good vibes, she thought, half amused. Certainly, there was a welcoming air, and Rachel was pleasantly surprised. She'd always expected the house of a psychologist to be tense, watchful.

'I've been looking forward to meeting you, Rachel,' Hazel said.

'You, too.' Ten minutes ago, it wouldn't have been true; but Rachel couldn't help responding to the sheer warmth of the woman.

Hazel arched one slender dark eyebrow. 'You don't have to be polite.'

Rachel flushed. Had her initial doubts been so obvious? 'I . . .'

Hazel merely grinned. 'Let's have a glass of wine, shall we?

There's a bottle of chardonnay in the fridge. I'll be back in a minute.'

Before Rachel had time to register anything else, Hazel returned with an opened bottle of wine and three glasses. Rachel sipped her wine, and her nervousness disappeared as Hazel began chatting lightly, explaining what she did at the university, and her interest in regression therapy.

'I've always thought that it was some kind of PR stunt, for people trying to relaunch a flagging career,' Rachel admitted.

Hazel chuckled. 'That's true for some, yes; but I've had some very odd experiences which make me keep an open mind. I've regressed people who've told me that they're from the ninth century or King Henry's court, and the historical detail's been amazing. It's not even as if the people concerned had ever been interested in that particular part of history, or had read about it somewhere and forgotten about it: there really was no explanation for how they knew so much. Some of my colleagues verified the historical detail for me, later, and they were just as surprised as I was.'

'That's the problem, in my case,' Rachel said. 'I've always been fascinated by Egypt, and I've read a hell of a lot about it. In fact, sometimes I think I should have read something like Egyptology instead of an English degree. So if I gave you any historical details, they'd be straight from my memory – not even my subconscious memory, at that.'

'It doesn't make what you're experiencing any the less valid. Maybe that's why you're so interested in Egyptian things, in the first place.'

Rachel thought about it. 'So you really can regress people, Hazel?'

'Certainly within their present life, yes. Sometimes people

have phobias about things – water or bridges – and regressing them can unlock some incident in their childhood that started the phobia in the first place. It's helped a lot of people; they've found out the root of the problem, dealt with it, and the phobias have gone away.' Hazel's brown eyes were kind. 'It's just another therapy tool, that's all: lowering people's defences so that they can tackle the problem properly.'

'I don't know if this is going to go away, like your patients' phobias.' Rachel took another sip of wine. 'Hazel, how much do you know about what's been happening to me?'

'Daniel's only told me a few very brief details.' Hazel glanced at Daniel, then back at Rachel. 'Rachel, would you rather that we regressed you when you and I are on our own?'

Rachel shook her head. 'It's OK. Daniel knows everything, anyway. I'd like him to be there with me.'

'So what happens?' Hazel asked softly. 'What happens when you have these weird experiences?'

'I feel as if I'm going to faint; it's almost like I'm blacking out, and the world's spinning. Then I'm in Egypt, and I'm me – but not me, at the same time. The woman has my face, but her hair and her eyes are different. I'm usually with a man, who has the same eyes as Daniel – and yet he's not Daniel. The first time it happened, it was before I'd even met him. It was so strange. I was in the British Museum, and suddenly I wasn't there any more, and I saw this man and woman together. I woke up, and Daniel had caught me. He said that I'd passed out. The moment that I saw his eyes, I nearly passed out again, I was so shocked. He had the same eyes as the man I'd seen in my – well, dream, or whatever it was.' The words tumbled out. 'The worst thing is, most of these dreams are highly erotic. It's getting to be a problem.

I'm starting to black out at work, or when I'm on the tube, and I just can't handle it any more.'

'Have you thought that it might be anaemia?'

Rachel nodded. 'I've been to see the doctor. I've had blood tests, and nothing's physically wrong with me. I'm not anaemic, I'm not epileptic, and I know that I'm not going mad, because if I were mad, I wouldn't even consider the idea that I might be insane.' She sighed. 'I just don't know what the hell's happening to me. My best friend suggested that maybe it was reincarnation, memories of a previous life filtering through into this one.'

'And although you think that the idea's completely ridiculous, you can't think of any other explanation – so you're trying regression, to see if there's anything in it.' Hazel finished.

Rachel flushed. 'Put like that, it sounds so . . . so . . .'

'Completely understandable,' Hazel said gently. 'I was a bit sceptical about it, as a student. I've never had any sense of *déja vu*, or anything like that, but some of my patients have – and it's changed my views about regression to past lives.' She paused. 'Look, why don't you come through to my study? It'll be more comfortable if we try regressing you there.'

Rachel nodded. 'All right.' She took another sip of wine, then put her glass on a low coffee table and followed Hazel through to the study. It was a comfortable room; there was a large battered oak desk in one corner, with a very up-to-date computer, a desk lamp and a pile of books on it and a high-backed office chair behind it. The walls were lined with bookcases, and there were a couple of comfortable chairs.

Hazel spun the office chair round to face the room, and sat down, motioning to Rachel and Daniel to take the easy chairs.

'Now,' she said, 'what we're going to do might cause you to have another of these visions, Rachel. If that happens, it doesn't matter; don't worry. No-one's judging you. It's between you, me and Daniel. It won't go any further.'

Rachel flushed. 'I ought to warn you. These visions, or whatever they are . . .'

'Are erotic,' Hazel finished. She shrugged. 'You've already told me that. I'm pretty broad-minded, so don't worry. Nothing you say is going to shock me, offend me, or upset me. I won't throw you out.' Her lips twitched. 'Unless you try to murder me, that is; I might have a bit of an issue with that.'

Rachel smiled back, suddenly relaxing. 'OK. So how do we start?'

'I'll put you in a light trance,' Hazel said, 'then I'll ask you a few questions. Gradually, I'll take you back to your childhood; and then, I'll see if I can regress you any further back, and if you have lived before and you're remembering a past life, we'll be able to find out who this woman is.'

'Right.'

'I'll tape everything, so if we do find something, and you want to review it later, it won't be a problem.' Hazel opened the drawer of her desk and took out a small tape-recorder. She plugged it in, checked that it was working, and switched it on. 'Now, Rachel, would you look at the light behind me?'

'OK.' Rachel concentrated on the desk lamp.

'It's bright, Rachel, very bright. It's so bright,' Hazel said, her voice soft and low, 'that you want to close your eyes, shut it out. Just close your eyes, and relax, and the light will stop dazzling you. Close your eyes, Rachel . . .'

Rachel found that the light was suddenly dazzling her, and closed her eyes.

'Now,' Hazel said, 'your left hand is so light, lighter than air. You can feel it rising, rising.' Almost exactly as she said it, Rachel's left hand rose up. 'And now it's falling down again, softly, like an autumn leaf.' Rachel's hand fell down gently onto her lap.

'Now, Rachel. Let's go back ten years. Tell me, where are you?'

'I'm in London, of course,' Rachel said.

'What are you doing?'

She wrinkled her nose. 'I'm working on my essay.'

'What's your essay about, Rachel?'

'*Antony and Cleopatra.*' Rachel grinned. 'Pretty much what everyone expected – that I'd choose the Egyptian play.'

Hazel smiled. Daniel had told her that Rachel's friends and colleagues called her 'Cleo', because of her Egyptian obsession. 'All right. Let's go back a bit further, say another ten years. Where are you now?'

'I'm at home,' Rachel said. 'It's the summer holidays, and I'm playing in the garden with my dog, Sam.'

'What's the house like?'

Rachel described the house in minute detail: a typical house in the stockbroker belt, with large windows and an immaculate garden.

'OK. Now we'll go back a few more summers. Where are you, now?'

'I'm at home. It's Christmas, and we're making decorations for the tree. I'm painting gold stars, and making silver bells out of egg-boxes.' Rachel's voice had become high and girlish; Daniel smiled. He could imagine her as a child, intense and eager, chattering endlessly.

'Now, Rachel, we're going back further. You're floating,

floating; and we're going back before the darkness. Where are you now?'

Rachel was silent.

'Back through the mists of time,' Hazel continued, her voice still gentle and regular. 'Where are you, Rachel?'

Still, there was silence.

Hazel gave it one last try. 'Rachel, you're going back, further back. Where are you?'

Still, Rachel said nothing.

Hazel sighed. 'All right, Rachel. I'm going to count to three, and when I reach three, you're going to open your eyes. You'll remember everything we talked about, and you'll feel relaxed and happy. One, two, three.'

Rachel opened her eyes.

'Hello,' Hazel said. 'How are you feeling?'

'Fine.' Rachel smiled back at her. 'So, did you get anything? Was I Cleopatra or Nefertiti?'

Hazel shook her head. 'I talked to you when you were eighteen, when you were eight, and when you were five. There was nothing before that. You haven't lived before, Rachel: and certainly not in ancient Egypt.'

'I guess that squashes the regression theory, then,' Rachel said ruefully.

'Yes.' Hazel nodded. 'You can have the tape, with pleasure, but I'm afraid that whatever you're seeing isn't you in a past life.'

'I see.' Rachel bit her lip. 'What else could it be? Am I tapping into someone else's memories?'

'Maybe,' Hazel said slowly. 'But I can only regress you as you: I can't do anything else. I'm sorry.' She was aware of Rachel's disappointment. 'Let's go back in the sitting room. It's more comfortable there, and we can finish the wine.'

'Yes. Thanks.' Rachel followed her back into the living room; she and Daniel spent the next hour or so chatting amiably with Hazel, talking about everything except Rachel's strange visions and the subject of regression. On one level, Rachel enjoyed herself: Hazel was good company. And yet she couldn't help wondering. If she wasn't living out her own past life, what the hell was she seeing? And why was she the only one who could see it?

On the way back to the tube station, Rachel was very quiet.

'Are you all right?' Daniel asked, squeezing her hand.

'Yes.' She sighed. 'I suppose I was just expecting too much.'

'And this is the woman who told me that regression was a load of rubbish, just a publicity stunt.'

'Yeah, well. Maybe some people have lived before. I'm just not one of them.' She shook her head. 'But Daniel, when I see it, it's real. So real, so vivid. At first, it was just like I was watching through a wall of glass; at the same time, I could feel what was going on. Now, I can hear things as well, hear the birds and the animals and the sound of people working. I can feel the heat of the sun. I can smell the river. I can hear people walking and talking and playing in the river. Cats miaouing, dogs barking – everything. It's like I'm there, in the past, part of it all. I don't understand what's happening to me, Daniel, I really don't.'

'No.' His fingers tightened round hers. 'I was hoping that Hazel would be able to help you, too.' He shrugged. 'I don't know, Rachel. We'll get to the bottom of it, somehow.'

'Maybe.' Rachel looked at him. 'Daniel, stay with me tonight.'

'Of course. Neither of us have to go to work in the morning, anyway.' He smiled at her. 'Look, why don't you come back to my place? There's nothing about Egypt there, so maybe you won't see anything tonight.'

'Maybe.' Rachel was grateful for the suggestion.

They turned back from the tube station, heading for Daniel's house instead. When they reached his front door, he unlocked it, then closed the door behind them and took her into his arms. 'I think,' Daniel said carefully, 'that you could do with a bit of pampering.'

'I'm all right.'

'Put it another way – so do I.'

She caught the note in his voice, and was suddenly interested. 'What exactly did you have in mind?'

'A long, relaxing aromatherapy bath. Together. By candlelight, listening to Mozart, drinking freshly-squeezed orange juice.'

'What, no champagne?' she teased.

He grinned. 'You'll need to keep your strength up. Vitamin C's better for you than alcohol – though it doesn't have quite the same effect, I admit.'

She grinned back. Everything was going to be all right. 'Candlelight, Mozart and orange juice.'

'Definitely.' He led her into the kitchen, collected a couple of glasses froma cupboard and a bottle of freshly-squeezed orange juice from the fridge, then led her upstairs. He made a swift detour to his bedroom, taking the cassette recorder and picking out a tape of Mozart piano sonatas, then plugged it in outside the bathroom, switching it on and adjusting the volume so that music filled the air.

Then he led her into the bathroom. He switched on the light, and set the glasses down carefully on the windowsill. He lit the thick beeswax candle on the windowsill, then switched off the bathroom light so that the room was lit only by the flickering flame on the windowsill.

Suddenly, it wasn't just Daniel's functional and rather masculine bathroom any more – it was a dark oasis, full of sensuous promise. The gentle music and the soft light made Rachel feel suddenly aroused: what they were going to do was going to be very good, for both of them.

'Rachel.' He took her hand, lifting it to his lips so that he could kiss her palm; then he sucked her fingers, one by one, keeping his smoky eyes fixed on hers.

Rachel felt a familiar kick in her loins. Whatever force had made their paths cross at the British Museum, she blessed it silently. Daniel was one of the sexiest men she'd ever had the privilege to meet; and she knew that they were going to make love all night, to chase all her demons away.

'Daniel,' she breathed softly, her voice husky.

'I know. I've been thinking about this all day. I've wanted to do this with you for a long time.' He slowly unbuttoned her shirt and let it fall to the floor. 'And although you're not my lusty seventeenth-century milkmaid, you're still beautiful, and lovely, and I want you very much.' His voice, too, grew husky. 'Your skin's like alabaster, and your scent drives me insane.' He hooked one finger under the thin shoulder strap of her ivory lace teddy. 'And this . . . this turns me on in a big way. I love the way you dress, the way you look, the way your skin feels under my fingers. I love your breasts, the way they swell and your nipples grow dark and hard.'

She swallowed, and he slid the thin straps of the teddy over her shoulders, rolling the lacy material over her breasts.

He cupped her breasts, lifting them slightly. 'God, you're so perfect,' he breathed, bending his head and drawing the tip of his nose down her cleavage. Rachel shivered, and he drew his tongue up the shadowed vee, teasing her and making her want more.

She tipped her head back, baring her throat to him; he nibbled along her collar bones, licking the soft hollows at the base of her throat. His mouth slowly drifted down to the hard peak of one breast, and she gave a sigh of bliss as he finally began to suck at her nipple, drawing fiercely on it.

Rachel closed her eyes as his fingers began to toy with her other nipple, arousing her to fever pitch. She suddenly wanted desperately to feel him inside her, and pushed her pelvis towards him.

Daniel smiled. 'Easy. We have all the time in the world.'

Rachel stroked his face. 'You started this, Daniel.'

'Yes, and I intend to finish it – all in good time.' He pulled away from her for a moment, putting the plug in the bath and turning on the taps. He added some aromatherapy bubble bath, which immediately scented the air with a mixture of orange and ginger; Rachel sniffed.

'That's lovely.'

'Aromatherapy bath oil – a birthday present from my sister-in-law. She's into this sort of stuff; it's meant to be revitalizing. And I think both of us need it, right now.' He took her hands, drawing them down to the waistband of his chinos. She undid the button, sliding the zip down, and curled her fingers round his cock through the soft cotton of his underpants.

It was Daniel's turn to close his eyes and push his pelvis towards his lover; she grinned. 'All the time in the world, you said.'

'Yes.' He helped her remove his shirt and the rest of his clothes, then dropped to his knees in front of her, rolling the teddy downwards until she could step out of it. Then he drew his hands slowly up the insides of her legs, until he reached her thighs.

Unable to help herself, Rachel widened her stance, and she felt him smile against her abdomen. She put her hands on his shoulders, for balance, and closed her eyes as he slowly peeled down first one stocking and then the other. She was already wet with anticipation, a fact that Daniel wasn't slow to discover when he cupped her mons veneris, letting his fingers drift over her quim.

'Oh yes,' she breathed, as he rubbed his cheeks against her inner thighs, then finally drew his tongue along her satiny cleft. She widened her stance still further, giving him greater access, and he rewarded her by making his tongue into a hard point, flicking it rapidly back and forth over her clitoris until her internal muscles went into spasms and she came, moaning softly.

'That was just for starters,' Daniel told her, standing up again and rubbing his nose against hers. 'I have something much nicer in mind.'

He tested the bath water, and added a little cold water before helping Rachel into the bath. 'It'll be easier if you kneel,' he said.

'Hm?'

'It'll be more comfortable,' he said. 'For both of us.'

Rachel did as he said, sitting back so that her buttocks touched her heels, and resting her hands on the sides of the bath. Daniel climbed in behind her and knelt in the same position. He reached for the soap, lathered his hands, and began to wash her back, smoothing his palms all the way down her spine, then rubbing up again in small circles. Rachel found the action incredibly sensual, and she couldn't help a small shiver of anticipation. Daniel was going to make love to her in the bath, she knew that; this pampering was only a prelude.

Daniel said nothing, but continued to wash her back: soaping her skin very gently, then sluicing the lather away again. His hands skimmed her buttocks, tracing their swell, then moved up over her hips to settle at her waist. Rachel closed her eyes as he drew his hands over her midriff, then slowly began to stroke upwards towards her breasts.

She arched back against him as he took the soap in one hand, rubbing it over her breasts, then dropped the soap in the bath and worked the lather up with his hands. His fingertips drew small circles on her skin, sensitizing her; by the time he started to sluice her down again, her nipples were hard, jutting out.

He traced the darker area of her areola, teasing her; at last, she could stand it no longer. 'Please,' she whispered huskily.

'Please what?'

'Please, touch me, Daniel.' The strange man in her dreams had vanished: all she could think of was the way Daniel would feel as he touched her, his mouth and his fingers probing her more intimate zones, and then finally sliding his cock deep inside her, filling her completely.

'Touch you?' His voice had grown husky. 'My pleasure, Rachel.' He rested his palms against her nipples, moving them in small circles; when she gasped, pushing against him, he took her nipples between finger and thumb, pulling gently until she tipped her head back, her breathing coming in small pants.

He buried his mouth in the corner between her neck and shoulder, taking tiny nibbles at her skin.

'Oh, God, yes,' Rachel moaned. She could feel the hardness of his cock thrusting between them, the muscle engorged and erect, and she longed to feel it pushing inside her, blindly exploring her.

She reached one hand between them, caressing his cock. 'Daniel . . .'

'Mm?' He licked her shoulder.

'You don't feel like reading my mind, do you?'

'Nope. If you want something, you have to tell me exactly what you have in mind.'

Rachel grinned. 'That wouldn't be in the style of a seventeenth-century milkmaid, would it?'

'In the style of a twentieth-century advertising copywriter would do.'

Her grin broadened. 'Then how about a good honest fuck, Daniel?'

'I thought you'd never ask.'

She leaned forward, grasping the edge of the bath and pushing her bottom back towards him. Daniel couldn't resist nuzzling the soft globes, then letting his tongue drift along the cleft of her buttocks, making his tongue into a hard point as he reached her anus. Rachel moaned, and Daniel continued to lap at her, teasing her.

At her impatient wriggle, he moved so that he was between her thighs, and guided his cock into the warm velvety depths of her quim. Rachel gave a sigh of pleasure, and tightened her internal muscles round him; he smiled, and rubbed his face against her shoulder.

The water swished gently round them as he began to thrust

into her, forming miniature tidal waves as his movements grew harder and faster. He steadied himself against the side of the bath with one hand, reaching round to fondle her breasts with his free hand, weighing the soft creamy globes in turn and then stroking the soft undersides. Rachel moaned softly, and his hand trailed down between her thighs, his fingers seeking and finding the hard button of her clitoris. He licked her earlobe and caressed the little nub of flesh, rubbing back and forth and then letting his finger move in a rapid figure-of-eight pattern which made her body jerk.

Just when Rachel thought that she couldn't take any more, she felt his seed pump hotly into her, and her internal muscles contracted sharply round him, prolonging the length of his orgasm.

'God, that felt good,' she said, shuddering.

He eased himself gently out of her. 'Mm. Though unless you want to look like a prune as well, I suggest we get out of the bath.' He clambered out, wrapped a towel round himself, and pulled out the plug. Rachel slowly got to her feet, and he was ready with a towel for her, wrapping her in it and lifting her out of the bath.

He dried her gently, paying minute attention to every inch of skin, then wrapped a bathrobe round her, and led her into his bedroom. 'Sorry, I'm not used to entertaining women here,' he said softly, 'so I can't offer you any moisturizing lotion.'

Rachel suddenly remembered what he'd said about his reputation as a would-be Trappist monk, and chuckled. 'Entertaining women, indeed.'

'Well.' His eyes held hers. 'Except in very special cases. Maybe you ought to keep a few of your things here.'

She tipped her head on one side. 'Are you asking me to move in with you, Daniel?'

He shook his head. 'Just suggesting that it might be – convenient, shall we say? – to keep a few things at each other's houses. To make life more comfortable.' His lips twitched. 'Though I do have a new toothbrush, which you can use in the morning.'

She chuckled. 'Oh, Daniel. You're so good for me.' He'd managed to rid her of the tension she'd felt since leaving Hazel's house, and discovering that she was no further forward in finding out why she was having the Egyptian visions.

'I hope so.' He tugged at the belt of the bathrobe, loosening it and pushing the garment to the floor. He'd left the cassette player on continuous play, and Mozart still filled the air; a shiver of delight ran through Rachel at the look in his eyes.

Slowly, Daniel traced the curve of her shoulder, his fingertips gliding along her collarbone and dipping into the hollows beneath it, then across the other shoulder. He let his hand drift up to curve round her throat, his touch still very light and gentle; finally, he cupped her chin, guiding her face towards his.

His kiss was gentle, his mouth nibbling gently at her lower lip until her mouth opened, allowing him to slide his tongue against hers. His hand moved round to caress the nape of her neck beneath her hair, and then he stroked her back. 'I wish that I could paint,' he said softly.

'Paint?'

'Mm. I'd love to paint you, like Degas. You know, the painting in the National: *Woman drying herself*. It's the most erotic picture I've ever seen.'

'Hang on. He's not a pre-Raphaelite,' Rachel teased.

'I don't care. I still love that painting.' His voice was husky.
'Your skin's so soft, so beautiful. I'd paint you by candle-light,
naked and with your back to me. All the time, I'd be hard,
wanting you, but wanting to paint you so I could see you
when you weren't with me. And then, when I'd finished, I'd
turn you round to face me, and take you in my arms. Like
this.' He kissed her again; Rachel pressed against him, sliding
one leg between his. Daniel's hands moved down to cup her
buttocks, returning the silent pressure of her body. She could
feel his cock, large and erect, against her pubis; she moved
her body slightly to rub against it.

'Christ, Rachel. I meant to take this slowly, to make it good
for you – but I just can't help myself. I want you so badly.' He
drew her over to the bed, pushing the duvet back and picking
her up, laying her gently on the mattress.

Rachel looked up at him, giving him a coquettish pout.
'Earlier, you wanted me as a seventeenth-century milkmaid.
Now, it's a French ballet dancer.'

He grinned. 'Actually, I'd settle for you as you.' He stretched
out next to her on the bed, lying on his side, and stroked her
fair hair away from her face. 'Rachel, I can't resist you.' He
lowered his mouth to hers, kissing her deeply, then slowly
tracked his mouth down her body. He licked the hollows of
her collar-bones, then moved down to nuzzle her breasts.
Rachel closed her eyes, tipping her head back against the
pillows and concentrating only on the way that he made
her feel.

She felt slightly dizzy, and squeezed her eyes tightly shut.
No. Tonight wasn't the time for Egypt: it was London, in the
twentieth century, and she was with Daniel. Nothing was going
to interrupt that. She wasn't going to let her mind slip back to

whenever it was, let whoever it was control her. She was going to fight.

The wave of dizziness receded, and she became aware that Daniel had made his tongue into a hard point, flicking it across her erect nipple. She gasped, and he moved to concentrate on the other breast, licking the hard nub of flesh and then blowing gently on it, making her arch up towards him.

'Daniel,' she murmured, sliding her hands into his hair.

He said nothing, but continued to kiss his way down her body, paying attention to her ribcage and making her wriggle when he traced a path with his tongue round her navel. He moved lower, to her abdomen, and she parted her legs automatically; to her relief, he didn't tease her by moving to her ankles and working his way up again. He nuzzled her thighs, and then she felt his tongue move along her quim, licking from the top to the bottom of her musky furrow in one smooth sweep.

She shivered, her internal muscles flexing; Daniel continued licking her, teasing her clitoris with the tip of his tongue, until she cried out and let her orgasm sweep through her. He continued to lap at her, until the aftershocks of her orgasm died away; then he eased himself back up her body, kissing and licking her skin as she moved. He placed his hands either side of her head, his fingers sinking into the deep feather pillow; he kept his weight on his hands and knees, aware that her frame was more delicate than his.

He rubbed his nose affectionately against hers, and she smiled at him. Then she eased her hand between them, her fingers curling round his cock as she guided it to her entrance. Daniel could feel how hot and moist her sex was against his glans; he gasped with pleasure as she slid her legs round his waist, pressing down on his buttocks with her heels, and lifting her own buttocks at the same time so that he slipped into her, right up to the hilt. He stayed still for a moment, luxuriating in the way she felt, and giving her body time to adjust to him again; then, slowly, he began to move inside her. Rachel matched him, moving with him and pushing up as he drove into her, releasing the grip of her thighs as he pulled out again.

'Oh, God,' he said, his voice drowsy with pleasure. 'Rachel. With you, I'm in paradise.'

A shiver ran through her. She'd heard that before: *with you, I'm in paradise*. Except that the phrase hadn't been Paradise. It had been "the Field of Reeds". The afterlife, land of pleasure and plenty, ruled by Osiris. And the words hadn't been spoken by Daniel, though they had been spoken by a man with aqua grey eyes . . .

Before she could hold onto that thought, she felt another climax sweep through her, an inner sparkling that grew stronger and stronger, until it felt like her body was splintering and floating away. She cried out, and heard Daniel's answering cry as he, too, climaxed. And then he was kissing her, holding her close. 'Oh, Rachel. Rachel.'

'I know. It's the same for me,' she said softly.

Again, she felt that weird shifting sensation. *It's the same for me*. Again, she was echoing the words of the past – but whose words? And why?

EIGHT

'You could,' Daniel suggested, the next morning, with Rachel curled into his arms, 'spend the whole weekend here.'

'I could,' Rachel agreed. 'But I do need some clothes.'

He grinned, stroking her face. 'I don't see why.'

She chuckled. 'Lecher. You know what I mean. I need a change of clothes, anyway.'

'Even if we're going to spend the whole weekend in bed?'

She shook her head. 'We can't. We have to get up, some time.'

'Why? If you're thinking about food, we can order pizza, and eat it in bed.' He grinned. 'And I rather like the idea of you padding round the house, naked.'

'Like a slave?' she asked, her voice acerbic.

He chuckled. 'Far from it. Like an empress. A queen.' His lips twitched. 'Cleopatra, perhaps.'

'Which makes you a fat and ageing Roman general making a fool of himself in a foreign country, and me a raddled old hag.'

'Age cannot wither her,' he quoted.

'Tough. Even if you pick the most gorgeous parts of that speech, and woo me with your knowledge of Shakespeare – which isn't exactly usual for a historian, I admit, and yes, I'm impressed – I'm still going back to my place, to get a change of clothes.'

'Are you sure?' he asked hopefully.

She laughed. 'Sure. Anyway, how come you know that speech?'

'One of my brothers was into amateur dramatics, in the sixth form. His drama group performed *Antony and Cleopatra*, that summer, and he played Enobarbus. He really fancied the girl who played Cleopatra. He learned the whole play by heart, so that he could quote the most romantic bits to her – and he drove us all mad in the process. "The barge she sat in", for breakfast, lunch and dinner ... I suppose a bit of it stuck,' he said. 'Like the other bit about "he ploughed her, and she cropped".'

Rachel smiled. 'How old were you? Fifteen?'

He was surprised. 'How did you know?'

'Because that's the sort of thing that stays in a fifteen-year-old boy's mind,' she said loftily. She stretched. 'Anyway, I'd better get dressed, so I can go back to Islington and collect my stuff.'

'I'll come with you, if you like.' He looked thoughtful for a moment. 'We can drop your stuff back here, then go out somewhere for the day. We could go to Greenwich, or Hampstead Heath, and spend the whole afternoon walking – nothing heavy, just a gentle stroll. Then we could go and see a film, or have something to eat, or both. Then, tomorrow, we can see what the weather's like. If it's grim, I'll go and get the papers, and we can spend the day drinking coffee and eating bacon sandwiches and slobbing round and fighting each other for the arts section. If it's nice ... Well, we could go for a drive.'

'I'd like that,' Rachel said. The way Daniel had pampered her in the bath the previous night, then made love to her so tenderly afterwards, seemed to have washed away all her tensions and most of her worries about the Egyptian dreams. Forgetting the odd twinges of *déja vu* she'd felt the previous evening, she felt relaxed and happy, looking forward to a whole weekend spent in his company.

After a late breakfast, they set out for Islington. They'd just walked through Rachel's front door, and she was saying to Daniel that he could always make them both a cup of coffee while she got her things together, when she stopped in horror.

'What?' Daniel asked, seeing the shock on her face. Then he reached her side, and his eyes widened as he saw the mess in her sitting room. 'Christ, you've been burgled,' he said.

She shook her head. 'I can't have been. Apart from the fact that I set the burglar alarm before I left and it hasn't gone off, the door wasn't open. How could burglars have got in?'

'The window?' he suggested.

'That's closed, too: and there's still the alarm. Like I said, it hadn't been set off. I switched it off myself when I opened the front door, just now.'

He swallowed. 'Christ, this is awful. Who the hell could have done this?' Every book had been thrown from the shelves, lying open and crooked on the floor; some had had pages ripped out. Several of Rachel's Egyptian artefacts lay in fragments on the floor, as though someone had stamped on them. Everything had been swept from the mantelpiece, which was scored with short deep grooves, and the cat mummy-case lay face up on the floor. The pictures all hung crookedly, some of them with a jagged streak through the glass; and along her low coffee table, there were distinct scratches.

Scratches, Rachel thought, that looked as though they'd

been made by a cat. A heavy, angry and very determined cat. She pushed the thought away. No, she was being completely ridiculous. Apart from the fact that the cat she shared with her neighbour was, quite literally, a fluffy and sweet-tempered pussy cat, no real cat could have done that sort of damage.

'Better call the police,' Daniel said.

She shook her head. 'I don't think anything's missing. Anyway, I don't have anything to steal. I don't have expensive jewellery, or original paintings; I don't keep any cash in the flat, either. And surely the first thing to go would be my stereo, or the television?'

'Even so. The police might be able to find fingerprints, and catch whoever did this.'

'Maybe.' Her idea of the cat wouldn't go away. She was about to say, 'What would they find, paw prints?', but stopped herself in time. This was not the place to tell Daniel about the night when she'd heard mewing and the cat had moved on the mantelpiece. It was all completely and utter supposition – a trick of her mind, nothing more than that. She rubbed her hand across her face. 'Oh, God. I can't believe this, Daniel.'

'Look, I'll make us both a coffee while you ring the police. Then, when they've checked it out, we can start sifting through this mess and see what damage has been done, and what we can save.'

'OK.'

Daniel headed for the kitchen while Rachel rang the police. A few minutes later, two burly constables rang the doorbell; Rachel explained the whole story to them, that she'd stayed at Daniel's, the previous night, but had left the alarm on. The alarm hadn't gone off, it hadn't been tampered with, and there was no sign of breaking and entering. They hadn't moved anything, but Rachel was sure that nothing was missing. There was no motive; she wasn't aware that she had any enemies. There were people who didn't like her very much, yes – she wouldn't have been human, otherwise – but no-one who hated her enough just to wreck her living room like that. And no other room in the house had been touched; no-one had rummaged through her bedroom drawers in search of jewellery or money.

One of the policemen checked for fingerprints, but found nothing; in the end, Rachel promised to call them if she found anything was missing. In the meantime, it would be logged as an unsolvable case. She ushered them out, then walked back into the sitting room.

'Christ,' she said, surveying the mess. 'It's going to take hours to sort this lot out.'

'I'll help you,' Daniel offered.

'Thanks.'

'Just tell me what you want me to do, and where you want me to put things.'

'I appreciate this, Daniel.' She bit her lip. 'But it's all such a mess. How the hell did it happen?'

'I don't know. But we'll sort it out, together,' he said comfortingly.

Three hours later, all the books were back on the shelves in the right place; there was a pile of damaged books by the coffee table, which Rachel thought could be repaired with invisible sticky tape, and the debris of the broken ornaments was hidden in a dustbin bag. 'Daniel, I think that this rather puts paid to our day out,' she said, staring at the pile of books.

'Hey, that's not a problem. We can go out any other time.' He took her hand and squeezed it. 'I'm sorry that all this happened in the first place.'

'You and me, both.' She swallowed. 'Daniel, I'm sorry, but I don't think that I can stay at your place tonight. I want to be here.'

'In that case, I'll stay with you,' he said. 'There's no way that I can let you stay here on your own. Supposing they come back for whatever it is they didn't find the first time?'

'I don't know. I really don't know. But if someone had broken in, surely either the door would have been open, or a window? But everything was closed, locked. Then there's my burglar alarm. The burglars would have had to disable that, too.'

'So what do you think happened?'

'I don't know,' Rachel said, not wanting to voice her suspicions. But it seemed odd that the only things to have been damaged were Egyptian artefacts, and books on Egypt. Nothing else had been broken; her other knick-knacks had been exactly where she left them, and although her other books had been thrown onto the floor, their pages weren't torn and their spines weren't broken.

'Tell you what, we haven't had any lunch. Why don't I sort out dinner, while you repair the books?'

Rachel appreciated his concern too much to tell him that she wasn't hungry. 'Thanks.'

Daniel set to work in her kitchen, making a casserole from the contents of her fridge and store cupboard, while Rachel set to work with some invisible tape and a pair of scissors, painstakingly repairing the books. She finished just as dinner was ready; the meal was good, but Rachel picked at it, still upset by the mess in her sitting room.

After dinner, Daniel suggested watching a video; he picked

one of her favourite films, but Rachel couldn't concentrate. She lay quietly in his arms on the sofa, brooding about what had happened, and wondering just what the hell was going on.

The more she thought about it, the more she was convinced that it had something to do with the cat. That, and their attempts at regressing her. Why else would there have been those scratch marks on her coffee table and mantelpiece? Yet, at the same time, she knew that it was completely ridiculous. The cat was an inanimate object. A reproduction, probably made of balsa wood or some synthetic material. It couldn't possibly move, or cause that sort of damage.

'Are you all right?' Daniel asked softly, as the film came to an end.

'Yeah.' She tipped her head back, and forced a smile to her face.

He sighed. 'You didn't watch a single minute of the film, did you?'

'I'm sorry.'

'Hey, I would have been the same. Don't worry. Whoever's behind this has gone now; if he comes back, he'll have me to deal with.'

Her lips quirked. 'Being macho, are we?'

'No. I just get angry with the sort of person who thinks it's their right to mess up the home of someone who's worked hard for what she has,' he answered seriously. 'Anyway, we might as well get some sleep.'

'Yes.'

Daniel didn't attempt to make love to her, sensing that what Rachel really needed was just to be held. She fell asleep in his arms, her head pillowed on his shoulder and her arm curved round his waist, her hand flat against his chest. The regular thudding beat of his heart made her feel safe, secure; at last she drifted off to sleep.

It was midnight, and they were taking their greatest risk yet. She wasn't sure if it was the excitement of the forbidden – being alone with him in his quarters – that made her heart beat so strongly, or whether it was the sight of her lover, naked, his skin glistening with a strange metallic light from the moonlight which streamed through the window.

He was magnificent, his body hard and firm, the muscles perfectly sculpted. If she was caught with him, like this, the consequences didn't bear thinking about. They all knew the punishment for adultery. And yet she couldn't stop herself. She needed him, needed the feel of his body pushing into hers.

She laughed softly, out of the sheer delight of being with him, and tipped some oil from a pot into the palm of her hand. She rubbed the oil between her hands to heat it. He would enjoy this, she knew, having his body smoothed with oil. What he didn't know was that she'd added certain spices to the oil, to bring them both greater pleasure. Spices which would make his body heat up even more, make his skin tingle and his cock rigid.

She had already painted her own body, decorating her hands with intricate patterns in henna, as well as her nipples and her inner lips. Before she'd decorated herself, she'd sugared her body to make her skin perfectly smooth, the better to slide against his oiled skin.

He stood quietly, watching her; when she was ready, she stood up, walking over to him with proud, confident steps. She placed a hand on his chest and began to smooth the oil into his skin. He closed his eyes, letting her fingers wander where she pleased, feeling his pectoral muscles and then sliding down over his ribcage, down over his abdomen. His cock reared up from the mat of hair at his groin, proud and demanding. With a smile, she went back over to the pot of oil, bringing it back to him. She knelt down to anoint her hands again, then curled her fingers round his shaft, moving her hand up and down so very gently.

He gasped, and she gave him a warning nip. They were to make no sound. He nodded, and then bit his lip very hard as she continued to masturbate him. She could see that the spices were already having an effect on him, making his cock even longer and harder. She bent her head, her hair swinging down to cover her face, and took the tip of his cock into her mouth, cooling his skin with her tongue. Automatically, he slid his hands into her hair, massaging her scalp and urging her on.

As she began to suck him, very slowly, she let her fingers drift across his perineum, to his buttocks. She slid one finger down the cleft and sought out the puckered rosy hole of his anus. She pressed gently at the forbidden entrance, and her oiled finger slid easily into him. His body tensed and jerked, and she began to suck him harder, pushing her finger in and out in the same rhythm. She could feel his body straining with the effort not to cry out, and she laughed inside, exulting in her power over him. Then she began to work him properly, moving her head rapidly and pushing her finger as deeply as she could into him, massaging his prostate gland so that he writhed beneath her.

She could feel his balls lift and tighten: he was almost ready. Just as she felt him about to come, she pulled back; she could see his face, contorted in an agony of pleasure. She withdrew her hand and then his seed fountained up, spraying over her body. She smiled at him, rubbing the pearly liquid into her skin, into her face and her breasts, cupping the soft globes of her breasts and squeezing and kneading and rubbing them. She heard him gasp, and then he was kneeling with her, kissing her strongly, his tongue invading her mouth.

His hands slid between her thighs, testing and probing her warmth. He was about to push her onto her back, but she shook her head. No. She wanted to play. She wanted to be taken like a slave girl, kneeling and with her head bowed down on her hands. He seemed to understand what she wanted without her having to tell him, and he eased her over onto her hands and knees. He stroked her back, making her arch against him, and then he pushed her hair away from her nape, kissing the sensitive spot at the back of her neck, and then tracing a line of kisses down her spine.

She arched again, dipping her head, and his hands lightly stroked down her sides, gripping her hips. And then, finally, he kneaded the soft globes of her buttocks. Still, his mouth drifted lower; she tensed as she felt the tip of his tongue touch her anus, and then relaxed as he began to probe her. It felt so good, so good, the warmth of his mouth against the forbidden entrance of her body. Then, at last, he straightened up, and she felt the tip of his cock nudging against her sex.

She stifled a moan against her hands as he entered her, pushing in as deeply as he could. He stayed there for a moment, letting her body get used to him, and then he began to move, using very slow, measured thrusts. She moved in the same rhythm with him, pushing backwards, and wanting him to take her harder. He slid one hand round her front, stroking her midriff and then letting the heel of his palm rest on her mound, sliding one finger between her labia and rubbing her clitoris. She gasped, and bucked against him; then he speeded up his rhythm, fucking her hard and deeply. She bit at her hands; her whole body seemed to quiver as she came. At the same time, she felt his cock throb deep inside her.

He withdrew, turning her round and enfolding her in his arms. They lay together for a while, relaxing; then he kissed her lightly on the lips and turned to the little pot of oil. Copying her earlier actions, he poured some into the palm of his hands, warming it; then he slowly began to rub her body with it. She pushed up against his fingers, like a cat, loving the way he touched her and the effect of the oil against her skin, tingling and teasing.

He anointed her nipples; she pushed her ribcage up towards him, offering him her breasts, and he smiled, bending his head and taking one nipple between his lips. He sucked hard, and she had to bite her lip hard to keep herself silent. It felt so good, so good, the way he touched her.

She almost wished that her other lover was there, wearing the tie-on dildo and pushing into her, while he knelt before her and filled her mouth with his cock. To be penetrated, all her orifices filled, her body fountaining with pleasure ... Yes, it would be good. One night, she'd arrange for that to happen. And then she'd watch her lovers playing together, bringing each other to a climax: and finally, she'd give her other lover something to really think about. Yes, she'd be wearing the strap-on dildo herself, penetrating her lover's quim while her lover's cock filled her forbidden passage ...

The thought was enough to make her come, and she bit her lip hard again, drawing blood. He licked away the tiny beads of red from her mouth, then knelt between her thighs, lifting her legs up and placing them over his shoulders. She supported herself on her elbows, and he slid his hands down her inner thighs, spreading her legs and letting his fingers glide across her moist channel.

She opened her mouth in a soundless moan of pleasure, and he fitted the tip of his cock to her quim, pushing deep inside. She closed her eyes as he began to move, tilting his hips and entering her even more deeply; she gritted her teeth as she felt his finger probing her anus, pushing rudely into her, stretching her and making her feel as though she were going to soil herself. And then the discomfort had gone, and she relaxed into it, gradually drawing her legs downwards so that her knees were pressed against her shoulders, and her lover was lying on top of her, thrusting deeply.

She jammed her mouth to his as she felt the beginning of her orgasm sweep through her; she kissed him fiercely, plunging her tongue into his mouth, and she felt his body stiffen for a moment, and then the warm wet gush of his seed inside her . . .

Rachel woke in Daniel's arms the next morning, and stretched luxuriously against him. Her body ached pleasantly, as though she'd spent the whole night making love, though she had no memory of it. All she could remember was curling into his arms and falling asleep. She stretched again, and cuddled back into Daniel, her hand flat against his midriff and her head on his chest.

He stirred, gave a small groan, and turned his head to kiss the tip of her nose. 'You're awake, then.'

'Mm,' she murmured lazily.

'What time is it?'

Rachel yawned, and looked over at the clock on her bedside table. 'Half past nine.'

'Mm. Half past nine on a Sunday morning.' He stretched, and yawned. 'I could do with some sleep.'

She chuckled. 'Oh, Daniel. You've been sleeping all night.'

'Hardly.'

She frowned. 'What's wrong? Did you wake up in the night? Was there a thunderstorm, or did you hear something outside?'

He grinned. 'Oh, come on, Rachel. Surely you haven't forgotten that quickly?'

She was completely lost. 'Forgotten what, Daniel?'

'You woke up in the night,' he said softly, 'and then you . . . I think the only phrase I can use is that you *ravished* me.'

'What?'

'Look.' He pointed at his shoulder. There was a line of small purple bruising on his skin.

Rachel frowned. 'I did that?'

'Don't you remember?'

'No. I'm sorry.'

'You don't remember a single thing about what happened?' He stroked her face. 'Rachel, do you—'

'No, just tell me what happened, please,' she interrupted.

He raised an eyebrow. 'Are you quite sure that you want to hear this?'

'Yes.' She bit her lip. 'I don't understand it. It's not as if we'd been drinking last night, so it's not because I was too drunk to remember what happened. All I can remember is falling asleep in your arms.'

'Hm, well. I was asleep, too, then suddenly I was aware that you were stroking my body – very gently, very softly.' He twined his fingers through hers. 'You were touching me all over, moving your fingertips on my skin in small circles. I loved it. It was a kind of soft massage – nothing deep, no pressure like Shiatsu massage – and I could feel myself getting turned on, particularly as your hands drifted lower. Then you discovered just how aroused I was, and you started stroking my cock.'

Rachel flushed. 'Um. I'm sorry, Daniel. I don't remember doing any of this.'

'Hey, no need to apologize. Like I said, I enjoyed it. Anyway, you pushed the duvet off the bed and opened the curtains.'

'I what?'

'You said that you wanted to see my body in the moonlight. It was nearly a full moon last night. Anyway, then you came back to bed. You were stroking me and caressing me, and you kissed your way down my body. It felt good, very good.' His fingers tightened momentarily round hers. 'In fact, it makes me hard even remembering.' He shifted slightly so that she could feel his erection pressing against her. 'Then you took my cock into your mouth. God, it felt so good. You started sucking me, and you licked my cock all over. You made your tongue into a hard point, probing me, then you started sucking me again. Licking and sucking, licking me until I was nearly coming. Then you twisted round, so that you were kneeling by my shoulders, your beautiful quim just inches from my mouth.'

Rachel's colour deepened. 'I, um . . .'

'Like I said, I enjoyed it.' Daniel's voice grew husky. 'You know I can't resist you. Having a treat like that next to my mouth . . . God, it was wonderful. Seashore and honey and vanilla. You were so turned on. I began to lick you, just like the way you were licking me. When you teased the head of my cock, I teased your clitoris. When you took me into your mouth, I put my tongue up you as deeply as I could. You were warm and wet, and it was like lapping honey. I think we came together, and you swallowed every last drop. Then you shifted round again and kissed me. You were straddling me, pinning me down to the bed. The next thing I knew, you were reaching over to your bedside cabinet, opening the top drawer, and taking out a silk scarf. You tied me to the bedstead.'

Rachel's eyes widened. 'Christ, why don't I remember any of this?'

'I don't know, but I swear to you it happened.' Daniel nuzzled her hair, breathing in her scent. 'And then, you kissed me again. You started biting my shoulder, licking my neck and nipping me gently. I couldn't do anything about it, because you had me tied: I was completely in your hands.'

'I'm sorry.'

'Stop apologizing. Like I said, I enjoyed it. You were rough with me, kissing and licking and biting. You used your mouth on my cock until I was hard again, and then you straddled me properly, slipping your hand between us and positioning my cock at your entrance. Then you sank down on me, and I could feel your lovely warm wetness pulsing round me. Then you rode me . . . like a Maenad. You kept to just the right side of the pain-pleasure barrier, but you kept going and going and going. You were rubbing your clitoris, and pulling at your nipples, and moving your body round mine, slamming down onto me and using your internal muscles as you lifted up again. I don't know what turned me on more – watching you, or feeling what you were doing to me.'

Rachel buried her face in his chest. 'I don't know what to say,' she mumbled.

He manoeuvred her so that she was lying on her back, then cupped her face in his hands so that she had to look at him. 'Rachel, it's all right.' He bent down to rub his nose against hers. 'Shock affects people in different ways. I just assumed that you went a little wild because of what happened to the flat. A release of tension, perhaps – after all, sex is good for headaches. It's probably good for other tensions, too.'

'Perhaps.'

He caught the look in her eyes. 'There's something you're not telling me, isn't there?'

She sighed. 'If you must know, the only thing that I remember last night was going to bed with you. I fell asleep almost straightaway; I felt warm and secure, lying in your arms. Then I was dreaming.'

'Don't tell me – the people in Egypt?'

She nodded. 'But I wasn't acting out the dream. There was no bondage. It was all fairly straight; except that I'd covered his body in oil and I'd mixed some spices with it – I don't know what spices, exactly, but they were aphrodisiac, designed to make us both even more turned on.'

'Right.'

She swallowed. 'Daniel, I don't know what's happening. My whole life seems to be teetering on the edge of a kind of abyss, and I don't understand why. If I'm doing things like this to you in the night, then what the hell do I do during the day if I have these bloody dreams then?'

'Hey, it's all right.' He stroked her face. 'Rachel, how long have you been having these visions?'

'The first one was when you caught me, in the British Museum.'

'So it all started just about the same time that you met me.'

She narrowed her eyes. 'What are you trying to say, Daniel?'

'I was just wondering if there was something between you and me that sparked this off. It could be related.' He paused. 'Is there anything else that's changed in your life?'

'Not really. Everything's been the same at work.' She thought hard. 'Nothing's changed at home; I suppose the only thing is the cat mummy-case.'

'Mummy-case?'

'The one on the mantelpiece. My friend Carrie brought it back for me from Lavenham – she found it in a little shop there. As you know, we see each other on Wednesdays; she just presented it to me, a couple of weeks ago. She saw it, thought that I'd like it, and bought it for me as a surprise.' She shrugged. 'It's just a replica, though. There's nothing spooky about it – nothing like the Curse of the Pharaohs.'

'Are you quite sure about that?'

'Well ...' She bit her lip. 'This is going to sound really silly.'

'Tell me anyway,' he invited.

'I didn't say anything before, because ...' She made a face. 'Well, I thought it was my imagination working overtime. Like I'd been watching too many sci-fi programmes on television, or something. But a few nights ago, I heard this cat miaouing at the window. It was going on and on and on; it wouldn't stop. I thought that it was the cat that I share with my next-door neighbour, and the last thing I wanted was a cold damp moggy warming himself up on me. So I put my pillow over my head and ignored it. The next morning, the cat mummy-case had moved on the mantel-piece. There was a trail in the dust behind it.' She wrinkled her nose. 'Though I'm being silly. I probably moved it the night before and forgot about it.'

'That's one explanation,' Daniel agreed, 'but supposing you didn't? Supposing that it's not a replica, Rachel?'

She shook her head. 'Original Egyptian artefacts don't just turn up in small rural antique shops.'

'But just supposing, somehow, this one slipped through,' Daniel said. 'There are all the Egyptian stories – the curse of Tutankhamun's tomb, and what have you. Maybe there's something attached to the cat.'

'I doubt it.' She rolled her eyes. 'The Curse of the Pharaohs is pure Hollywood invention.'

'Not necessarily,' Daniel persisted. 'I can remember reading a story about a hotel that was being renovated. The builders were knocking through to an old fireplace, and they found a mummified cat buried in the chimney-breast. They took it out.' He shrugged. 'The next day, there were all sorts of accidents and illnesses in the renovation team. It was only when the cat was brought back and replaced that everything was all right again.'

'That sounds like one of the modern urban myths,' Rachel said tartly. 'You know, like finding a tarantula among the bananas in the supermarket, or the one about the axe-murderer sitting in the back of the car and the woman thinking that someone was chasing her, but the driver of the other car had really seen the guy with the axe and was trying to warn her. No way, Daniel.'

'But what if? Isn't it worth getting it checked out?'

'Maybe. If you want.'

'I could talk to someone at the university. A specialist in Egyptology. Someone in the archaeology department could probably take a look at it,' Daniel said. 'Then, if there is anything, we'll know what it is.'

'I suppose you're right.'

'Anyway.' He dipped his head, kissing her lightly. 'How about I make us both some breakfast?'

'That'd be nice.' Rachel smiled at him as he stood up, pulled on his boxer shorts and padded out of the bedroom. She settled back against the pillows, and thought. Maybe Daniel had a point. Maybe there was something about the cat; if it really was an original artefact and not the replica she believed it to be ... then maybe it could be a curse.

But from what she knew of Egyptian magic, most of it worked on the same principle as voodoo or witch-doctors. It was suggestion in the minds of the people who'd been cursed or whatever. Even so, there were unexplained tales of accidents befalling the early archaeologists, mysterious illnesses and premature deaths, if they'd disturbed the wrong tomb.

She was still deep in thought when Daniel returned with two mugs of steaming coffee, a pile of buttered toast, and the cat mummy-case. He handed her a mug of coffee, then put the tray on the floor, removed his boxer shorts, and slid into bed beside her. He put the mummy-case between them, on the duvet. 'Have you ever noticed these inscriptions on the bottom of the case, Rachel?'

'No.' She put her coffee on the bedside cabinet and picked up the cat, examining it more closely. 'I can't read them, though. I can just about work out hieroglyphics, with the aid of a book, but I think that this is in heiratic. I can't read it.'

'Will you let me lend it to someone who could? A friend of a friend?'

Rachel sighed. 'If you really think it's that important – all right.'

'It could be that important,' Daniel said slowly.

Her lips twitched. 'Says the historian.'

'Exactly. This is more my field, Rachel – piecing information together and working out what really happened. This could be the clue we've been waiting for, Rachel: it could lead us to the answer.'

'And on the other hand, it could simply be a joke, someone writing "Made in Taiwan" in mock-heiratic.'

He chuckled. 'Cynic. So will you let me take it to work, and see if someone can help?'

'All right.'

'Good.' He ruffled her hair. 'And if that fails, we'll try something else. We'll find out what's happening.'

NINE

Daniel was on nodding acquaintance with several members of the archaeology department. When he flicked through the departmental directory, he was pleased to discover that the specialist in Egyptology, Kate Berry, was someone he'd met a couple of times at parties given by mutual friends. They'd been introduced, partly as a match-making idea by the said mutual friends, but although they'd liked each other on sight and spent the evening chatting, it had been a platonic relationship only. There hadn't been that spark of desire between them.

He knew that she was an archaeologist, but he'd forgotten that she specialized in Egyptology. He smiled to himself. At least it would be easier to explain some of what had been happening to someone he knew. He walked down the corridors to Kate's office, carrying a brown-paper-wrapped parcel under his arm, and rapped on the door.

'Come in,' a quiet and well-spoken voice answered.

He opened the door. 'Hello, Kate. Long time, no see.'

'Not since Denis and Michelle gave that party, last term.' She smiled at him. 'Well, Daniel, it's not often that we see an historian in these parts. What can I do for you?'

He smiled back. 'It's a professional thing – but nothing to do with Victorian excavations of Egyptian tombs, I promise!'

'Have a seat and tell me about it.' She gestured to one of

the grey plastic moulded chairs common to all the lecturers' offices. 'Would you like a coffee?'

Daniel wrinkled his nose. 'I'd love one, but I have a tutorial in about ten minutes, so I'd better not, thanks.' He cleared his throat. 'Actually, I wondered if I could ask you a bit of a favour.'

'Oh?' She tipped her head on one side, the gesture reminding Daniel of Rachel. Kate's hair was dark rather than fair, and her eyes were brown rather than blue, but the shape of her face was similar to Rachel's, and she had that same bright, interested air about her. That, and the posters and postcards which were blu-tacked to the shabby walls, British Museum prints of mummy cases; the carved black cats which sat on her bookshelves and the windowsill, the small facsimile of the Rosetta Stone. Kate Berry obviously loved Egypt as much as Rachel did.

'Well, a friend of mine was given a present by her best friend.'

'And this is the same present that's wrapped up on your lap?' Kate asked, seeing the package that Daniel had on his knee.

'The very same.' He smiled. 'I think that you and Rachel would like each other, because she's obsessed with Egypt. She's probably got more Egyptian things in her sitting room than you have in your office – and that's saying something! Anyway, this present was a replica of a cat mummy case, and Rachel wants to find out its history. I wondered if you could maybe point us in the right direction?'

'Well, sure. If I can.' Kate spread her hands. 'Would Rachel mind lending it to me, so I can have a proper look at it?'

Daniel nodded. 'We were hoping that you'd say that. I

brought it with me.' Rachel had lovingly wrapped the mummy case in bubble-wrap and brown paper. 'There's an inscription on the base. Rachel says she can work out rudimentary hieroglyphics, but she can't work this out. It's in some kind of script she doesn't know – heiratic, I think she said.'

'I'll have a look at it, then. I probably won't get a chance until the weekend,' Kate warned, 'but can I get back to you, next week?'

'Sure.' He felt slightly guilty; he'd only told Kate half the story. But if he told her about Rachel's weird experiences, he'd be pre-judging everything. He wanted to see if Kate could shed some light on what was going on. 'Thanks. I owe you dinner, for this.'

She grinned. 'You're on.'

'How about next Tuesday night, at my place? I'll invite Rachel, too; I'm sure she'd love to meet you.'

'Next Tuesday night it is,' Kate said warmly. 'I'll bring the cat back with me. What sort of time?'

'Half past seven?'

'Fine.'

Daniel took a pen from his pocket. 'If I can scrounge a bit of paper, I'll give you my address, and directions.' Kate handed him a pad; Daniel wrote his address and directions quickly and neatly. 'Tuesday evening,' he said. 'And I'd better go, or my students will be hanging around and muttering darkly.'

Kate chuckled. 'First years, are they?'

'Mm.' Daniel rolled his eyes. 'Most of them have settled down now, but I could still cheerfully strangle one or two of them.'

'Tell me about it,' Kate said feelingly. 'I have a couple who are exactly the same. Usually the ones who were top of the class at school, and they can't understand why I'm only giving them fifty-three per cent for an essay, when they're used to getting an A plus.'

'Give them a few more months, and they'll have grown up. I hope.' He smiled. 'Well, see you later.'

'OK.' As he left the room, Kate looked at the package. Half of her was tempted to open it there and then, but she knew that she could spend too much time on it, deciphering the strange inscription Daniel had told her about and then trying to date it. She looked at the pile of essays on her desk; after a brief struggle, duty won. With a sigh, she pulled the essays towards her, took a red pen, and began to read.

That evening, Daniel rang Rachel. 'Hi, Rachel.'

She smiled as she recognized his voice. 'How are you?'

'Fine. I just thought I'd ring you and let you know how I got on with Kate.'

'Kate?'

'The Egyptologist I was telling you about. I'd met her at mutual friends' parties, actually.' Daniel decided not to tell Rachel about the match-making. Rachel wasn't the jealous type, but it was irrelevant anyway. 'She's very nice.'

'Oh, yes.' Rachel waited expectantly.

'She's promised to have a look at it. I've invited her over to my place, next Tuesday, for dinner. She's going to give us the verdict, then.'

'Right. I'll look forward to that.'

'How are you feeling?' Daniel asked.

'All right. A bit tired, because it's been one of those days, but OK.'

'No more of those flashbacks?'

'No.' Daniel had stayed the previous night and she hadn't dreamed; but since he'd taken the cat, she'd been thinking about it. 'I can't help wondering, though, Daniel. Do you think that all this really is something to do with the inscription on the bottom of that cat?'

'We'll find out next Tuesday, with any luck.'

His voice seemed to have changed, grown slightly deeper. 'What are you thinking?' she asked softly.

'I was thinking,' he said, 'about you. And what I could imagine you doing.'

The husky note of desire in his voice thrilled her. 'Tell me more.'

He chuckled. 'It's just a fantasy. I won't bore you with it.'

'No, tell me.'

'All right, if you really want to know. But you might regret this,' he warned.

She laughed. 'I don't think I will, somehow. Tell me.'

'You're in this room, on a bed.'

'My bedroom, or yours?'

'Neither. It's a room in a hotel, or something like that. A posh hotel. The sheets are pure silk, soft against your skin.' His voice held the ghost of a smile. 'They ought to be navy, really, but they're white.'

Rachel, remembering her fantasy about Daniel on navy silk sheets, when she'd first met him, smiled. 'Mm.'

'The bed's big, probably a king size, with a black wrought-iron frame. You're sitting down and leaning back against a pile of thick feather pillows. You're wearing black silk hold-up stockings with lacy welts, and long black lacy gloves that come halfway between your elbow and your shoulder, and a black lace basque. The basque is underwired, pushing your breasts up and together, and it's beautifully cut, revealing and teasing at the same time. You're sitting there on the bed with your knees drawn up and your feet flat on the mattress. Your eyes are closed, and you're thinking of me and what we do together.

'You open your eyes and you see a mirror in the corner. It's a cheval mirror, framed in mahogany, and it's angled so that you can see yourself on the bed. You can't resist it: you part your legs, watching yourself. You can see your quim, beautiful pinks and vermilions and crimsons merging into each other. All glistening and shiny, because you're beginning to be aroused, just by remembering what we do together. And slowly, so very slowly, you slide one hand down your body, hearing the lace of your gloves hiss against the lace of your basque. You put the heel of your palm on your mound, and then you part your lips with your index and ring fingers, and let your middle finger glide down your slit.

'It feels good, the roughness of the lace against your skin, so you do it again, and again, and again. Suddenly, your sex is all slippery and gleaming, because you're aroused. You begin to rub yourself in earnest, working on your clitoris, but you want more. Your nipples are so hard that they hurt; they rub against the lace, but the friction isn't enough for you. You slip the fingers of your free hand inside one of the cups, and pull the lace down, exposing your breast. You're aroused, so your breast is swollen, and your nipple is dark and hard.

'You knead your breast, and then you start pulling at the nipple, rolling it between your forefinger and thumb. You do the same with your other breast, and you look so beautiful, masturbating in front of the mirror and watching yourself, the way your fingers dip into your beautiful cunt. You look incredibly lewd and wanton, and you're enjoying yourself. Your sex is all glistening and puffy, and you want more.

'There's a small bedside cabinet next to you. You know that it contains something that will make you feel better, so you reach over and open the top drawer. All there is inside the drawer is a thick, gold vibrator. It's big, and you know that it's just what you need, so you smile and take it. Again, you part your labia, and you watch yourself sliding the thick gold tube very gently into yourself. It's so big, stretching you as it goes in, and it feels good, so very good. You almost come, right then, but you hold yourself back. You're not ready, yet: you want to be nearer to the peak before you let yourself come. You begin to pump the vibrator in and out, very slowly, teasing yourself a little so you can draw the most pleasure from it. You withdraw it until it's almost out; then you push it back in again, hard.

'You're not sure what turns you on more, fucking yourself or watching yourself doing it. You keep going, and it's good, but you still want more. So you flick the switch on the end of the vibrator; with one hand, you pump it in and out, and with your other hand, you rub your clitoris. You're lying there, imagining that you have half a dozen men seeing to your every need – one with his cock inside you, one fingering your clitoris, two sucking your nipples, one kissing your mouth, and one sliding his finger into your pretty little arse. The fantasy excites you, and makes you use the vibrator harder and faster until, at last, you come. You open your eyes, and watch your reflection in the mirror: you can see the muscles of your cunt flexing round the vibrator, contracting hard.'

By the tone of his voice, Rachel knew that Daniel was masturbating, and the thought thrilled her. Daniel, thinking of her, was rubbing his cock. Suddenly, she wanted him to tell her. She wanted to know exactly what he was doing, and how it felt. 'What are you doing, right now?' she asked softly.

'Talking to you.' There was a hint of amusement in his voice, as if he knew that she knew what he was really doing, and he was teasing her.

'No, I mean, really, what are you doing?'

'I'm not sure if you'd like to know.'

'I would. Tell me,' she coaxed. 'I want to know everything.'

'All right. I'm lying on the sofa, talking to you. I'm stretched out; and when I was telling you about my fantasy ... well, what do you think?'

'I think,' she said slowly, 'that you're lying there, and while you were describing how I was using a vibrator, you were so turned on by the picture that your cock became hard. It was so hard that it almost hurt, and you had to do something about it. So you undid your zip and pushed down your jeans and your pants, all in one movement. Your cock was hard and hot; you curled your fingers round the shaft. It throbbed in your hand, and you started to rub it, thinking of what you wanted to watch me doing.'

'That's pretty accurate,' Daniel admitted. 'And I do it a lot, if I'm on my own and I end up thinking of you. I have to touch myself, and I imagine that it's your beautiful fingers wrapped round my cock, not mine; and that you're kneeling beside me, and you're just about to bend down and take me into your mouth. I've even had to bring myself off at work, and I'm sure that my students can smell sex in the air, sometimes.' His breathing grew faster, more ragged; Rachel knew that he was near the edge.

The thought thrilled her and, unable to help herself, she slid one hand under the waistband of her leggings, burrowing under the waistband of her knickers. She was already wet, and her finger slid easily into her; she leaned back, closing her eyes, and began to rotate her thumb over her clitoris. 'Then what happens?' she asked.

'And then . . . I imagine how it feels, your beautiful mouth working on me, sucking me. I can smell your perfume, and I can smell your arousal: it's honey and spice and musk. Having you touch me like that is wonderful, but I want more. I want to taste you as you're tasting me. So we change position slightly, so I can reach you; I stretch out my tongue, drawing it down your slit, and you taste so good. You shudder and wriggle slightly as I lick your clitoris; then you begin to work on me even harder. You wet your finger, and you start stroking the crease between my balls and my anus. I know what you're going to do, and the thought turns me on even more; I want to do the same to you, fill you and drive you wild with desire.

'You slide a finger deep into me; at the same time, I lift my head, replacing my mouth with my hand, and I begin to kiss your lovely soft buttocks. You wriggle again, shifting slightly because you know what I want, and then I can taste you, feel your flesh puckering beneath my tongue. I push into you as hard as I can, all the time working my fingers in your cunt, and you moan round my cock. Then I go back to sucking your clitoris, and push a finger into you, the same way that you're penetrating me. We work in synch, in and out, in and out.'

'Then what?' Rachel asked.

'Then . . . oh.' His 'oh' was long and drawn out; Rachel knew that her lover had just climaxed. 'And then,' he said, long moments later. 'Then, I come.' Almost at the same time, Rachel felt her own climax pour through her; she stilled her hand, letting her internal muscles flex round her fingers.

She sighed, and Daniel chuckled. 'I guess we're still in synch,' he said softly.

'Mm,' she agreed, feeling suddenly lazy and fulfilled.

'I'll see you tomorrow night,' he said softly. 'Sleep well.'

'You, too,' Rachel said, equally softly.

Two days later, Rachel met Carrie in the wine bar, as usual.

'Well, you seem in good spirits,' Carrie said, looking at her friend.

'Yes. I am.' Rachel smiled at her. She felt brighter than she had done for weeks: something like the high one of her friends had said she'd felt after the first three months of pregnancy, when the morning sickness had finally lifted.

'Any more of these awful blackouts?'

'Actually, yes, but there's something worse than that.' Rachel explained about the weekend, and how her flat had been smashed up.

'Bloody hell.' Carrie was shocked. 'Did the police find anything?'

'There was nothing missing. There was no entry or exit point, and they couldn't find any fingerprints. And the burglar alarm hadn't been tampered with; so God only knows how it happened.'

Carrie shivered. 'That's spooky. God, I don't know if I could live there, knowing that someone had been in the flat and poked around my things.'

'I don't think that anyone had actually been in the flat.'

'But the place was smashed up.'

'I know. There were deep gouges in the furniture, some of my Egyptian things were smashed, and pages were torn from my books.'

'So it had to be burglars.'

'Not necessarily.'

Carrie frowned. 'How do you mean?'

'You know that cat you found for me . . .'

'Yes?'

'Well, I'm beginning to think that it's all connected with that.'

Carrie frowned again. 'I'm being dense, Rach; because I don't follow you.'

'Well, I started having these visions or what have you on the weekend after you gave me the cat – the minute I stepped into the Egyptian section of the British Museum. There's an inscription on the base of the cat that I hadn't noticed before.' Rachel shrugged, and sipped her wine. 'Anyway, Daniel knows an Egyptologist at the university. She's agreed to have a look at it for us, and tell us what it says.'

'I'm surprised that you haven't been able to work it out yourself, Cleo.'

Rachel shook her head. 'No. I love Egyptian things, but I don't kid myself that I can translate ancient scripts.'

'You were good at languages. When we went to evening classes to learn Spanish, you picked it up quicker than me – quicker than anyone else in the class.'

'There's a big difference between modern and ancient languages. And yes, I know you bought me that book on hieroglyphs for my birthday one year, but this script is different – and anyway, there are thousands and thousands of different hieroglyphs. It'd take me forever to translate.' She smiled at her friend. 'Anyway, enough of all that. I don't have any proof for my theories, yet. So how are you? And how's the luscious Ralph, or shouldn't I ask?'

'He's fine.' Carrie's dark eyes crinkled at the corners. 'Actually, I've seen quite a lot of him, lately.'

Rachel was surprised and pleased. 'Don't tell me that you're finally getting serious with someone?'

Carrie shrugged. 'Well, it's about time I settled down, I suppose. And if I have to be with someone permanently—' she wrinkled her nose '—much as I hate the idea of being tied down, I'd rather it was with someone like Ralph.'

'What – tall, dark, handsome, incredibly rich, intellectual, and good in bed?' Rachel teased.

'Something like that. Though not necessarily in the same order,' Carrie agreed, laughing. 'Though any relationship I have won't affect my career. I still want my own agency by the time that I'm thirty-five.'

'And if anyone can do it, you can,' Rachel said, being honest as well as loyal to her friend. Carrie was ambitious, and bright with it; Rachel had always known that her friend was a true high-flyer.

'So, to change the subject onto something more interesting, when am I going to meet the famous Daniel?'

'Soon. Actually, you could make it Saturday night, if you like. Dinner at my place.'

Carrie shook her head regretfully. 'Sorry. I'd love to, but I'm already booked.'

'And for the next three months?' Rachel teased. Carrie's social diary was almost as full as her business diary. 'Let's synchronize diaries later.' She topped up their glasses. 'Anyway, here's to good friends.'

'To good friends,' Carrie echoed, lifting her glass in a toast. 'And new lovers.' She took a sip of wine. 'Dare I ask if you've had any more – well, experiences?'

'You mean, have I screwed any more of my clients?'

'Well.' Carrie spread her hands. 'Yes. Or suppliers.'

'No, I haven't.'

'But you said you'd still had some dreams?'

'With Daniel.' Rachel coughed. 'I – er – was rather rough with him the other night. I couldn't remember a thing about it: all I could remember was the dream I'd had, making love with the man in Egypt. But Daniel had a few marks on him – all caused by me. He told me the next morning that I'd ravished him.'

Carrie's eyes widened. 'So you're becoming a wild woman in your sleep, then?'

'Ha, ha.' Rachel pulled a face at her friend. 'And when am I going to meet Ralph?'

'Don't change the subject,' Carrie admonished, laughing. 'These dreams of yours—'

'Are just dreams,' Rachel said firmly. 'I'm not going through them in blow-by-blow detail.'

Carrie's lips twitched. 'Blow. Rather an appropriate choice of phrase, methinks.'

Rachel laughed back. 'Your imagination's a hell of a lot wilder than mine. You'd just find them tame. Anyway, I'm starving. Time for dinner.'

'All right, all right. We could try that new Mexican near my place, if you like,' Carrie suggested.

'Deal,' Rachel said with a smile. 'And no more talk about that cat, and the dreams.'

'Pity,' Carrie said. 'I was looking forward to hearing all about it . . .'

'Well, tough.' Rachel pulled a face at her, and finished her wine. 'The only thing on my agenda right now is food.'

'You're a hard woman,' Carrie teased, finishing her own wine. 'Food it is.'

The rest of the week was more normal than Rachel had experienced for a while. She was relieved to be rid of the dreams and the blackouts; and the fact that the cat was no longer in her flat made her even more convinced that whatever had been happening to her was something to do with the mummy-case. Maybe Daniel was right, she thought, and it was an original. Or maybe the inscription on the base was some kind of curse, and it had somehow transferred to the replica.

She tried to put it out of her mind until the following Tuesday, when she was to meet Kate. Kate was slightly late, and Rachel was curled up on Daniel's sofa, her legs tucked under her and a book in one hand, while Daniel – who had shooed her out of the kitchen, earlier – was busy putting the final touches to dinner.

When Kate arrived with the cat mummy-case, in a breathless flurry of apologies, Rachel warmed to her straight away. Within minutes, they were talking as if they'd known each other for years, their shared love of Egypt giving them an instant rapport. Daniel watched them both, smiling to himself. As he'd thought in Kate's office, there was something similar about them, though he still couldn't quite put his finger on it.

'So, about the cat—' Rachel began.

'No,' Daniel cut in. 'Dinner first. No Egyptian talk until after we've eaten.'

'OK, OK. If you insist.' Rachel spread her hands in submission, laughing.

Daniel had cooked wild mushrooms in cream and garlic, followed by salmon poached in white wine, with early summer vegetables. Both women were warmly appreciative.

'If this ever gets out at work,' Kate said, 'you'll have people begging you to ask them to dinner. Or to marry them, even – and I'm talking about the blokes as well as the women. You're the only man I know who can cook this well, particularly when it comes to lecturers.'

'Well, I like good food, so I learned to cook.' Daniel grinned. 'You think that I'd make a good housewife, then?'

'Mm. When you've had the day from hell, and you've a pile of essays to mark, the last thing that you want to do is faff around in the kitchen. To have a good meal like this waiting for you . . .' Kate gave a blissful smile. 'Well. I envy you, Rachel.'

'We don't live together,' Rachel hastened to explain. 'In fact, we haven't known each other that long.'

Kate looked at her. 'Well, you seem pretty settled together.'

'Mm. Apart from that bloody cat,' Daniel said.

Kate chuckled. 'And who was it who said that we weren't to talk about it until we'd finished dinner?'

'Yeah, I know.' Daniel went to fetch the *tarte aux framboises*, admitting that he'd cheated and bought it from the local deli.

'It's still excellent,' Rachel said.

'Hear, hear,' Kate agreed.

After coffee, Kate stretched. 'Mm, that was lovely, Daniel.'

'Pleasure.' He smiled back at her, and refilled her cup.

'So,' Rachel said, 'can we talk about the cat, now?'

Daniel rolled his eyes. 'All right, all right. If you must.'

They both turned expectantly to Kate.

'Well,' she said, 'I thought that it was a replica at first, but then I changed my mind. Somehow, you've managed to get hold of a genuine artefact.'

Rachel was shocked. 'You mean, it's original?'

'Yes. Where did you get it?'

'I didn't. A friend of mine – Carrie – bought it for me, as a present. She went to Suffolk for the weekend, and she found it in some curio shop. At least, I think that she said it was in Lavenham.' She frowned. 'But normally, dealers ... Well, surely they'd know if it was an original?'

'You were fooled as well, and from what Daniel tells me, your flat is filled with Egyptian stuff. You're less likely than the average person to be taken in.'

'I suppose so. But Carrie didn't buy it as an original, because this sort of stuff's priceless.' She paused. 'How old is it?'

'I'd say,' Kate said slowly, 'that it was probably Third Intermediate period, in the twenty-second dynasty.'

Daniel coughed. 'Can you translate that, for a non-Egyptophile?'

Kate grinned. 'Somewhere between 945 and 755 BC. Actually, there was a pharaoh around then called Pamiu.' Her eyes sparkled mischievously. 'Pamiu means "tom-cat"; apparently he was called after the similarities between him and a tom-cat. Quite what that says about him, I'm not sure!'

Rachel chuckled. 'I think that we can guess.'

'Anyway, around that period, Bast – she's the goddess with the head of a cat – was very popular. I think the cat's from around that era. And as you guessed, Rachel, the inscription on the bottom is in heiratic. It's a pretty standard curse, against anyone who harms the goddess or the family she's protecting.' She tipped her head on one side. 'So are you two going to tell me the real story about why you asked me to look at this?'

Rachel winced. 'This is going to sound completely crazy.'

184

'Tell me anyway,' Kate invited.

'Well, before Carrie gave the cat to me, everything was fine. I have this bad habit of spending my spare Sunday afternoons in the Egyptian section of the British Museum. Anyway, a few weeks ago, I went there, and I seemed to black out. I thought maybe it was because it was so hot and stuffy out there – it was a really airless day – and Daniel caught me. Which is how I got to know Daniel.' She bit her lip. 'The thing is, when I blacked out, I was me and yet not me. It was like I was some kind of Egyptian princess, and the man I was with . . . he had eyes exactly like Daniel's. But I hadn't met Daniel, at that point.'

'I see,' Kate said slowly. 'There's more to it than that, isn't there?'

Rachel nodded. 'I've been having a lot of dreams. Even during the day, I keep blacking out and seeing these people together. There's a woman who's me and yet not me, and a man who's Daniel and yet not Daniel.' She decided not to mention the fact that Hazel had tried to regress her. She also decided that it wasn't worth mentioning what had happened in her flat; that would only muddy the waters. 'Anyway, I just wondered if that cat was something to do with what I kept seeing.'

'Could be,' Kate said thoughtfully. 'Have you had any of these dreams since Daniel gave the cat to me?'

Rachel shook her head. 'Why do you ask?'

'Well.' Kate frowned. 'Ever since Daniel brought it to my office, I've been having weird dreams. I haven't been blacking out during the day, or anything like that; it only happens at night. The people you saw – would I be right in saying that he was like Daniel, facially quite similar, with the same eyes, and you had the impression that he wasn't Egyptian? Whereas the woman – she was about your build and your height, facially almost identical to you, but with dark hair and dark eyes?'

Rachel's face whitened. 'You mean, you've seen them, too? And felt what happened?'

'I've only seen things, not felt them,' Kate said. 'I've been an onlooker. Why? Isn't that the same as you had?'

'No.' Rachel shook her head. 'I could feel everything that was going on, as well. It's like it was happening to me: and yet, at the same time, I was somehow watching what was going on.'

Kate's lips twitched. 'They must have been some dreams you've been having, Rachel, because mine were pretty raunchy. The guy has a very inventive imagination.'

Daniel flushed as he realized that both women were looking speculatively at him. 'Leave me out of this, you two,' he said.

'Even so, it's pretty odd. I didn't experience anything like this until I met you,' Rachel said. 'It seems that it's the combination of you and the cat.'

'But if it's a bog standard curse,' Daniel said, 'then I don't understand why Rachel is being affected by it in this way. Or you, Kate, for that matter.'

'I don't know.' Kate was thoughtful. 'There are a lot of tales, Daniel, about Egyptologists who've had strange things happen to them – strange illnesses, strange deaths, strange visions. Maybe it's something to do with that. Like I said, this is an original, not a replica.'

'As it's an original,' Rachel said, 'I shouldn't even have the thing. It should be where everyone can see it, in the British Museum.' She frowned. 'But the question is, the place where Carrie bought it – where did *they* get it from?'

'There's only one way to find out,' Daniel said. 'Ring her up, ask her exactly where she bought it, and we'll go there this weekend and see what we can find out.'

'What, now?'

Daniel nodded. 'We have to know.'

While Rachel was out of the room, he looked at Kate. 'These dreams you had – they were erotic, as well?'

Kate nodded. 'Very. In fact, I almost envy Rachel.'

Daniel's eyes widened. The spark of desire that hadn't been between them at the party ... it was definitely there, now. 'Kate, I—'

'Hey, I'm not about to muscle in,' she said softly.

Daniel nodded. 'Back to safe topics, I think. This goddess, Bast ... How's she involved?'

'Bast was the goddess of fertility. Rachel could probably tell you all this, but in about 400 BC, the time of the early Ptolemies, the festival of the goddess Bast was one of the biggest and most popular in the country. Somewhere in the fifth century, Herodotus described seven hundred thousand people attending the festival. There were lots of river boats on the way to the city, full of men and women singing and clapping their hands and making music. He mentioned that a lot of the women pilgrims made inviting erotic gestures to the people on the riverbanks.' She grinned. 'They drank an awful lot of wine during the festival, I can tell you that much – so whether the gestures were because Bast was goddess of the erotic, or whether it was because they were all drunk, I don't know.'

Rachel came back into the room as they were talking, caught the references, and grinned. 'Like Chaucer making his pilgrims bawdy, I'd say.'

Daniel looked at her. 'So, what did Carrie have to tell you?'

'She found it in a place called Serendipity, in Lavenham. She's given me the name of the owner, and the phone number, so maybe we could ring.'

Daniel shook his head. 'It'd give him a chance to weasel out of it. No, I think that we should go down there, take the cat with us, and see what the guy has to say for himself.'

'And,' Kate said, 'I think that I'd be as interested as you two are in finding out the truth.'

'Why don't you come with us?' Rachel offered.

Kate shook her head. 'Thanks for asking, but I can't make this weekend.' She smiled at them. 'Come to dinner at my place on the Monday, though. You can tell me everything, then.'

'Deal,' Rachel agreed.

TEN

'Hello, Rachel.' Kim Price, David Foster's secretary, smiled at Rachel as she walked into the office. 'David's expecting you. He's free, now.'

'Thanks, Kim.' Rachel felt slightly nervous. Just what did David Foster want to see her about? Usually, the head of their agency was happy to let his staff get on with the job; they saw him for regular appraisals, but impromptu meetings like this were very rare. If David wanted to see you, it meant either that you were just about to be promoted, or that he was going to ask you, very nicely, to leave the agency.

Rachel didn't think that a promotion was likely; at the same time, she knew that she had done nothing wrong. She hadn't had a row with clients, or with any of the account handlers. There was no reason for David to carpet her, or to suggest that she should leave her job. So what the hell was going on? She steeled herself, and opened his office door.

David looked up from his desk. He was a handsome man in his mid-forties, although he looked younger. Any grey hairs were lost in his mop of curly blond hair, and his face was remarkably unlined. One or two people joked that David had a picture of a mean-tempered, ageing roué in his attic; the only signs that David had worked and played hard were the faint shadows beneath his bright blue eyes. Plus the fact that he'd started his own agency at the age of thirty: only the very best could afford to do that sort of thing. And his gamble had paid off handsomely. DFA was one of the best agencies in London.

'Hello, Rachel. Sit down,' he said, nodding to the chair opposite his desk.

She did so in silence, folding her hands in her lap and waiting with a mounting feeling of dread.

'I imagine you already know why I wanted to see you.'

Rachel swallowed. Actually, she had no idea. 'I'm sorry, David, I'm afraid that I don't.'

He looked faintly disappointed. 'Oh. Well, Rachel, you've been with us for nearly eight years. You've done a lot of good work for us, in that time.'

Rachel stared at the floor. It was obvious what was coming next: one hell of a 'but'.

'But I'm sorry to say that things have changed over the last few weeks.' He looked at her, his eyes filled with concern. 'Rachel, to be honest, I'm worried about you.'

'Why?'

'Some of the clients have said that you've been dreamy in meetings, not paying attention: it's just not like you. You're normally on the ball. I wondered if there was something wrong, or if there's anything that I can do to help. Do you want to talk about whatever it is that's bothering you?'

Rachel couldn't look at him. How could she possibly tell him what was wrong? He'd think her insane if she said that she thought she was being haunted, and it was all to do with a cat mummy case that was nearly three thousand years old. She sighed. 'I'm sorry, David. I've been in another world, lately. I'll pull myself together.'

'But it's not like you, Rachel,' he persisted. 'Look, would you like a coffee?'

She shook her head. If he shouted at her, it would be easier; this niceness – particularly as it was genuine – made her want to cry. 'No, thanks. I'm trying to give the stuff up.'

'Rachel, I wish that you'd talk to me. I don't want to let you go. I like the work that you've done for me in the past.'

Rachel lifted her chin. 'But if I don't buck my ideas up, I'll have to go?'

David sighed. 'Look, ten years ago, advertising was a perfect career if you liked having three-hour lunches, spending most of your time in wine bars, and spending huge sums of money. Nowadays, for most of us, a lunch-break means a sandwich grabbed at your desk, and lunching a client means having a meeting in our board room, with a buffet and a long list of action points. We're fighting harder battles, pitching for work which used to be ours without comment, and we're having to keep costs as low as we can, just to survive. I can't afford to keep on someone who doesn't pull their weight – even someone as good as you, Rachel.'

She lifted her chin. 'So do you want me to leave?'

'I've already told you, no.'

'Then what do you want, David?'

He sighed. 'What I'm saying, Rachel, is that maybe you've been working too hard, and a holiday will do you good. Take a week off, and use it to sort out whatever the problem is. If there's anything I can do to help, just tell me; then come back to work as the Rachel Meaden we all know and love.'

'All right, David. I'll work until the end of today, then take a week off.'

'Good. Because I don't want to lose you, Rachel. I want to make that clear, right now.'

To Rachel's horror, at that precise moment, she felt the familiar sweeping dizziness. Everything went black, and she was back in Egypt. Her lover was there with her, dressed in pure white linen. He was sitting down, looking into the distance, deep in thought. She smiled, and walked over to him, cupping his face in her hands. When he looked up at her, his face brightening as he realized who had interrupted his reverie, she lowered her face to his.

His lips were warm and gentle against hers; his mouth opened as she slid her hands round the nape of his neck and pressed against him. She slid her tongue into his mouth, exploring him, deepening the kiss. Her nipples began to grow hard; she knew that he could feel them through the thin cloth of her dress, and that he was just as aroused as she was.

She broke the kiss, looking at him; his eyes were filled with a deep sadness, something that she didn't understand. There was one way, she knew, that she could bring a smile to his face. She shook her sistrum at him, the ceremonial rattle making a shimmering sound in the air, and grinned. 'You said that Isis was always on the side of lovers. Bast, too.'

He sighed. 'Yes, but—'

'But nothing.' She began to dance before him, a ceremony she'd performed so many times before. But this time, she infused her movements with eroticism, the sway of her hips designed to draw attention to what was covered by the long skirt of her dress, the moist delta that he'd touched and kissed and penetrated so many times with his fingers and his cock, until both of them were shaking with pleasure. She continued dancing to the music in her head, shaking the sistrum, the rattle keeping beat with her steps. And then slowly, slowly, she loosened the top of her dress, letting it fall to reveal the generous swell of her breasts, her hard dusky nipples.

With one hand, she began to massage her breasts, squeezing and kneading the soft flesh. Her nipples grew harder as she continued to pleasure herself; she pretended not to watch him but, all the time, her gaze was trained on his face. She needed to know if the way that she pleasured herself pleasured him, too, and took the sadness from his eyes.

It seemed to be working; she smiled to herself and continued to dance with abandon, letting her dress fall further and further downwards until she was able to kick it away and dance before him, completely naked. She continued to move sinuously, weaving her hips and rattling her sistrum. A lewd thought popped into her head, and she couldn't resist it. She knew that what she was going to do could cause real problems for both of them if they were caught, but she didn't care. The sacrilege of what she was about to do was beyond punishment.

She slid one hand between her legs, seeking and finding her clitoris. She began to rub the little button of flesh, kneading her mons veneris at the same time. Her flesh grew slippery and liquid beneath her fingers; then, when she was sure that she was ready, she drew the sistrum between her legs. Like most ceremonial rattles, it was shaped like an ankh, the handle smooth and rounded at the tip; it was warm from where she'd been playing it. Slowly, she put the tip of the handle to the entrance of her sex, and slowly slid the sistrum deep inside her.

She stood before him, the sistrum buried in her quim to the hilt; as she moved her hips very slowly, flexing her internal muscles round the smooth golden handle, it made the rattle play. She lifted her hands to the nape of her neck, exaggerating the movements, making the rattle louder and faster; then, suddenly, she was coming, her internal muscles flexing sharply round the rattle's handle. She tipped her head back, biting her lip to stifle her cry of pleasure; and then he was there before her on his knees, removing the sistrum so very gently, and jamming his face into her crotch, lapping and lapping the scented nectar from her quim.

The movements of his tongue lengthened her orgasm, pulling her to another plateau. She gasped as he pulled her down on top of him. He was still kneeling, and she was kneeling astride him, his cock pressing hot and hard against her pubis. Swiftly, she uncovered his cock, curling her fingers round the shaft. He nodded, and she lifted herself slightly, fitting his cock to the entrance of her sex and then sliding down onto him. It felt so good, so good. She leaned back experimentally, loving the way the angle of his penetration changed and deepened her pleasure.

He eased one hand between their bodies, stroking her belly, pushing one finger between her labia and teasing her clitoris from its hood. 'Ah yes,' she moaned as he began to rub her, instinctively finding the pattern she liked. She began to ride him then, hard, pulling up and slamming down onto him again, grinding her pubis against his. All the time, he kept up the relentless pressure on her clitoris, rubbing her and rubbing her.

Sensing that she was about to cry out, he jammed his mouth over hers; she could taste herself on him from where he'd licked her, seashore and honey and nectar, and it turned her on even more. Her body seemed to splinter and then she was climaxing, her body shaking and quivering. At the same time, she felt his body tense, felt the hot gush of his seed inside her . . .

Rachel opened her eyes to find herself looking straight into David's flushed face. And, worse, she was sitting astride him. His cock was still twitching deep inside her. She realized with horror that she'd more or less acted out the scenario she'd just seen, though without sliding anything into her body while she danced for him.

'Oh, Christ,' she said. 'What have I done?'

David stroked her face. 'Rachel, I think that you have a little explaining to do.'

She sighed. 'David, I'm so sorry. I just don't know where to start.'

'Try the beginning,' he suggested gently. 'That normally helps.'

She was about to pull herself from him, but he shook his head, wrapping his arms round her and tightening his hold so that she couldn't move. 'Rachel, this has never happened before. As far as I was concerned, you never thought of me in a sexual sense.'

'Of course not. You're my boss.' Rachel bit her lip. 'And now . . .'

He rubbed his face affectionately against hers. 'Rachel, you don't have to worry. I know that this is a one off. You don't usually behave like this.' He grinned. 'In fact, some of the clients have complained to me about you, saying that you're almost like an ice-maiden. Friendly and animated when talking about work, happy to keep things on a platonic level – but the moment that one of them asks you out, there's a flat refusal and you're a little formal with them from then on.'

'You know the rules,' she said. 'If you want to get on by merit, you don't sleep with clients – and you don't sleep with colleagues, particularly ones senior to you.'

'So what's caused this sudden change? Why did you – well, how come we've just made love, if you feel that strongly about it?'

Her eyes met his. 'David, I'm not going mad.'

'I didn't say that you were.'

'No, but if I tell you what's been happening . . .' Her words tailed off, and she looked away.

He cupped her face in his hands, turning her so that she was forced to meet his eyes. 'Tell me what?' he asked gently. 'Talk to me, Rachel. I promise you that I won't laugh at you, and I won't make judgements. Just tell me.'

She sighed. 'Well, I warn you, this is going to sound completely crazy.'

'Tell me anyway.'

'Well, a couple of weeks ago, Carrie bought me a present.'

'Carrie? Carrie Taylor?'

Rachel nodded. 'She's my best friend.'

'And one hell of a woman.' The words were out before he could stop them; Rachel's eyes widened in surprise. She hadn't realized that Carrie and David had had a fling. Though it would have been after Carrie had left DFA: Carrie was inflexible in her rule. The same rule that Rachel herself had just broken.

Rachel decided not to push the subject. 'Well, she'd been away for the weekend. She found this mummy case of a cat, and she thought that, knowing my tastes, I'd like it.'

'Yes.' David smiled at her. 'Cleopatra's cat.'

'Since then, I've been having disturbing dreams – at least, I thought that they were dreams. I keep blacking out, and seeing these people. They're in Egypt. And then, the next thing I know, I'm acting out what I've just seen. Like what happened between us, just now.'

'Have you talked to anyone professional about this?'

She nodded. 'A friend of Daniel's. She works in psychology. Anyway, she couldn't help. We're no nearer finding out what's going on.'

'Daniel being your boyfriend?' David questioned.

'Yes. I met him in the British Museum – which is where it all started. I blacked out; when I opened my eyes, he'd caught me, and . . .'

'And what?' David persisted.

'His eyes were the same as the man's I'd seen in this vision, or dream, whatever you want to call it. It was uncanny. I was a bit scared; I just don't know what's going on, David. It's been getting worse.'

'Have you been to see a doctor?'

She nodded. 'In the early days, I thought that maybe I was anaemic, or something like that. I fainted in the office, and Charlie threatened to set Sara on me if I didn't go to see a doctor.'

'And?'

'I had some blood tests; there was nothing wrong. I'm perfectly healthy.'

'But I bet that you didn't tell the doctor about these visions, did you?'

Rachel shook her head. 'I couldn't. I feel like I'm going crazy, David, but I know I'm not. Because if I was crazy, I wouldn't even consider the thought that I might have a problem – I'd think that it was everyone else who was crazy, not me.'

'Yes.' His eyes narrowed. 'So is this why some of the clients have said that you're being dreamy?'

'Probably. But I do have another lead.'

'Which is?'

'I know that the cat came from Lavenham. There was an inscription on the base of the cat; Daniel knows someone in the archaeology department who could translate it.'

David looked puzzled. 'Archaeology department?'

She nodded. 'Daniel's a lecturer in history at the University of London. Anyway, one of the archaeologists is a specialist in Egyptology. She looked at the cat for us, and the inscription turned out to be a bog standard curse. So we thought that the next thing to do was to trace the history of the cat – go back to where Carrie bought it, find out where the dealer bought it, and trace it back from there until we can get some answers. We're planning to go there this weekend.'

David nodded. 'Well, why don't you take some time off, now? Take as long as you need, and don't worry about using holiday, or anything like that.'

Rachel remembered what he'd said about keeping costs low. 'Are you sure?'

He nodded. 'I don't particularly want to lose my best copywriter; and I'd rather like to have you back to normal.' He licked his lower lip. 'Even though this little interlude's been extremely pleasant, I know that it's not the way you normally work, Rachel. I won't refer to it again.' He leaned forward to kiss her very lightly on the lips. 'Go and tidy yourself up, then go home. Try and find out what you can about this damned cat, and come back to us when you've sorted it all out.'

'Thank you, David. I do appreciate this.'

'I know, Rachel.'

She paused. She knew that asking was dangerous – it could open up all sorts of things that were best kept closed – but she had to know. 'David ... What exactly did happen, when I blacked out?'

'Well.' His blue eyes filled with concern. 'One minute you were talking to me; the next, your eyes glazed over and you stood up, almost as if you were sleep-walking. You came round to my side of the desk, cupped my face in your hands, and kissed me.' His mouth twitched. 'I don't kid myself that I'm irresistible. Something was obviously going on. I didn't think that it was drugs, because you're not the type – yes, I've seen you a bit merry at the odd Christmas party, but you've never been one to overdo it. So I waited to see what was going to happen next. I tried saying your name, but you ignored me. Then you undid my trousers, pushing my pants down as well.' He raised an eyebrow. 'Are you quite sure that you want to hear the rest of this, Rachel?'

'Yes. I have to know what happened, David.'

'Well, you curled your fingers round my cock, and started rubbing me. When I was hard, you hoisted up your skirt, pulled the gusset of your knickers aside, and just sank down onto me. You were already wet, so I slid into you very easily. Again, I tried saying your name – I even tried shaking you – but you didn't hear me, didn't react. It was almost as though you were in another world.'

'Oh God.' Rachel flushed with shame, closing her eyes and tipping her head forward to rest against his shoulder. To her surprise, she felt David kiss the curve of her neck.

'Hey, it's all right, Rachel. Though I have to admit, I did feel a bit used. It was obvious that you didn't know that you were making love with me.'

She kept her head buried in his shoulder, unable to look at him. 'I'm so sorry.'

'Like I said, it's OK.' He regarded her speculatively. 'Just out of interest – have you done anything like this with a client, or a supplier?'

Her flush deepened. 'I don't want to talk about it. Like I said, the number one rule is that you don't sleep with a client, or anyone in the business.'

'I know.' He smiled wryly. 'I think that you'd better sort this out before you break all your rules. But, first . . .'

Rachel lifted her head again and opened her eyes, looking David full in the face. 'What?'

'First, I think that we should take the taste of this dream, or whatever it was, from both our mouths.'

Rachel didn't quite follow, until he smiled at her – a slow, gentle smile that lit up his whole face. She suddenly realized how very attractive David Foster really was: like a young Robert Plant, with that same sweet and sensual curve to his lips, those same bright eyes. At the same time, she realized that his cock was hardening inside her again.

'Rachel,' he said softly; then he kissed her, very gently, his lips exerting only a slight pressure on hers. It was a coaxing kiss rather than a demanding one, and Rachel found herself responding, opening her mouth to give him the access he wanted. By the time that he broke the kiss, she was shaking. When she opened her eyes, she realized that his had been open all along – a hot, intense blue of desire.

Gently, he lifted her from him, and pushed his chair back, standing up. At a little over six foot, he was considerably taller than Rachel; but she didn't feel intimidated by him. His fingers were very gentle as they finished undoing her shirt; he took it from her, hanging it over the back of his chair. Her skirt followed; he stroked the soft flesh of her inner thighs, just above the welts of her stockings. 'I think we'll leave these on,' he said softly, the tip of his finger tracing the tops of her stockings. 'I never realized how good your legs were, Rachel. Beautiful.'

Then he shed his clothes, his movements swift and sure. Rachel couldn't take her eyes off him. She'd never considered David in a sexual way before, but she could see now that he had a good body. He was single, having dedicated himself to his career, and when he wasn't working on his business, he obviously worked out at a gym. Maybe even Vivace, she thought. She could imagine him working out with Ellis.

His body was beautifully sculpted, and would have graced a man twenty years his junior; and his cock was impressively large and thick. If he saw her staring greedily at him, he made no comment; he merely stooped slightly to kiss the tip of her nose.

She shivered again as he unclasped her bra, dropping it to the floor, then cupped her breasts, pushing them up and together slightly, squeezing them. Her nipples hardened, and he laughed, dipping his head to take one rosy peak of flesh into his mouth and sucking gently. Meanwhile, his hands stroked down her sides, moulding her hips; his fingers hooked into the sides of her knickers, and he began to peel them downwards.

Christ, Rachel thought. David might not be in a relationship – that she knew of, anyway – but he certainly knew how to make love. He had the sort of skill that came with a great deal of practise. She closed her eyes, tipping her head back, and his mouth drifted upwards, kissing the curve of her throat, making her arch against him.

Then he lifted her slightly, placing her on the edge of his desk, and gently urged her backwards, finally removing her knickers. He traced each areola with the tip of his tongue, then blew gently onto them, so that her nipples became even harder – so hard that they almost hurt. Rachel willed him to suck her nipples to ease the ache, but he didn't: he moved lower, tracing a path over her abdomen with the tip of his nose.

She felt a pulse beat hard between her legs. Was he going to do what she thought he was going to do? Her excitement grew as she realized that yes, he was; she widened the gap between her thighs, bending her knees to give him easier access. He rubbed his face on her inner thighs; he'd shaved that morning, but there was a faint trace of new stubble on his face, and the slight roughness thrilled her. He breathed against her quim, teasing her; then, at long, long, last, he stretched out his tongue and drew it the full length of her musky slit.

Rachel almost cried out, it felt so good; he explored her thoroughly, tracing every fold and crevice with his tongue in a way that made her blood beat faster. She was shaking by the time that he began to tease her clitoris from its hood, catching it between his lips and sucking on it, then lapping at her again.

Her climax took her by surprise, splintering through her; he kissed her nether lips gently, then tracked up her body again. She could feel the hardness of his cock rubbing against her pubic bone, but he made no attempt to penetrate her. He simply continued kissing her and stroking her, arousing her until she felt her quim grow puffy, ready to receive him. Then he lifted one of her legs, stroking it and manoeuvring her so that her ankle was resting on his shoulder. He repeated the action with her other leg; then she felt him fit the tip of his cock to the entrance of her sex.

Rachel was already wet, so he slid easily into her; then he began to move, very slowly, with long and deep measured thrusts. Rachel couldn't help opening her mouth in a long drawn-out "oh" of pleasure; David began to move his hips in small circles, changing the angle of his penetration. She felt the familiar shimmering of her orgasm slide through her body again, but David didn't stop: he kept going, bringing her up to a higher peak. She climaxed again, so sharply that it almost hurt; at the same time, she heard him give a small moan of pleasure, and she felt his cock throb deep inside her.

Gently, he slid one leg from his shoulder, then the other, and pulled her to him; he was still inside her. He stroked her hair, holding her close, burying his face in her shoulder. The gesture was so cherishing that Rachel felt unexpected tears prick her eyelids.

When he could feel that the aftershocks of her orgasm had died away, he rubbed his cheek against hers and pulled back slightly, so that he could look her in the eyes. 'OK?' he asked quietly, his voice slightly unsteady.

'Yes.' Rachel's voice was equally shaky.

He smiled at her. 'Well, I think that that made it feel better, for both of us.'

'Mm.'

He stroked her face, gently withdrawing from her. 'Go home now, Rachel. Take some time off, and sort out whatever it is that's haunting you.' At her widened eyes, he smiled. 'And before you start worrying, no, I'm not expecting a repetition of this. Though I'd very much like to repeat it—' his voice grew husky '—and though I'd like to taste your body all over, touch you and taste you until you were almost delirious, I don't think it'd be fair to either of us. We have a good working relationship, and I don't want that spoiled just for the sake of a few moments of pleasure.'

'No.'

They both dressed swiftly. Rachel's skirt was still crumpled from where she'd hoisted it up around her waist earlier to ride David, but she smoothed herself down as best as she could.

'Off you go, Cleo,' he said softly. 'And call me if you need anything.'

'Thanks.' Rachel avoided Kim's speculative look as she left the office, and went to the ladies', cleaning herself up properly; then she returned to her desk.

Charlie and Sara both stopped what they were doing the moment they saw her, and came over. 'Are you all right, Cleo?' Charlie asked.

'Yeah, I'm fine.' She smiled at him.

'So, what did David want?' Sara asked excitedly. 'Did he give you a promotion?'

She shook her head. 'No. He says that I've been a bit dreamy recently.'

'You have.' Charlie looked at her. 'But you haven't been having any more of those blackouts, have you?'

'No,' Rachel lied.

'That's the important thing. Did you tell him about that?'

Rachel nodded. 'He told me to take a week or two off.'

'Well, we've already worked out most of the stuff we're going to do between us for the next couple of weeks.' He wrinkled his nose. 'I can't think of any copywriter I'd rather work with, but I'll muck in with the others until you're back.'

'Thanks, Charlie.'

'So when are you going? Now?'

'I was going to work until the end of the day, but David told me to go now.'

Charlie glanced at his watch. 'It's more or less lunchtime. And considering that neither of us has had a proper lunchbreak for the past three weeks, I vote we go to the wine bar.'

Rachel chuckled. 'Trust you to think of that! Seriously, Charlie, I think I'd rather just go home.'

'You're not feeling well again, are you?' Charlie accused.

'I'm OK,' she said.

'Well, you're taking a taxi home, not the tube, and that's an order,' Sara chipped in. 'And before you argue, I'm going to book one now.'

'And I'll pay for it,' Charlie added. 'Then you can take me out to lunch, Sara, seeing as Cleo stood me up.' He ruffled Rachel's hair. 'Take care of yourself. If you need anything, you know where we are.'

'Yes. Thanks.'

Within five minutes, the taxi arrived; Sara and Charlie bundled her into the taxi and paid the driver. Rachel knew better than to argue with them, making a mental note to treat them both to lunch when she was back at work. She let the taxi driver take her back to Islington.

ELEVEN

When Rachel told Daniel what had happened at work that day – leaving out the erotic interlude with David – he was immediately sympathetic. 'The guy's got a point. He wants whatever it is that's affecting you to be sorted out; so do I, and so do all your friends.'

She wrinkled her nose. 'Yes, but I still feel almost as if I've been sacked.'

'Of course you haven't. If anything, it proves how much they value you at DFA – otherwise your boss wouldn't have given you the time off to sort things out.' He smiled at her. 'And because you're free tomorrow, it means that we don't have to wait until Saturday before going to Lavenham.'

Rachel didn't follow him. 'How come?'

'Because I can call in a couple of favours and get someone else to cover my tutorials tomorrow. I don't have any lectures, and the one session that I had booked with my MA student can easily be re-arranged.'

She bit her lip. 'Daniel, I can't ask you to skip work for me.'

'You're not asking. I'm offering.' He stroked her face. 'Next week, all this will seem like a bad dream.'

'I hope so.'

So do I, Daniel thought, but he kept his doubts to himself,

knowing that Rachel needed all the support that she could get. 'Look, why don't you make us both a coffee while I make a couple of phone calls?'

'OK.'

When she returned, bearing two large mugs of steaming coffee, Daniel had just put an old favourite on the stereo and was curled up on the sofa. Rachel's lips twitched. 'A couple of phone calls, you said. I thought that you'd still be talking.'

'Men don't spend anywhere near as long as women do on the phone,' he teased.

She didn't rise to the bait, but handed him the coffee. 'And this song isn't very tactful, in the circumstances.'

Daniel grinned. 'Who was it who said that she didn't believe in reincarnation?'

'Hm. Well, I like the Alan Parsons Project, anyway.' She curled up beside him, listening to Colin Blunstone's soulful voice. *Old and Wise* was one of her favourite tracks, too; she found herself relaxing into the mellow mood of the album. Daniel didn't start a conversation, sensing that she wanted to be quiet; he merely slid his arm round her and sipped his coffee. Once they'd gone to Lavenham and found out the history of the cat, everything would be fine . . .

The next day saw them driving down the A12 to Suffolk in Daniel's Golf.

'I still think that you ought to drive a Morris Minor,' Rachel said with a grin. 'Or a battered Renault 5.'

Daniel chuckled. 'I'd need to wear brown corduroys, a Fair Isle sweater and a battered tweed coat with leather patches on the elbows, too. Anyway, that's more a geography lecturer's outfit than a history lecturer's.' His lips twitched. 'And if we're talking stereotypes, how come you don't drive a little red Porsche or a shiny BMW?'

'Because I'm a copywriter, not an estate agent,' was the immediate retort.

Daniel smiled. The more time he spent with Rachel, the more attractive he found her. Without the cat, things would be even better. 'Well, then.' He switched on the stereo.

Rachel tipped her head on one side, trying to place the music; eventually, she gave up. 'Tell me,' she said, 'what's this?'

'Fleetwood Mac.'

'Never.'

He chuckled. 'Everyone always thinks of *Rumours*, or *Man of the World*. This is in between – just after Peter Green left the band.'

'I like it,' Rachel said.

'It's one of my favourites. If I could play the guitar, I think this would be the first one I'd learn. *Sands of Time*.'

'You're going to make me into a blues lover if it kills you, aren't you?' Rachel teased.

'Something like that.'

They lapsed into a companionable silence; Daniel concentrated on the road, while Rachel looked out of the window, relaxing and taking in the scenery. As Daniel turned off onto a side road, the landscape grew more beautiful, the soft folds of the Suffolk countryside shown to its best advantage, cornfields and trees and churches set against a very blue sky.

Rachel smiled to herself. Had it not been for that damned cat, she would have considered herself perfectly happy; but until she found out the truth about the cat and what was happening to her, she wouldn't be able to relax.

Her eyes widened as they drove into Lavenham. The narrow streets were lined with higgledy-piggledy timber-framed buildings, the windows and doors and timbers leaning at crazy angles. The white plaster between them looked firm and solid, though: these houses were built to last. The windows all had tiny frames, some with diamond-patterned leading and others with neo-Georgian white-painted sash windows, and the front gardens were filled with spring flowers.

Rachel was entranced. 'Daniel, this place is gorgeous!'

'Have you never been here before, then?' he asked.

'No – and Carrie didn't say that much about it, only that it was the sort of place that I'd adore, and that I ought to take a trip here some time.'

Daniel nodded. 'It's full of antique shops and tea rooms. Perfect for pottering around and indulging yourself.'

'Do you come here often, then?'

'Not often, exactly – but I've brought some of my students here on visits, when I had to take a few terms of medieval history. Lavenham was an important wool town in the fourteenth and fifteenth centuries, so it was a fairly rich place – which is why they could afford to build a village like this.' He shrugged. 'It's hardly changed in appearance over the years; though, obviously, the roads have improved. The church is amazing.' He looked appealingly at her, tipping his head slightly to one side. 'We've got plenty of time. We could always have a proper wander round before we start tracing the cat.'

'Yes, I'd like that,' Rachel said.

He turned off the main street and into the courtyard of a hotel. 'This place used to be an old coaching inn,' he told her.

Rachel eyed the expensive-looking cars in the courtyard: BMWs and Mercedes, and a gleaming red MGF sports car. 'Are you telling me that you stayed here with your students?'

He chuckled. 'No. Even if London wasn't such a short drive away, they couldn't have afforded it. But I've earmarked this place for years as somewhere ... I dunno.' He wrinkled his nose. 'Romantic, I suppose. Somewhere special. I thought you might like it.'

When they'd parked the car, Daniel ushered Rachel into the reception.

The pretty dark-haired woman behind the desk smiled at them. 'Can I help you?'

Daniel smiled back. 'Yes. I have a double room booked. My name's Daniel Sinclair.'

Rachel stifled a giggle. She'd half expected him to book them in as Mr and Mrs Smith, or even as Mr and Mrs Sinclair. But Daniel was too honest for subterfuge like that. Besides, they had nothing to hide.

'Certainly. We've booked you into room seven.'

After they'd signed in, the receptionist gave them directions to their first-floor room. Rachel noticed the thickness of the plush carpet and the fresh flowers everywhere: this place, she thought, was far from cheap.

'Before you start nagging me, I'll let you take me somewhere nice for a weekend next month,' Daniel said softly in her ear. 'This is my treat, OK?'

Rachel winced. 'I'd be a lot happier if we went halves.'

'Well, tough. I feel like spoiling you – and myself, for that matter,' Daniel said, sliding an arm round her shoulders. 'And before you say anything else, yes, I can afford it.'

'Then thank you very much.' She smiled at him. 'I think that this is going to be a great weekend.'

When they reached their room, Rachel was delighted to discover that the view from their window was trees and fields and a small stream, and that there was a large four-poster bed. She sat on it, swinging her legs. 'Did you know that I've always fancied sleeping in one of these?'

'Who said that I had sleeping in mind?' Daniel asked, his voice slightly husky. 'I know we need to look round and find this antique dealer, but, first . . . Well, seeing you sitting there like that is giving me ideas. Very pleasant ideas.' He walked over and sat beside her, cupping her face in his hands and lowering his mouth to hers.

His lips touched hers very gently at first, a light and warm pressure which coaxed rather than demanded. Rachel couldn't help opening her mouth under his; then she took the initiative, sliding her tongue against his lips until his mouth parted, and then kissing him deeply.

Daniel broke the kiss and pulled her to her feet. She was wearing faded jeans and a short-sleeved purple silk shirt; slowly, he unbuttoned her shirt, stroking every inch of skin as he revealed it, and let the soft material fall to the floor in a rustle, not caring that it would crumple. Rachel slid her hands round his neck, lifting her face invitingly. He lowered his head to kiss her again, this time taking control and being the one to kiss her thoroughly.

Rachel was shaking when he stroked her midriff, undoing the button of her jeans with one hand and sliding the zip down. He eased the soft faded denim over her hips; she wriggled slightly, helping him push them down past her knees and then, when her jeans were at her ankles, she stepped out of them, kicking off her shoes at the same time. Daniel held her at arm's length, looking at her, his aqua grey eyes burning with desire.

She thrilled to the intensity of his gaze. He drew one finger very slowly along the edge of her lacy bra, tracing the contours of one breast, then letting his finger dip in the valley between her breasts, rubbing up and down once or twice to tease her, then tracing the edge of her bra across her other breast. Rachel couldn't help arching against him; he smiled, and undid his own shirt, tossing it to the floor. Then he stripped off his denims while she watched him.

She could already see how aroused he was, the outline of his hard, thick cock clearly visible through the soft cotton of his navy boxer shorts. Suddenly bold, she stepped forward, hooking her thumbs into the sides of his boxer shorts and drawing them down. He stepped out of them, and she dropped to her knees before him, pushing her hair back and then bending her head, tracing the tip of his cock with the tip of her nose.

It was Daniel's turn to shiver, then. She smiled, shifting position very slightly, and curling her fingers round his long thick shaft. She opened her mouth, stretching out her tongue, and slowly traced his frenum with the tip of her tongue. Daniel gasped, and she noticed a small clear bead of fluid appear in the eye of his cock. She lapped at it, liking the slightly bitter taste, and then slowly eased her mouth over the head of his cock. Daniel groaned, sliding his hands into her hair, and she began to fellate him in earnest, her head moving up and down rapidly, and her fingers curled into a tight ring so that she could work his cock in the opposite direction to her mouth.

Daniel cried out softly as he came, filling her mouth with

warm salty liquid. She swallowed every last drop, then got to her feet. Daniel pulled her into his arms, kissing her fiercely, the taste of his seed mingling in both of their mouths. Then he lifted her up, carrying her over to the bed. He pushed the blankets and quilt aside, and gently put her down on the crisp white cotton sheet. 'Rachel Meaden, you're the most desirable woman I've ever met,' he said quietly, his voice ragged and intense. 'I want you so much, it hurts.'

She noticed with pleasure that his cock was hard again, and then he was kneeling between her thighs. She was still wearing her bra and knickers; it didn't seem to bother him. He merely smiled, and slid his fingers under one of the cups of her bra, pulling it down to expose her breast, then doing the same with the other cup. 'You're utterly adorable,' he said softly. 'I love the way your body curves. I love the shape of your beautiful breasts, the way your nipples harden and grow dark when I touch them.'

He bent his head, drawing a trail of kisses down her throat. She arched against him, and he laughed softly. 'I love the way you respond to me. I love the texture of your skin, so soft and smooth, here.' He bent his head, licking her breasts. 'And it's different again, here.' He traced her areolae with the tip of his tongue. 'And here.' He pushed the tip of his tongue against her engorged nipples. 'And then, here.' He continued tracking downwards, nuzzling her midriff. He took the side of her knickers between his teeth, and began to tug gently.

Rachel chuckled. 'Now you're trying to be macho.'

'Yeah. And failing,' he added, his eyes sparkling with amusement. He hooked his thumbs into the other side of her knickers, and gently drew them down over her thighs. He smiled at her, leaning over to kiss her lightly, then lifted her legs up and together, so that he could remove her knickers properly. 'And here, you taste different again.' He bent down, putting his mouth to the hollow of her ankle.

Rachel shivered as his mouth drifted over her calves. 'And here. And here, you're sensitive.' He licked the back of her knee, and she wriggled impatiently, wanting him to kiss her more intimately. 'And here.' He parted her legs, and nuzzled her inner thigh. 'Here is where I start to get really excited, thinking of what's just inches away from my mouth. I love the taste of you there, Rachel. Like seashore and honey and vanilla and musk, all rolled into one. It's the most exotic perfume, and it tastes even better than the scent.'

A pulse was beating hard in Rachel's quim. She longed for Daniel to stop talking, stop teasing her, and start making love with her properly. She could almost feel his breath against the softness of her sex-flesh, and closed her eyes in anticipation; then he shifted again, kissing the back of the ankle on her other foot, and then slowly kissing his way up her leg.

'Please, Daniel.' The words burst out of her.

'Please what?'

She groaned. 'You know what I want.'

'You'll have to tell me.'

She swallowed. 'I want you to . . . I want you to lick me. I want you to use your mouth on me, make me come.'

'Just my mouth?' he queried.

She shook her head. 'I want more than that. I want you to touch me. And I want you to fill me with your cock, while I'm still coming. I want you to make me come again and again and again.'

'Seems pretty clear to me,' he said equably; and then he lowered his mouth. Her legs were still at right-angles to her body. Slowly, very gently, he widened the gap between her thighs, still keeping her legs up. She could feel him breathing against her quim, and she pushed impatiently upwards. She heard him chuckle, and then he bent his head properly, stretching his tongue out and drawing it from the top to the bottom of her musky furrow in one slow, delicious movement. He repeated the action again and again; Rachel felt her sex grow warm and puffy, ready to receive him. Then he was lapping her in earnest, one moment working on her clitoris until she was near to coming, and then plunging his tongue as deeply as he could into her.

Within moments she was coming. As her internal muscles spasmed sharply against his mouth, she felt him smile. He moved suddenly, and she felt the tip of his cock pressing against her contracting sex. She gave a small moan of pleasure as he pushed inside her, his cock buried right up to the hilt.

'Rachel, you feel so good,' he told her huskily. He rested her ankles over his shoulders, and then he began to move with long, slow, rhythmic strokes, pushing deep into her and then pulling out so very slowly until his cock was almost out of her, then pushing back in again. He rested his weight on one hand; with his other, he stroked Rachel's breasts, his fingertips tracing her areolae and then pinching her nipples very gently until she groaned and pushed against him. As his pace quickened, she felt the inner sparkling of her orgasm begin again, her flesh rippling. She could almost see stars as she came; at that precise moment, she felt Daniel's cock throb deep inside her, his climax melding with hers.

Very gently, he moved her legs, sliding them down his body; she twined them round his waist, pulling him deeper into her. He smiled, and rolled over onto his back so that she was straddling him. He wrapped his arms round her, holding her close; she lay content, her cheek resting against his.

'I don't know about you,' he said softly, 'but I feel a lot better for that.'

'Yes,' she admitted quietly. 'I've never slept in a four-poster bed before, let alone anything else.'

He grinned. 'I have all sorts of pleasurable ideas about later tonight. I thought that maybe we could order dinner through room service – because I don't know if I can keep my hands off you for long enough to eat in the restaurant.'

She chuckled. 'Oh, Daniel.'

'Yeah.' He rubbed his cheek against hers. 'Much as I'd like to sleep now, then make love with you again when I wake, I suppose we'd better start looking for this shop.' He kissed her lightly on the mouth. 'Shower first, I think. Though I daren't take one with you, because I know what will happen.'

She grinned. 'You don't say.'

He slapped her lightly on the rump. 'Off you go.'

After they'd both showered and changed, Daniel asked Rachel if she wanted lunch, before they started looking for the antique shop.

She shook her head. 'To be honest, I'm not that hungry.'

'Fair enough.' He slid one arm round her waist as they left the hotel, and they wandered down the high street, browsing in all the shop windows. 'So what's this place called, then?' he asked. 'I know you told me the other day, but it's slipped my mind.'

'Serendipity.'

'A lucky find.' He chuckled. 'That's the sort of name I'd associate more with – I dunno, a charity shop run by a vicar's wife, or something like that.'

'Well.' She raised an eyebrow. 'And I'm not sure whether the cat was a lucky find or not.'

'We might not have met without it,' he reminded her softly.

'Then I suppose that it does have its plus points.' She paused. 'It'll be interesting to find out what else is in that shop besides the mummy case.'

'Yes.'

'The owner's name is Brian Fletcher. I hope that he's there.'

'It's Friday. It's not early closing day or anything like that. He's bound to be there.'

They found Serendipity tucked away in the corner of a small courtyard. An old-fashioned bell rang as Daniel opened the door and ushered Rachel inside. No-one came to greet them; they looked at each other in resignation, shrugged, and began to walk around the shop.

The place was a veritable Aladdin's cave; Rachel's eyes widened as she came across a pile of other Egyptian artefacts, shabti figures and scarabs and a bracelet. Were they copies, she wondered, or were they originals, like the mummy case?

Eventually, a young girl came from the back of the shop to the cash desk, and looked shyly at them. 'Can I help you?'

'We're looking for Brian Fletcher,' Daniel said. 'Is he free to see us for a few minutes, please?'

The girl shook her head. 'I'm afraid he's gone to Bury St Edmunds for the afternoon, to see a client.'

'Will he be back tomorrow?' Rachel asked.

The girl nodded. 'Yes.'

'What time do you open?'

'About half past nine. Do you want me to give him a message?'

Daniel shook his head. 'Thanks, but there's no need. A friend of ours bought something from here, a few weeks ago, and we were wondering if he had anything else like it, that was all.'

'You'd best come back tomorrow morning,' the girl said.

'Yes, all right.'

When they left the shop, Rachel was frowning. 'What's up?' Daniel asked.

'There are quite a lot of Egyptian things there,' she said. 'Scarabs and shabti figures, some jewellery. I was looking while you were over the other side of the shop. I'm not sure if they were copies, or originals.'

'If the mummy case is, surely everything else is?'

'Probably – but where the hell did he get the stuff from? Copies are cheap and easy to come across, especially in the shops outside the British Museum, but originals . . . Well, Kate will tell you. Things just don't turn up like that, Daniel.'

'So what do you think? Is Brian Fletcher part of some international crime ring?'

She glared at him. 'Don't take the piss.'

'I'm not. Sorry. It was just a suggestion.'

'Hm.'

He stroked her hair. 'Rachel. Lighten up; we'll find out what's going on, tomorrow.'

'Yeah. I'm sorry.'

They spent the rest of the afternoon wandering around Lavenham. Daniel told her more about the history of the town, then gave her a guided tour of the fourteenth-century church, pointing out the one hundred and forty-one foot high tower and other points of architectural interest.

'What?' he asked, catching the amusement on her face.

'I was just thinking,' she said. 'I'd love to sit through some of your lectures.'

'How do you mean?'

'Well, you must bring it alive for your students.'

'You mean, this is a nice way of telling me that I'm boring you stiff?'

'No, not at all.' She smiled, and tucked her arm through his. 'I'm enjoying myself, Daniel. Very much so.'

'Good.'

They headed back for the hotel; Daniel looked at Rachel. 'So shall we have dinner in our room tonight?'

She shook her head. 'I'd like to eat in the restaurant.'

'Oh.' He looked faintly disappointed.

She grinned. 'But I have something else in mind, for later.'

'What?'

'You'll have to wait.'

Daniel could see the determination in her face: she wasn't going to tell him what she was planning. But whatever it was, he knew that it would be very pleasurable indeed.

'I think I'll have a shower before we eat,' Rachel said as they closed the door to their room. 'Alone.'

'Spoilsport.'

'Yup.' She grinned. 'You first.'

'Why?'

'Because I'm sorting out what I want to wear tonight.'

He rolled his eyes. 'You mean, you're not even going to offer to wash my back?'

'No.'

'OK. We'll play it your way, then,' he said, and stripped swiftly. Rachel watched him appraisingly; he caught her glance, and smiled. 'You can always change your mind,' he said.

'Not on your life.'

While Daniel showered, Rachel rummaged through her case. She'd brought a good dress with her, and she'd invested in certain items of underwear which she thought that Daniel would appreciate. She had intended wearing them in London, but their planned trip to Lavenham was the perfect opportunity. Particularly as they were sharing a four-poster bed.

She took something else from her case, slipping it into the drawer of the table next to the bed. It was fairly unlikely that Daniel would look in the drawer before they went to dinner; even so, she hid the item underneath the hotel writing paper, just in case. This was one thing she didn't want him guessing about. Then, smiling, she gathered her clothes together, and waited for Daniel to finish.

As soon as he emerged from the bathroom, she went in, smiling sweetly at him, and locked the door behind her. She showered, then dressed carefully and did her make-up, putting her hair up and pushing a pin through it, before emerging.

Daniel looked at her, his eyes widening as he took in her outfit. She was wearing a little black dress with no sleeves, and long black lacy gloves which she'd borrowed from Carrie. Her stockings were sheer and black, and she was wearing a pair of high-heeled black patent leather shoes which she'd also borrowed from Carrie. 'Rachel, you look gorgeous! Let's forget dinner.'

'Not a chance. I'm starving.'

'If you insist.' He sniffed. 'And you smell gorgeous. What is it?'

'Lilith. The new perfume we did the launch ads for the other week.'

'I thought I recognized it. All I can say,' he told her huskily, 'is that I hope their service is bloody quick, here.'

She grinned. 'Indeed.' And when he found out what else she was wearing, he'd enjoy it even more, she thought.

The restaurant was secluded and romantic; the tables were covered with white damask cloths, and there was a spray of white lilies in a white vase in the middle of the table. Rachel thought of the story that Carrie had told her, and hid a smile. She might relay that to Daniel, some time – but not before he'd actually met her friend.

The service was efficient and unobtrusive, and the food was excellent. Daniel had indulged them both by ordering margaux, which Rachel sipped with pleasure. 'Mm. The wine's perfect,' she said. The crab-stuffed mushrooms were excellent, as were the game casserole and the crème brûlée; the coffee was perfect, too, dark and rich and aromatic.

When they'd finished, Rachel stretched. 'Mm. Must be all the country air, because I'm tired.'

Daniel nodded. 'Let's go up.' He slid his arm round her shoulders as they went up to their room; Rachel leaned against him, feeling suddenly relaxed and happy. And what she had planned, for the rest of the evening ... Daniel wouldn't be expecting it, but he'd certainly enjoy it, she thought.

When they'd closed the door behind them, she turned to him. 'Daniel.'

'Mm?'

'Go and sit down. At the foot of the bed.'

He frowned. 'Why?'

'Just humour me, will you?'

He nodded. 'All right.' He pulled the chair to the foot of the bed, and sat down, crossing one leg over the other. 'Is this what you want?'

'That's perfect.' She smiled, and slowly removed her dress, unzipping it and letting it fall to the ground.

Daniel's eyes darkened with pleasure as he saw what she was wearing. 'Wow.'

'Remember our conversation on the phone, the other night?' she asked.

'Mm.'

'Well, I thought that you might enjoy this. Except that the sheets are cotton, not silk; the bed's a four-poster, rather than wrought iron; and you're taking place of the mirror.'

As realization dawned, he smiled. 'I see.'

'So.' She sashayed over to the bed, kicking off her shoes, and pulled back the sheets. She leaned over so that she could pile all the pillows together, then turned her back to Daniel, bending over to remove her knickers. At his sharp intake of breath, she smiled to herself. If he liked what he was seeing now, he'd really enjoy the rest of it.

Her stockings were black silk, the hold-up type with lacy welts, and her basque was exactly as he'd specified in his fantasy, as were the gloves. She smiled again, and sat on the bed with her knees drawn up and her feet flat on the mattress. She closed her eyes. 'Mm, Daniel. I'm thinking of you, and what we do together. I'm thinking of the way we make love, the way you make me feel.' She opened her eyes again, and looked at him; then, with a coquettish smile, she parted her legs.

Daniel gave a sharp intake of breath as she exposed herself to him; she was so beautiful. He was silent as, so very slowly, she slid one hand down her body. Both of them could hear the lace of her gloves hiss against the lace of her basque, and it sent a shiver of pure pleasure through them. Rachel put the heel of her palm on her mons veneris, and then she parted her vaginal lips with her index and ring fingers, letting her middle finger glide down her slit.

'How do you feel?' Daniel whispered huskily. 'How does it feel, Rachel? Tell me.'

'It feels good, the roughness of the lace against my skin,' she whispered back, repeating the action until her sex was slippery and gleaming with her arousal. She began to rub herself in earnest, working on her clitoris, but it wasn't enough: she wanted more. Her nipples were so hard that they almost hurt; the friction of the hard peaks of flesh rubbing against the lace wasn't enough for her. She slipped the fingers of her free hand inside one of the cups, and pulled the lace down, exposing her swollen breast, her dark and hard nipple.

She kneaded her breast, and then she started pulling at the nipple, rolling it between her forefinger and thumb. She did the same with her other breast, and then she looked at Daniel. 'Do you like the show, so far?'

'Yes. You look so beautiful, masturbating in front of the mirror and watching yourself, the way your fingers dip into your beautiful cunt. You look incredibly lewd and wanton,' Daniel told her.

She grinned. 'I'm enjoying myself. Though I haven't finished, yet.'

'Oh?'

She grinned again, and reached over to the bedside cabinet, opening the top drawer and extracting the item she'd put there earlier: a thick, gold vibrator. Daniel groaned as he saw her part her labia, and watched her sliding the wide gold tube very gently into herself. 'It's big,' she said. 'Like you. It's stretching me as it goes in, and it feels good.' She leaned back against the pillows, and began to pump the vibrator in and out, very slowly, teasing herself a little so that she and the watching Daniel could draw the most pleasure from it. She withdrew it until the tube was almost out; then she pushed it back in again, hard.

She made a small moan of pleasure. 'Oh, it's good, Daniel,' she told him hoarsely. 'But I want more. I want so much more.' She flicked the switch on the end of the vibrator; with one hand, she pumped it in and out, and with her other hand, she rubbed her clitoris. 'I'm the queen of my empire,' she said, 'with all my slaves ready to do my every bidding. I've picked the most attractive for my private use: I have half a dozen of them with me, now, and they're so in tune with my needs, I don't even have to tell them what I need.'

'What are they doing?' Daniel asked.

'One's kneeling between my thighs, his cock pushed into me up to the hilt. He has one sitting either side of him: one's fingering my clitoris, and one's sliding his finger into my anus. Two more are by my sides, sucking a nipple each, and one's kissing my mouth. All my pleasure-centres are being stimulated at once, and it feels wonderful. They'll keep this up for as long as I need it, touching me and licking me and sucking me and fucking me, until I've come so much, I'm almost comatose. And then they'll take me to the edge once more, until I scream with pleasure.'

She began to use the vibrator harder and faster until, at last, she came, her internal muscles contracting hard around the thick tube. Daniel watched her; when her breathing had

Evelyn D'Arcy

slowed, he stripped swiftly, joining her on the bed. 'God, that was so good,' he said softly.

She smiled at him. 'I thought that you might enjoy it.'

'Very much so.' Gently, he removed the tube from her quim, and brought it to his mouth, licking the glistening nectar from it. Then he threw it to one side, pulling Rachel towards him and kissing her hard. She responded immediately, twining her hands round his neck and opening her mouth under his, pressing her body against his so that she could feel the thick hard length of his cock pressing into her pubis.

Daniel broke the kiss and gently turned her onto her front, guiding her onto her hands and knees. 'Do you have any idea how good you look, dressed like that?' he asked.

She grinned. 'You're the one who specified it, in your telephone call, the other night.'

'Mm, and I'm glad that I did. You were fantastic,' he said. 'And as for your six slaves ... well, I can't do everything at once, but there are a few things I can do. Like this.' He pushed the hair from the nape of her neck, kissing her skin and making her shiver. She was still aroused and wet from the vibrator, and when he pressed the tip of his cock to the entrance of her sex, he slid easily inside her. 'You feel so good,' he told her, his voice cracking with desire. 'I love the way you feel, so wet and tight and hot around me.' He slid his hands round to her front, cupping one breast and her delta; he nuzzled her shoulder. 'I love touching you, Rachel. I can't get enough of you.'

'I think it's mutual,' she said.

'Good.' He began to rub her clitoris, and thrust deeply into her, moving his hips in small circles; Rachel groaned, and pressed back against him. He quickened his pace, still rubbing her clitoris, and she began to moan, writhing in pleasure underneath him and using her internal muscles to good effect.

And then, at last, they were coming, their bodies melting into fluid pleasure; Daniel held her close, his head still buried in her shoulder, until the aftershocks of their climax had died away. Then he withdrew, rolling onto his back and pulling her into his arms. Rachel cuddled into him, smiling; he stroked her face. 'Rachel. Lovely, adorable Rachel.'

'You're pretty adorable, yourself,' she said.

He smiled, content to lie in silence with her; finally, they drifted into sleep.

TWELVE

Daniel looked at Rachel, and smiled. She was absolutely dead
to the world, he thought. But he had no intention of waking
her. She needed her sleep after what had been happening to
her lately: plus the fact that they'd woken twice more in the
night and made love again.

At the same time, he really needed a cup of coffee. If he made
himself a cup of coffee in their room, the noise would disturb
her, which wasn't fair. Though he really couldn't wait for
Rachel to wake before he went down to breakfast. Carefully,
he slid out of the bed, dressed in near-silence, and padded out
of the room. He'd have some coffee and do the Telegraph
crossword; then, if Rachel wasn't up by ten, he'd send up a
tray of coffee and croissants for her, via room service.

It was warm, so very warm; Rachel moved restlessly. It was
the kind of hot, sultry, sticky night which banished sleep,
making you toss and turn to try and find a cool place. Even
the air was thick and hot. She groaned, turned over – and then
she suddenly realized that she wasn't alone. Lying next to her,
on her side, was her lover from the waterfall, watching her.
Her lips curved as she discovered that Rachel was awake.

'Hello, beautiful.'

Rachel smiled back. Part of her wanted to ask what the

other woman was doing there – she hadn't been there when Rachel had gone to sleep – but she didn't want to make a fool of herself. There was obviously a good reason for it. If only her memory wasn't so bad, nowadays.

'When you look at me like that,' her lover said, 'you're irresistible.'

'When I look at you like what?'

'Your eyes are all soft, and your mouth's slightly open, as if you're waiting to be kissed.' As if impatient with herself, her lover leaned over and kissed her hard on the mouth. Rachel couldn't help responding, flicking her own tongue against her lover's and letting her hands slide up her lover's sides, cupping one full breast in her hand.

The other woman's nipple was already hard and erect, pressing against Rachel's palm. Rachel rotated her palm very gently against the hard peak of flesh and was rewarded with a groan of pleasure. She continued circling her palm until she felt her lover's breast swell even further; then she bunched her fingers, drawing them back towards her palm and arching her hand until her fingertips reached her lover's nipple, allowing her to roll the peak of flesh between her fingers.

'Ah, yes,' her lover groaned, rolling onto her back. 'Touch me. Do it to me. Now.'

Memories of the waterfall surged through Rachel and, the next thing she knew, she was kneeling between her lover's thighs, letting her hair trail softly along her lover's belly, and then taking one hard nipple into her mouth, sucking hard, while she rolled its twin between a finger and thumb, distending it.

Her lover's body jerked beneath her, and Rachel sucked harder, using her teeth to graze the sensitive tissues. At her lover's moan of pleasure, Rachel began to move lower, nuzzling her midriff, and finally reaching her mons veneris. The other woman drew her knees up, putting her feet flat on the ground, and widened the gap between her thighs, exposing herself to Rachel. Her quim was already warm and puffy, glistening in the dim light. Rachel let a finger drift down the musky crevice and was rewarded with another moan; her lover's hips bucked slightly.

Rachel pressed harder this time, slowly drawing her finger up and down her lover's quim; the other woman began to twist her head from side to side, pushing her pelvis up. 'Do it to me,' she begged. 'Don't tease. You know I want you.' Rachel teased her lover for a little longer; then she relented, and slid one finger deep into her lover's warm, wet, willing channel.

'Oh yes, yes. More,' her lover moaned, writhing beneath Rachel's ministrations.

Rachel remembered the dildo her lover had used in the cave. What would it feel like, she wondered, to have the implement tied to her, to fuck her lover as if she were a man?

Almost as if her lover knew what was going through Rachel's head, she opened her eyes, lifting herself from the bed and propping herself on her elbows. 'I want you,' she said softly, her eyes dark and sultry, and her mouth full and passionate. 'I want you to take me like a man, like I took you behind the waterfall. I want you to fill me. I want you to fuck me. Fuck me hard, make me writhe and moan and cry under you.'

Rachel's mouth was suddenly dry with excitement. She'd never done this before. She wanted to do it, oh, so badly. If only her other lover was there – the man with the beautiful eyes. Then she could kneel between her lover's thighs, thrusting into her like a man, while her other lover took her from behind. It was a delicious thought, one that she knew she'd act out one day. Now wasn't the time, but the very idea of it made her breasts tingle and her quim feel wet.

'Over there, in the chest,' her lover directed. 'You'll find what you need, there.'

Rachel stood up and slowly walked over to the chest, opening it. There was an amazing series of harnesses and toys, things that made Rachel's eyes widen. She wasn't sure how half of them were used; but what she did know was that every single item was used for pleasure. Pleasure which she needed so badly, herself.

In the middle of the jumbled pile was the item she remembered: the dildo which she could tie onto herself. Swiftly, she picked it up and put it in place. She realized with a sudden jolt of pleasure that the leather triangle to which the phallus was attached was more than just a holding piece or decoration. There was also a prominent nubby ridge which went between her own legs, and would stimulate her clitoris every time that she moved her hips.

A thrill ran through her at the thought. This was going to be good, so very good, for both of them. She tied the thongs around the tops of her thighs and her waist, letting the phallus jut out from her mons veneris, then went to join her lover again, who was lying back in a prone position, one hand behind her head and a look of sensual expectation on her face.

Rachel realized with a mixture of amusement and surprise that her lover's other hand was firmly lodged between her thighs, teasing her clitoris. She put her hand over her lover's hand at her groin. Immediately, the other woman stopped moving and looked at Rachel, her eyes challenging. Rachel lifted her lover's hand, and slowly drew her fingers into her mouth, one by one, licking off every scrap of glistening musky juice and revelling in the spicy taste. Then she knelt between her lover's thighs, positioning herself so that the phallus was ready to slide into her lover.

So this was what it felt like to be a man, she thought. The surge of power as you were about to penetrate your lover ... She wasn't sure if it shocked or excited her more. Experimentally, she moved her hips, letting the dildo slide along the length of her lover's quim. The other woman shivered, and lifted herself slightly, ready to receive the phallus. Rachel let the phallus slide along her quim again and again, until her lover was writhing, bucking her hips and pushing upwards. Rachel knew how that felt: when you wanted to be filled, when you wanted your lover's cock to stretch you and take you to the limits of pleasure. She smiled, inserted the tip of the phallus at the entrance of her lover's warm, wet channel, and pushed.

The dildo slid in easily, up to the hilt. Rachel licked her suddenly dry lips, and began to move. As she thrust into her lover, the nubby prominence between her legs began to rub her clitoris. The faster she thrust, the more enjoyable it felt. Like she was masturbating, but even better.

Her lover wrapped her legs around Rachel's waist, pulling her closer; Rachel tilted her hips and thrust harder, harder. God, this felt good, she thought: this feeling of power and overwhelming lust. She groaned as her lover cupped her buttocks, digging her nails in slightly to urge her on; then, with rising excitement, she realized that her lover had an implement of her own in her hand. A long, thin phallus which was meant for a quite different orifice.

She shuddered as she felt the tip of the thing pressing against the rosy puckered hole of her anus: then it was inside her, being pushed inexorably into her. Her bowels grumbled, and she stiffened, afraid.

'Shh, it's all right. Let it go. You won't do anything to disgrace yourself,' her lover whispered softly. 'I like it when this is done to me. I like a man to do it to me – first with this, while his cock's deep inside me, and then I like him to take it out, spill his seed over my arse and rub it in. Then I like him to put his cock back in me, right here.' She pushed the dildo in slightly deeper, and Rachel cried out. 'I like to feel him stretch me, take me.'

Rachel moaned, and continued to thrust; her lover kept the dildo inside her, using the same rhythm as she moved the implement in and out.

'I have other toys,' her lover told her quietly, her voice husky with pleasure. 'Other toys to pleasure us both at the same time, like two cocks facing away from each other. We can do it that way, taking each other like a man, but with the warmth of a woman.'

'Yes,' Rachel said, her excitement growing.

'I want to do it with you. I want to take you – and I want to watch him take you at the same time. I want to feel your body rocking between us, like you're drowning in the waters of pleasure. I want to see you come until there's a river flowing between your legs.'

'Oh, yes,' Rachel said. She wanted it, too.

'He's watching us now,' her lover told her wickedly. 'Hidden. I won't tell you where, but he can see everything we're doing. His cock's hard, so hard that it hurts, but he dare not move, because he doesn't want to give himself away. He wants to take his cock in his fist and rub himself hard, pleasure himself like you're pleasuring me, but he dare not. He doesn't want you to know that he's there.'

'Where?'

Her lover chuckled. 'I said that I won't tell you where. But he's excited. He's watching what you're doing to me, and it turns him on. He can see what I'm doing to you, and it turns him on even more. Especially because he knows that he's going to do it to both of us later. He's going to fill you and fuck you, until you're writhing like a bitch on heat, wanting more and more and more. He's going to fill your cunt, and then he's going to take your pretty little arse. We're both going to touch you and lick you and suck you and fuck you, until you don't know where you are, until your whole body's rippling with pleasure.' Her lover began to move the thin dildo in and out, taking Rachel to fever pitch. 'He'd like to be beside us right now. He'd like to be the one pleasuring your arse. And he'd like to have us both together. Do you know what he told me, the other day?'

'No.'

'He said, he'd like to take you from behind, having you kneel before him; and I'd be standing in front of you. You'd eat me while he fucked you, and you'd be doing to me what I'm doing to you. The three of us, giving and taking so much pleasure. Or maybe he'd be taking me, while you took him like a man, filling his arse.'

Rachel swallowed. 'I . . .'

'We can do it all. It's so easy. Just the three of us. We'll go behind the waterfall where no-one can find us. We'll take my treasure-chest, and we'll make each other come time and time and time again. I'll teach you everything I know about pleasuring a man – and a woman. He can watch us together, mouth to cunt, licking and sucking each other to paradise. He'll be so hard, by the time he's finished, that we can ride him until we've reached another orgasm, and another.'

'Uh,' Rachel groaned, as she felt her orgasm rising through her. Almost at the same time, her lover bared her teeth, clenching her teeth together as though stifling a cry of passion. Her body went rigid for a moment, and then she relaxed, smiling, and reached up to kiss Rachel, hard.

Marie walked up the stairs, carrying the tray of coffee. She could imagine why the woman in room seven was still asleep. If she'd spent the night with a man as gorgeous as Daniel Sinclair – Marie had been unable to resist looking up his name in the register, after she'd taken his order for breakfast – then she would have been sleeping, too, exhausted after making love until she'd lost count of how many times she'd come.

She rapped on the door. 'Room service,' she called, her soft voice speaking perfect English with only a hint of her native French accent.

There was no answer, so she opened the door. Her eyes widened in shock as she saw the woman lying in the middle of the four-poster bed, the sheets and covers pushed back. She didn't think that she'd ever seen a more beautiful sight. The fair-haired woman was lying there, writhing on the bed, one hand working madly between her legs while the other caressed her breasts roughly, pulling at her dark and distended nipples.

No wonder there had been no answer, Marie thought, closing the door behind her and putting the tray down on the dressing table. The woman hadn't heard her. She seemed completely oblivious to anything happening around her, she was so tuned in to her own pleasure. Marie found it irresistible. She knew that what she was about to do could cause her no end of problems, and maybe even lose her her job, but she didn't care. She couldn't help herself. She sat down on the edge of the bed and gently rested one hand on the woman's abdomen.

Rachel opened her eyes in utter shock, and realized that she was naked, she was masturbating, and there was a woman she'd never met before, dressed in a maid's outfit, sitting on the bed next to her.

'Christ, I . . .'

'Shh, it doesn't matter,' Marie said, her accent thicker, now. She bent down and lowered her mouth to Rachel's.

It was almost where Rachel's vision had ended, her female lover kissing her hard. This new woman – Rachel realized, with a flash of insight, that she was from Room Service – was softer, gentler than the lover in her dream. But Rachel was still so aroused, she couldn't help responding, opening her mouth and letting the other woman kiss her properly, tongue pressing against tongue.

At last, Marie broke the kiss, and her mouth drifted down to caress Rachel's throat. 'So beautiful. So very beautiful,' she murmured.

Rachel arched against her, suddenly shameless, offering her breasts to the strange woman. The woman with the accent so like the woman in her dream . . .

Marie nuzzled her breasts, rubbing her face between them and breathing in Rachel's scent. She could smell sex on her skin – not just from the masturbation she'd witnessed, but no doubt from lovemaking with Daniel Sinclair, Marie thought wryly. This was a woman with a powerful libido. Someone who would respond, give her the passion she craved and had missed so desperately since leaving France.

She took one engorged nipple into her mouth; Rachel gave a sigh of pleasure and wound her hands into Marie's hair, urging her on. Marie let one hand drift further, stroking Rachel's midriff, then cupped her mons veneris. The heel of Marie's palm rested on Rachel's belly, and her fingers lay along Rachel's sodden quim. Rachel wriggled impatiently, and Marie pressed her fingers down harder, letting her middle finger glide along Rachel's hot moist quim. 'So beautiful,' she breathed.

Rachel didn't care that the other woman was fully clothed. She was aroused to fever pitch, and she wanted to come. She wanted to feel someone deep inside her, someone stroking and licking and sucking her pleasure points. She had no idea what had happened to the vibrator she'd used in front of Daniel the previous night, and she couldn't be bothered to look for it: she wanted to feel the other woman's hands and mouth working on her. She tipped her pelvis up, splaying her legs and exposing herself to Marie. The Frenchwoman chuckled. 'So impatient, little one.'

Rachel drew her legs up, flaunting herself as her lover had in the dream, and Marie touched her quim reverently. Marie had never met an Englishwoman this prepared to abandon herself to pleasure, and she was impressed.

'Please,' Rachel said huskily. 'Do it to me. Do it to me, now. Touch me. Make me come.'

Marie dipped her head, rubbing her cheeks against the soft skin of Rachel's inner thighs, and put her mouth to her quim. Rachel moaned as the other woman teased her clitoris from its hood with her tongue, then took the hard bud of flesh between her lips and sucked, hard. Her breathing began to come in ragged pants as she felt Marie insert one finger into her vagina, and then another, then move her hand back and forth to simulate the movement of a cock.

Then, somehow, the other woman had changed hands, and Rachel felt something wet and hard and slippery pressing against the puckered rosy hole of her anus. Not the long, thin, hard dildo of her dream, but something smaller, something gentler. She cried out as Marie's finger slid inside her, up to the second joint, then began to move, using the same movement as her other hand in Rachel's quim. While her bowels seemed to churn in protest, a sharp spike of pleasure ripped through the feeling. It was good, so good. She cupped her own breasts, stimulating her nipples, pulling roughly at them as the penetrating fingers thrust into her. When she came, she almost howled, the pleasure was so sharp.

Her new lover shifted again, kissing her lightly on the lips. 'I'm sorry. When I walked in and saw you, I couldn't resist you.'

Rachel flushed as awareness suddenly hit her. 'We don't even know each other's names.'

'Marie Duval,' Marie said.

'You're French.'

Marie smiled. 'Yes. Though I've worked in England for two years, now.' She looked enquiringly at Rachel, her dark eyes gleaming. 'And you?'

'Rachel Meaden.'

Marie smiled at her. 'Rachel.' She stroked Rachel's face. 'I think that we both enjoyed that, hm?'

'Yes,' Rachel admitted.

'Though you're shocked at yourself, needing to make love

with me, when your beautiful man is waiting for you down-stairs.'

'Daniel.'

'Daniel,' Marie echoed.

Rachel's flush deepened. 'I didn't know that you were there, at first.'

'It must have been some fantasy you were having,' Marie said. 'You were already so hot, so wet, so ready to be touched.'

Rachel licked her lips. 'Yes. I was dreaming.'

'Of Daniel?'

Rachel couldn't speak. How could she tell Marie that she was fantasizing about another woman, a woman she'd never met?

Marie didn't press the subject. 'I think,' she said softly, 'that we both need a shower.'

The waitress stood up; Rachel realized that her new lover was extremely attractive. She had long, long legs, which she showed to advantage in a short black skirt and white frilly apron. Her dark nipples were obvious through the thin white silk of her shirt.

She was wearing an old-fashioned maid's hat; with a grin, she lifted her hands to it, removing it and then shaking her long dark curly hair free. She was one of the prettiest women that Rachel had ever seen – even more attractive than Jasmine. She lay back against the pillows, a smile on her face, as she realized that Marie was performing for her, stripping to arouse her again. She had a fairly good idea what Marie meant by a shower. Mutual pleasure. Like the pleasure she and her mysterious female lover had shared, under the waterfall . . .

Marie, seeing the glint of interest in Rachel's eyes, smiled to herself, and began to move slowly, swaying her hips sinuously as she undid the frilly apron, hanging it over the back of the chair. She slid down the zipper of her black skirt, letting it fall to the floor, turning round and bending over to pick it up, giving Rachel an eyeful of her well-shaped bottom. She turned round again and began undoing her shirt, finally removing it to reveal a skimpy white lace underwired bra and matching g-string.

She was wearing black hold-up stockings; she suddenly wished that she was wearing black patent leather high-heeled shoes, rather than the practical flat loafers she wore for work. High-heeled shoes that would tip her ever so slightly off balance and show off her legs and her hips to her best advantage ... But that was beside the point. Slowly, she reached behind her, undoing her bra. She slid her hands across to cover the cups of her bra, then let the garment drop to the floor, covering her breasts with her spread hands; then she moved her hands to let her hard nipples peep through her fingers. Rachel smiled in approval, and Marie smiled back, turning round once more.

She peeled her g-string down, then bent over to step out of it, giving Rachel the perfect view of her glistening quim. She rolled down her stockings, again moving so that Rachel could see how hot and wet she was; then straightened up, turning round to face Rachel and standing with her hands on her hips and her head tipped on one side.

'A shower,' she said softly.

Rachel looked at the contents of the tray. 'The coffee will get cold. And I'm hungry.' She smiled appealingly at Marie. 'How about some breakfast, first?'

'All right.' Marie nodded, and walked back to join Rachel on the bed. She poured out a cup of coffee. 'Sugar?'

Rachel shook her head. 'Just milk, thanks.'

'You should try drinking your coffee the proper way, some time,' Marie said, 'No milk.'

Rachel shrugged. 'Okay. How about now?'

'Now.' Marie smiled, taking a sip and then passing the cup of black coffee to Rachel.

Rachel took a draught of the coffee. It was surprisingly good.

'Croissant,' Marie said, breaking off a corner of the crumbly pastry, and adding butter and jam. She held it in front of Rachel's lips; Rachel smiled and played along, letting Marie feed her. Then she did the same for Marie, adding butter and jam to a piece of croissant, feeding her. Marie ate gently, delicately; Rachel watched her mouth, fascinated. And then her gaze dropped lower, to Marie's beautiful breasts, her still-hard nipples.

On impulse, she dabbed jam over Marie's dark nipples, and bent her head to lick it off.

Marie chuckled, dipping her fingers into the jam and then smearing it over Rachel's bare breasts, bending her head and licking the sticky mixture from Rachel's skin. Rachel shivered, tipping her head back in pleasure as Marie continued to lap her skin; then she pushed the Frenchwoman back against the pillows, crumbling some of the still-warm flaky croissant over her body, and nibbling her way down, licking up the crumbs.

'That tickles,' Marie said, laughing.

'How about this, then?' Rachel asked, dipping her head and rubbing her cheeks against the softness of Marie's thighs, in exactly the same way that Marie had touched her, earlier.

'Oh, yes,' the Frenchwoman sighed, closing her eyes and

splaying her legs wider. 'Oh yes, *chérie*, do it.' She slid her hands into Rachel's hair, urging her on; Rachel smiled, and put her mouth to Marie's quim. She heard Marie moan as she probed her with her tongue, exploring her folds and hollows; then she teased Marie's clitoris from its hood, sucking gently on the engorged bud of flesh.

Marie groaned, her breathing becoming ragged; Rachel smiled, sliding a finger into Marie and moving her hand back and forth.

'Do it,' Marie hissed. 'Do it like I did it to you.'

Her accent became stronger as her arousal grew; Rachel smiled, and began to rub Marie's quim with her other hand, letting the first nectar-soaked hand drift over the other woman's perineum, then pressing gently against the forbidden portal of her anus. Marie sighed with pleasure as Rachel's finger slid into her; Rachel began to move in earnest, pushing Marie closer and closer to the brink of orgasm.

The Frenchwoman stiffened, then gave a small gurgling moan; Rachel felt her flesh jolt beneath her fingers. And then Marie was smiling, stroking Rachel's hair. 'So good, so good,' she said softly. 'Thank you.'

Rachel smiled back, and sprawled on the bed next to Marie, letting the other woman cuddle into her. 'Pleasure.'

'For both of us,' Marie purred softly. 'You enjoyed it as much as I did.'

'Yes.'

They lay together in silence for a few moments; then Rachel stretched. 'A shower, you said.'

'A shower. Yes.'

Rachel sat up, and Marie followed suit. Marie held out her hand, and Rachel took it. They slid off the bed; together, they walked to the bathroom. On the way, Marie double-locked the door. 'I don't think that either of us wants to be disturbed,' she said softly. 'Not this time.'

A thrill ran through Rachel. Was there to be a next time – with Daniel? Acting out the vision she'd seen before, the beautiful woman and the man with her, making love, touching and kissing and caressing each other?

'Vision?' Marie queried.

Rachel flushed. Despite the intimacy of what they'd already shared, she didn't want to tell Marie the truth about her visit to Lavenham. 'Sorry. I didn't realize that I was speaking aloud.'

'Something you don't want to talk about, hm?'

Rachel was relieved at the other woman's perception. 'Yes.'

'Then we won't talk.' Marie tipped her head on one side. 'We'll just take a shower.'

When they walked into the bathroom, Rachel realized that there was a mirror opposite the bath and shower – a mirror which would give them a full view of whatever happened in the shower. Excitement kicked in her stomach. She would see everything that Marie did to her – and everything that she did to Marie.

As if oblivious to the possibilities, Marie pulled the shower curtain across, then switched on the shower.

'No,' Rachel said softly. 'I want to see.'

Marie looked at Rachel, then the mirror; realization dawned, and she grinned. 'You want to watch us together.'

'Yes,' Rachel said, a flush staining her cheeks. Put that way, it sounded so perverse, so shameful. Watching herself in a mirror making love to another woman . . . It was way outside the usual realm of Rachel's experience. And yet she craved it.

She wanted to see Marie's dark hair against her skin, see her own fair hair against Marie's skin.

'Then we'll watch, together.' Marie tested the temperature of the water, then took Rachel's hand. 'Come on.'

Rachel climbed into the bath beside Marie, who picked up a bar of soap and began lathering Rachel's skin. Then she turned, making Rachel face herself in the mirror, and stood behind her. 'Like this,' she said softly, her fingers caressing Rachel's breasts.

Rachel swallowed as her nipples began to harden again. Watching themselves in the mirror . . . It was something she'd never done with any of her lovers. Ever. But with Marie, she couldn't get enough. She wanted more. She wanted it all.

She watched in the mirror as Marie's hand slipped downwards, rubbing the soap into her skin; automatically, she widened her stance as Marie's hand drifted lower, lower. She closed her eyes for a moment as Marie's hand inserted itself between her legs, and then she opened her eyes again, meeting Marie's dark and sensual look in the mirror.

Marie slid her other hand downwards, and nuzzled Rachel's neck. 'Play with yourself,' she said softly. 'Touch your breasts, like you were doing when I walked into the room.'

Rachel lifted trembling hands towards her breasts, and began to play with her nipples, hesitantly at first, and then with abandon. All the time, Marie was working on her quim, rubbing her clitoris and pushing one finger deep into Rachel's moist channel. Rachel began to shiver, and then to moan, her legs feeling weak; she could feel Marie's pubic mound pressed tight against her buttocks, and it turned her on even more. Just as she was about to come, she saw Marie unhook the shower nozzle, turn it to a fierce jet, and then hold her vulval lips apart, directing the jet of water straight at her clitoris.

She cried out, her internal muscles contracting sharply at the unexpected invasion, and Marie smiled. 'Better?' she asked softly.

'Better.' Rachel was still shaking. 'Time to change places.'

Marie spread her hands. 'If you're sure.'

'I'm sure,' Rachel said huskily. She moved to stand behind Marie, and rested her chin on Marie's shoulder, watching herself soap Marie's body. The Frenchwoman's skin was so soft, so supple. Rachel wasn't sure what turned her on more – touching Marie, or watching herself touch Marie. Just as the Frenchwoman had done to her, Rachel soaped Marie's breasts, teasing the nipples into hardness, then let one hand drift down over her abdomen.

Marie widened her stance, as Rachel had done, and Rachel licked her earlobe. 'Touch yourself,' she said softly. 'I want to watch you touch your breasts. Just like you watched me.'

Marie grinned, and did as she was asked; meanwhile, Rachel slid her hand between her lover's legs, seeking and finding her clitoris. As she began to rub the hard nub of flesh, she pulled Marie back against her, liking the feel of her body pressing close to hers. Marie tipped her head back and continued rubbing her breasts; Rachel felt her lover's quim grow liquid and puffy with the impending approach of orgasm, and smiled.

Just as Marie had done, she picked up the shower nozzle, turning the jet onto its fiercest, and used her ring and index fingers to part Marie's vulval lips. Marie moaned as Rachel let the jet play along her quim, teasing her to a climax: then she shuddered violently. Rachel watched her lover's face in the mirror, seeing Marie bare her teeth in passion; and she smiled as the familiar rosy mottling spread across her lover's skin.

'Better?' she asked softly.

'Better.' Marie twisted round and kissed her, hard. Then she hooked the shower back into its proper position, and began to wash Rachel, soaping her skin and then sluicing the suds from her. Rachel did the same for Marie, and it ended with Marie washing Rachel's hair, massaging her scalp tenderly.

When they were both rinsed clean, Marie switched off the shower, and they stepped out of the bath. They dried each other in turn, and then Rachel wound her hair into another towel, turban-style. Marie smiled at her. 'I would offer to rub body lotion into your skin, but I think we both know what will happen if I do.'

'And you're on duty,' Rachel said, suddenly feeling guilty. 'God, if someone's missed you . . .'

'Don't worry.' Marie stroked her face tenderly. 'I can deal with it.'

Rachel had a sudden flash of insight into exactly how Marie would deal with any problems, and smiled. 'Yes, I see.'

'Well.' Marie led her back into the bedroom, and kissed her lightly on the lips. 'Daniel is waiting for you, downstairs.'

'Right.'

Marie smiled. 'You can ring room service and ask for me, any time.'

'Thank you.' Rachel felt suddenly awkward.

'I believe the phrase is, "have a nice day",' Marie said, a teasing glint in her eyes. 'But if you don't get dressed soon, I think it'll be "have a nice night", instead!'

Rachel chuckled, at ease again. 'Something like that. Take care.'

'You, too.' Marie winked at her, dressed swiftly, and left the room.

THIRTEEN

Rachel dried her hair and dressed swiftly, choosing a midnight blue cotton shirt and another pair of faded denims. She left the room, locking the door behind her, and went downstairs to meet Daniel.

He was sitting in the lounge, waiting for her; he looked up from his newspaper as she walked into the room and smiled at her. He stood up, folding the paper and leaving it on the table. 'Hi. How are you feeling?'

'Fine.' She smiled back at him. 'The coffee and croissants were lovely.'

'Good.'

'Thanks for sending them up. I appreciated it.'

'Any time.'

Rachel decided not to tell him what had happened with Marie. There would be time enough for that, later. The most important thing was to go back to Serendipity, talk to Brian Fletcher, and find out about the cat. Where he'd bought it, if he knew its history, or if he could at least give them the name of the previous owner so that they could trace it back from there.

It was as if Daniel had read her mind. 'Are you ready to go and talk to Brian Fletcher, then?'

She nodded. 'Had we better take the cat with us?'

'Good idea. Then he'll know that we're genuine.' Daniel tipped his head on one side. 'Do you want me to nip up and get it?'

'Thanks.' She handed him the keys; Daniel went upstairs to retrieve the mummy case, and returned with it tucked under his arm.

'Let's go,' he said.

The streets were already crowded with weekend trippers, out to enjoy the sunshine and browse in the shops. Even so, the courtyard where Serendipity was sited was off the main track, and the shop was empty.

The bell clanged as Daniel and Rachel walked into the shop. A man in an ancient tweed jacket with leather patches at the elbow, thinning grey hair and half-moon gold-rimmed glasses was sitting by the cash desk, poring over what looked like an auction catalogue. Daniel walked over to him. 'Excuse me, please. Would you be Brian Fletcher?'

The man looked up, his face suspicious. 'Who wants to know?'

'A potential client. My name's Daniel Sinclair.' Daniel held out one hand.

The dealer took it gingerly, shaking it. 'What can I do for you, Mr Sinclair?'

'A few weeks ago, a friend of ours bought something from your shop. We'd like to know if you have anything else like it – and if you could tell us a little more about the history of it.'

'History of what?'

'This.' Daniel placed the parcel on the desk, and unwrapped the brown paper and bubble wrap to reveal the cat. Neither he nor Rachel mentioned that they already knew something about the cat – and the fact that it was an original rather than a copy. From Brian Fletcher's slightly nervous air, they both knew that it would be wise to take this one slowly.

As soon as the dealer saw it, he grimaced. 'I might have known that that damned thing would turn up again.'

Rachel looked at him, her eyes narrowing slightly. 'What was the problem with it?'

'With that?' The dealer rolled his pale blue eyes and made a sound of distate. 'I was glad to get rid of it. I had to sell it at a loss, in the end, but I can live with that. I just wanted the thing out of here.'

'Why?' Rachel asked.

'Well, you know what they say about mummies. They're cursed, they're bad luck.'

'And the cat brought you bad luck?' Rachel's voice was soft and sympathetic.

He nodded. 'You can say that again. I could never find anything I put in the shop – it always moved from where I knew that I'd put it, only minutes before. I wasted hours and hours looking for things, hoping that I'd find them before the client who'd bought them turned up. I lost a whole box of receipts, the first week I bought the thing, and I've had the taxman on my back about it ever since. Then we had a burst pipe which ruined some of the stock, and we had to rewire part of the shop.' He shrugged. 'Oh, I know that it's probably just coincidence that it all started from when I bought the cat. Burst pipes can happen any time, and in a place as old as this, there's always something that needs doing. But my grand-daughter's superstitious. She's read a lot about Egyptian mummies and what have you. She thought that our bad luck was something to do with the cat, so she persuaded me to sell the thing cheap, to get it out of here.'

'And things have been fine ever since?' Rachel asked.

'Yes. Though it's probably just coincidence.' He laughed shortly. 'I mean, what harm can a bit of painted wood do?'

'Not a lot,' Daniel agreed with a smile.

'Where did you find it?' Rachel asked.

'If you want to know if there's more where this came from, then no. That was the only one, I'm afraid. It came from Egypt. It's a copy made in the last century.'

'That's what I thought,' Rachel lied. 'I've always been interested in Egyptian things, so when my friend came to Lavenham for the weekend and saw it in your display, she bought it for me, as a present. I just wondered if you had anything else.'

'Well, there are a couple of bracelets and a few carved stones – they're over there on the middle shelf of the dresser, if you want to take a look.'

'Thanks. I'll do that.' Rachel wandered over to the display he'd pointed out; Daniel remained by the cash till.

'We'd be interested in tracing the history of the cat,' he said.

Brian Fletcher shrugged. 'Well, I'm sorry, I can't help you there.'

'Look, we're not dealers. All we want to do is know a bit more about the cat, that's all,' Daniel said. 'Where you bought it – and maybe we can talk to the original owners, and trace it back from there.'

He shook his head. 'I don't think I can do that.'

At that moment, Rachel returned with a couple of scarabs. 'I'd like to buy these, please,' she said. 'Who shall I make the cheque payable to?'

'B Fletcher,' the dealer said. Almost as if Rachel's decision to buy had loosened his tongue, he sighed. 'All right. I bought the Egyptian stuff from a country house sale, about ten miles away. All I know about it was that the original owner was an archaeologist. He went to Egypt in the late 1800s to work on a dig, and died insane, some time in the 1930s.' He shrugged. 'The stuff he brought back from Egypt was passed down the family, but they've fallen on hard times – death duties, and all that. These mouldering old piles cost a fortune to maintain, and when you've got to pay taxes on top of it ... Well, it's too much. So they sold a few bits of porcelain and silver, a picture or two, and the Egyptian stuff. I managed to get the Egyptian stuff as a job lot. I've sold some of the scarabs, and the cat, but the rest of it has stayed put.'

'I'd like to talk to the previous owners,' Rachel said. 'They could tell me more about where it came from.'

He shook his head. 'I wouldn't bother, if I were you. They probably wouldn't know. It's from years back, and papers get lost, that kind of thing. You're wasting your time.'

'Please,' Rachel said. 'I can't just put the cat on the shelf and think that it looks nice. I need to know more about it.'

'I don't know.' The dealer frowned. 'It wouldn't be fair to give you the address. They might not want people dropping in on them.'

'Please. We're not going to cause any trouble. All we want to do is find out a bit more about the cat.'

The dealer looked at her for a moment, as if assessing her; finally, he nodded. 'All right, then.' He ripped a piece of paper from a pad, and scribbled an address on it. 'Here. There's no guarantee that they'll talk to you, mind. And mentioning my name won't do any good – they don't even know who I am. Like I said, I bought the stuff at a sale.'

'Thank you very much.' Rachel slipped the piece of paper into her pocket. She handed him her cheque and cheque card, took the paper bag of scarabs, and rewrapped the cat while Brian Fletcher wrote her card number on the back of the cheque.

'Pleasure,' the dealer murmured automatically.

Daniel slipped his arm round Rachel's shoulders as they left the shop. 'So where's this place, then?'

She retrieved the piece of paper. 'Melbury Hall.'

'He said that it was only about ten miles away.'

'Mm. He didn't give me a name, though.'

'He probably didn't know one. Let's go there, anyway.'

Rachel wrinkled her nose. 'You heard what he said. They might not even talk to us.'

'But we have to try,' Daniel said. 'We've come this far. We can't stop, now.'

'OK.' A feeling like ice slid down Rachel's spine. Part of her was scared to find out too much about the cat and its history; part of her knew that, if she was ever to get any peace, she had to know what had really happened.

They went to Daniel's car, and Rachel placed the cat and the bag of scarabs on the back seat. Daniel retrieved the map from his glove-box and studied it for a moment. 'Mm, he's right: it's about ten miles away, if we use the back roads.'

'Do you want me to navigate?' Rachel asked.

He shook his head. 'No, it's pretty easy. I think it'll be signposted, when we're out of Lavenham.'

'All right. If you're sure.'

'Mm. But you can sort the music out, if you like.'

'OK.' Rachel fiddled with the radio, tuning it in to Radio Three; a Mozart piano sonata was playing, and she lapsed into silence, concentrating on the music and trying to calm herself down. Her heart was racing, as though she were on the edge of an important discovery; she held her breath, trying to slow her pulse down.

Eventually, Daniel glanced at her. 'What's the matter?' he asked softly.

She shook her head. 'Nothing.'

'Come on, Rachel. I can see it in your eyes. You're brooding about something.'

'I was just thinking about what the dealer said. You know, about the cat being bad luck.'

Daniel laughed shortly. 'He also said that it was probably coincidence. It's the fact that everyone thinks about Egyptian curses that made him get rid of it. It's like medieval seers – say, if someone in the village stole a goose, the original owner would go to the village wise woman for advice. The wise woman would look in her glass, and say that she knew who it was; and, nine times out of ten, the rumour would go round the village that if the goose wasn't returned, the wise woman would put a spell on the thief. The threat was enough to make the thief return the goods. It wasn't the fact that the wise woman had seen who it was – she probably hadn't – but her reputation was enough to do the trick. It's the same with voodoo, witch doctors, and Egyptian curses. Belief's the most important thing.'

'I suppose so.' Rachel sighed. She'd said it enough times, herself, about Egyptian curses: although there were still so many unexplained stories about the early archaeologists and their experiences. Not to mention her own. 'Though so many weird things have happened to me since Carrie gave me the cat, it makes me wonder if there is something in it.'

'Bad things?' Daniel questioned.

'Apart from my flat being wrecked, and David carpeting me—'

'He wasn't carpeting you, exactly,' Daniel interrupted. 'He was concerned about you. There's a difference.'

'I know. It's just . . .' She winced. 'I don't know how to explain this, Daniel, but I'm not behaving like me. I'm doing things that I would normally never do.'

'Such as?'

'Well, sleeping with you within a couple of hours of meeting you, for one thing.'

He smiled. 'And very enjoyable it was, too.'

'But it's not like me, Daniel. And the things that have happened, since . . . Like the dreams of me with another woman.'

'Dreams?' Daniel enquired silkily.

Rachel flushed. 'I told you about one of them, the one I had in the shower.'

He nodded. 'I remember.' He shrugged. 'Think of it as broadening your horizons.' Then his brain registered what she'd said. '*One* of them. You've had more?'

'Yes.'

'When?'

'Last night.'

'Last night?'

'Well, this morning,' Rachel amended. 'It was the same woman I saw, last time. We were in a bedroom. I think it might have been her bedroom, or it might have been mine – I'm not sure. I was very confused, in the dream.'

'And you ended up making love with her.'

She nodded. 'And when I woke up, I was masturbating.' She

swallowed. 'That's not all. There was a woman sitting on the bed next to me.'

'A real woman,' he said softly. 'Not a dream.'

'Not a dream,' she confirmed. 'She told me that her name is Marie. She's French, and she works in the hotel. She brought up the coffee and croissants for me.'

'And you woke up to find yourself masturbating, with her sitting next to you on the bed.'

'Yes.'

Daniel licked his lips. 'Was she . . . Did she touch you?'

'Yes,' Rachel said.

'How?'

'She put on hand on my abdomen. That's what woke me up.'

'Then what happened?'

'She stopped me, before I could say anything.'

'How?'

'She kissed me.' A pulse began to beat in Rachel's quim at the memory. 'I was still so turned on from my dream, that I kissed her back.'

'And then what happened?'

She started to kiss her way down my body. She sucked my nipples, and stroked my skin.' Rachel closed her eyes, her voice becoming husky as she recalled what had happened. 'She cupped my delta in her hand, her fingers pushing against me. I didn't care that she was fully clothed and I was naked – I needed her to touch me. I wriggled underneath her, and tipped my pelvis up, spreading my legs for her.' She swallowed. 'And then I begged her to do it to me. I wanted to come, Daniel; I was so turned on, so near the edge. I needed someone to touch me properly.

'Then she moved down the bed, rubbing her cheeks against my thighs. I knew then that she was going to lick me, and I wanted it so badly. She played with my clitoris, using her lips and her tongue, then she put one finger inside me.' She licked her suddenly dry lips. 'It was good. And then she pushed a finger in my anus. She worked my quim and my arse at the same time; and I worked on my breasts. My nipples were so hard, they hurt. And then I came. It was so good, so strong; then she moved up the bed and kissed me. That's when she told me her name.'

'Marie,' Daniel said softly.

Rachel nodded. 'Marie Duval. She'd already noticed you, downstairs. She said you were beautiful. I think she wanted you, too, Daniel: but seeing me there in the middle of the bed, the covers pushed back and my hand between my legs, was too much for her.

'Then she undressed. It was more of a strip-tease, really, calculated to turn me on again. She was amazing. Just watching her strip made me wet again. She came back to join me on the bed, and we drank the coffee out of the same cup, and ate the croissants. We fed each other; I know it sounds childish, but it was really erotic. It gave me all sorts of ideas. I smeared jam over her nipples, so I could lick it off again. We ended up rubbing jam into each other and sucking it off: then I crumbled a croissant down her stomach, and ate it off her. Then I took her in the same way that she'd taken me, earlier.' Rachel swallowed. 'I couldn't get enough of her, Daniel. She felt so good, she tasted so good.

'Then we had a shower together. She stood behind me and made me rub my breasts, while she slid her hands between my legs. We watched everything in the mirror. She made me come again, rubbing my clitoris until I was moaning and then directing the spray from the shower nozzle on it. I came so hard, it was untrue. Then I did the same for her, standing behind her and working her quim while she touched her breasts, using the shower nozzle on her so that she came. Then she washed me, and I washed her, and we dried each other. Then she dressed.

'She told me that you would be waiting for me downstairs. And she said that I could ring room service and ask for her, any time.'

Daniel swallowed. 'I'm going to have to stop the car, Rachel.'

'Pardon?'

'I'm going to have to stop the car,' he repeated.

'Why?'

'Well, you can't tell me something like this, and expect me to drive.'

She opened her eyes and looked at him. There was a dark flush across his cheekbones, and his eyes were wide and glittering. She looked down, to see the tell-tale bulge at his groin, and smiled. 'So it turns you on, then? The idea of me and another woman making love?'

'Oh, Christ.' Daniel spied a gateway ahead, and put his foot on the accelerator. He turned sharply into the gateway, then drove along the bumpy track into a copse. He put the handbrake on, then switched off the ignition. Then he turned to Rachel, his eyes glittering. 'Get out of the car.'

Her eyes widened. 'What, here?'

'Yes.'

'But, Daniel, it's private property.'

'I don't care,' he said simply. 'Besides, I don't think anyone's going to come and interrupt us, do you?'

'Daniel—'

'Get out of the car, Rachel,' he repeated softly. The tone of his voice made it more of a request than a command; Rachel found herself complying. Daniel, too, left the car. He unlocked the boot, taking a rug from the back.

Rachel's lips quirked. 'Daniel, are you telling me that you planned all this?'

'No. I suppose it's habit; I've always carried a rug in the car. My parents live in the country, so a torch and a rug and a shovel are usually kept in the boot of their car.'

'You live in London,' she reminded him.

'Exactly. Like I said, it's habit: though I think it's going to come in very useful today, don't you?'

She raked a hand through her hair. 'Daniel . . .'

'Rachel, I want you,' he said. 'I want you so badly, it hurts. I want to be inside you, sink into your warm sweet depths. And I want to do it right now.' He spread the rug on the ground, beneath the trees. 'Come here,' he said softly.

'We're supposed to be going to Melbury Hall,' she reminded him.

'I don't care. I want you, Rachel. I want to make love with you. Now.' He pulled her into his arms, sliding his hands down her back and stroking her buttocks. Rachel couldn't help responding, sliding her hands round his neck as he lowered his mouth to hers.

His kiss was gentle, coaxing rather than demanding; the pressure of his lips was warm and soft and sweet. She made no protest when Daniel tugged her shirt free of the waistband of her jeans, burrowing under the soft material and stroking her back and her midriff. She shivered as he undid the button of her jeans and slid the fly downwards, and arched against him.

Then she let her hands drift down over his shoulders, onto his chest, and began to unbutton his shirt. She pulled his shirt from his jeans, and pushed the soft cotton from his shoulders, smoothing her fingertips across the light covering of hair on his chest. Daniel gave a small moan of pleasure, and removed her shirt, drawing his finger through the deep vee of her cleavage and smiling when she gave a sharp intake of breath and tipped her head back. She was already aroused, her dark nipples prominent through the lace of her bra; he smiled again, and finished removing her jeans, pushing the faded denims over her hips.

Daniel helped her remove his own jeans, then made short work of the rest of their underwear; when they were both naked, he drew her down onto the blanket. The slightly rough surface of the material tickled her skin, but she didn't care. They way Daniel was touching her was enough to make her forget everything else.

'Is this what Marie did with you?' he asked softly, nuzzling her neck and stroking her midriff.

'Mm.' She arched against him, and his mouth tracked downwards until he reached her nipples. He took one hard peak of flesh into her mouth, sucking gently on it. At her small gasp of pleasure, he began sucking harder, teasing its twin between his thumb and forefinger, pulling it gently and then harder as he felt her breathing grow ragged.

She pushed her pelvis up towards him, and he chuckled. 'Oh, Rachel. You're irresistible, do you know that?' He continued kissing his way down her body, and made her giggle by licking round her navel, then he pulled back slightly. 'Show me,' he said huskily. 'Show me how you were with Marie. You said that you spread your legs for her.'

Rachel lifted her legs, exposing herself fully to him. He gave a sharp intake of breath. 'Christ, Rachel, you're so beautiful.' Her sex was already growing liquid and puffy; he drew one finger experimentally down the musky slit, testing her arousal. She groaned, tipping her head back and arching her pelvis towards him again.

'And this is what Marie did next?' he continued huskily, sliding one finger deep into her vagina.

'Yes,' Rachel admitted.

'And this?' He dipped his head and drew his tongue along her quim, teasing her clitoris from its hood and sucking it gently.

Rachel's breath became uneven. 'Yes,' she said.

'And then this . . .' Daniel wetted the little finger of his other hand, and drew it over her perineum, pressing against the rosy puckered hole of her anus.

'Oh,' Rachel moaned as he pushed gently at her forbidden portal; her flesh gave way beneath his invading finger, and he began to piston his fingers in and out of her, in perfect time. She reached up to cup her breasts, pulling at her nipples. Had it not been that Daniel's fingers were longer and thicker, she could have imagined herself back in the hotel room with Marie.

Her climax took her by surprise; she cried out, and her internal muscles contracted sharply round his fingers. Daniel waited until the aftershocks of her orgasm had died away, then removed his fingers and shifted up so that he could kiss her again. She could taste herself on him, and she kissed him fiercely. 'Daniel . . .'

He tilted his hips, and she could feel his hard erection pressing against her. He shifted again, and rolled her over onto her front. She frowned in surprise. Just what did he have in mind? He guided her onto her hands and knees, and knelt behind her. 'This is what I want,' he said softly, fitting the tip of his cock to the entrance of her sex. Then, slowly, oh, so very slowly, he eased himself inside. 'God, Rachel, you're so hot and wet,' he murmured huskily. 'It nearly makes me come, just pushing into you and feeling your beautiful cunt wrapping round me.' He began to move, with small rocking strokes.

He reached round to her breasts, stroking them with one hand, and squeezed her buttocks with his other hand, moulding the soft globes of flesh. Then Rachel felt his finger slide down the crease of her buttocks, pressing against her anus again. She was still stretched from where he'd touched her before, and his finger slid easily into her. He began to move his finger back and forth, quickening his rhythm to match.

Rachel closed her eyes in bliss; and suddenly the rich blue summer sky and the lush green grass were replaced by something hot and arid. She was still on her hands, in the desert. The man with the beautiful aqua grey eyes was kneeling in front of her, his cock hard and erect, and behind her was another man, his cock filling her to the hilt and his finger inserted rudely into her anus.

As the body behind her lowered itself slightly to rub against hers, she smiled. It wasn't a man behind her at all – it was her other lover, wearing her favoured tie-on harness and the large dildo. Their bodies were moving in perfect synchronization; as one lover thrust deep into her, the man with beautiful eyes pulled back; and as the woman penetrating her withdrew, so he pushed forward, his cock pushing as deeply into her mouth as she could allow it.

All the time, the sun beat down on their naked bodies; she could feel the warm air moving against her, rousing her passion. They were skating closer and closer to the edge. If they were discovered like this, it would be the end for all of them – she knew that. And yet they couldn't help themselves. These splintering moments of pleasure were more important to the three of them than anything else. They needed this, the release that only their bodies could give them.

She began to move with them, faster and faster, harder and harder, until at last, she came. She heard the lover behind her cry out as she reached a climax; and her internal muscles were convulsing sharply around the thick hard dildo and the penetrating finger. And then she felt the warm salty liquid flow from her lover's cock into her mouth . . .

Then Rachel was aware of being in an English field again, stretched out on Daniel's picnic rug and curled into his body. He stroked her face. 'Ah, Rachel. I'm sorry about that.'

'Sh, it's all right.' She reached up to trace the curve of his lip with her forefinger.

'Still, you were right. We ought to be going to Melbury.' Gently, he disentangled himself from her, standing up; then he helped her to her feet. He dressed her; Rachel submitted to his ministrations, secretly touched by the cherishing gesture.

When he'd finished dressing her, he raked his fingers through her hair. 'I think you're going to need a comb,' he said with a grin. 'You look like you've been rolling in a haystack.'

'On a picnic rug, actually,' she answered, laughing.

He dressed swiftly, completely unselfconscious. When he'd

finished, he bundled up the rug and threw it in the boot of the car, then opened the passenger door for Rachel. He slid into the driver's side, and turned the car round, driving back onto the main road. Then they continued towards the village of Melbury.

Melbury Hall turned out to be a square, eighteenth-century building in what had once been honey-coloured stone, but it had grown darker over the years. The narrow sash windows looked shabby, in need of cleaning as well as painting, and the wooden front door could have done with rubbing down and being given a coat of protective resin.

The front garden was laid mainly to lawn. In more prosperous times, Rachel imagined, it had probably been landscaped properly, with shrubs and trees and flowers in neatly weeded borders. There was a long gravel drive and a small gravelled area to the front of a house, where a battered and elderly mini stood. Daniel parked next to it.

'I almost wish that we'd phoned, first,' Rachel said. 'Do you think that anyone's actually at home?'

'There's only one way to find out,' Daniel replied. 'And we'd better take the cat with us.'

'Yes.'

They both got out of the car and went up to the front door. There was an old-fashioned bell pull at the side of the door, rather than a push-button buzzer; Daniel pulled it hard, and they heard a faint jangling. They waited a few minutes; when there was no answer, Daniel pulled the bell again.

At last, they heard an irritable, 'All right, all right, I'm coming,' and the door was flung open to reveal a woman whom Rachel guessed was about her own age. She had cropped dark hair, very blue eyes, and a scowl. 'Yes?' she said, looking at them both.

'Would this be Melbury Hall?' Rachel asked diffidently.

'What of it?' The woman was obviously not the housekeeper or domestic help, because her accent was cut-glass; judging from her sloaney dress of tailored trousers, loafers, sweater and pearls, Rachel guessed that the woman was part of the family.

'Er, I'm Rachel Meaden, and this is Daniel Sinclair. We wondered if we could talk to you about your recent sale,' Rachel said.

The woman rolled her eyes. 'Look, there isn't anything else to sell. I can tell you that, now. And I don't want Gran upset by dealers.'

'We're not dealers,' Daniel said. 'And we don't want to upset anyone. A friend bought the cat mummy case for us, and we're trying to find out about its history. The dealer she bought it from told us that he bought it from you, so we wondered if you could help.'

'I certainly can't. I don't know anything about the thing, and I won't have you bothering Gran. The last thing she needs is people poking around and asking questions.'

'Like I said, we don't want to bother anyone,' Daniel said. 'All we want to do is know a bit more about where the mummy case came from.'

'Egypt,' the young woman said rudely. 'Where do you think?'

Daniel was about to make a sharp comment of his own, but Rachel forestalled him, pulling his arm. 'Daniel, leave it. Obviously these people are too busy to talk to us. We'll have to think of some other way of finding out about the cat.'

'Yes. Starting with the local press,' Daniel said.

'Jesus Christ, give me strength,' the woman burst out. 'You're not wanted here. Can't you take a hint?'

'Imogen, who is it?' a voice quavered from the other end of the hall.

'No-one, Gran. Just a couple of people who are going.'

An elderly woman came to the doorway, saw Rachel, and gave a gasp of fright. 'You're back!'

Rachel and Daniel looked at each other in surprise. 'I've never been here before,' Rachel said quietly.

The old woman's face grew white as she saw the cat under Rachel's arm. 'I knew it. I knew that you couldn't rest, even after all this time. I knew that you'd be back, some time.'

'I'm sorry. I really haven't been here before – I haven't even been to Suffolk, let alone this part of it.' Rachel shook her head. 'Look, I'm sorry for bothering you. I'll go, now.'

'You'd better. You've done enough damage,' Imogen said sharply, taking her grandmother's arm.

'No, Imogen. This is something that happened a long, long time before you were born. I always knew that the day of reckoning would come. She's here because of the cat. I have to talk to her.'

Rachel and Daniel looked at each other with a mixture of surprise and dismay. Just what the hell was going on?

'Look, I really don't want to cause any—' Rachel began.

'No, come in.' The old lady beckoned Rachel and Daniel inside. 'Imogen, be a dear and make a pot of tea, will you? There's some cake in the cupboard.'

Imogen frowned, but stomped off to do her grandmother's bidding. The old lady led Rachel and Daniel through to a sitting room.

'I'm afraid that Melbury's terribly shabby now,' she said apologetically. 'That's one of the reasons why we held the sale. After my father died, there was barely enough to cover the death duties. The place has gone to seed a bit, since then. It's such a monster to keep up. We don't use most of the rooms, because it costs too much to heat.'

Rachel's eyes filled with sympathy. 'I'm so sorry.' She held out her hand. 'I'm Rachel Meaden, and this is Daniel Sinclair.'

'Augusta Morgan,' the old woman said, taking Rachel's hand. Her skin felt like thin dry paper against Rachel's fingertips. 'Imogen's my grand-daughter. Her mother bolted, and left me to bring up the child. I'm the only real family she has, and I'm afraid that she's rather protective about me.'

'That's understandable,' Rachel said.

'Even an old woman like me doesn't always need molly-coddling,' Augusta said, though her tone was wry rather than sharp. Rachel was pleased to note that she had recovered her colour.

'I really haven't been here before,' Rachel said. 'Not to Lavenham, not to Melbury – nowhere in Suffolk, to be honest.'

'Suffolk isn't on the way to anywhere, except Norfolk,' Augusta said, her lips quirking. 'There's no reason for you to come here. But you gave me a shock, because you look so much like *her*.'

'Who?' Rachel asked. 'You said that it was something to do with the cat, and that was why I was here – did you overhear me talking to your grand-daughter?'

Augusta shook her head. 'The minute I saw you, I knew why you were here. It couldn't have been anything else.'

FOURTEEN

'You knew?' Rachel asked.

Augusta nodded. 'There could only be one reason why you're here. The cat.'

'Where did it come from?' Rachel asked. 'I know that it was from Egypt, and I know that it isn't a copy.'

'No, it's certainly not that. I believe the fool dealer who bought the stuff thought that it was a Victorian facsimile. And the idiot who organized the sale thought the same, so he sold it off at a knock-down price.'

'Why didn't you offer it to one of the museums, instead? The British Museum, the Fitzwilliam – or even Cairo?' Rachel asked. 'They might have given you more money for it.'

'I was ill at the time. Imogen did her best, but she wasn't to know. She didn't know just how important the cat is.'

Imogen, as if on cue, stalked into the sitting room carrying a silver tray with a Sèvres china tea-pot, matching cream jug and sugar bowl, plus tea-cups, saucers and plates. Daniel stood up immediately and brought a low occasional table over to Augusta's side. 'Are you really sure that you're up to this?' he asked Augusta. 'Believe me, we don't want to cause any trouble.'

'I'm sure,' Augusta said softly. 'And I'm ready to talk now. I've kept it quiet for so long.'

'You don't have to tell them anything, Gran, if you don't want to,' Imogen interrupted.

'I know.' Augusta's eyes turned faintly steely. 'But it's time that the truth was out.'

'Hm.' Imogen handed round the cups of tea as Augusta poured them; both Daniel and Rachel refused sugar, but accepted milk.

Rachel tasted the tea, and smiled with pleasure. 'Russian Caravan, isn't it?'

Imogen softened a fraction. 'Yes. It's Gran's favourite tea.'

There was also a slightly dry seed-cake; Daniel's eyes widened. 'I haven't seen this since I was a child.'

'It was one of my favourites when I was in India,' Augusta informed him. 'That was after Egypt, of course.'

'You lived in Egypt?' Rachel asked.

Augusta shook her head. 'No, no. I was born here in 1913. I was in India after I married. Anyway, the cat – that was my father's. He found it on a dig, and he kept it – he couldn't bear to put it with the rest of the things his team found. He was an archaeologist, and he worked on a dig in Egypt in the late 1890s and early 1900s.' Her face grew wistful. 'I didn't find out the whole story until after he died. He always hated cats – he refused to have them in the house, ever. He wouldn't have harmed one, of course. He never drowned kittens, or anything barbaric like that – he was far too kind a man to do that sort of thing. But he just couldn't bear the thought of cats in the house. If one crept in, he'd make me take it to a neighbour or a friend's house. He didn't care where I took it, as long as it was away from him.

'Just before he died, he kept talking about cats. He kept saying that he could smell one in the house and asking me to take it out. He said that one was sitting there and watching him, though of course none of us could see anything.'

Rachel shivered, suddenly remembering what the dealer had said: that the archaeologist had died, insane. Or had he really been haunted by something that no-one else could see? 'That's creepy.'

'At the time, I thought that it was just an old man's mind wandering.' Imogen was sitting next to Augusta on the floor; Augusta ruffled her hair affectionately. 'You know how old people are. Always wandering off at a tangent.'

Imogen smiled at her grandmother. 'You know I never say that about you, Gran.'

'You think it, though. Just as I did, about my father.' Augusta smiled back at her. 'Well, after my father died – after my mother had died, for that matter – I was going through their papers. I found a locked trunk. I was younger, then, more curious, so I had the groom break the lock. It was full of papers about his time in Egypt, plus the mummy case and a few odds and ends. Shabti figures, jewellery, scarab seals. He shouldn't have taken them, I know, but I suppose it was either that or leave them to be looted.

'Anyway, I thought maybe I could make a book about it, when I sifted through them. His sketchbooks and journals were all very neat, very precise: that's the kind of man my father was. I read them, and that's when I found out what had really happened.' She closed her eyes. 'It seems that a young girl in the village had been hanging round the archaeologists. Her father worked on the dig, and she wanted to help. Pretty young thing, she was, and bright. My father befriended her. She helped him discover a few things, including the cat mummy case.' She looked at Rachel. 'Her face was identical to yours. Obviously, she had dark hair and darker skin and dark eyes, not blue eyes like yours, but she really was lovely. My father sketched her again and again. Her face is all over his sketchbooks, among the drawings of wall-paintings and arrangements of tombs.

'He fell in love with her. The inevitable happened, and she became pregnant. She told my father, thinking that he would marry her.' Augusta bit her lip. 'That's when he told her that he was already married, to my mother. My mother had been ill, so she hadn't gone to Egypt with him. She'd lost a child, I think, and my father longed for a child of his own. When the Egyptian girl told him that she was carrying his child, he wanted to do something for her, but there was nothing that he could do. He couldn't betray my mother and divorce her – he had no grounds – and he couldn't have both of them. His first duty was to my mother, and he was a man who took duty seriously.'

'Like most Victorians,' Daniel said quietly. 'He was in an impossible position.'

'Exactly.'

'What happened to the girl?' Rachel asked.

Augusta winced. 'It was a terrible business. She killed herself. She couldn't bear the shame. Her family knew what had happened, though, and they cursed my father in the name of the goddess Bast.'

'The cat-headed goddess,' Rachel said softly.

Augusta nodded. 'You know about Egyptian things, then.' It was a statement, not a question: as if the old lady wasn't at all surprised.

'For years, ever since I was a tiny child, I was fascinated by Egypt.' Rachel shrugged. 'There was no reason. Nobody I knew had ever been there. And the cat . . .'

'Yes, the cat. I think that's what they used for the curse,' Augusta said quietly. 'You know the rumours about Egyptian curses. Look what happened to Howard Carter.'

'Gran, that's all stuff and nonsense. The curse of the mummy's tomb – it's all so Hollywood,' Imogen interrupted.

Augusta ignored her. 'Even so, my father felt bad about what had happened. He never really got over it. I knew that something had happened in Egypt, but my parents never talked about it. My father never spoke of his time there. And then, after his death, when I found the trunk ... His diaries were in there, too, saying how he regretted what had happened and he wished that there was something he could do.' Augusta smiled ruefully. 'Of course, there was nothing he could have done.' She looked at Rachel. 'The cat came from the tomb in Bubastis where my father first met the girl. She helped him to find it. According to him, it was from the twenty-second dynasty.'

'That's what Kate said,' Daniel said.

'Who's Kate?' Augusta queried.

'A colleague of mine at the university. She's an Egyptologist.'

'She's seen the cat?' Excitement flickered in Augusta's eyes. 'Did she say what the curse was? My father couldn't decipher it.'

Daniel nodded. 'She said that it was a general curse in the name of Bast, on the head of anyone who hurt her or the family she was protecting.'

'That figures,' Augusta said. 'We hurt their family. And we were cursed for it.'

'Gran, that's superstition,' Imogen said.

'Even so, after that, my family had bad luck. My father, William, was the second son; he wasn't brought up to inherit or run Melbury. He was encouraged to do what he wanted to do – so he became an archaeologist, a scholar. Then my grandfather died, and my father was asked to come home, to help sort out family matters. His elder brother, James, inherited Melbury, but he was killed during the Great War, which meant that my father had to look after Melbury. He would have been happier pottering around at a dig, finding pieces of the past; but he knew his duty. He did what was expected of him.' She shrugged. 'He was never happy. He always wanted a son, to carry on the line and relieve him of the burden of Melbury. My mother miscarried seven times before she had me.'

'And you did just as good a job of looking after Melbury as any man could have done,' Imogen said hotly. 'Better.'

'No-one's disputing that, little one,' Augusta said, ruffling her hair. 'Anyway, my father never really forgot Egypt, even though he never talked about it. His heart was there. He lost a lot of money on stocks and shares, in the Wall Street Crash, and this house eats money.' She pulled a wry face. 'Just like all the others of its type. My father fell into ill health, after that. Worry and regret did for him, in the end. My husband died in the Second World War, and I reverted back to the family name, running Melbury like the other Morgans before me. I never met anyone who could take Malcolm's place, but at least I had Margaret – Imogen's mother – with me.'

'I'm sorry,' Rachel said quietly.

'No-one could have helped. Just circumstances,' Augusta said, matter-of-factly. 'Would you like to see his notebooks?'

Rachel's eyes gleamed. 'We'd love to,' she said warmly. She looked at Imogen. 'If we're not intruding?'

'I think that you should see them.' Augusta was about to haul herself to her feet, but Imogen forestalled her.

'Sit down, Gran. I know where they are.' She threw a look at Daniel and Rachel, which both interpreted correctly as *just hurry up, and leave Gran alone*. But the chance to learn more about the cat was too tempting. They stayed put.

'She's a good girl, Imogen,' Augusta said. 'Hot-headed, like her father, but she means well.'

Daniel was embarrassed. 'I . . .'

'Don't take her rudeness to heart,' Augusta advised. 'It isn't personal. She doesn't like to see me upset – and she thinks that talking about my father upsets me.' She smiled. 'It doesn't, really. Not now. Though when I first read his diaries, it made me cry. I hated him for what he'd done to that Egyptian girl – and for how he'd betrayed my mother. But she stood by him; and, once he was back in England, he did his best by her. That's all that matters, now. He did his best to make amends.'

Imogen returned with an armful of notebooks, all filled with tiny neat handwriting in sepia ink. She handed them to Augusta, who flipped rapidly through them, then eventually found what she was looking for. She passed the open book to Rachel, who looked at the pages, and blanched. The face of the girl sketched on the pages was identical to her own.

Daniel's eyes widened as she passed the book to him. 'My God. Rachel, if I didn't know better, I'd swear that this was you.'

'It's uncanny,' Rachel said.

'Would you like to borrow the books and read them properly?' Augusta offered.

'May we?' Rachel asked.

'Hang on. We don't know these people from Adam,' Imogen

interrupted. 'How do we know that we'll ever see the books again?'

'That's true, but I promise you that we'll take good care of them, and we'll return them safely,' Daniel said. He fished in his wallet and handed her a card. 'If you need to contact me at work, that's my direct line.'

'Doctor Daniel Sinclair, history department,' Imogen read.

'I lecture at the University of London,' Daniel said. 'I have my ID card with me, if you'd like to see it. You can see from the photograph that I'm who I say I am.'

It was enough to quell Imogen's doubts. She nodded. 'All right, but we'd like them back within a week, please.'

'Of course,' Daniel said. 'That gives us enough time to photocopy them so that we can study them in more depth and make notes.' He smiled at Augusta. 'Thank you very much. It's very kind of you.'

'It's the least that I can do,' Augusta said.

'Look, we've taken enough of your time. We'll leave you in peace – but thank you.' Rachel picked up half of the books, and Daniel picked up the other half. 'Thank you very much, Mrs Morgan.'

'Augusta,' was the immediate response. 'Like I said, it's the least I can do. You look like the Egyptian girl, and you bought the cat: so I think that I owe you the answers.'

Rachel was quiet on the way back to the hotel, and refused Daniel's suggestion that they should go out for a walk, wander round the rest of the town. 'I'd really rather not.'

'Do you want to go straight back to London?'

'You've already paid for the room.'

'That doesn't matter.' He sat down on the bed next to her. 'What do you want to do?'

'To be honest – I know it sounds silly, but I don't want to leave these notebooks on their own with the cat.'

'Right.'

She saw the scepticism in his eyes, and winced. 'Look, remember what happened to my flat, that time? I can't let that happen to Augusta's father's notebooks, can I?'

'No.'

'I don't want to lug the books around with us, or the cat; so I think the only solution is that I should stay with them both.'

'Here,' he said softly. His lips twitched. 'What you really want to do is to sit down and read those notebooks, isn't it?'

'Yes,' Rachel admitted.

'Then that's what we'll do. I'll go out and get some paper, so we can start making notes when we find something about the cat, or about the Egyptian girl.'

She smiled at him. 'Daniel. I do appreciate this.'

'Hey, any time.' He smiled at her, and left the room. Rachel shifted so that she was lying face down on the bed, propping herself up on her elbows and swinging her legs behind her. It had been her favourite studying position when she'd been a student, and she was surprised and amused at how easily she could slip back into it.

By the time that Daniel returned with two pads of paper and a supply of pens and pencils, Rachel was engrossed in one of the notebooks; without saying a word, he placed a pen and pad before her, sprawled on the bed next to her, and picked out another of the notebooks. He began to read, occasionally pausing to take notes; they worked solidly, in silence, until Daniel stretched, feeling the muscles in his back protest at the length of time he'd spent in one position, working.

'I need a shower,' he said, stroking Rachel's hair. 'Care to join me?'

She rolled over onto her back. 'Maybe later.'

'OK.' He paused. 'This not wanting to leave the cat and the books alone together – does that include having dinner in the restaurant, tonight?'

She bit her lip. 'I know it's crazy, but – yes.'

'All right. How about I order us something nice from room service? Champagne, smoked salmon canapés, that sort of thing?'

'Mm. That sounds good. Thanks.' To her surprise, Rachel found that she was hungry.

He smiled at her. 'Let me have my shower, and then I'll call room service.'

While Daniel showered, Rachel continued to read the notebooks. He returned, his hair still wet and smelling faintly of lemons, and sat on the bed next to her while he rang room service and ordered champagne and a trayful of delicacies. Then he swung round to lie beside her, sliding his arm round her and resting his chin on her shoulder. 'So how's it going?'

'Well, I'm only at the early stages. I haven't found out anything about the cat, at the moment – just that William's working in Bubastis and how excited he is at finding some of the tombs.' She shrugged. 'I imagine it'll be another couple of notebooks before I get to the cat. But I want to do this properly, not just skip to the bit I know is about the cat. I might miss something.'

'Very true.' Daniel nuzzled her earlobe, and she smiled, closing the notebook and rolling over onto her back.

'Daniel.'

'Mm.' He lowered his face to rub his nose against hers, then kissed her gently. 'Funny, I wasn't expecting to find anything like this. I was expecting the dealer to give us the name of another dealer, perhaps, and we'd spend the whole weekend on a wild goose-chase – not that we'd end up with a treasure-trove like this.'

'Me, too.' Rachel looked at him, her eyes clear. 'It's funny that Hazel didn't pick up anything about the girl in Egypt.'

'You're not a reincarnation of her,' Daniel pointed out. 'The fact that you look like her – well, it's said that everyone has a double. It doesn't necessarily have to be someone from the same culture, or even the same era.'

'So why am I picking up what happened to her? Assuming that the man with the eyes like yours is Augusta's father?'

'I don't know,' Daniel said. 'Sympathetic vibes, maybe?'

'Maybe.' Rachel was thoughtful. 'I wish now that I'd asked Augusta to see a picture of her father. Just to see if he was the man I keep seeing.'

'Dare you brave Imogen, tomorrow?'

She chuckled. 'No. Maybe next week, when we return the notebooks.'

'Rather you than me. Actually, she's more likely to talk to you than to me. I get the impression that she doesn't like men very much.'

'And what are you insinuating?' The teasing note in Rachel's voice took the sting from her words.

'Nothing. Just that she's more likely to talk to you than to me, because you're not male.'

'Even though it was seeing me that made her grandmother nearly faint?'

'Mm, you have a point.' Daniel lowered his head again,

drawing a trail of tiny kisses across her face until he reached her lips. 'Talking of faint . . . I'm hungry.'

'Maybe we should have had lunch.'

'I don't mean just for food.' His eyes glittered. 'For you.'

'Indeed.'

'And I think that we should move these books over to the dressing table so they don't get spoiled by food – or anything else,' he added.

She grinned. 'What do you have in mind, Dr Sinclair? And talking of which, you didn't tell me that you were a doctor.'

'You didn't ask.'

'That's not fair.'

He chuckled, sitting up again and gathering the books together. 'All right. I didn't want to put you off and make you think that I was a stuffy academic.'

'Now that,' Rachel said as he took the notebooks over to the dressing table, 'is the last phrase I'd use to describe you.'

'So how would you describe me, then?'

She grinned. 'That'd be telling.'

'I'm asking.' He rejoined her on the bed, putting his arms round her waist and kissing her. 'Tell me.'

'OK.' Her lips quirked. 'You're a tall, dark and handsome lecturer, with incredible eyes, a gorgeous bum, and an acceptable performer in bed.'

'Terribly clichéd. Just as well you're not running an ad campaign on me, hm?'

'I wouldn't want to advertise you,' Rachel said, sliding her hands round his neck.

'Because you want to keep me to yourself?'

'Something like that. Though I could be persuaded to share you, in the right circumstances.'

'The right circumstances,' he repeated softly. 'And what would those be?'

'I'll know what they are, when they happen,' Rachel said.

'Indeed.' He tugged her shirt from the waistband of her jeans, smoothing his hands over her back. 'Well, we'll have to wait and see, won't we?' He kissed her again, lightly at first, and then deepening the kiss as she opened her mouth, responding to him. He undid the buttons of her shirt, sliding his fingers under the edge of the cups of her bra to release her breasts from their constriction, while keeping the bra in place. 'Oh, Rachel. I can't resist you,' he said huskily, nuzzling the side of her neck.

She arched her back, tipping her head back and closing her eyes; Daniel began to nibble the sensitive spot at the side of her neck, cupping her breasts at the same time and smiling to himself as her nipples hardened beneath his touch. He bent his head, the trail of kisses moving lower; as she pushed against him, he took one nipple into his mouth, sucking hard and then releasing her, blowing gently on her wet flesh to increase the sensations.

Rachel moaned, and Daniel worked on her other breast, teasing the nipple with his lips and his tongue, nipping playfully and then drawing fiercely on the hard peak of flesh, making her cry out with pleasure.

At that precise moment, there was a rap on the door. 'Room service.'

'Shit,' Daniel said, sitting up. 'That's incredibly bad timing.' Rachel pulled the open front of her shirt together. 'Come in,' Daniel called.

The door opened, and Marie walked in. 'Room service, with your order, sir,' she said with a smile.

Rachel's eyes widened. Circumstances . . . She smiled. 'Hello, Marie.'

'Hello, Rachel.' The waitress smiled back. 'Did you have a nice day?'

'Interesting,' Rachel said. 'How was yours?'

'Busy. But this is my last call, today.'

Rachel smiled. 'Why don't you stay and have a drink with us, then?'

Daniel looked at his lover, and suddenly remembered what she'd told him earlier. This was the Marie she'd mentioned. The Marie who'd made love to her, on this very bed. He looked appraisingly at Marie; Rachel had told him very little about the Frenchwoman. Yet she was beautiful: olive-toned skin, dark hair which gleamed in the light, dark intense eyes, and a beautiful mouth. 'Yes, have a drink with us,' he said.

Marie shook her head. 'There are only two glasses.'

'That doesn't matter. We only need one,' Rachel said.

Marie paused, as though considering the offer, then smiled. 'Yes. All right. Where do you want the tray?'

'Here,' Daniel said, standing up and moving the low coffee table next to the bed.

Rachel gave a greedy smile as she looked at the tray. 'Smoked salmon. Mm.'

'I'd eat the Brie parcels now, while they're still hot,' Marie advised.

Rachel took one, and bit into it. 'Absolute bliss. Filo pastry, Brie and redcurrant sauce,' she said.

Daniel, too, took one. 'You're right,' he said. 'Marie, help yourself.'

'You ordered for yourselves, not for me.'

'But there's plenty here,' Rachel said. 'Easily enough for three.'

Daniel poured two glasses of champagne, handing one to Rachel and one to Marie. 'Cheers.'

'What about you?' Marie asked.

'I'll share.' Daniel's eyes met Rachel's, and she nodded imperceptibly. The circumstances were right.

They ate and drank in near-silence, Daniel feeding Rachel with tiny morsels and sharing her glass. Eventually, her head buzzing with champagne and a relaxed smile on her face, Rachel reached out to touch Marie's hand. 'Marie. I told Daniel about this morning.'

'I wondered if you might.' The Frenchwoman's face was impassive.

'She told me when I was driving – when I couldn't do much about it,' Daniel said.

'And?'

Rachel smiled. 'He had to pull off the road.'

'I see.'

Rachel hadn't bothered doing up her shirt; she let the front fall open, revealing her bared breasts. 'Marie. This morning, you said that I could call you for room service, any time. You also said that you thought Daniel was beautiful.'

The Frenchwoman smiled. 'Yes.'

'So wouldn't you like to see more?'

Daniel's eyes widened. He hadn't expected Rachel to be quite this relaxed about things. He cleared his throat. 'Which means?'

'Which means, Daniel, that I think you should strip for us.' Rachel lay back on the bed, propping one hand behind her head, and pulled Marie down next to her. 'Don't you agree, Marie?'

Marie grinned. 'Leave me out of this!'

'Oh, no. You're part of this, as much as we are,' Rachel said softly.

'Well.' Daniel took a gulp of champagne, then stood up. 'So you want a show, then?'

'Uh-huh.' Rachel nodded.

'I'm no Chippendale, you know.'

She grinned. 'You're a real man, not a plastic himbo.'

Daniel grinned back, and began to move for them to the rhythm of a soft bluesy tune in his head. He undid his shirt, very slowly, swaying as he pulled the soft cotton from his shoulders and dropped it onto the floor. His jeans were next; he undid the button and then the fly, then slowly eased the soft denims to the floor. He kicked off his shoes and socks, then stepped out of the jeans; then he stood before them in his boxer shorts.

'All the way, Daniel,' Rachel said softly.

'Not while you two are wearing so much.'

'Now, there's a challenge,' Marie said softly. She smiled at Rachel, who sat up, and allowed Marie to remove her shirt. She supported her weight on her hands and feet, tipping her pelvis up while Marie undid her zip and pushed her jeans over her hips; then she sat down, helping Marie remove the jeans properly. Then, still wearing her lewdly-positioned bra and her knickers, Rachel turned to Marie. She removed Marie's cap, combing her fingers through Marie's dark hair so that it fanned over her shoulders. Then she undid the apron, dropping it to the floor, and slid down the zipper of Marie's skirt. Marie copied Rachel's actions, supporting her weight on her hands and feet while Rachel removed her skirt; then Rachel undid Marie's shirt, letting it, too, fall to the floor.

Then the two women sat up, looking at Daniel. 'Happy?' Rachel asked.

'Not quite.'

'You'll have to come over here, then,' she said, patting the bed. She and Marie shifted slightly, making room for Daniel, who climbed onto the bed between them and sat down. Rachel smiled at Marie: then, in perfect synchronization, they each took the waistband of Daniel's boxer shorts between their fingers, and slowly drew the material down. He lifted himself so that they could remove his boxer shorts properly, and his cock sprang up, hard and erect. Marie made a small sound of approval as she looked at him.

'Do you like what you see?' Rachel asked.

'Yes,' the Frenchwoman said.

Rachel ran her hand down Daniel's chest. 'He feels as good as he looks.'

Marie copied her actions, and smiled. 'You're right. He does.'

Daniel swallowed. 'Rachel. Marie. You're both still wearing too much.'

'Let's see.' Marie tipped her head on one side, then straddled Daniel, so that he could feel the silk gusset of her knickers gliding against his cock. She smiled at Rachel. 'Up you get,' she said softly.

Rachel did as she was bidden, kneeling up, and Marie reached over to pull her knickers down to her knees. 'I think that your bra should stay as it is,' she said. 'A sweet disorder in the dress, as they say.'

Daniel groaned as Marie moved back to the side, and Rachel

finished removing her knickers and took the Frenchwoman's place, resting her quim very lightly against his cock. He could feel how hot and wet she was, and yearned to be inside her – but this was her show. She was the one dictating the pace.

Rachel reached across to Marie, deftly undoing the clasp of her bra, then stroking the material away from her body. She bent her head, nuzzling Marie's breasts and taking one hardening nipple into her mouth; Daniel groaned again. 'Christ, watching you both like this is sheer torture.'

Rachel chuckled, and deliberately moved so that his cock travelled the length of her quim. 'I haven't finished, yet.' She beckoned Marie to kneel so that she could remove Marie's knickers. 'I think that the stockings should stay, though.'

'Definitely,' Marie agreed.

Daniel swallowed. 'I don't know how much more of this I can take.'

'There's the whole night ahead,' Rachel warned him, her voice husky.

'Kiss me,' Daniel begged.

'Who?'

He closed his eyes. 'One of you. Just kiss me.'

Marie smiled, and moved to his side. She beckoned to Rachel, who leaned over to kiss Daniel, her lips moving gently against his; he cupped her face in both hands, sliding his tongue into her mouth and deepening the kiss.

Meanwhile, Marie crawled down the bed and began kissing her way up his legs, starting at his ankles and moving up to his thighs. Daniel gasped as Marie cupped his balls in one hand, and ringed his cock with the thumb and forefinger of her other hand, gently masturbating him. Rachel couldn't help opening her eyes and turning her head to see what

Marie was doing; she, too, caught her breath as she saw her working her mouth all the way down Daniel's magnificent cock. Marie was obviously an expert at this, she thought: she'd never considered herself to be a novice, but Marie could teach her a lot.

Daniel continued kissing Rachel, moving his hands down to caress her breasts and play with her nipples, while Marie sucked him. Rachel felt his body tense, but then Marie stopped, and squeezed gently just below the head of his cock to delay his orgasm. 'So, Daniel, what do you want?'

'I want to be inside you, Marie,' he said, his voice hoarse with longing. 'I want to feel your quim move round me.'

She nodded, moving to straddle him; she coaxed the tip of Daniel's cock to her sex, and slid down onto him.

'Rachel,' he said softly, stroking his lover's back. 'Let me pleasure you, too. Straddle my chest, and face Marie.'

She did as he said; he urged her buttocks back towards him slightly, and buried his face between her thighs, licking her quim with long, slow strokes, matching the rhythm of Marie lifting and lowering herself onto his cock.

Rachel shivered, and Marie smiled at her. She leaned forward, still moving around Daniel's cock, and touched her lips to Rachel's. Rachel could taste Daniel, mingled with Marie's own sweetness, and suddenly found herself kissing Marie properly, opening her mouth and pressing her tongue against Marie's.

Marie made a small sound of approval, and reached up to caress Rachel's breasts, circling the areolae with her middle fingers and then pulling on Rachel's hardened nipples. Then she gently pulled on them, rolling them between forefinger and thumb.

Rachel, in turn, touched Marie's breasts, remembering their lovemaking of that morning and wanting more. The Frenchwoman felt warm and soft, the skin around her areolae raised in tiny pimples. Rachel cupped the other woman's breasts, lifting them up and together, and pinching her nipples gently with her fingers.

Marie gasped, and put her hands over Rachel's, squeezing them gently and dragging them downwards. Rachel instinctively knew what she wanted, and let one hand cup her mons veneris, her middle finger sliding between Marie's labia and searching for her clitoris.

She could feel the hard rod of Daniel's cock sliding in and out of Marie's quim, and it was enough to remove her last inhibitions. She began to rub Marie in earnest, her fingertip describing a rapid figure-of-eight around the hard nub of flesh. Marie cried out, and Daniel's mouth worked harder on Rachel in response.

'Oh God!' Marie cried. 'Yes!' She climaxed, her face contorting with pleasure, then slid her arms round Rachel's neck and drew her face to hers, kissing her hard. At the same time, Rachel felt her quim flex, and her own orgasm bubbled through her. Daniel's body jerked under hers, and she felt him groan against her flesh as he, too, climaxed.

When their pulse-rates had subsided, Marie and Rachel climbed off Daniel, who sat up, raking a hand through his hair. 'Christ. That was every bit as good as I'd dreamed.'

'How about "thank you, darling, the earth moved for me"?' Rachel suggested, laughing wickedly and sitting down beside him.

'Something like that,' he agreed, taking her hand and kissing it. He took Marie's hand, too, and pulled her down onto his other side. 'Bliss.' He kissed them each lightly. 'Thank you.'

'We haven't finished, yet.' Rachel smiled at him. 'Not by a long way.'

'Let's drink to that,' Marie said, moving to pick up a half-filled glass of champagne. 'To long nights, and *l'amour*.'

'To long nights, and *l'amour*,' the others echoed, taking the glass in turn and sipping from it.

FIFTEEN

'Hello?' Carrie's voice sounded slightly sleepy.

'Hi, Carrie. It's Rachel. I haven't woken you, have I?'

'Rachel!' Carrie's voice brightened. 'Actually, yes, you have. It's Sunday morning, so I suppose I was pretty much comatose.'

'Sorry.' Rachel bit her lip, cross with herself. Of course Carrie would have been asleep at half past ten on a Sunday morning. It had been bloody selfish of her to ring Carrie.

'Oh, it doesn't matter,' Carrie said, dismissing it. 'What can I do for you, then?'

'I just – um – wondered. Are you busy this afternoon?'

'Not exactly. I was planning to sprawl out with the *Sunday Telegraph*, but that's about it. Why?'

Rachel paused. 'Um – I need a favour.'

'Which is?' Carrie prompted.

'You know we came to Lavenham this weekend to find out more about the cat?'

'Yes. Are you still there, now?'

'Mm, we're in the hotel. We've just had breakfast. Anyway, we've found the original owner of the mummy case, and she's lent me her father's notebooks – he was the one who found the cat. So I wondered if I could borrow your photocopier to take copies of the notebooks, so that I can study them properly and make notes on them during the week?'

'Yes, of course you can!' Carrie said. 'Look, why don't you come over for lunch?'

'Lunch?'

'Well, knowing you, you'll want to make those copies as soon as you can.'

Rachel chuckled. 'Right.'

'And bring Daniel with you. I'd like to meet him. It's about time I made his acquaintance, anyway.'

Rachel had a sudden thought. 'Are you on your own at the moment?'

Carrie chuckled. 'No. But you said that you wanted to meet Ralph, did you not?'

'Definitely.'

'That settles it, then. See you here at about one?'

'That's fine,' Rachel said.

'Have a good trip back.'

'Cheers.' She put the phone down and looked at Daniel. 'It looks like we have a lunch date.'

He was surprised. 'A lunch date?'

'With Carrie, in Docklands.' Rachel's lips quirked. 'I'm not sure whether she's going to cook something herself, or whether she's going to be her usual lazy tart of a self and get a takeaway.'

'She's not a good cook, then?' Daniel asked.

'Oh yes, she's brilliant. Carrie is good at just about every-thing she tries to do,' Rachel told him. 'The only thing is, she lives her life at about a thousand miles an hour, so she doesn't have the time to cook. Most of the time, she eats out or gets a takeaway.'

'Fine.' Daniel paused. 'Is it just Carrie I'm meeting?'

Rachel shook her head. 'Her new man's going to be there, too. I don't know much about him, apart from the fact that he's fairly high-powered – a marketing director, or something like that.' And that he was extremely inventive when it came to sex – not that she was going to repeat to Daniel what Carrie had told her. 'Carrie met him through business.'

Daniel ruffled her hair. 'Tell you what, you have a shower while I go and settle our bill, and we'll have a leisurely drive back to London.'

'Sounds good to me.' Rachel watched him as he left the room. She felt more relaxed and happy than she'd felt in weeks. The explosive encounter between Daniel, Marie and herself, the previous night, had drained away all her tension. The fact that she was nearer to finding out the truth about the cat was a bonus.

She showered quickly and washed her hair, still thinking about Marie. The previous night had been a one-off. Apart from the fact that they were unlikely to see Marie again – the Frenchwoman had refused to stay the night, saying that it was better to keep it as a short and sweet memory – and although she'd enjoyed what they'd done, she didn't particularly want to share Daniel. Not now.

By the time that she'd finished drying her hair and had dressed in some tailored navy trousers and a bright yellow silk shirt, Daniel returned. They packed and left the hotel, heading back for London. They stopped at an off-licence en route to Carrie's flat, and Rachel bought a couple of bottles of Chardonnay and a selection of Belgian chocolates. 'Carrie's favourites,' she explained to Daniel with a grin. Then she directed Daniel to Carrie's flat.

Carrie opened the door to them, smiling. She hugged Rachel, kissing her. 'Hi, how are you?'

'Fine,' Rachel said, hugging her friend back. 'Right: introduction time. Carrie, this is Daniel Sinclair. Daniel, this is Carrie Taylor – my best friend from way back.'

'Pleased to meet you,' Daniel said politely, holding out his hand.

'And you,' Carrie said, her eyes sparkling wickedly as she surveyed him. 'I've heard a lot about you.'

Daniel merely chuckled. 'Likewise.'

'Oh God,' Carrie said, laughing. 'Depending on whether Rach was drunk or sober when she told you about me, you'll think that I'm either a raving nymphomaniac or a lush.'

'A schizophrenic, perhaps,' Daniel suggested wickedly. 'Because I also know that you're a hot-shot businesswoman.'

'Or I like to think I am,' Carrie said. 'Anyway, come in, come in. There's a bottle of wine chilling in the fridge, unless you'd prefer a cup of coffee?'

'Wine would be lovely, thanks. And these are for you,' Daniel said, handing her the wine and the chocolates.'

Carrie looked at them, and smiled. 'Thanks. My favourites. I can guess who picked these!' She led them into the flat; a tall, dark-haired man with very blue eyes was lounging on the sofa. He stood up as they entered, and shook hands with Rachel and Daniel. 'Hello. You must be Rachel and Daniel.'

'And you must be Ralph,' Rachel said. Her eyes widened. Carrie had said that the man was sexy – but not *this* sexy. Not only did Ralph have virtually film-star looks and a perfectly toned body, he also had a voice which Rachel could imagine only too easily whispering outrageously erotic things. From what Carrie had told her, Ralph had as gorgeous a personality as he had looks, and a sharp brain to go with them. No wonder that Carrie was smitten with him.

Rachel also noticed the way that Ralph looked at Carrie: their feelings were entirely mutual. Rachel made a mental note to lay a wager with Carrie that they'd be moving in together within the next three months.

'Now the introductions have been made, we can have lunch,' Carrie declared. 'We'll do your photocopying later, Cleo.'

Rachel sniffed the air, and was surprised to discover the scent of roast lamb. 'Carrie, don't tell me that you actually cooked lunch yourself?'

'Hey, I can cook.' Carrie held up her hands, laughing. 'No wonder poor Daniel thinks that I'm a lush. You've told him that all I do is eat out or order takeaways.'

'Which is true,' Rachel said, laughing back. 'You work such ridiculous hours, and you spend the rest of your time socializing, that you don't get time to cook.'

Carrie accepted the nagging good-naturedly. 'Well, you can come and give me a hand dishing up.'

Rachel smiled. That was Carrie's shorthand for saying that she wanted to find out what Rachel thought of Ralph, and to tell her what she thought of Daniel – in private. 'OK.'

They went into the pristine kitchen; Carrie closed the door behind them. 'I do like your man,' she said approvingly. 'His eyes are incredible.'

'Yours isn't so bad,' Rachel said. 'With looks like that, he'd be the darling of Hollywood. Charlie Sheen, eat your heart out.'

'I'd rather eat a different part of Charlie Sheen's anatomy,' Carrie said, with a wicked grin.

Rachel groaned. 'Oh, God, I've started you off again.'

Laughing, they dished up, and carried the food through to the dining room. Ralph and Daniel were talking together as though they'd known each other all their lives; Rachel and Carrie exchanged a smile. They chatted lightly through lunch; over coffee, Ralph turned to Rachel. 'Carrie said that you had some important photocopying to do. Work, is it?'

'Not exactly,' Rachel said, 'though it is important.'

'It's all my fault, really,' Carrie said. 'I found this mummy-case of a cat, in Lavenham. I thought that it was a reproduction. I bought it for Rach, because I thought that she'd like it, being so heavily into Egypt. Anyway, it's turned out to be an original.'

'We've been trying to trace its history,' Rachel said. 'One of Daniel's friends at the university dated it for us; then we went back to the shop where Carrie bought it. The dealer told us where he'd got it, so we paid a visit to the woman who sold it at this country house sale. It turned out that her father brought it back from Egypt around the turn of the century – he was an archaeologist, and worked on a few digs out there. Anyway, she's lent us his diaries about his Egyptian years.' She shrugged. 'I can't really photocopy the stuff at work. Apart from the fact that I'm supposed to be having a few days off, I'd much rather stay out of the office at the moment. I know that Ms Workaholic here has her own up-to-the-minute kit at home, so it was the obvious place to come.'

'Exactly,' Carrie said. 'And I'd be more than happy to help.'

'Have you ever been to Egypt?' Ralph asked.

'No,' Rachel admitted. 'I've always wanted to, but somehow I've never got round to it.'

'I've been to Luxor,' Ralph said, 'and you'd adore it. Go, Rachel. Visit the place.'

'I will. One day, soon.'

'Why don't you two go and do the photocopying while we wash up?' Ralph suggested.

'Good idea,' Daniel agreed.

'You mean, while you wash up with the help of a bottle of wine,' Carrie teased. 'See you in a bit, then.' She and Rachel headed for her study; while they were waiting for the photocopier to warm up, Carrie looked enquiringly at her friend. 'You didn't tell me that you had a few days off.'

'They weren't exactly planned,' Rachel said.

Carrie's eyes narrowed. 'Come on. Tell me the whole story.'

Rachel sighed. 'David called me into his office. He said that some of the clients had complained about me, saying that I was being dreamy and not listening to them.'

'They *what*?' Carrie was outraged.

'It's probably true. I've had this Egyptian stuff so much on my mind, I haven't been able to think straight. Anyway, I was talking to David and, the next thing I knew, I had another of the blackouts.'

Carrie caught on immediately. 'You mean, you ended up making love with David?'

'Yes.'

Carrie whistled. 'So what's happened? Did he throw you out?'

'No.' Rachel smiled wryly. 'He said he knew that it wasn't the way that I normally behaved. I felt that I owed him an explanation, so I told him what's been happening.' She paused, not wanting to tell Carrie that they'd made love a second time, afterwards. 'He said that I should take a week or so off, to try and get it sorted out, and that if I need anything, I should give him a ring.'

'That's more in character. He's a nice bloke, really,' Carrie said.

Rachel chuckled. 'Considering that you used to fight like cat and dog with him, when you worked there.'

'Yeah, well.'

'I got the impression,' Rachel said, 'that you did something similar. After you left the company, that is.'

Carrie was surprised. 'Is that what he said?'

'He didn't have to. It was the look on his face when he said your name,' Rachel said softly.

Carrie grinned. 'All right, I admit it. I did spend a night with him – but it was one night, only. Not to be repeated.' Her lips twitched. 'He's a more than acceptable lover, but it wouldn't have worked between us, long term. We'd have clashed badly within a week, and I prefer my home life to be a bit more relaxed.' She paused. 'Did you have any more of those dreams, in Lavenham?'

Rachel nodded. 'And how. But I don't know if I want to go into that, right now.'

Carrie took her hand and squeezed it. 'Hey, it's all right. Any time you want to talk about it, I'll be here. I won't judge you. You know that.'

'Mm. Cheers. Though I think somehow, now that I'm beginning to know the truth about what happened, the dreams will stop.'

'So what did this woman have to tell you?'

'You're not going to believe this,' Rachel said. 'When she saw me, she nearly fainted. She said that I was the spitting image of this woman.' She quickly flicked through the notebooks until she found the sketch of the Egyptian girl, then handed it silently to Carrie.

Carrie studied it, looked at Rachel, then studied it again. 'That's incredible,' she said softly. 'I can't believe that you're so alike.'

'It isn't really reincarnation, because Daniel's friend Hazel regressed me – I told you about that, on the phone – and she didn't manage to find any past life for me. The only thing I can think of is that, for some reason, I'm picking up whatever happened to this girl.' Rachel bit her lip. 'She had an affair with Augusta's father.'

'Who's Augusta's father?'

'The archaeologist. The one who found the mummy case. Augusta told me what had happened between her father and the Egyptian girl. They became lovers; the inevitable happened, and when she found out that she was pregnant, he told her that he was already married. She couldn't bear the shame, and killed herself. Then her family cursed him in the name of the goddess Bast.'

'Hang on. You're saying that this is turn of the century stuff, and the family cursed him?' Carrie was surprised.

'Yes. But Winifrid Blackman did a study of Egyptian villages, in the mid-nineteen twenties. I can't remember the name of the villages, right now, but I've got a book about it at home. Anyway, she discovered that the people in the villages were still using the old charms and amulets. They even used her cast-off clothes as amulets, protection against childhood diseases and that sort of thing.' Rachel shrugged. 'Anyway, now that the truth has come to light, maybe things will be better with the cat. I don't know.'

'Do you know anything more about the cat?'

'It's from the twenty-second dynasty. Daniel's friend Kate had a look at it for us. There's an inscription on the base of the cat, in heiratic; it's a bog-standard curse against those who harm Bast or the family she protects.'

'Right.'

'We're seeing Kate tomorrow night, and we'll show her the notebooks. I think that she'll find them pretty interesting.'

'Actually, I wouldn't mind having a read, when you've finished with them,' Carrie agreed.

Rachel grinned. 'Don't tell me that I'm finally giving you the Egyptian bug.'

'Er – no. I think that that's just you, Cleo,' Carrie said, laughing.

They finished the photocopying and went back to join the men. They spent the afternoon talking – avoiding the subject of Egypt and the diaries – and, later that evening, Carrie called a taxi for Rachel and Daniel.

Daniel gave the taxi-driver Rachel's address, and they returned to Islington with the cat, the notebooks and the photocopies.

'What did you think of Carrie?' Rachel asked.

Daniel nodded. 'I liked her. She's everything you said she'd be – lively, fun, very attractive.'

'Mm, that's Carrie.'

He stroked her face. 'Mind you, there's only one woman I really have eyes for, at the moment.' He nibbled her earlobe. 'Despite what happened between us and Marie.'

'I'm glad to hear it.'

He slid his arm round her. 'Come on. I think we could both do with an early night.'

She grinned. 'That's one way of putting it . . .'

The next morning, Rachel was sprawled on the rug in front

of her fire, a pile of photocopied paper and a pad and pen before her. The sheaf of closely-written papers next to her testified to how long she'd been working; though she was oblivious to both time and the tiredness of her muscles. All she could concentrate on was Augusta's father's journals. William Morgan's diaries were very thorough, minutely detailing life on a dig in Egypt, around the turn of the century, and his excitement at finding the tomb in Bubastis.

She had already shared with him the disappointments of seeing how the grave-robbers had already been there before him and despoiled the tomb, and the excitement of finding what had been left. Treasures which had been meaningless to the thieves in their search for gold, but which had told the late Victorian archaeologists so much about the past.

Suddenly, her vision blurred, and it was as though she were seeing double: William's words bringing the diaries to life before her eyes, and yet also seeing the scene from the viewpoint of someone else: a young girl, who was fascinated by the handsome archaeologist. Seeing William's thick black hair, his pale skin – so unlike the brown-skinned Egyptian men – and his eyes, an unusual aqua grey.

She was to be married to a boy in her village, and yet she couldn't bear the idea of his hands touching her, violating her body. Whereas the tall and handsome stranger, the man who'd barely noticed the fact that she was around, except to boss her about as the daughter of Makhbar – she could imagine only too easily what it would be like to feel his hands upon her skin, stroking her and touching her and bringing her pleasure. She'd pleaded with her father to be allowed to help on the dig. Although her mother had scolded her, saying that she should be occupying her time with useful things, learning household skills for her marriage, she had persisted. She wanted to work on the dig; and she also wanted to know more about William Morgan, though she didn't tell her parents that.

Eventually, Makhbar, secretly proud of his clever daughter, had agreed that she could help with the dig. She'd only been allowed to fetch and carry, at first; but then, when William Morgan had seen how careful she was, how she could brush delicately and gently, uncovering more lost treasures, he'd started noticing her and letting her help more. Gradually, over the weeks, they'd begun to work together. She'd caught him looking for her, on one or two occasions, and it was enough to make her heart want to burst with pride and some other, unknown, feeling. Love? Lust? She didn't know what it was, but it was so different from her feelings for the other men she knew, the boys in her village and the next.

They'd worked together more and more, just the two of them. And then, the day that she'd found the mummy case . . . It was of a cat, and William had been so pleased, he'd actually hugged her. And then, suddenly, he'd been aware that his arms were round her. He'd drawn back, apologizing stiffly for his forwardness; she'd said nothing, simply stared at the floor in agonized embarrassment. Being in his arms had felt so good: and yet she knew that she mustn't appear too eager, too forward. Then William had cupped her chin in his hands, gently lifting her face so that her eyes met his. A long, long moment later, he'd lowered his mouth to hers. The moment his lips had touched hers, it had felt like she was seeing stars.

'Amy, Amy,' he kept saying. It was his pet name for her. Although she knew that he was perfectly capable of pronouncing her name, he persisted in calling her 'Amy', an affectionate kind of diminutive. Some weeks later, he'd told her that 'Amy' meant 'love'; but at that moment, all that she could see, all that she could feel, was William Morgan. His mouth moving gently over hers, opening her lips; and then his tongue sliding into her mouth. It was the first time that anyone had kissed her like that, with that kind of passion. Several of the village boys had tried it, and she'd pushed them away; but with William ... With William, it was different. She found herself sliding her hands round his neck, kissing him back.

His hands moulded her sides; even through the thin stuff of her clothes, she could feel the heat of his hands, and she suddenly wanted to feel it against her bare skin. A pulse was beating heavily between her legs. She wanted him so badly; she wanted him the way that she'd refused others, the way she'd seen the pharaohs taking their favoured ones on the wall paintings – paintings from which she should have averted her eyes, as a modest girl, but which had fascinated her and made her wonder what the artists were like who drew the scenes, and whether they were working from imagination or fact.

She wanted him so badly. She could feel the bulge of his erection pressing against her; then, the next thing she knew, she was completely naked, and he was kneeling before her, rubbing his face against her midriff. She arched against him, wanting him to use his mouth on her body; he was so much taller than she was that it was easy for him to stretch up, take one hard nipple into his mouth and play his tongue against it. She nearly cried out at the sheer pleasure of it, but managed to bite her lip: if they were heard, and others came to see what was happening, it would bring disgrace upon her father. She didn't want that; but she definitely didn't want to stop. Not now.

His fingers were plucking at her other nipple, rubbing and teasing, until she was writhing beneath his hands and mouth, wanting him to touch her more intimately. As his mouth drifted downwards over her abdomen, she froze for a moment, half-shocked, and not quite sure what to expect. Then, gently, he parted her legs. She could feel his warm breath against her moist quim, and although part of her was scandalized, a greater part of her welcomed it when she felt the first long, slow sweep of his tongue down her musky furrow. She slid her hands into his hair, urging him on, and he began to lap in earnest, sometimes making his tongue into a sharp point and pushing it as deeply as he could into her, sometimes taking it long and slow, and then flicking his tongue quickly over her clitoris, making her moan.

He lifted his head as he heard her soft cry. 'Sh, it's all right,' he said, his eyes glittering.

'I'm sorry,' she whispered. 'I'm sorry, William.'

He smiled at her. 'You're adorable. My Amy.' And then he resumed his attentions, licking her and licking her, until her whole body felt as though it was on fire, molten and fluid. Then she seemed to splinter into a thousand fragments: she opened her mouth in a soundless wail of pleasure, and then William was naked, too, pulling her down next to him. His cock was thick and hard; she touched it with wonderment, and he sighed.

'Oh, Amy, I need this. I need you so much.'

And then he was lying between her legs, stroking her, arousing her to fever pitch. She felt the tip of his cock rest against the entrance of her sex. It felt so good as he pushed inside her, filling her and stretching her. Almost by instinct, she wrapped her legs round his waist, tilting her pelvis up so that he could penetrate her more deeply. He began to move, very gently, withdrawing until his cock was almost out of her and then pushing slowly back in, taking it gently, easy, riding her.

The damp, the musty air and the gloominess of the tomb was forgotten by both of them. All she could see, all she could feel, was her lover: belly to belly, cock to cunt. It felt so good, so very good. And then her flesh dissolved again, contracting hard around the thick, rigid muscle of his cock, and she felt his cock twitch deep inside her, the warm gush of his seed. He was kissing her hard, his tongue plunging deeply into his mouth, just as his cock filled her, stifling her cries of pleasure . . .

Rachel surfaced to find herself lying on her back, her hand working between her legs. She groaned as she climaxed, and rolled over onto her side, suddenly thoughtful. She'd just seen the first time that William and Amy had made love . . . And now she knew the girl's name, a name which wasn't in the journals. Though even if Amy's name had been written in that neat sepia handwriting, Rachel knew that Augusta would still have referred to Amy only as 'the Egyptian girl'. Giving her a name would have made things so much worse, emphasizing again how badly William had treated her.

Amy. Rachel shivered. Years ago, her mother had once said that she had nearly called her 'Amy', after Amelia Earhart, her childhood heroine. Was that just coincidence, or something more sinister?

She pushed the thought aside, and continued reading. When she reached the section about the cat, the flat dissolved around her, and again she was with William and Amy, in Egypt. They were lying naked on a blanket, in each other's arms, still flushed from recent love-making. The evidence of their hard work on the excavations was all around them, but neither of them was showing any interest in the artefacts they'd uncovered. They were only interested in each other.

'So there's a story attached to this cat, then?' William asked.

Amy nodded. 'It's probably one for someone like you to smile at.'

'Someone like me?'

'You're not Egyptian. You don't believe the same things that we do.'

William rolled his eyes. 'You don't believe in the Egyptian gods, any more than I do. You're not like the others, Amy, and you know it. If anything, you're more ... Oh, I don't know. European, I suppose.'

Amy was thoughtful. 'Mother says that I'm too clever for my own good.' There was a slight frown on her face. 'She was so against my joining Father here. She said that someone of my age should be married, looking after my husband and children, not digging around in the dirt, with a bunch of men who act like schoolboys.'

William grinned. He'd met Amy's mother, and although she'd been perfectly courteous to him, he'd always suspected that she felt that he was a bad influence on Amy's father – that if Makhbar hadn't been mixed up with the archaeologists, he would have had a proper job, something that she could be proud of. A farmer, working with his hands – anything but this digging and delving into the past. Amy's mother thought that it was somehow disrespectful. 'You were telling me the story of the cat,' he prompted.

Amy smiled wryly. 'It was a long time ago. I'm not sure how long ago. An Egyptian princess fell in love with a stranger. He wasn't from these lands: he had pale skin, though his hair was dark, and his eyes were so strange.' She reached up to stroke his face. 'Like yours, a kind of greeny-grey, the colour of the Nile on a stormy day.'

'So what happened?'

'She disobeyed her father. She should have remained pure, but she ended up making love with the stranger. In the end, he betrayed her, and she was thrown out of her home. Her family disowned her. She crawled into the desert, to lay down and die under the hot sun, weeping her penitence: but Bast took pity on her, and changed her into a cat, so she could go back to her family home and be accepted as part of the household once more, without revealing who she really was.'

'What happened to the man?' William asked.

'The stranger? He left Egypt. None of the cats in the village would go near him, so the King persuaded him diplomatically to return to his homeland.'

'Hang on. He betrayed her, he seduced her, and yet they allowed him to walk free?'

Amy shrugged. 'He came from powerful lands. Her people would have lost any war that they'd started against his people. Besides, they thought that she was dead. It was easier to let him go. Though they do say that on his journey home, his party was surprised by a pack of wild cats. He was torn to death. Bast looks after her own.'

William stroked her face. 'Well, you know that I'll never betray you, Amy. Never.'

Amy chuckled. 'Scared of being plagued by cats, are you?'

'No. I promise I won't betray you. And promises, I always keep.'

* * *

Rachel's eyes widened. No wonder that William Morgan had been so nervous of cats. Amy's story of the man with strange eyes who'd betrayed his lover and been torn apart by wild cats – particularly as the man had had the same colour eyes as William's – was enough to worry anyone. Especially an old man who was feeling guilty about the way he'd behaved. Thank God that Daniel wasn't like them ... Or was he?

She shook herself, and read on. For the next few pages of the diary, William had concentrated on his finds at Bubastis. And then there was an odd entry: *The worst day of my life. I have to leave. Now.* And the journal stopped.

Again, Rachel found herself sliding back to Egypt. Amy and William were together, in his quarters, taking their biggest risk yet. If they were found together, there would be trouble for both of them. And yet they couldn't bear to be apart.

Amy was curled into William's arms, and his hand was jammed between her thighs, his finger gliding along the moist flesh of her quim. 'Amy, Amy. I could drown in your pleasure-garden,' he told her softly.

She smiled, taking his hand and sliding it onto her belly.

He frowned. 'What? Don't you like what I was doing?'

'Of course – but I wanted you to feel something, too.'

'Feel what?'

'Our child is lying beneath my heart,' she told him quietly.

'Our child? You're with child?' He looked at her in wonder. 'Amy, you're carrying my child?'

She nodded, torn between tears and smiles.

'But – how long have you known?'

'Today. My monthly courses ...' Amy swallowed, flushing. 'I think it must have happened the first time we lay together.'

'Oh, God.' William kissed her. 'God, I can't believe this.'

'You're happy?' Amy relaxed. 'Though my father: he will want us to marry.'

A sudden cloud crossed William's face, and he rolled over. 'William, what's wrong?'

He closed his eyes, swallowing hard. 'Amy, I don't know how to tell you this.'

'Tell me what?'

'Back in England, I'm married. My wife has never been able to give me children.'

'But William, you lay with me. I thought that you wanted me to be your wife. I thought . . .' Her voice cracked.

'Amy, I can't divorce Mary. She's done me no wrong. I can't—'

He was cut off by Amy standing up and dressing swiftly. 'I should have known better,' she said, 'than to trust a stranger with eyes the colour of yours.' She said no more, but left William's quarters.

'You callous, callous bastard,' Rachel said, tears in her eyes. 'You were so much older than she was. You knew exactly what you were doing. She was a child of sixteen, and she trusted you. You should have known better . . .'

SIXTEEN

When Daniel rang Rachel's doorbell, a few minutes later, she answered it in tears.

'Hey, what's the matter?' he asked, pulling her into his arms and holding her close.

'William and Amy.' She dashed the tears from her eyes. 'I know what happened between Augusta's father and the Egyptian girl.'

'Well, Augusta told us more or less. The affair, then she fell pregnant, and killed herself when William told her that she was married.'

She shook her head. 'No. I mean, I had flashbacks. I saw it as it happened.'

Daniel's eyes widened. 'Flashbacks? Look, do you want me to ring Kate and tell her that we'll make it some other night, instead?'

'Kate! Christ, I'd forgotten that we were going to see her this evening.' She shook her head. 'It's OK. We'll go.'

'Are you sure?'

'Yes. I just want to wash my face, first. I'm sorry. I just got so upset for Amy.' Rachel bit her lip. 'I think that I know how she died.'

'Augusta said that she killed herself.'

Rachel shook her head. 'I don't think so. She wasn't the sort to do that. I think she had a back street abortion, and it went wrong.'

'Christ.' He stroked her face. 'Oh, Rachel. I'm so sorry.'

'Yeah, me too,' she said. 'It was all so unnecessary. If only he'd been honest with her from the start, and told her that he was married ... God, she was a mere child, Daniel. She trusted him. How was she expected to know what he was hiding from her?'

'I know,' he soothed her, stroking her back. 'Look, before we go to Kate's, do you want me to get you a coffee, or a glass of water, or something?'

'No. Thanks for the offer, but I'm all right.' She pulled back. 'There was something else.'

'What?'

'There's a story about Bast. I hadn't heard it before, but apparently there was an Egyptian princess who fell in love with a stranger, a man with aqua grey eyes. Eyes like yours, like William's. Anyway, he seduced her, and something happened – I don't know what, probably that they were caught together making love, when she'd made a vow to be chaste – and he betrayed her. The princess was cast out from her family, and she went out to die in the desert. The goddess Bast rescued her and turned her into a cat so that she could go home and live with her family again, in peace – because cats, as you know, were treated like the Goddess incarnate in Egyptian homes. The stranger went back home, but his party was ambushed by wild cats in the desert, and he was torn to pieces.'

'That's pretty gruesome,' Daniel said.

She looked at him. 'Daniel, you're not a cat person, are you?'

'No – but that's probably because I was always brought up with dogs.' He held her at arm's length. 'If you're worried that just because I happen to have the same colour eyes as the man in the legend and William Morgan – and let's face it, if the resemblance had been that close, surely Augusta would have said something – then don't. I'm not like either of them.'

'I know. I'm sorry. I'm just a bit overwrought. I've been concentrating too hard on the journals.'

'You don't have to make excuses,' he said gently. 'In your position, I'm sure that I'd feel the same.'

'Mm. It's irrational, I know. Stupid. You're not like them, and our relationship's based on something different, not the illicit and hidden coupling of William and Amy, or the stranger and the princess.'

'Exactly.' He looked at her. 'I don't know what would reassure you, make you feel happier. If you want a ring, that can easily be arranged.'

Rachel shook her head, smiling wryly. 'I hope that if you ever do decide to propose to me, Daniel, then you'll do it with a little more finesse.'

He chuckled. 'Yes, it was pretty badly worded. I suppose that I just wanted to make you see that I care.' He stroked her hair away from her face. 'There is one way that I know I can make you feel better . . .' He lowered his mouth to hers.

Rachel froze for a moment, remembering how it had felt when William had kissed Amy, that first time: and then she relaxed. This wasn't the same. It was a different age, a different culture, and the circumstances were different. Everything was different. And Daniel had always been completely straight with her, apart from not telling her that he had a doctorate – and that was hardly important, in the scheme of things.

She opened her mouth beneath his, and his tongue slid into her mouth, pressing against hers, exploring the soft contours of her mouth. He pulled her shirt loose from her jeans, sliding his fingers up over her back; she arched against him and, deftly, he undid the clasp of her bra. She pulled back. 'Daniel . . .'

'Sh, it's all right,' he said. 'Kate won't mind if we're a little late. But I think that we both need this. Call it reassurance – for me, as well as for you.' He pulled her back into his arms, and started stroking down her spine again, his fingertips brushing her skin lightly in a way that made her shiver. He let his hands drift round to her midriff, sliding upwards until he could cup her breasts. Her nipples were obviously erect, pushing through the lace of her bra; he brushed the material out of the way and cupped her breasts properly, skin to skin, his thumbs tracing her areolae.

Rachel shuddered, and Daniel broke the kiss, moving one hand so that he could unbutton her shirt. 'Mm. I've been thinking about this all day. How perfect you are, how I love your curves. I could drown in your body, Rachel . . .' He pushed her shirt from her shoulders, then removed her bra, letting it drop to the floor.

'Daniel . . .' She suddenly realized that they were in her hallway. They hadn't even waited until they were in her bedroom.

'Sh. No-one can see us, and I want you here, I want you now. I can't wait, Rachel. I want to touch you, to taste you.' He cupped her breasts again, pushing them up and together to deepen her cleavage, then stroked the hard peaks of her nipples with his forefingers. 'Rachel, you're so beautiful, so adorable . . .' He dipped his head, kissing the curve of her throat and licking the soft hollows of her collar-bones.

She arched against him, and he let his mouth drift downward so that he could suckle one breast, drawing fiercely on the erect nub of flesh while rolling its twin between his thumb and forefinger. Rachel closed her eyes and slid her hands into his hair, urging him on. This time, she didn't feel the weird blurring she'd felt all day, or see William making love with Amy: this was just the two of them, in twentieth-century Islington.

He unzipped her jeans and pushed the soft denims down over her hips; then he hooked his thumbs into the sides of her knickers, pulling them down, too. Rachel lifted one foot and then the other, balancing herself against him so that he could remove her clothes properly; and then he drew her down onto the floor. He looked at her for a moment, taking a sharp intake of breath at her sheer beauty, the voluptuous curves that haunted him when he wasn't with her; then he bent his head, licking her areolae and breathing on them in turn so that she shivered and arched against him. Then his mouth tracked slowly southwards, nuzzling her belly.

Rachel sighed with pleasure as Daniel licked the soft skin of her inner thighs; he smiled against her skin, and blew lightly along her quim. He could tell how excited she was: he could feel the heat of her quim, so close to his mouth, and he could smell her arousal, a sharp musky scent which made him itch to taste her.

'Don't tease me, Daniel,' she murmured softly. 'Make love with me.' She pushed her hips up to meet him, and he drew his tongue along her quim, licking from the top to the bottom of her musky divide in one smooth movement. As his tongue flickered across her clitoris, she tipped her head back against the floor, her lips parting in a silent groan of pleasure. She slid her hands into his hair, massaging his scalp and urging him on; Daniel made his tongue into a sharp point, working rapidly across the hard nub of flesh, bringing her swiftly to the edge of orgasm.

'Oh God, yes,' she moaned, and she felt her climax ripple through her, her internal muscles contracting sharply.

He stayed where he was until the aftershocks of her climax had died down, then rubbed his face against her belly. 'Rachel. Lovely, lovely Rachel.'

'Oh, Daniel.' She shifted so that she could kiss him, her tongue sliding into his mouth; he tasted of her, and it thrilled her. She undid his shirt, smoothing the muscles of his chest and his upper arms as she removed the garment and threw it to one side. Then she pushed him onto his back, undoing his belt and the button at the top of his chinos, then slowly pulled the zipper downwards. Daniel kicked off his shoes, then lifted his buttocks off the floor so that she could slide the soft material down his thighs; she removed his underpants and socks at the same time.

Naked, he was beautiful, she thought: in some respects, like William Morgan, but so much better. Because he was real, he was now, and he didn't have the streak of cowardice so evident in William. She slid her hands down his midriff, over the flat planes of his stomach; then curled her fingers round his cock, pulling his foreskin back and forth. 'Mm. Have I ever told you, Dr Sinclair, just how gorgeous you are?' she asked.

'You can say it as often as you like,' he told her huskily.

'I like touching you, Daniel,' she informed him. 'And it's you

I'm touching, you I'm making love with – not William Morgan or the Egyptian stranger.'

'I'm very glad to hear it.' His arms came round her, and he pulled her on top of him.

Rachel rested against him for a moment, delighting in the feel of his hard cock against her quim. Then she lifted herself slightly, sliding one hand between their bodies so that she could position the tip of his cock against the entrance to her sex. Slowly, very slowly, she slid onto him; he gave a small moan of pleasure as he felt his cock slide into her warm wet depths, and reached up to touch her breasts, teasing her nipples so that she arched her back and tipped her head back.

She began to move over him, lifting herself very slowly, then slamming down onto him again; his hands drifted down to her hips, and he urged her on, steadying her rhythm. He felt so good inside her, she thought; she loved the way he filled her. The weird blurring sensation began, but she fought it. No. Amy and William were in the past; this was here and now.

Daniel cupped her mons veneris, sliding his finger between her labia; she was still aroused from her recent climax, and she gave a sharp intake of breath as he touched her clitoris. He found her rhythm quickly, teasing the sensitive nub of flesh with his middle finger, and then rubbing harder as her pleasure grew.

'Oh, yesssss,' she groaned, as she felt the inner sparkling begin again. Her whole body felt fluid and, as pleasure exploded deep inside her, the shudders of orgasm seemed to travel down every nerve-end, making her whole body quiver.

She felt him stiffen slightly, and then his cock twitched deep inside her as he reached his own climax. He wrapped his arms round her, pulling her back against him and cradling her, resting his cheek against her hair.

Neither of them spoke, unwilling to break the spell; finally, Daniel softened and slipped out of her. He stroked her face. 'Oh, Rachel.'

'Daniel.' She moved slightly so that she could kiss him.

'Better, now?' he asked softly.

She nodded. 'Much better.'

'Good.' He kissed her lightly. 'I suppose we'd better get going, or Kate'll think we've got lost.'

'I need a shower, first,' Rachel said. She surveyed her crumpled clothes. 'And I can't wear these out, now. I'll have to change.'

'Not necessarily. I could iron them for you, while you're in the shower,' he suggested, surprising her.

'Hang on, let me get this straight.' She stared at him. 'You're offering to iron my clothes?'

He chuckled. 'Oh, dear. You really do know some undomesticated types, don't you?'

'I don't know if I'd call you domesticated, exactly,' she said. 'Even though you're a better cook than I am.' She smiled. 'But I'll take you up on your offer. I hate ironing.'

'Just tell me where your iron is, and I'll sort it out.'

She took him into the kitchen, showing him where she kept her iron and ironing board, then headed for the shower. She soaped herself thoughtfully. Daniel was really nothing like William Morgan, or the stranger from the legend: neither of them would have been so thoughtful, so caring. Maybe the cat had brought them together to make amends for the past, she thought idly; then grimaced, sluicing the suds from her skin. She was being superstitious, and just a little too fanciful.

Mirage

She dried herself quickly, then padded into her bedroom, putting on clean underwear before heading for the kitchen, where Daniel was waiting for her. He smiled at her. 'Your clothes, madam.'

'Thank you, Jeeves,' she teased.

'I think you'd better put them on yourself,' he said. 'Otherwise they'll end up being crumpled again as I take them off you, and we definitely won't get to Kate's tonight.'

'OK.' She dressed swiftly, then took a bottle of wine and a box of Belgian chocolates from the fridge. 'Let's go, then.'

They headed for Kate's flat in Holborn; it was only when they'd rung the doorbell that Rachel realized that she'd left the journals behind. 'Damn,' she said. 'I meant to bring William's journals with me. I thought that Kate might like to see them.'

'Never mind.' Daniel squeezed her hand. 'There's always another time. Or maybe I could take them in to the university tomorrow.'

'Mm.'

Kate opened the door, and smiled at both of them. 'Hi. Come in, come in.'

Rachel handed her the chocolates and the wine. 'For you.'

'Thanks.' Kate's face glowed with pleasure. 'Would you both like some wine?'

'Yes, please,' Rachel said.

'Go and sit down, then.' She ushered them into the sitting room. 'I'll be back in a minute.' She returned with three glasses, a corkscrew and a bottle of chilled white wine. She removed the cork and poured the wine, handing a glass to each of them. 'I almost rang you today, Daniel, to see how you got on,' she said. 'But then I thought that you'd probably be in lectures all day, so I didn't bother.' She looked expectantly at both Rachel and Daniel. 'So how did it go? Did you find out anything else about the cat?'

'Actually, it went even better than we'd hoped,' Rachel said. 'We spoke to the dealer, and he told us that he'd bought the cat from a country house sale, along with a few other Egyptian bits and pieces.'

'Rachel was considering buying up the whole shop,' Daniel said, with a grin.

'Except that payday's a little too far off, so I limited myself to a couple of scarabs,' Rachel said, giving him an arch look. 'I think that they're probably originals, too, Kate.'

Kate whistled. 'So what else went in that sale, I wonder?'

'Porcelain, silver and paintings, mainly, from what the dealer told us.' Daniel said. 'He got the Egyptian stuff as a job lot.'

'But he gave us the name of the family who'd held the sale, and we paid them a visit. The woman's father had been an archaeologist in Egypt at the turn of the century, and he'd found the cat while he was on a dig,' Rachel said.

'That's incredible,' Kate said. 'Did she know anything about its history?'

'Only that it was twenty-second dynasty, found at Bubastis – which gives you a gold star for getting it spot on,' Daniel said with a grin.

'It wasn't that hard,' Kate told him, her eyes twinkling. 'It's like you could tell the difference between, say, Victorian art and sixteenth century art.'

'Ye-es.'

'Well, it's the same kind of thing. You know what to look for.'

'It's better than that, though,' Rachel said. 'Augusta – she's the woman who owned the cat – lent us her father's journals. It's a complete record of his excavations at Bubastis, including sketches and diagrams.'

'A complete record?' Kate asked, her voice rising with excitement. 'Rachel ... Do you think that I could see them, some time?'

'Of course. I meant to bring them with me tonight, but ...' Rachel coughed, not wanting to admit to Kate just how she'd been distracted. 'I photocopied them yesterday, at my friend Carrie's.'

'The one who found you the cat, in the first place?'

Rachel nodded. 'Anyway, we promised Augusta that we'd have the journals back to her by the end of this week.'

'If you could lend them to me for a day – either the copies or the originals, it doesn't matter which – I can take a copy at the university,' Kate said.

'I could bring them in to work tomorrow morning,' Daniel said.

'Thanks.' Kate looked thoughtful. 'Do you think that Augusta would let me do some work with them?'

'I think there would be a fight over that, between your department and mine,' Daniel said, with a grin.

'Tough. It's about Egypt, so it's my lot's prerogative – right, Rachel?'

'Right,' Rachel agreed, laughing.

'Anyway, these journals – did they tell you any more about the cat?'

Rachel nodded. 'It's all very weird, Kate. I have this theory, though it sounds pretty crazy.'

'Tell me, anyway,' Kate invited.

'Well, while I was reading them, I kept getting these flashbacks. I could see what William was writing, and yet I could see it all unfolding from someone else's perspective.'

'Someone else?'

'The Egyptian girl. That's what Augusta called her, anyway, though Rachel believes that William called her "Amy".' Daniel slid his arm round Rachel's shoulders. 'You won't believe this, Kate. When you see the journals – as well as the tombs and the wall paintings and what have you, William Morgan sketched this woman's face. And I swear that if I didn't know better, I'd have said that he drew Rachel: Rachel with dark hair and dark eyes.'

'That's exactly what I saw, when I had the cat for those few days,' Kate said slowly. 'A woman who was so like Rachel, but with darker colouring, so I presume that the man with her was William.' She paused. 'He was fairly tall, with black hair, eyes the same colour as Daniel's, fairly pale skin, and a gorgeous mouth. He looked clever and vulnerable, at the same time: the sort of man that women would find hard to resist. Especially a young and naive girl from a provincial village in Egypt.'

'That sounds like the man I saw,' Rachel said. 'I only wish that I could get hold of a picture of Augusta's father. I'm sure that we've both been seeing William.'

'You could be right,' Kate said slowly. 'Is there any chance that she'd have a photograph of him?'

'Yes, but we'll have to brave the grand-daughter to get hold of it.'

'What grand-daughter?'

'Augusta lives with her grand-daughter. Imogen's a real terrier; she's fiercely protective of her grandmother,' Daniel said. 'I can understand it, up to a point, but she's way over the top. And I don't think that she likes men very much.'

'That's where you come in, Rachel,' Kate said.

Rachel shook her head. 'The thing is, Augusta nearly fainted when she saw me, because I look so much like the Egyptian girl, Amy.'

'Amy's not a very Egyptian name,' Daniel said.

'No, it's an anglicized diminutive,' Rachel told him.

'And as for being unEgyptian – did you know that Susan was a very popular name?' Kate asked. 'As were flower names.'

'Susan was a popular Egyptian name?' Daniel was astonished.

'You'd be surprised,' Kate said. 'Anyway, Rachel: what's the rest of your theory? Why have we both seen William and Amy?'

'Well,' Rachel said, 'there are two things. I don't know if you've ever heard a legend about an Egyptian princess who was seduced by a stranger? She was cast out by her family, and went to die in the desert, but was turned into a cat by Bast. Then, when he left the country, his party was attacked by wild cats and he was torn apart.'

Kate shook her head. 'It doesn't ring a bell with me. The best-known one about someone being dismembered is Osiris, and how Isis searched for his body and put him back together again.'

'I have to admit, it didn't ring a bell with me, either; but Amy told the story to William. The thing is, his eyes were the same colour as the stranger's in the legend. I don't know whether she was re-living some kind of curse, or something.'

'How do you mean?' Kate asked.

'The same sort of thing happened to Amy. She fell pregnant,' Rachel said slowly, 'and then William told her that he was married. The official story is that she killed herself, for shame, but I think that it's more likely that she died having a back street abortion.'

'God, how awful,' Kate said.

'Augusta said that her father couldn't bear cats to be in the same house as he was, and he was haunted by a cat that only he could see, towards the end of his life. It's quite a parallel.'

Kate's eyes flicked to Daniel. 'And his eyes are the same colour as—'

'Pure coincidence, before you say it,' Daniel interrupted. 'And the circumstances are completely different.'

'Then maybe,' Kate said, 'this is history repeating itself – except that, this time, there will be a happy ending.'

'Mm, that's my theory.' Rachel shrugged. 'I told you that it sounded crazy.'

'But it's logical,' Kate agreed.

'The question is,' Daniel said, 'what happens now?'

'Well, we can't keep the cat,' Rachel said. 'Not now I know that it's an original. Apart from the fact that I'd never be able to afford the insurance, I think that I'd feel a lot happier if we gave the cat to the British Museum, or somewhere like that, where the cat can be on display and everyone can see it.'

'What about Augusta?' Kate asked.

'I don't think that she'd want it back,' Rachel said. 'It's too much of a reminder of what happened.'

'Maybe we should ask her, first,' Daniel said. 'When we return the journals.'

'If she doesn't want it, the British Museum has quite a good collection of mummified cats,' Kate said thoughtfully. 'And I know one of the curators from the Egyptian department, Annie – I met her at a conference, a couple of years ago. I could have a word with her, if you like, and ask her if they could display it.'

'Thanks. I'd appreciate that.' Rachel nodded gratefully.

'Don't mention it.' Kate smiled at her. 'In your position, I'd do the same. Maybe they can give you a replica in return, or something.'

Rachel shook her head. 'After all this, I'd rather just see the cat in the museum. I don't want anything like it back in my flat.'

'I understand. I'll ring Annie tomorrow.' Kate glanced at her watch. 'Anyway, I invited you both for dinner. It should be ready by now; let's eat.'

'And no more talk about William and Amy,' Daniel insisted, 'or the colour of my eyes.'

Rachel and Kate smiled at each other. 'OK,' Rachel said.

The following Sunday, Rachel and Daniel drove down to Melbury. To their relief, Imogen wasn't there; Augusta welcomed them warmly, insisting on giving them tea and more of the seed cake that Daniel had enjoyed the previous week.

'So you read the journals?' she asked.

Rachel nodded. 'They told me everything I needed to know. I didn't tell you, last week, but I kept having these dreams, and I saw everything so clearly. I think I could see a lot of what had happened between your father and the Egyptian girl. At least, I think that it was your father.'

'Would you like to see a photograph of him?' Augusta offered.

Rachel's eyes widened. 'Are you sure? I mean, it won't upset you, or anything?'

'Of course not. Don't take any notice of Imogen, last week. She sometimes forgets her manners – and forgets that I might be old, but I'm not that fragile.' Augusta walked over to the sideboard, taking out an old photograph album. She leafed through a couple of pages, smoothing out the tissue paper, then handed the album to Rachel. 'Here. This is my father at a dig.'

Rachel's face paled as she looked at it. It was indeed the man from her dreams. 'My God, it's amazing. That's the man I've been dreaming about.' She looked at Daniel. 'This isn't a colour photograph, but I'm sure that his eyes were the same colour as yours.'

Augusta peered at Daniel. 'Now you mention it, yes. They are.' She smiled. 'I inherited my mother's eyes.'

Rachel handed the album back to Augusta. 'Thank you for lending us the journals. I took copies, so that I wouldn't damage the originals.'

'I knew that you'd take good care of them,' Augusta said.

'We showed the copies to Kate, my friend who looked at the cat for us,' Daniel said. 'She'd be very interested in working on them, maybe writing a paper on them – but only with your approval, of course.'

Augusta looked thoughtful. 'Maybe. But I'd rather that it wasn't in my lifetime.'

'We understand,' Daniel said immediately. Of course Augusta wouldn't want to see her father's seamier side made public.

'So, what are you going to do with the cat?' Augusta asked.

Rachel swallowed. 'Well, would you like it back?'

Augusta shook her head. 'It's had its time with my family. It's yours, now.' She tipped her head on one side. 'It was unlucky for us, but maybe it'll bring you good luck. Now that the curse is finally over.'

'Maybe. But I don't think it's fair for me to keep it where only I can see it. I'd like to give it to the British Museum,' Rachel said.

Augusta nodded approvingly. 'I think that's what my father would have wanted, too. Now that the truth is out in the open.'

'Though it's a truth that doesn't have to be told to the curators,' Daniel added.

'Thank you,' Augusta said quietly. 'I'd like him to be remembered for the good things he did. He wasn't all bad. I don't think he ever wanted to hurt that young girl; it was just the way things turned out. And he did his penance, through the cat.'

'One hell of a penance,' Daniel agreed. 'There was a legend, about a man with eyes his colour, who betrayed an Egyptian princess.'

'So my father told me, towards the end – though I thought at the time that he was delirious. I'd never heard the legend, before,' Augusta said. 'It must have preyed on his mind, ever since he left Egypt.'

'Hardly surprising. I think it would have haunted me, too,' Daniel said.

'Anyway, we ought to let you get on,' Rachel said. 'We've already taken up enough of your time.'

Augusta chuckled. 'Making a quick getaway before Imogen returns, eh?'

'Something like that,' Daniel admitted. 'I don't think that she approves of us.'

'The arrogance of the young,' Augusta said. 'When she's

my age, she may have learned to keep her temper in check.'
She smiled at them both. 'Well, I wish you both all the best.
Stay in touch. It'd be nice to learn what happens to the cat,
in the end.'

'Of course.' Rachel smiled warmly at her. 'Thank you,
Augusta. It can't have been easy, telling us what really
happened, all those years ago.'

'No. But it's set my mind at rest, too,' Augusta told her.
'Guilt weighs heavily on the old.'

Three Saturdays later saw Rachel, Daniel and Kate at the
British Museum, in Annie Woodford's office. Kate had passed
the cat to Annie a week or so before, together with a partial
copy of William Morgan's diary, showing the origins of the
cat. 'We're absolutely delighted to have this,' Annie told Rachel
warmly, with a glance at the cat. 'Thank you very much.'

'No problem,' Rachel said. 'But it's a joint bequest – from
Augusta Morgan and me. Augusta was the original owner,
and my friend bought it for me from a dealer who'd bid for
it at a country house sale. We thought that it was a replica;
though obviously, it isn't. Augusta's father was the man who
excavated it, so I think that it should be her bequest as well
as mine.'

'We can certainly do that,' Annie said. 'Though I've been
doing a little research, since you brought it in, and I've found
something interesting. The case came from the same tomb as
one of the mummies on display, here.'

'Really?' Rachel was intrigued. 'Which one?'

'Come into the department, and I'll show you.'

They followed Annie through to the Egyptian section;
Rachel's eyes widened as they came to a stop in front of

a recess. The case where she'd first nearly passed out, and Daniel had caught her . . . 'This one?' Rachel asked.

Annie nodded. 'It's the most beautiful example we've ever had. Twenty-second dynasty.' She smiled. 'It's my favourite, out of all our pieces.'

'Could the cat be displayed here, do you think?' Rachel asked.

'I'm not sure,' Annie said. 'My boss might insist on it being with the rest of the mummified cats, but as these two come from the same tomb, it would be a shame not to have them together. I'll do what I can, anyway.'

'Thanks.' Rachel smiled at her. 'I appreciate the fact that you've spent so much time with us; I know you're busy.'

'Any time. And if you have any questions, you know my number,' Annie said, returning the smile.

'We'll let you get on, then.'

Annie nodded. 'See you later. And thanks again, for letting us have the cat.'

Daniel squeezed Rachel's hand as they left the department. 'Full circle,' he said softly. 'It ends where it all began.'

'Yes.' Rachel nodded. The visions that had haunted her were all over: Amy and William would both be at peace. And as for herself and Daniel: she had a feeling that this wasn't an ending. It was going to be the beginning of something even better . . .